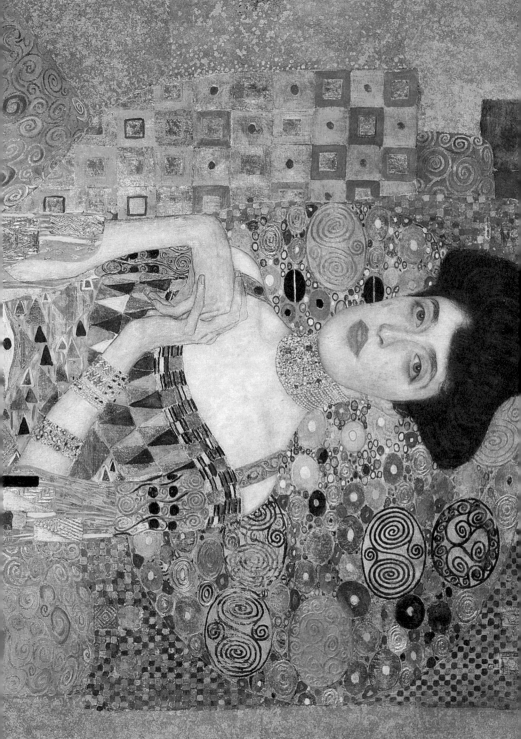

STOLEN BEAUTY

ALSO BY LAURIE LICO ALBANESE

The Miracles of Prato (cowritten with Laura Morowitz)

Blue Suburbia: Almost a Memoir

Lynelle by the Sea

STOLEN BEAUTY

A NOVEL

LAURIE LICO ALBANESE

ATRIA BOOKS

NEW YORK   LONDON   TORONTO   SYDNEY   NEW DELHI

ATRIA BOOKS

An Imprint of Simon & Schuster, Inc.
1230 Avenue of the Americas
New York, NY 10020

First Atria Books hardcover edition February 2017

ATRIA BOOKS and colophon are trademarks of Simon & Schuster, Inc.

For information about special discounts for bulk purchases, please contact Simon & Schuster Special Sales at 1-866-506-1949 or business@simonandschuster.com.

The Simon & Schuster Speakers Bureau can bring authors to your live event. For more information, or to book an event, contact the Simon & Schuster Speakers Bureau at 1-866-248-3049 or visit our website at www.simonspeakers.com.

Interior design by Kyoko Watanabe

Endpapers: (Front) *Portrait of Adele Bloch-Bauer I,* 1907 (oil, silver & gold on canvas), Klimt, Gustav (1862–1918) / Neue Galerie, New York, USA / De Agostini Picture Library / E. Lessing / Bridgeman Images; (Back) Map of Vienna © Antiqua Print Gallery / Alamy Stock Photo.

Manufactured in the United States of America

10 9 8 7 6 5 4 3 2 1

Library of Congress Cataloging-in-Publication Data

Names: Lico Albanese, Laurie, 1959- author.
Title: Stolen beauty : a novel / Laurie Lico Albanese.
Description: First Atria Books hardcover edition. | New York : Atria Books, 2017.
Identifiers: LCCN 2016023119 (print) | LCCN 2016028839 (ebook) |
ISBN 9781501131981 (hardcover) | ISBN 9781501131998 (softcover) |
ISBN 9781501132001 (eBook)
Classification: LCC PS3562.I324 S76 2017 (print) | LCC PS3562.I324 (ebook) |
   DDC 813/.54--dc23
LC record available at https://lccn.loc.gov/2016023119

ISBN 978-1-5011-3198-1
ISBN 978-1-5011-3200-1 (ebook)

For my great-grandmother
Regina (née Solitar) Falcone
1888–1980
She was born Jewish
in the Austro-Hungarian Empire
and quilted a bridge for her family
between two worlds

To every age its art; to art its freedom

—SECESSION GALLERY INSCRIPTION, CIRCA 1899

STOLEN
BEAUTY

*T*he portrait of Adele Bloch-Bauer I *measures 54" by 54" unframed, and weighs 22 pounds, 8 ounces. She has sixteen eyes, fifteen grams of gold, and seven grams of silver. Her dress is decorated with erotic signs and Egyptian symbols: the eyes of Horus to defend against evil, the three-sided ka that infuses the portrait with an indelible spirit. She's a queen and a seductress, a Jewess trapped in a lost world. Her lips are parted, as if she is about to say something that we will never hear.*

MARIA

1938

I was a love-struck newlywed when Hitler came to Austria.

Outside, the Ringstrasse was streaming with cars, trams, and pedestrians in belted trench coats. Inside, we were waltzing and drinking French champagne. My dear friend Lily had just become engaged to a Catholic man, and the glittering ballroom was in full swing. Music was playing—it was Schubert—and men in bow ties were circulating with trays of crab cakes and miniature mushroom tortes. Someone toasted the happy couple. There was crystal, and dresses the colors of hyacinths and tulips. The dance floor was a blur of pastels.

It was a long time ago, but I can still see everything clearly.

I was wearing violet perfume, and dusk was approaching. Fritz moved like a panther in his tuxedo as he crossed the room toward me. My mother was wearing a shimmering gray dress, and my father was holding his bow over the cello strings when someone shouted, "The chancellor is making a speech."

Aunt Adele was long in her grave, but I saw my uncle Ferdinand put out a hand to steady himself near the cocktail bar.

"Schuschnigg is on the radio," the man shouted again in an angry voice. "Silence, everyone."

The violinists ripped their bows from the strings, and our host turned up the volume on the radio. The chancellor's voice rang across the room just as Fritz reached my side. Every bit of my husband's childhood in the Jewish ghetto had been polished away by then, replaced by elegant manners, a starched white shirt, and a clear, operatic baritone. He put his arm around my shoulder and his ruby cuff link brushed my cheek, a cool spot in the warm room.

"Men and women of Austria: this day has placed before us a serious and decisive situation," Chancellor von Schuschnigg said.

He took a choked breath that we could hear through the radio waves. Men I'd known since I was a girl turned pale. They lowered their champagne flutes and balled up their cocktail napkins. Lily wilted against her father's thin frame. Someone tipped over a glass, and it shattered.

The chancellor said that Hitler's army was at our borders, and for one more second I believed our small country was about to go to war. I thought we would fight the Germans, and that we could win.

"We have decided to order the troops to offer no resistance," the chancellor said. "So I take leave of the Austrian people with a German word of farewell uttered from the depth of my heart—God protect Austria."

A strange sound came from my husband's throat. I saw my mother mouth my father's name—*Gustav*—and my father mouth hers—*Thedy*—in a single moment that seared itself into my mind like a photograph. A woman fainted, and sirens began to wail in the streets outside. I saw Uncle Ferdinand waving in my direction, but my parents circled around us saying *Secure your money. Secure your jewels. Go home. Lock your doors. Get your passports. Get out* and then Fritz and I were pouring outside into the fading evening with everyone else.

Church bells were ringing, and hundreds of people were crowding into the streets waving Nazi flags. I had no idea there were so many Austrians just waiting for the Führer. But there they were, hordes of ordinary Gentiles who thought Hitler was right and the Jews were to blame for their problems—poverty, sadness, cold, whatever it was they were angry about, Hitler wanted them to blame us. And they did. They were smiling and laughing and waving their swastikas. They were shouting, *Germany is united—long live Hitler.*

We all knew what had been happening to the Jews in Germany, but until that moment it had seemed a world away. If that makes us willfully ignorant or foolish and naive, then that's what we were. There's no other way to say it.

Behind the wheel of our new black sedan, Fritz stared straight ahead. Men in brown uniforms marched arm in arm through the street as if they'd stepped right from the thick walls of the Ringstrasse buildings. Soldiers stood like hard marionettes with their chins thrust into the air. I wanted to ask Fritz where they'd been hiding with their pressed uniforms and shining swastika pins, but when I saw tears on my husband's face I bit the inside of my cheek and swallowed my words.

By the time we reached the Altmann Textiles factory grounds, where we lived in our newlywed apartment, Fritz had composed himself and looked as much like the vice president of the business as he could manage.

"Four men were here asking for you," the gateman said. Otto was a strong man with a clean, square jawline and two lovely children. He secured the padlock behind us, and for the first time in my life it occurred to me that I was locked inside the gates. "They wanted to see the man who runs the factory."

"What did you tell them?" Fritz asked.

"I said Bernhard Altmann is away on business, and Fritz Altmann is here in Austria."

"What did they say?"

Otto blanched.

"They said, 'There is no Austria anymore.'"

Inside the apartment we bolted the door, turned off the lights, and crawled under the blankets. We'd been married only four months; I was twenty-two and Fritz was thirty, but we held each other like frightened children.

"You'll leave right away," Fritz whispered. "Tomorrow, if it's possible. You go with Uncle Ferdinand, and I'll join you as soon as I can."

My uncle Ferdinand and Fritz's brother Bernhard had both tried to warn us about Hitler, but their fears had seemed hazy and improbable and we'd listened the way most of Austria had listened: with one hand on the radio dial, searching for music and entertainment.

"I'm not leaving without you," I said. "We'll wait until your passport is renewed."

I had a valid passport, but Fritz's had expired after our honeymoon. We'd filled out the paperwork, filed for a renewal, and forgotten about it. That had been a month ago.

"I'm not going to get a passport now," Fritz said. Lights from the factory grounds shone through our bedroom window, illuminating his face in zigzagged shadows. "The Nazis aren't going to give me one. You go first, and I'll come as soon as I can."

"Go where?" I asked. "I don't want to go anywhere without you."

"Go with your uncle to Jungfer Brezan," he said. "That's where he said he would go if Hitler came. Czechoslovakia will be safe."

Only then did I remember my uncle waving to me on the dance floor.

"I'll call Uncle Ferdinand in the morning," I said. "He'll make sure we can get out together."

I pressed my cheek against Fritz's, and recalled the faint cinnamon of his aftershave on the night we'd met. There had been music and men in tuxedos that night, too—a cool breeze coming through an open window at the Lawyers' Ball, and a line of women holding their dance cards and waiting for the second waltz.

"Just look at him," I'd breathed to Lily when Fritz walked by. He'd moved as I thought a lover might move when he wanted a woman, as if there was velvet under his feet. And there was the cinnamon scent, like warm bread and breakfast in bed, lingering in his wake.

"That's Fritz Altmann," Lily had whispered. "He's an amateur opera singer and a real charmer. I admit he's a looker, but don't waste your time on him—he's crazy about a married woman."

I might have heeded my friend's warning if Fritz hadn't climbed onto the music stage just then and silenced the room with Schubert's aching love song: *You are peace, the gentle peace—you are longing, and what stills it.* Maybe he was a playboy, but his voice had the warmth of a roaring fire. He sang about longing, pleasure, and pain. He sang as if he wanted a home, and that very night I'd made one for him inside myself.

I wouldn't leave Austria or Vienna without him. To even think of it was terrifying.

I was swallowing a bite of dry toast the next morning when a delivery boy in a blue hat hammered at the kitchen door. The sky was flat as Fritz gave the boy a silver coin and read the cable from his brother.

Safe in Paris. Secure the books. Come immediately or await my instructions. Stop. Bernhard.

"Of course," Fritz said in a tight voice. "I have to secure the ledgers."

The newspaper was unopened on our table, with a photograph of Hitler's motorcade crossing the Danube River above a boxed notice that read: *EFFECTIVE IMMEDIATELY Jews must report all property, holdings, and cash to the Central Offices of the Reich. Those failing to cooperate will be subject to seizure and imprisonment.*

"I'm calling Uncle Ferdinand," I said. I hit the telephone receiver once, then twice. The line was dead, and that gave me a new sense of urgency. "I'm going over there. He might already have a passport and papers for you."

"You can't go out there," Fritz said. "We have no idea what's happening in the streets."

I buttoned up my coat and pulled on my scarf and gloves. My resolve was a metronome clacking inside me: *I can't leave without you, I won't leave without you, I can't leave without you, I won't leave without you.*

"You get the ledgers. I'll see my uncle, and then I'm going to check on my parents," I said. "I'll be home in three hours, maybe less."

The Altmann Textiles factory was set on four acres in Vienna's Margareten District, southwest of the city center. The buildings were yellow and whitewashed brick connected by a maze of smooth pathways. There was a modern cafeteria where everyone ate lunch together, and Fritz and Bernhard knew each of their three hundred employees by name.

Fritz walked me to the front gate, when we found Otto still on duty at the guardhouse.

"Where's the morning man?" Fritz asked.

The workers usually began arriving before eight in the morning, but that day the grounds were still empty.

"He didn't show up," Otto said with a shrug. He looked at my sturdy shoes. "Frau Altmann, the streets are dangerous. I hope you're not going out there."

"Wait," Fritz said. "I'll go with you later."

"I'm going now." I pressed my face against his. "You take care of the books."

Outside the gates, our street was deserted and the houses silent. Shades pulled low across dark drawing room windows seemed to flutter and blink as I walked away from home. I was much more frightened than I'd let on to Fritz. At the tram stop I kept my eyes on the ground and pulled my collar up around my face. I tried not to think of anything. I tried only to breathe and stay calm.

There was no ticket taker on the tram. The seats were full of silent workmen and servants in white starched uniforms. I shoved my ticket into my pocket and held on to a leather strap as the rail rolled beneath me. As we rounded the Mariahilf District, there was an angry red Nazi banner hanging from a tall building. We all turned to look, and the car buzzed with something that seemed to hang between anticipation and terror.

At the stop near the Naschmarkt, a big man in a black uniform stepped onto the streetcar and shouted, *Heil Hitler.* The entire car saluted back, but I hesitated. The man barked again, *Heil Hitler,* and stared until I put up my arm and mouthed the words. As I did, I saw the Secession gallery slide by on my left. Soldiers stood in a line across the museum steps, unfurling a red banner that covered the slogan that had been there all my life. I struggled to recall the words, but they slid away as quickly as the golden dome slid from view.

The next stop was Karlsplatz, where the Church of St. Charles anchored the square. I got off without looking back. The church doors were flung open, the bells were ringing, and there was a crowd of people in front of the fountain. I turned the other way, clutched my handbag to my side, and tried not to run through the streets.

My uncle's house was on Elisabethstrasse, overlooking Schiller Park.

As I rounded a stand of naked shrubs, I nearly tripped over a line of old women on their knees. The women were dressed in fur coats and patent leather boots, and they were scrubbing the sidewalks with toothbrushes. I lost my footing and came to a full stop, nearly retching in the street.

"If you do a good job, filthy Jew, maybe I'll let you keep that fat diamond ring," a soldier barked. He butted a woman with his rifle, and I felt a sharp pain in my jaw, as if he'd struck me, too. The woman cried out, and he struck her again. I scanned the old faces, praying I wouldn't see anyone I knew.

"Join us, fräulein," a soldier leered at me. Another one laughed, and I thought I might faint. "We can use a pretty young one like you."

I fled from the park, hurried up the steps at 18 Elisabethstrasse and banged on the door.

"Uncle Ferdinand?" I called first for my uncle, then for his butler. "Georg? Are you in there? It's Maria—it's me, please open the door."

A gunshot rang out in the park behind me, and my knees went weak.

The door opened and my uncle's cook was standing in her white uniform, a dish towel over her shoulder. I was prepared to throw myself into her arms, but she looked at me with a cool eye.

"Your uncle isn't here," Brigitte said. "He left before dawn. He's probably across the border by now."

"Left?" I asked numbly. It had not occurred to me that my uncle might leave without us.

"Without a word to anyone." Brigitte's mouth twisted. "Georg saw him pack his papers and lock up the safe. He's probably gone to Jungfer Brezan."

"Did he leave anything for me?" I asked. "A package or an envelope?"

She shrugged.

"I'd like to check his study." Even to my ears, it was clear the words were a plea.

"Suit yourself," she said, and stepped aside.

The grand *palais* was silent. The furniture seemed to cast long shadows across the parlor, and the grandfather clock on the landing kept time like ticking dynamite. Upstairs, my uncle's desk was impossibly tidy. I tried the desk drawers, but they were locked. I looked under the radio and the ink blotter and ran my hand along the clean bookshelves. There wasn't even a layer of dust.

I could smell my uncle's cigars, but very quickly it was clear that he'd left nothing for me. My last chance was Aunt Adele's sitting room, where her golden portrait hung. The room was a shrine to my aunt, filled with her favorite paintings and books. The curtains were drawn, and the air inside was stale. Her portrait was filled with gold and silver baubles and strange symbols I'd never been able to puzzle out. I'd often had coffee and cake in that room with my uncle, nibbling on sweets while he talked about the wife who'd died when I was only nine.

"She was celebrated throughout Europe and the empire. One day that legacy will belong to you, Maria," my uncle had said. He'd leaned over and brushed my cheek. "You're the daughter we never had. The daughter she longed for."

Outside the *palais* a woman screamed, and gunshots followed. I pushed aside thick curtains and saw two women lying in pools of blood. My knees buckled, and for a moment my eyes went black. An engine roared, a horn blared, and there was the sound of dogs' frenzied barking.

I pulled away from the window and grabbed for Adele's letter opener in a panic. I felt sure there was something hidden in the room for me— perhaps behind the portrait or slipped into a picture frame.

Another shot rang out, and a jeep screeched to a stop outside. I heard heavy boots on the landing, and loud knocking. Men barked my uncle's name, and blood pounded in my ears like a loud siren.

"Ferdinand Bloch-Bauer? We're here for Herr Bloch-Bauer."

"He's gone," I heard the cook say calmly. "But his niece Maria Alt-mann is upstairs in the dead wife's sitting room."

ADELE

1886

I was born on the third floor of our summerhouse just outside of Vienna, and learned to read there the year I turned five. The day was lazy and sunny and smelled of the briny Old Danube in the distance. Everyone else had gone up the hill to ride horses near the monastery, but Karl and I stayed behind with a fat copy of *Grimm's Fairy Tales*.

"I hate this thing," my brother said, tugging at the starched collar of his blue-and-white sailor suit. He was fourteen years old and desperate for long pants and a button-up shirt. "I'd rather wear a dress and corset than this."

Karl plucked two buttermilk scones from the silver tray and spread them with blackberry jam. I draped myself over a sturdy wicker chair on the shady veranda and kicked off my shoes. When I rolled down the long cotton stockings, my toes looked like ten white, skinny fish. They made me very happy, and I wiggled them in the air. Karl offered me a bite of his scone, and held his hand under my mouth so I wouldn't drop crumbs on my apron dress. Then he wrote the alphabet on a slate.

"I already know my letters," I said. I swatted at a mosquito that had bitten my foot, and rubbed away a spot of blood. "I practiced outside with a stick in the dirt."

"Then see if you can write them."

Karl handed me the chalk, and I traced each letter carefully. *A* was for *Adele*. *B* was for *Bauer*. It was easier than I thought it would be.

"See here." Karl wrote out the letters of his name, and when the

kitten mewled against my bare leg, he wrote out the word *K-A-T-Z-E*.
Soon everything fell into place, and I was lost in the swirl of letters and
symbols, the possibility of entire words and sentences already forming
like a boat on a distant shore, when the others came back and Mother
appeared on the porch. My sister, Thedy, stood behind her.

"Get up at once," Mother said. Her face was pinched, her hair still
tightly wound under her riding cap. "Put on your shoes and stockings.
And where is your hat?"

Mother thought I was too young to be taught to read, but the deed
was done, and within a few weeks, I was sounding out long words on
my own. I didn't like making my mother cross, but it happened so often
that I'd gotten used to it. I loved the letters that jammed against one
another like *tsch,* the soft *c* nestled against the tall *h* making a sound
that could chug across the page or whisper softy enough to put a kitten
to sleep.

"You're much too clever for a girl," Thedy said when she found me
puzzling out the words to a fairy tale at the end of August.

Thedy was my only sister, and she was very kind. Her eyelashes
curled up twice as long as anybody else's, and when she spoke, she
sounded like she was almost singing. She was three years younger than
Karl and content to play the piano and dress up as Mother liked. She
pleased her tutors but never asked for more books to read or spent extra
time on her lessons, as Karl did.

I wasn't sure if Thedy meant it was good to be clever, or if it was bad.
I looked to her for a clue, but her face revealed nothing.

"Adele is the smartest girl I know," Karl said. He was bent over his
desk, tracing out small ferns and tiny edelweiss for his botany scrapbook. When *he* said it, I was positive that being smart was a good thing.
"Maybe as clever as me."

"Yes," Thedy said with a sigh. "I suppose that's true."

We had no pets in the city, but kept two kittens in the country because
Mother said they calmed her nerves. The cats slept on the veranda in
the daytime, and under my bed at night. Thedy named the kittens after
the emperor and empress: Franz was skittish and playful, not at all like

the emperor with his stiff red jacket and big black bucket hat; Little Sisi had beautiful, mottled green eyes and warm brown fur.

In the blanched heat of my seventh summer, I studied a portrait of the empress that hung in Father's library and decided to try my own hand at art. With two sharp pencils and a single piece of watercolor paper, I sat cross-legged on the veranda and worked for hours drawing my Little Sisi with a ring of white clover looped around her ears just like the flowers the empress wound through her hair.

When I showed the drawing to my sister, she laughed.

"It's darling," Thedy said, when she saw that her merriment had made me cross. "Truly, Adele, it's a very pretty picture."

When I showed the sketch to Karl, he considered it with the utmost seriousness.

"You've got the proportions just right," my brother said. His praise rang in my ears for days.

In Vienna we lived in a white stone house directly across from the university. Because I was the youngest, I had the smallest room, but it had a bright cupola where I kept my green chaise pushed against the windows. From my bedroom, I could see the emperor's palace and St. Stephen's Cathedral in the Graben, and beyond it the sweep of green toward the Nineteenth District, where we summered. When I was alone, I climbed often into the windowsill and peered down to watch university students rushing to and from their classes with books tucked under their arms and neckerchiefs flying.

Although I looked very long and hard, I never saw a single woman among the scholars. Even among the best families, few girls continued their education beyond the age of twelve. Girls who sat for the university entrance exam were gossiped about over breakfast tables and afternoon teas, and only a rare few managed the coursework. Still, I dreamt of studying philosophy, anatomy, and biology, attending lectures and talking about them around the supper table with my brothers.

When the first gymnasium for young women opened in Vienna when I was twelve, Mother enrolled me—probably because the school was very exclusive and the talk of all of her friends.

The first day, I was up and dressed in my blue uniform before anyone else. Nanny coiled my hair atop my head instead of wrapping it in two braids, tucked a lavender sachet into my pocket, and pinched my cheeks so they wouldn't look pale. My stomach was nervous, and I was too excited to eat.

"Toast, at least," Mother insisted. Karl winked at me, and I hurried with my nanny to the school on Hegelgasse, where I entered through glossy brass doors without looking back.

The building smelled of soap and ink, and the halls were lit with gaslights. The classrooms were set with tables instead of little desks, and I was given an assigned seat next to two girls whom I knew because our fathers were in business together. The headmistress wore a white dress with a black smock over it and took attendance from her desk. My name was first, and I called out, "Present."

"What are you?" the headmistress asked. She didn't look up until I begged her pardon. Then her face turned to a prune and she said, impatiently, "Come now, Jewess or Catholic, it's not a difficult question."

"Jewess," I said, although I'd never called myself a Jewess before.

Most of my classmates were Catholic, and straightaway at recess they asked if I'd studied Hebrew or spoke Yiddish—as if I wore a shawl over my head and smelled of cabbage and herring like the poor shtetl Jews in the Second District.

"Papa says he hears you Jews wailing your religion songs on Fridays," one of the girls said. She had bright yellow hair, and when she tossed her head and laughed, a whole gaggle of girls around her did the same. At that moment I resolved that I would never cackle around with a goose parade of silly girls.

Anyway, my family wasn't the least bit observant. Like all of our friends, my parents had declared themselves *konfessionslos*—without faith—because it was better for my father's banking business, and for our standing in society. Emperor Franz Joseph had made it easy for us to leave our religion behind. At Christmastime we had a tall tree in our front parlor and exchanged gifts at the stroke of midnight on Christmas Eve. We didn't go to church, but we didn't go to synagogue, either. While my Catholic classmates at gymnasium attended religion class on

Mondays and Thursdays the three other Jewish girls and I sat on a hard bench outside the headmistress's office and waited in silence. I didn't like that one bit, but there was nothing to be done about it.

Like all of our friends in Vienna, my family had dinner together every afternoon at two o'clock. Mother sat at one end of our table and Father at the head, the maids served meat and potatoes, and my four brothers took up the center of the table with loud debate.

"God is dead," Karl announced one afternoon when I was still in my first year at the gymnasium.

Nobody blinked an eye. My mother passed the potatoes, and the butler ladled gravy onto Karl's plate.

"Darwin certainly agrees with that," Eugene said, waving his fork in the air. The other boys all joined in. I wanted to participate, and to know what the boys knew, but I was a girl, and no one paid any attention to me.

Karl had begun reading for philosophy and anatomy at university that same year, and soon after he told us that God was dead, I asked if he would let me read one of his philosophy books.

"Nietzsche is too much for a girl," Karl said. "Even one as clever as you."

"Darwin, then?"

He raised both eyebrows and shook his head.

"Well then, anatomy." I popped out my lower lip in a trick that sometimes worked with him. "Teach me that. I want to know what you know, and learn what you learn."

"Anatomy is worse than philosophy," Karl said. "You know a girl can't have that kind of education."

"Why not?" I asked.

"Because it will frighten you," he said. "Your mind isn't ready. It may never be ready."

My brother had never said such a thing to me before. I was more furious than hurt. I left his room without a word, put on my boots and coat, and asked Nanny to walk with me to the Museum of Art History on the Ringstrasse.

"I'd be delighted, Miss Adele," she said, and found her best hat and gloves for the occasion.

It seemed half the city was at the museum looking up at the colorful murals or marveling at ancient artifacts collected from the tombs of dead Egyptians. I pretended to study the formal portraits that ran up the fresh red walls, while really I peered sideways at a tall oil painting of Adam and Eve standing naked and unashamed beneath an apple tree.

What was dangerous about anatomy? I wanted to know. Why should a girl not learn about the mind and the body, or what lay beneath the skin?

I was never permitted to visit the museum without a chaperone, but at least Mother and Nanny—or Thedy, when I could convince her to go with me—did not insist on standing beside me while I wandered through the cool galleries. Up and down the marble staircase, I searched for large, sweeping paintings of mythical events and stood in awe of pale flesh and naked buttocks. I contemplated Adam and Eve as they covered their bodies in shame, and the three phrases of man as he matured and withered away.

Vienna was a city of music, but my interest in art was an acceptable diversion. Mother went so far as to arrange for me to have drawing lessons, which I promptly gave up when I realized I would only be drawing landscapes and flowers, and not the human body.

Karl and I were waving good-bye to Father in the country house courtyard the following summer when his carriage pulled away with a start and my hand was caught in the wagon wheel. It happened very quickly. I saw just a small bit of what was beneath my skin—red blood, a loop of blue vein, something that looked like string—before I passed out and Karl caught me. When I woke, my hand was wrapped in a fat white bandage and I felt as if I were floating.

"I'm sorry," Karl said. His face was woozy, as if he were a ghost.

"It's not your fault," I said before I fell back asleep.

My hand healed, but the scar was purple and my thumb permanently twisted. Everyone said it was barely noticeable, but I felt otherwise. At school I tucked my right hand in my lap when I wasn't writing, and raised my left hand whenever I wanted the headmistress to call on me. Karl was especially kind to me that autumn, and on a snowy evening just past the New Year of 1894 he invited me into his study and told me to close my eyes.

I pretended to do as he asked, but kept one eyelid open just a tiny sliver.

"No peeking," he said.

My brother was twenty-three. He had a thin mustache and serious brown eyes. He had begun courting a girl who was often a guest at the Wittgensteins' music parlor, although he didn't seem to have much enthusiasm for her. His bedroom smelled like freshly starched shirts, and the books on his desk smelled of ink and dust and the mill where the paper had been made.

I ran my fingers blindly over the book he'd slid across his desk. I wanted to eat the words, to feel the paper turn back to pulp in my mouth, to swallow the letters and make them mine.

"Is it anatomy?" I asked.

"Tell me again why I should show it to you."

I was ashamed of the way my fingers had been twisted and scarred by the accident. That's why I thought Karl was being kind to me. But that's not what I said.

"Because I'm clever, and because I want to learn what makes us human," I said. "And because you cannot think of a good reason why I should not be allowed to study what you study."

"But you can't tell Mother," he said. "She can't know I've shown you. Ever."

"You can trust me with your life," I said.

"I believe I would," Karl said. "I believe you would be worthy of it."

He told me not to cry out when I opened my eyes, and so I was prepared for the worst thing I could imagine, like my hand when it had been ripped open.

Instead I saw a man without skin, his blue and red veins beneath his skull as if his very thoughts were mapped beneath my fingertips, the whole universe of his nerves and the very breath in his lungs and the heart right at the center of his chest where I felt my own heart beating beneath my shirtwaist at that very moment. This was what I had been waiting for—a glimpse of what was invisible and yet right there below the surface of everything. In a flash, I understood there was a world of hidden knowledge in books, under clothing, and in hallowed lecture halls—entire universes that I did not even know existed, and questions I would never know to ask.

"Look here, Adele." Karl's hand hovered over the red and blue lines that crisscrossed through the skull. "Here, especially, a man and a woman are the same."

My brother spoke to me about ligaments, sinews, tendons, veins— the long torso and the nervous system that moved through the spine, connecting everything. It was all much more splendid than I had imagined. He put his hand upon my mangled one, and traced the two bent fingers. He told me to pulse my fist, and traced a line on another page where the hand muscles and ligaments were drawn.

"You can make your hand stronger," Karl said. "Beneath the skin, everything is already being repaired."

When I next saw *Adam and Eve* in the museum, I knew how bones, muscle, and tendons kept the pair standing even when God banished them from the Garden of Eden. I knew their bodies completed one another's like hand and glove, so that even after God was dead—in my naive way, I understood that somehow God had existed but was now gone—their children, and their children's children, were able to cover themselves in clothing and to go on.

This is not to say I understood the working of the genitalia, for clearly I did not. But I knew what made a man and a woman different, and that it was not the mind or the heart that distinguished one from the other.

I was in my bedroom reading a Jane Austen novel one cool afternoon when the front door burst open and there was shouting on the landing and a scramble of feet up the stairs.

"Hold his head, don't let go of his feet, damn it!"

I ran into the hallway and saw Karl stretched out between my brothers, his body limp and his eyes rolling up into the back of his head. I started crying *no, no,* but very softly, so I wouldn't scare my brother. He had on a morning coat and striped gray pants, and one shoe had fallen off. His sock had a tiny hole in the toe. It had been a very long winter, and the house was still damp and cold.

"Call the doctor," Eugene shouted. "And, Adele, get back in your room."

Someone sent for Father, who came home and hurried directly into Karl's room, banging the door shut behind him. I heard worried voices, and my mother telling something to the cook. Thedy came into my bedroom and sat with me. I was shaking and struggling to breathe, and my sister said I was imagining the worst.

"He'll be fine," Thedy said, stroking my hair. "He has a fever, he should have stayed home instead of going to his lectures."

Soon the doctor swept through the kitchen and up the back staircase, carrying his black bag and the smell of medicine and sickness. Mother was sent from Karl's room, and the whole house was quiet. The church bells rang five o'clock, and then six. I thought the silence was a good thing, and finally stopped crying and curled up into a ball under my blankets. Light drained from the day, and I could hear the university boys rushing and shouting in the streets.

When Karl's door opened and the doctor came out, Thedy and I jumped up to eavesdrop on the landing. We pressed against the wall and gripped one another around the waist.

"It's pneumonia," the doctor said. "I've given him a cold enema, and he has to stay wrapped in warm blankets."

Mother's voice was high and frightened, and my father's sounded flat as a wooden plank.

"Will he be all right?" Father asked. "What else can we do?"

"You can pray," the doctor said. "If his fever doesn't break tonight, I'm afraid we'll lose him."

"Lose him?" Father asked. Mother broke into a loud sob. Thedy and I ran into the hallway and flung our arms around her. The other boys came, too, and stood in a stunned circle around us until my mother began to gasp for air.

"Leave your mother be," my father said. His voice was choked, his face ashen. He put an arm around Mother's shoulder, and they went together into Karl's bedroom.

Father didn't leave Karl's side, and sometime during the night I crept in and slipped beside him. I'm sure Father saw me, but he didn't say a word. He didn't touch me. The room was hot and stuffy, my brother's face was pale and blank, and every few minutes he opened his mouth and groaned. I knew Father would make me leave if I cried, and so I made myself very strong.

I reached beneath the sheets and took Karl's hand. It was hot to the touch.

"You're going to be fine," I said. We were the same beneath the skin, but he was hot and I was cold, he was sweating and I was shivering, and he smelled of unwashed sheets.

I closed my eyes and prayed with all my might. I'd never prayed before, but I'd heard the girls at school during their catechism and knew the words by rote: *Holy Mary, Mother of God, pray for us sinners,* I whispered. I told myself that if I believed in God, he would help.

"Addie," Karl whispered. I jumped. My prayers were working. "Addie, listen to me."

I had to put my ear right next to his lips to hear.

"Don't let them box you in, do you hear me? Don't let them do that."

I didn't know what he meant. I was fifteen, he was twenty-six, his hand was limp and damp in mine.

"I won't," I said.

"Promise me."

He coughed, the sound of angry crows in his lungs.

"You're the cleverest girl I know," he said.

I didn't think he was going to die. I believed he was going to get better. I prayed and prayed for his fever to break, and fell asleep with my face on his bed, the sheets and blankets wrinkled under my cheek.

I woke to my mother's hand on my shoulders, leading me out of the room.

"Is he better?" I asked. "Is he awake?"

The room was cold, and my mother was weeping softly.

Karl's room was locked, and the servants packed away his books and clothes.

"His Darwin?" I asked my brother Eugene. "And his anatomy text, too?"

Eugene nodded sadly, and pressed a slim copy of the *Homeric Hymns* into my hands the next morning. It had a blue linen cover and Karl's bookplate with his signature inside. I slid it beneath my pillow, and at night I buried my face between the pages, where I inhaled the pulp and ink that had always been part of my brother and that I'd always believed would be part of me, too.

I didn't sit for final exams that year at school. Instead, I sank into my green chair and refused to leave. My brothers threw themselves back into work and studies, and Father spent long days in his offices. Thedy played *Moonlight Sonata* on the piano in the foyer every afternoon, and I thumbed through art books I'd dragged out of Father's library. I turned page after page of tinted lithographs, examining saints and goddesses and the way Italian painters depicted heaven among the clouds peopled with winged cherubs. Although I knew heaven was a lie, the pictures comforted me.

Mother came every morning to ask what I wanted for dinner, and every day I told her the same thing: potatoes mashed with butter, the way Karl liked them. Then I sat at the table, moving the potatoes around on my plate and drying my tears on the edge of my white napkin.

"You *will* get better," Thedy said.

"You said Karl would get better," I said. I didn't mean it to sound cruel, but I knew it did.

"That's not very kind." Thedy's eyes teared.

"I'm sorry," I told her. "Please, just leave me alone."

I read *The Odyssey* and Ovid's *Metamorphoses*, and tried to take some comfort in the idea that somewhere there was an eternal castle of dark and light memory where Karl might be reading his books at the same time, pondering the same words and phrases. God and my brother were both dead, but I wanted to believe in something more powerful than myself, and I read until I'd worn myself out trying.

Still, my body insisted itself, and every morning my bosom seemed to have grown a tiny bit. When my bleeding came, it was a shock to feel my insides churning and to see the angry red spot on my knickers.

"It's here," I told Thedy. "Just like you said. But you didn't say I would feel so sick."

"That will pass." Thedy put her cool lips to my forehead. "Just rest for today, and tomorrow you'll feel better."

She let me have her belt and a clean supply of rags, but of course I needed my own, which meant I had to tell Nanny, who told Mother, who came to my room and said it meant that I was a woman.

"I'm not," I said.

I didn't want to be a woman if Karl wasn't there to be a man. When he was alive, I'd believed that somehow he would convince Father and Mother to send me to university. With him gone, I felt everything slip away. I was half child, half woman: a sad, thin sprite. I refused to make my debut in the January season—Mother didn't have the heart to argue—and even the museum, with its silent columns and life-size murals, did not appeal to me.

"You'll have suitors anyway," Thedy said. "You know Mother will make sure of it."

"I only want to go to university," I reminded her, but we both knew that wouldn't happen. I wasn't courageous enough. I yearned to study, but I also wanted to have children one day—a boy and a girl who would love one another as I'd loved Karl, and he'd loved me. Without my brother, I could not imagine defying convention and having both.

*B*y order of Emperor Franz Joseph in 1881, Gustav and Ernst Klimt climb a ladder above the center stairwell in Vienna's sparkling new Museum of Art History and slide onto the wooden scaffolding that abuts the arcades and spandrels. The black-and-white-tiled floor is at a dizzying distance below. The brothers wear loose white overalls; their pockets are filled with measuring instruments and straightedge blades. Each young man carries a tubular spirit level in which a tiny air bubble floats in a minute amount of oil and rum. The museum is closed. Light streams through the high windows on either side of the new building. The elder brother unrolls the first long canvas while Ernst opens and mixes the pot of glue.

Their mural is on four pieces of painted canvas, a total of sixteen feet tall and thirty feet wide. The centerpiece is two Egyptian women: one holds a black ankh, the other a raven. The women's eyes are ringed in heavy black kohl, their costumes are golden and feathered. The painters start at the north end of the spandrel and work slowly, carefully, measuring and attaching the mural to the walls. The mythical figures tower above them, almost dancing across the museum walls.

MARIA

1938

There were footsteps on the staircase: the Nazis were inside my uncle's *palais*. I tried to hide by pressing between the silk curtains in my aunt's sitting room, but in an instant two men in black uniforms filled the doorway.

I recognized the younger one immediately: he'd been a lackluster suitor of mine when I'd been pining for Fritz. Now he wore a swastika armband.

"Where is Ferdinand Bloch-Bauer?" he demanded.

"I don't know," I managed to say.

"You don't live here, do you?" I could see he recognized me, and that he didn't wish me ill.

"Of course not. I live in the Margareten District."

"Then get out of here." He dismissed me with a snap of his wrist. "Go home where you belong."

Before the other soldier could stop me, I was flying down the stairs, past the shelves stacked with my uncle's precious porcelain, and out the front door into the shrill morning. If my uncle had left anything for me, it had slipped through my hands.

I didn't dare turn into Schiller Park. Instead, I went into the Ring and walked toward my parents' house. People were crowding into the streets waving flags and calling to one another as if they were waiting for a carnival. In the distance, I could hear drumbeats and the thrum of a parade.

I pulled my scarf tight around my ears and kept my eyes to the ground. Near the Belvedere Castle I passed a skinny old rabbi chained to a bench with a crooked sign around his neck that read *Filthy Jew*. Yeshiva students were on their hands and knees barking like dogs while soldiers yelled, "Louder, bitches, or we'll whip you." A young man shouted, *Die, Jews! Hitler is coming*, and schoolgirls in white knee socks threw rocks at two old men who cowered on a bench.

By the time I turned onto Stubenbastei, I was freezing and my face was wet with tears.

When the maid didn't answer, I fumbled for my key I found Mama alone in the kitchen, still in her bathrobe. There was a cup of coffee on the table, and the newspaper unopened beside it. The air smelled stale.

"Uncle Ferdinand is gone." I blurted it out, even though I knew it would frighten her. "Did you know that?"

My mother shook her head, and I told her what the cook at Elisabethstrasse had said.

"I hope he's safe." My mother began to cry. "Ferdinand wouldn't have left us unless he was in terrible danger."

I put my arms around her.

"What about Leopold and the others?" I asked.

My sister Louise lived in Yugoslavia with her husband and daughters. My brother Robert was an attorney, and Leopold was the head accountant at Uncle Ferdinand's sugar company. With my uncle gone, Leopold would be his highest-ranking company officer in Vienna. If Uncle Ferry was in danger, then my brother Leopold was in danger, too.

"Louise is safe where she is. Robert and Leopold should be at home or at their offices," she said. She wiped away her tears. "No one called, Maria. No one's been here but you."

"And Papa?"

"He's hardly said a word since we left the party last night."

I found my father in the library cradling his cello. The shades were drawn, and the room was dark.

"Papa?" I fell to my knees in front of him. He reached a hand toward my face the way a blind man might reach for the sounds of someone's voice. It was as if he couldn't see me.

"You should go home and lock the doors. Stay inside until it's over," he said, and then he shut his eyes.

Back in the kitchen, my mother was threading a needle with a shaking hand. I asked what she was mending, but she lifted a napkin to reveal a small pile of colored jewels.

"Not mending," she said. "I'm getting ready."

My mother had been raised with dressing maids and cooks. She was one of the most fashionable women in her circle and had two seamstresses in the Graben who made dresses on custom forms to her exact measurements. Yet she put the thread through the needle easily and deftly tied it with a bit of spit. Then she turned a black glove inside out, slit the lining, and tucked two emeralds and a small diamond into the tiny pocket she'd made.

"My sister was never interested in sewing or cooking," Mama said. It was true—my aunt's passion had been for art, books, and what she'd called a ferocious need for freedom and education. "But I learned what I needed to know."

My mother handed me a needle, and I threaded the eye as she had done. I watched her sew the glove back up, her neat black stitches disappearing into the seam. I did the same. The needle stuck on the first stitch, but then it moved smoothly. The rhythm of the stitches soothed me, and as we worked I told her about Bernhard's cable.

"Yes, Paris will be safe." Mama nodded as if it had already been decided. "Go to Paris right away. Everyone who can get out is leaving."

When she handed me the black gloves, the seams were perfect.

"Wear these. When you go home, pry the diamonds out of your rings and sew them into your brassiere just like this."

"You'll need the gloves," I said. "You're leaving, too. We'll go together."

"You've seen your father. He's too frail to travel."

I knew she was right, and yet I argued until finally she spoke the lie that neither of us believed.

"You and Fritz go first. When your father is stronger, then we'll find you."

———

The next day Hitler marched into Vienna with hundreds of thousands of German soldiers. While the streets filled with tanks, motorcars, cheering crowds and marching bands, Jews across the city lit bonfires and burned their bankbooks and business files. Fritz and I didn't leave the house, but we could smell the fire and ash in the wind.

The following morning my brother Robert was dismissed from his law firm with a single sentence—"you're a Jew"—and the contents of his desk emptied into the trash while he watched. Robert was tall and ordinarily calm, but he was close to hysterics when he knocked on our apartment door in the middle of the afternoon.

"Leopold's gone," he said. His jacket and tie were askew, as if he'd been out all night. "He's not at his apartments, and he's not at the offices. I went to 18 Elisabethstrasse—Uncle Ferry's place is crawling with Nazis."

"What do you mean, Leopold is gone?" I asked.

"I went to his apartment just before I came here," Robert said. "A stranger answered, and when I asked her about Leopold, she slammed the door in my face."

I felt close to hysterics.

Robert said, "I'm not going home—Katrine and I are taking the baby to Grinzing with my in-laws. You'll have to tell Mother and Father for me, Maria."

We didn't know how to say good-bye in those early days. There was too much uncertainty and too much at stake. So we only said, *Be careful, take care of the baby, take care of yourself.*

"When you see Leopold, tell him where to find me," Robert said.

"And if you see him first, tell him to stay away from Elisabethstrasse," I said.

Days passed with no word from Leopold or Uncle Ferdinand.

"Maybe they're together," I told my parents as I sat in their cold kitchen. It seemed important to keep up their spirits. "Maybe they've gone to Czechoslovakia and are at Jungfer Brezan right now, sleeping in those delicious, big beds."

But our phone calls to the country house were never answered, and no word came.

A work-stop notice was left at our factory gatehouse that week, and for the first time since we'd been married, the whistle didn't blow at eight the next morning. Fritz sat in the bedroom, nervously paging through the stack of account books he'd retrieved, adding sums and copying them onto small pieces of paper.

"We'll need the records," he said. "But I have to burn the books."

I took apart a diamond bracelet and hid the jewels piece by piece. I tucked the heart-shaped locket my father had given me into a garter belt lining, and used my mother's needle and thread to sew a few small gold coins into the padded lining of my favorite brassiere.

It wasn't enough: our most valuable jewels were in the jewelers' vaults, where we'd always felt they were safest. We'd even divided my jewels between two jewelers in case one was compromised—as if we had known something bad might happen.

After I'd washed our lunch plates and wrapped the leftovers in brown paper, I tucked my safety box key inside the top of my girdle and set out for the jewelers. Fritz was going to send a cable to his brother in Paris. He'd decided on a simple phrase—*we await instructions*—that could give nothing away.

At the gate, Fritz put his hands on my shoulders and rubbed his nose against mine.

"Take everything," he said. "Don't leave anything in the vault—the jewelers can't be trusted now."

"The best pieces are at Werner's shop," I reminded him.

"That's right—get your aunt's necklace and earrings from Werner, too."

I studied Fritz's long nose and heavy brow.

"Remember to salute when they walk by," I said.

"I won't salute the Germans." His eyes were blazing. "I may not be much of a fighter, but I won't surrender everything the first week."

We parted ways at the corner of Talgasse and Mariahilferstrasse, and I walked four long blocks more before I saw the crush of patrons outside the jewelers.

"The Germans are inside," a woman said. She pointed at a ring of soldiers in long coats with shiny brass buttons. "Those guards bloodied three men who tried to ask a question."

I was stunned to see a familiar face among the guards: it was Rupert, the gateman who'd failed to show up that first morning.

"Get away, filthy Jews!" Rupert shouted. "This store is under German ownership."

Old and young women with their errand coats and market bags were pressed together, smelling of onions and coffee and something unfamiliar. I could smell my own fear coming up from inside my coat.

"He's going to shoot," someone cried. The crowd surged forward and back. A shot rang out, and another shot seemed to come from behind us. I felt trapped. A woman screamed, and a man yelled. "She's been shot. They've shot my Elsa!"

I smelled blood in the air, and all I could think was to get away. I didn't let myself look at the fallen woman. I inched backward. I ducked under elbows waving in the air and moved past men comforting their wives. I moved blindly, not seeing where I was going, until finally there was nothing but empty space behind me. I almost fell, but at the last second I turned. I made every effort to make myself look carefree. With my light hair and round face, I knew I could pass for a Gentile as long as I didn't see anyone I knew.

I reached home to find my apartment door open, and two strange men standing in my living room. One wore a black suit, the other a brown uniform.

"Felix Landau," the suited man said. He had dark hair, and a long scar on his cheek. I sought Fritz's eyes, but they were glazed and unfocused.

"Frau Altmann, your husband fully understands why we're here and what is to be done."

Again I looked to Fritz, but his expression was blank.

This Landau had a clipboard and a gold pen, and he waved them in my direction.

"As I've explained to your husband, we've cataloged and Aryanized your assets—they belong to the Reich now, not to you. This is in accordance with the new law. Do you have questions for us?"

My mouth was dry. I shook my head. I'd read everything I needed to know about Aryanization in the morning newspaper. It meant that they could take anything from us, at any time. Any Jew who refused to cooperate would be arrested.

"You have very nice taste in furnishings, Frau Altmann," Landau said. He reached for my hand and turned my engagement ring between his thumb and forefinger. I forced myself not to pull away. "This is a very fine diamond, finer than anything I've been able to buy for my own wife."

My hands were damp, and the ring slid easily off my finger.

"Of course the Reich has a full list of your jewelry, but I'll feel so much better if you can give me a full accounting on your own." He dropped my ring into his coat pocket. "I believe you inherited a number of significant pieces from your aunt, didn't you?"

A car horn in the courtyard startled me. Fritz and I jumped at the same instant.

"The Koloman Moser necklace," I said. I felt as hollow as a ghost. Fritz made a small noise, but I didn't look at him. "There's a very valuable golden choker that belonged to my aunt Adele."

"Adele Bloch-Bauer." Landau nodded. "And matching earrings, I believe."

"I'll phone Hans Werner's shop, he'll send everything over."

"Of course he will," Landau said. He produced a paper that looked like a receipt, and told me to sign it. "Your cooperation is noted, Frau Altmann. Now pack your things."

I opened my mouth to speak, but he held up his hand.

"You're being relocated to other rooms on the third floor," Landau said. He looked around the apartment, and ran his hand over my leather chair. "I'm going to quite enjoy my new home."

ADELE
1898

"Mother will let you do almost anything right now," Thedy said. "Just to see you smile."

"Even this?" I asked with a thrill. I held up a sheath of white silk and wrapped it around myself like a toga. "Will she let me dress as a spring nymph?"

I was seventeen, my legs coltish in their new excitement, my hips still slim as a boy's.

"I think we can convince her," Thedy said. "I think you're still young enough to get away with it, too."

My sister was planning a party to celebrate her engagement to Gustav Bloch.

Engraved invitations had gone out, white lilies ordered, the menu planned. It was in vogue to have parties with Greek themes, and ours was to be a spring bacchanal. It was our first party since Karl's death more than a year ago, and even I knew it was time.

Thedy's long hair was newly oiled to make it shine, and her complexion was powdered to a smooth ivory. At twenty-three, she was almost too old to be a bride, but she'd waited through a period of mourning and then made an excellent match for our family. Gustav was considerably older than my sister and had already proven himself steady, reliable, and secure thanks to his family's sugar beet fortune.

Their love and tenderness thrilled me, but it was the suitability of the union that pleased Mother and Father.

31

People didn't marry for love, at least not the people we knew. They married for station, dowry, and dynasty. Even the Wittgensteins and the von Rothschilds carefully cultivated their social standing with marital alliances, annual society balls, and favors for the imperial family. And yet things were changing—there were hints of passion and rebellion everywhere, if only you wanted to see it. The crown prince had committed a stunning murder-suicide for love, and the emperor's cousin had run off to Switzerland with her young paramour. My friends and I had been deliciously shocked by a play at the Burgtheater about a man who takes a prostitute as his lover, and Gustav Klimt's new Union of Austrian Artists had been raising an uproar with their Secessionist show at the old Botanical House that spring.

The new art was said to be seductive and crude, and Father had forbidden me to see it. I was still too young to go anywhere without a chaperone, and I couldn't have properly asked one of my suitors—even if Thedy had agreed to accompany us—without causing a ruckus.

The suitors bored me, anyway. Fair-haired Klaus Fleischer was frightened of my father, Edward Krauss was handsome but unadventurous, and it was impossible to talk with the lawyer Pieter Nebel about anything artistic. They all thought I'd be a sweet, steady girl like Thedy, enchanted by domestic life and eager to be a bride. But I was not. I still felt my brother's spirit urging me on, telling me I was clever and warning me not to be put in a box. I'd begun to suffer terrible bouts of insomnia that year, and neither the suitors nor Mother and Father understood my nervous impatience or the dark circles under my eyes.

Thedy understood me, though. Thank God there was dear, tender Thedy.

"I have an idea," my sister said. "If you tell Mother you want to recite a poem for the party, and dress as a spring nymph—"

"Athena," I said, interrupting her. I still had mythology books stacked beside my bed, and had worn the pages thin reading through the night. "The goddess of wisdom and poetry."

"Nothing too complex," Thedy said patiently. "Just a spring nymph, reciting a poem. That will appeal to Mother's sense of proper aesthetics."

"I'll write a love poem for you and Gustav," I said. I don't know what prompted me to say that. I'd had few crushes in my short life, and sometimes wondered if perhaps I'd be passed over when it came to romantic longing. But Thedy smiled, and that was that.

"A love poem," she said. "I like that idea. I'll tell Mother you've written it for us already. The rest will fall into place, I promise."

She reminded me that I would meet Gustav Bloch's brother at the party, and that she thought he would make an excellent match for me.

"Ferdinand's not a very cultured man, but he's smart and rich, and he built the family's sugar beet fields into a dynasty," Thedy said. "He needs a young wife—someone like you, Adele, who can give him élan and style. If we marry brothers, the family will be united through blood on both sides," she added. "And you'll find you have a lot more freedom as a young bride than you have here at home with Father."

I was happy for my sister, but had no intention of letting Gustav's brother court me. My head was full of myths and poetry about unrequited love and passion that swelled but was never satisfied, and I wrote a poem that I thought answered those ideas with a rebuttal: Thedy and Gustav, at least, had found love together.

Ferdinand Bloch wasn't handsome, but he was substantial and striking in the newest style from London—black tuxedo, ruffled shirt, and a velvet trimmed top hat, which he handed to the maid when he arrived the following Saturday for my sister's party. His beard was laced with bits of gray, his eyes were soft brown, and his lips were full. He was old—nearly forty—and looked more like one of my father's important friends than the sort of sharp young man I expected to marry.

I felt light and unencumbered in my white toga when I greeted him at the foot of the iron staircase.

"Please come with me, Herr Bloch," I said, slipping an arm through his. When he smiled, he revealed a gap in his front teeth. He wore cologne, and a medal of honor from Emperor Franz Joseph pinned to his lapel. I wore a wreath of hyacinth and violets, and in my bare feet I led him to a seat between the groom-to-be and my brother David.

Mother had ordered the parlor decorated with white orchids hung from the ceiling, ferns in pots along the windows, and thirty white folding chairs adorned with paper flowers and netting. A pianist began to play Beethoven, and on cue I ducked out from behind a white curtain and recited the verses I'd written.

"Do you know me?" I called out. I was holding a cornucopia of greenhouse lilies and orchids across my chest. "I bring you joy," I said. "I bring you lust for life!"

The poem was juvenile, but I was very proud of it. When I was finished, there was applause, red roses for the pianist, and then dinner my mother and sister had carefully planned. We started with cold Grüner Veltliner from Father's favorite vineyards, shrimp and oysters on beds of ice, little blintzes with caviar, and pickled asparagus that I saw Ferdinand spit into his napkin.

When Ferdinand caught me watching him, he winked and I giggled. I hated pickled asparagus, too.

"Your sister tells me that you appreciate fine art," Ferdinand said later.

Dessert had been served, and he was stirring sugar into his coffee. At Mother's insistence, I'd been laced into a proper corset and gown before sitting for dinner, and I felt a bit breathless. We'd been in a hurry, and I think the corset was laced too tight.

"Did you see the Secessionist show at the Botanical House?" he asked.

"No." I was surprised that he would mention the modern art show, and flattered to be asked. "Although I wanted to. And I'd like to see the new gallery they're building over on Friedrichstrasse, too."

"Would you?" Ferdinand let out a small laugh. "I suppose it's quite a sight to see the emperor's artisans working alongside Magyar laborers."

I cast about for a word I'd read in an obscure French journal that one of my brothers had brought into the house.

"It sounds quite *avant-garde*," I said. "I admire that, Herr Bloch."

"As do I," he said. I couldn't make out if he was humoring me or not, but I liked the easy way he said it. "I admire ingenuity, and anything that advances the empire."

The intelligence and tenderness in Ferdinand's face appealed to me. So many people I knew were dull or cruel. Ferdinand was neither. I tilted my head at him and smiled. He put down his coffee, and folded his hands on the table.

"I hope you don't think me too forward, Fräulein Bauer," he said. "I'd be honored if you would come for a ride in my carriage to see how their work on the new Secession gallery is progressing."

It was a formal and proper invitation. Because he was my future brother-in-law, he was all the chaperone I would need—and that, alone, was novel for me. I was tired of being tethered to my mother and sister. When I glanced over at Mother, she was nodding approvingly at me.

"I would enjoy that very much, Herr Bloch."

He smiled broadly.

"I have a friend who's a great admirer of Herr Gustav Klimt's," he added. "Frau Berta Zuckerkandl, do you know her?"

Berta Zuckerkandl was the daughter of a newspaper publisher, and the only female writer in Gustav Klimt's new circle of artists. I had read her cultural commentary and was dazzled by her acceptance of all that was dauntless and modern.

"People say she's quite radical for a woman." I dared not look at him. The thought of romantic love with Ferdinand did not excite me, but intellectual and artistic freedom surely did.

"A strong man has no need to fear a woman with a strong mind." Ferdinand sounded almost jolly. "I think that's what you mean by your French words," he added, and then butchered the expression *avant-garde* into four distinct syllables.

It was clear his French was terrible, and when I barely suppressed a smile, I saw a flash of annoyance and what I would learn, soon enough, was his bottomless pride.

Ferdinand's Lipizzan horses had been trained at the Spanish Riding School with the emperor's own stallions, and when we rode along the Ring in his carriage the following week, heads turned and children waved as if we were royalty ourselves. Even my father's wealth paled in comparison to Ferdinand's, and that gave me a heady rush. I could feel what such wealth might do for a young woman of uncommon ambitions.

I watched out the carriage window as we approached the Vienna River, where the new Secession gallery was a brilliant white building rising at the edge of the proper city. On one side of the construction site were fishmongers and bakers stocking their wooden stalls, and on the other side, only a short distance away, the Academy of Fine Arts stretched the length of Schiller Park. The old Elizabeth Bridge had just been demolished, and there was a huge field of dust where new roads were being built on raised platforms that crisscrossed a winding patch of the river.

"It's outside the Inner Districts, so the building isn't a blemish on the Ringstrasse," Ferdinand said. "I think it was a wise decision to keep it at a distance from the palace."

The Secession gallery was much smaller than I'd expected, a fraction of the size of our grand art history museum with its dazzling marble columns and enormous murals. Square and sleek, the new gallery looked as if it had been built of small geometric patterns and white rectangles piled atop one another like a bright white wedding cake. I said as much to Ferdinand.

"You have a language for art that I don't have," he said as he motioned for the driver to stop on the square.

Set directly atop the center of the gallery, an intricate gold dome rose like a moon on the horizon. Men in white overalls balanced on a maze of scaffolding supported by pulley ropes, and we watched as they worked with small tools, chipping away to reveal a delicate filigree of golden leaves.

It was a warm day, and some of the men were working in their shirtsleeves, their hard muscles rippling in the sun. I couldn't help but notice how much older Ferdinand looked in the daylight, and how soft his body was in comparison to the young laborers.

As if he'd realized suddenly that it was rather scandalous to have me in the midst of so many workmen, Ferdinand directed his carriage driver across the road to the Church of St. Charles, where we stopped at the edge of the green square. He produced a small silver cup so that I could take water from the public drinking fountain, and we walked away from the noise and dusty gallery construction. The church square was full of nannies and nursemaids with their charges, and older couples who were taking the air. We found a bench closer to the Ring, and watched a woman with a purple feather in her hat walk by with a little dog on a leash.

"Have you been to Paris?" Ferdinand asked.

"I've never traveled beyond Lake Attersee or Bad Ischl. I've spent most of my summers in the house where I was born."

"If you were my wife, I would take you to Paris," Ferdinand said. I was startled by his directness, but I don't think that showed on my face. "And it would be in your power to bring the avant-garde here, to Vienna, if that's what you wanted."

His French pronunciation was remarkably improved—as if he'd studied and prepared to say that word for me. Beyond that, all I could do was smile and look away. The subject of marriage had been broached, and if I wanted to cut off such an idea, I would have had to tell him right then and there that he was wasting his time with me. And I didn't. It was exciting to be at the edge of Vienna, where shirtless workmen were building a gallery and women with boa feather hats were walking little dogs alone, by themselves, without an escort or chaperone.

I'd feared that I would be lonely when my sister married. Instead I was free to go about with my new brother-in-law as I pleased. We went to an outdoor symphony on the great lawn behind the Schönbrunn Palace, and rode into the countryside with his horses flying along gravel roads. We spoke about the great architectural accomplishments along the Ring, and debated the new, simple styles that Olbrich and Wagner were bringing to Vienna.

"The Ringstrasse buildings are majestic," Ferdinand said. "I applaud cultural advancement, but I'm not sure how Vienna is improved with a building that resembles a cake, or one that's decorated with red poppies like Wagner's new apartments."

The chance to have my opinion taken seriously excited me.

"The opera house and the new history museums are grand and beautiful," I agreed. "But what's the purpose of simply repeating what's been done before? Vienna deserves an identity of her own, separate from Rome and whatever the Germans are doing in Berlin now."

Ferdinand seemed to weigh my words carefully. Then, he smiled.

"Frau Zuckerkandl wrote something quite like that in last week's *Tagblatt*," he said.

"I read it," I said. "And I agree with her."

He asked me to say more; to explain why, exactly, the new style appealed to me.

"Perhaps you'll think me improper," I said, although I knew that simple declaration would arouse his curiosity.

He urged me to go on.

"I wore a white toga the night of Thedy and Gustav's party," I said. "It was loose and free—a very simple Greek design."

The edges of his ears pinked, and I felt a strange new power.

"The new architecture seems the same, to me," I said. "Pure and also simple."

"Less structured," he said.

I had to resist the urge to add the word *uncorseted*, but I believe we both understood the allusion, and that I had somehow made my point in the most proper and yet personal way.

In early June, Ferdinand and I spent a long afternoon in the *heuriger* wine gardens in the hills of Grinzing, where I enjoyed too much chilled Muscat and paid the price the next morning.

Father was off on business, but at breakfast my mother quizzed me about the colored lanterns hanging in the trees in the wine gardens and the subject of my conversations with Ferdinand.

"All I can tell you, Mother, is that he's a gentleman at all times," I said. Then I excused myself and went back to bed with a terrible headache.

Ferdinand lived in a light-filled apartment not far from the Belvedere Castle, and collected landscapes by the best old Austrian painters. While Thedy and Gustav were honeymooning in Switzerland, he invited Mother and me to see his collections. His prized paintings were by Waldmüller and Alt, each a sentimental representation of the idyllic days I'd been enjoying that very season: rolling hills, red-cheeked girls, landscapes with yellow wheat fields and fat apple trees. The works hung in a huge parlor filled with stately furniture and wine-red carpets, where tall white shelves displayed dozens of beautiful pieces of gold-rimmed ivory porcelain from the eighteenth century.

"What inspired you to collect porcelain?" Mother asked.

Ferdinand was a practical businessman. I expected him to speak of the value of the collection or its connection to imperial history. Instead, he reached for a delicate teapot, and traced the slender spout.

"It's important to preserve what's old and beautiful, even as we welcome what's new." He glanced in my direction and added, "The porcelain is a valuable part of the empire's heritage. By bringing together as many pieces as possible, they can be appreciated together in splendor."

"Like a great extended family," Mother said, with one of her satisfied nods.

Ferdinand had my mother's approval, and he knew it.

Not long after Thedy and Gustav came home from the Alps, he took me to meet Berta Zuckerkandl in a new café near the art museum. Women didn't generally visit coffeehouses, and I knew Father would forbid it—but Ferdinand held open the door for me, and I entered with a high head.

"Welcome to Café Central," a young woman in a starched white apron said in a bright voice.

The tall, arched ceiling and marble columns resembled a museum or library, but instead of studious silence there was a cacophony of piano music, clanking tableware, carts rolling across smooth floors, the sharp smell of boiled coffee and bubbling cocoa, a ribbon of cakes and pastries arranged on plates along a zinc countertop, and men in crisp shirts waiting to serve the pastries topped with fat dollops of whipped cream.

Ferdinand put a hand on the small of my back and guided me through the crowd. The gold-embossed wallpaper made the room glow like the inside of a treasure box. Dozens of men sat at round white tables drinking coffee, smoking, reading the newspapers, and arguing.

The swell of their voices reminded me of the chorus of voices I'd often heard around my family's afternoon dinner table. From each group there were names and words that meant something to me—*the empire's greatest . . . Parisian women . . . the exposition . . . dancers . . . medical training . . . Schopenhauer . . . damn the Italian count . . . plans for the Jubilee Ball,* and so on. It was hard to keep my head from spinning around at each enticing conversation.

I was wearing a smart blue cape and a new hat, and some of the men looked up as we passed. It was clear they didn't often see a young woman there, even in the afternoon, and I rather enjoyed the shocked expressions on their faces.

We found Berta in a red booth, sitting beneath a large portrait of Emperor Franz Joseph. She had a sweep of dark hair coiled loosely around her face, and a square jaw that made her more handsome than beautiful. She wore a bright shawl over her dress—a touch of the bohemian that I'd never seen another woman dare to wear in Vienna. And she was smoking a cigarette. In public.

In that instant I not only wanted to know and impress Berta but, as much as possible, I wanted to *be* Berta Zuckerkandl.

"My brother Karl was a student at the university," I told her after we'd been properly introduced. "He was reading anatomy with your husband, Herr Doctor Zuckerkandl."

Berta seemed to know all about my brother, and I wasn't surprised. Our circle in Vienna was small enough so that we had a passing acquaintance with all the best families, and knew their histories even if they weren't on our regular social calendars.

"My husband said your Karl was very promising," she told me. "We were all sorry when he passed."

Dark mirrors hung on the walls, and overhead there were gaslight chandeliers. At a nearby table, a group of young men had opened up a passel of sketch pads and were talking heatedly about Josef Olbrich and his design for the Secession gallery.

"It's about ornament and function," someone said, and another replied with a sharp observation about the contrast of the simple square foundation and intricate gold dome.

"Like a white wedding cake," Ferdinand murmured so that only I heard.

"It's a temple," another one of the young men said. "A place of refuge."

I told Berta I admired her opinions, and asked what she knew about Gustav Klimt and the artists he had gathered around him.

"Klimt is the most daring and innovative artist in Europe," she said without hesitating. "He's single-handedly changing modern art in Vienna, but I'm afraid he may pay a price for his vision."

I wanted to know more, but Berta would only say that Klimt's new murals for the university were going to be bold, dark, and startling.

"He's a very well-liked man," she said. "That may serve him in the end, but one can never tell how useful popularity is in the face of one's critics."

"In the face of critics, one needs powerful allies," Ferdinand said.

Berta smiled, and patted his hand.

"It's wonderful to see you cultivating a patron's attitude," she said.

Coffee was served on a silver tray, with glasses of cold water and a pretty bowl piled with sugar cubes—"from your factory, Ferdinand?" Berta asked—and the taste of the chocolate cake was made only richer by the dense cigarette smoke that filled the air. As we were finishing our cakes, Berta pointed out the writer Peter Altenberg sitting at a corner table, scribbling away.

"Schnitzler and Salten should be arriving in about an hour," she said. "The three of them start with coffee and end with cognac. Sometimes they read aloud to one another, and bits of poetry land on my table like beautiful birds."

The café windows looked out onto Herrengasse as if upon another world.

"I do so admire you," I told Berta impulsively. Just being with her made me feel emboldened. She reached across the table, and I barely had time to pull back my mangled hand before she took the good one in her own.

"And I admire you," she said. "You're beautiful and intelligent, with your whole life ahead of you."

She promised to invite me to coffee as soon as she returned from the country, and she hugged me good-bye.

"Thank you, Ferdinand," I said after we'd stepped out into the balmy evening and watched Berta disappear into the streets. "I've never met anyone like her before."

"You are like her, Adele." He stared at me intently. "Don't you see that you have just as much spirit, and just as fine a mind?"

Two nights later, Ferdinand took me to ride on the Ferris wheel in the Prater, where we stood in a huge red car the size of two carriages and watched Vienna's rooftops spinning below us. Maybe it was nerves, maybe it was meeting Berta and thinking of all those years at Karl's side, yearning to learn everything he knew. Soon I was going on and on to Ferdinand about the books I'd read and the things I still hoped to discover.

He looked at me with great kindness as I spoke about the Eternal Return, about time as a circle, about loving one's fate.

"*Amor fati*—love your fate," I said as the Ferris wheel came to a stop and I stepped onto a ground that seemed to buckle and spin beneath my feet. I felt free, and terribly intelligent. "That's Nietzsche, in case you didn't know."

"I didn't know," he said with what seemed like an indulgent smile. "But now I do."

Ferdinand bought me a cold lemonade and found us a quiet bench in one of the gardens. A line of tall trees towered over us like sentinels from another world, polka music from a brass band floated through the air and dropped its tinny notes at our feet, the last dogwood blossoms blew across the gardens and accumulated at the edges of the graveled promenade.

He cupped my gnarled fingers as he might have held a tiny bird. It's strange how it's all so clear and yet so otherworldly, as if he'd manufactured that moment the way his factory manufactured sugar cubes in neat rows and perfect stacks.

"You're beautiful, and I'm very fond of you," Ferdinand said gently.

"You can trust me, I'll take good care of you, and I'll give you as much freedom as you want."

He looked at me steadily, his brown eyes searching my face. My brothers played chess, and David had taught me the game one summer in the country. He'd checkmated me dozens of times, and always there was that moment when my heart dropped into my feet and I could see the pieces closing in and could not find a way out. I felt something like that, at that moment.

"Our families are already joined," Ferdinand said. "The Blochs and the Bauers are among the best families in Vienna. If we marry, our union will make us a dynasty."

He said it quietly. I saw the Ferris wheel circling in the distance and could almost feel the artists on the other side of Vienna, chipping away at the golden dome.

I'd read all the fairy tales when I was a girl and knew the princes were supposed to be handsome. I'd seen the men working outside the Secession gallery and felt myself stirring in response. Yet younger men had courted me, and they'd been like bumblebees on flowers, easily swatted away and easily replaced.

Ferdinand had much to offer. I had encouraged his affection, and I knew it. And then there was Thedy, my dear Thedy, telling me what a great honor it would be to marry into the Bloch family.

"I can't give you an answer now," I said.

"Of course you can't," he said. "There's no rush. You'll have all the time you want. All the time you need to consider, and to weigh it all out."

I stayed up all night, my stomach churning. I wondered what it meant, that I'd been more drawn to Berta's intelligence and charm than to Ferdinand or any other man that I'd ever met. How I wished Thedy were sleeping in her old room instead of in her new home, with her new husband. I wanted to ask her so many things that I knew I would never be able to ask her in the light of day—about love and passion, about intimacy and yearning.

Ferdinand was twice my age, but he was wealthy, kind, and unafraid of new ideas. I didn't think I loved him. But did that matter? Should it matter? I thought he would make a fine husband, and an excellent father for the children I wanted to have.

When dawn broke, I made my way downstairs and asked Cook for a boiled egg and a cup of tea. It was a warm day, and the servants were preparing to move everything to the summerhouse. My head ached, and the place where my fingers had been caught in the wagon wheel throbbed as if every wound were open anew.

Soon Mother took her regular seat at the table, and opened the newspaper. She let me be, and I wondered if she knew about Ferdinand's proposal. I wondered about my sister and Gustav, and about Berta and her husband. I thought about what it would mean to have the power to do what Ferdinand had promised, to go where I wanted and read what I wanted. I thought of the years I'd heard Mother crying in her room, about the mistresses that I'd heard whispered of, and about women in loveless marriages. I didn't want that for myself.

I was thinking about mistresses and marital intimacies when Father came into the room and pointed a finger at me.

"You were seen in the neighborhood of the Secession gallery, watching the men working in their shirtsleeves," Father said. He didn't even sit down. Mother rushed to tell him that I'd gone with Ferdinand Bloch, but he didn't give her the chance to speak. "I was willing to let that go, until Dr. Bratislav told me you were seen in the Café Central with a woman who was smoking cigarettes."

"Yes, Father," I began. "That's Frau Berta—"

He cut me off.

"I don't care who it is. You cannot go where you do not belong," he said in a hard voice. "I will not tolerate it. Not as long as I'm your father and you live in my home."

I felt the brightness in me fading, and that frightened me far more than Ferdinand's marriage proposal had. I tried again.

"Frau Zuckerkandl is married to Dr. Zuckerkandl. Karl read with him at university."

At the mention of Karl's name, my father's face purpled.

"Karl is dead, Adele. And the rebel painters and books, the philosophers, the art journals—those aren't for you. Those are not for a young woman on the verge of marriageable age. You'll learn to behave decently, or you will have a very difficult time in this world."

In a shaking hand, I wrote Ferdinand a long note that afternoon. I said that I wanted to read philosophy and anatomy, to study art and go to Paris. I said that if those things were acceptable to him, and if in fact he meant what he said about the avant-garde, then I would be his wife and glad of it.

"*Amor fati*," Ferdinand wrote in return. "If I'm your fate, Adele, I hope you will love it—and me."

"Maybe you don't love him now," Thedy said when I told her, "but you will have a good life with him, and you can learn to love him, Adele. I believe you can and that you will."

I had found a suitable and respected man with whom I could have a family. A man who held the keys to all those doors and books I wanted to open. I believed—at least I hoped—that all good things were to come for me.

MARIA

1938

As Fritz and I gathered our belongings for the move upstairs, I found a copy of *Grimm's Fairy Tales* my aunt had given me when I was young. I'd been a six-year-old princess then, prepared to kiss a lot of toads before I found my prince. I'd worn my hair in a fat braid like Rapunzel, and imagined one day it would be long enough to toss out the window for my true love.

I'd grown into an equally romantic young woman with fairy-tale ideas—and when I met Fritz at the Lawyers' Ball, I'd known it was love at first sight.

"You sing beautifully, Herr Altmann," I'd told Fritz on that first evening. "My father is a musician, and I hope we'll hear you perform again."

His eyes swept from my face down to my gown and up again. He smiled. I was twenty-one. He was considerably older—just shy of thirty, as it turned out—which appealed to me. I wanted a worldly, musical man.

"That would be very nice," he said. "I hope we'll meet again."

I made certain that we did. I dragged Lily and my sister to every party that season and flirted shamelessly with Fritz whenever I could. I'd heard all about his married lover, but he was always alone when I saw him, and that gave me hope. He had been raised among the shtetl Jews, and my family was one of Vienna's wealthiest. I felt sure that he would call on me, if only I made it clear that he was welcome.

When he finally came to our *palais* on a Sunday afternoon at the end of June, I had nearly given up hope. He wore a brown cashmere jacket and carried a huge bunch of yellow tulips, which he handed right to Mama.

"Your home is lovely," he said. "And so is your daughter."

It was 1937, and I'd seen my share of romantic movies by then. Fritz was my idea of the perfect leading man, and the gazebo my mother had set up with refreshments and fresh flowers was the ideal setting for our first true rendezvous. I introduced him to my sister Louise and her new husband, and to my brothers, who shook his hand with too much enthusiasm. I had just given him a glass of punch when my uncle Ferdinand rushed in carrying one of his anti-German newspapers.

"Picassos, Pissarros, Cézannes, and Beckmanns," Uncle Ferdinand said, even before he'd taken off his hat. "They're purging art museums and private collections in Germany now."

A few of the guests peeled away, but the rest of us gathered round as my uncle delivered the news.

"A new German law lets the Nazis confiscate anything they call Degenerate Art," Uncle Ferry said. "They can walk right into anyone's house and take the art right off the walls."

My uncle had an extensive art collection—my aunt's portrait was his most treasured piece, but all the pieces were important to him.

"That's in Germany, Ferry," my father said. He put aside his cello and rubbed his hands together. "Your art collection will be fine."

"This is bigger than my collection," Uncle Ferdinand said. He sounded indignant, as if maybe my father didn't understand what was at stake. I glanced nervously at Fritz. I didn't want anything to ruin the afternoon. But Fritz, too, seemed unperturbed. He asked to have a look at the newspaper, and read the story slowly.

"It says the German minister of propaganda is going to put on a Degenerate Art Show in Munich," Fritz said. "Maybe when the paintings are all together, people will see how splendid they are."

My uncle looked at Fritz for the first time. He said that made some sense, but that it didn't comfort him one bit.

"Let's not talk about Germany," Mama said. She took my uncle's hat and walking stick, and handed them to the maid. "We've all come to hear music."

"If Adele were alive, she wouldn't let you change the subject so quickly," my uncle said.

Mama put on a sunny voice and indicated with her eyes that Uncle Ferdinand should not ruin her party. I took my cue from my mother and turned a bright smile on Fritz.

"We'll live to regret it," I heard my uncle say.

"I wouldn't worry about things in Munich," Fritz said to me. By then we'd taken a window seat in the next room, and our knees were only inches apart. "I've always preferred Paris, anyway."

"I hear Paris is full of jazz now," I said. "Do you like jazz?"

I didn't know much about jazz, but I so wanted to impress him.

"Jazz is exciting—but it's confusing," Fritz said. "I love opera, to be honest."

"So do I." I gushed like the girl I was, and pretended it was music that was making me giddy. "I'd give anything to see Lotte Lehmann sing Wagner."

"I'd give anything to take you dancing," he said. I felt as if the top of my head would explode.

I waited a week and then let him take me to a nightclub near the Old Danube. I'd only been to a nightclub once before, and as we walked beneath the bright yellow lights and through a narrow doorway I was so overcome with lovesickness that I could hardly make a sound.

The club was hot and crowded. The jazz band was from Paris, and all but one of the men was black-skinned. Until then I'd only heard jazz on the radio. Fritz was right; jazz was exciting but confusing. It was impossible to waltz to the beat, and we laughed at our own clumsiness as we tried to imitate the dance moves of more chic and graceful couples.

When we'd had enough, Fritz guided me to a table in the corner. I ordered a whiskey sour because I thought it was sophisticated.

"I work for my brother's textile business now," Fritz said. "But I aspire to the opera. I know it's a dream, but I can't seem to let go of it."

I took a careful sip of my drink, and the tart lemon surprised me.

"You shouldn't let go of your dream," I said. "To my father, music is the most important thing in the world."

When Fritz walked me home that evening, I put a hand on his arm and tipped my face. When he put his lips on mine, I tasted cinnamon and stars. Yes, I did. I tasted cinnamon stars.

At my near-hysterical insistence, my mother put off our move to the country house that summer and hosted music brunches and cocktail parties twice weekly through July. Fritz came to most of them, and paid special attention to me, but there were no stolen kisses besides the ones in my imagination.

"He will hurt you," Lily warned me again. "I've asked around; he's crazy about that Czech woman. Her name is Mathilde."

But Mathilde was married, and I was not. He was sweet on me, I felt sure of it. One Sunday afternoon, as he was waiting for his hat, I slipped him a love letter that I'd toiled over alone in my room.

Darling Fritz, I want you to know that I love and admire everything about you. If you make yourself known to my father as a suitor, I promise you won't be disappointed.

I lost six pounds waiting for him to reply, and when he did, it was by telephone several days later. It was hot, and even the ceiling fans did little to cool the house.

"You're sweet, Maria, very sweet and pretty," he said. "But I don't think I'm good enough for you. Don't waste your heart on me when you can have any man in Vienna."

I hung up and wept, but I didn't give up. I'd set myself on him, and the gentleness in his voice had only convinced me that he was right for me.

All through August, the Germans mounted their Degenerate Art show in Munich (millions waited in line to see it, just as Fritz had predicted). I hiked through the Alps with my cousins Eva and Dora and pretended Fritz was with me. At night I kissed my pillow for practice, and one afternoon I begged Dora to show me what she did when a man held and kissed her. My cousin Eva, who was only four-teen, giggled.

"You mean you've never been kissed before?" Dora asked. She'd traveled to Rome and Florence, and whispered to us that she'd had an Italian lover. She was twenty-three and I was twenty-one, but she was decades more sophisticated than I.

"Of course I've been kissed," I said. "But that's all I've done."

"Well, you better learn what's what," Dora said, "if you're going to catch a man with a married lover."

Sitting under a tree with my eyes closed, my cousin nuzzled my neck, I murmured Fritz's name, and she broke into peals of laughter. Somewhere behind her, Eva laughed, too.

It wasn't funny to me. I ran away from them, my eyes burning.

When I returned home that September there were two dozen white roses waiting at the house, with a card signed, *With love from Fritz.* I ran down to Papa's library to show him the note, and found Fritz's brother Bernhard and my father drinking whiskey together.

"Maria, I'm sure you know Herr Altmann," Papa said. He looked very pleased with himself. "He's come to speak to me about his brother."

Bernhard had a long nose and none of his brother's elegant looks. But he was wearing a very fine suit and had a silk handkerchief in his pocket. He stood, and kissed my hand.

"You're even prettier than I remember," Bernhard said.

Bernhard was considerably older than Fritz, and had nearly raised him from the time he was small. It was Bernhard who'd turned their father's tailoring shop into a thriving textiles business. I could imagine only one reason why he'd come to see Papa. I went to my room and jumped up and down until I was out of breath.

After Bernhard was gone, my father sent Mama to my room to speak with me. I already had an inkling of what had happened: Bernhard had put a stop to the affair with Mathilde and urged Fritz to marry me. My mother knew how I felt about Fritz, but wanted to be sure I was in agreement with what had been proposed.

"I've watched you when you're with him, and I have no doubt that he's won your heart," Mama said. "I just want to make sure that he deserves it."

I told her I would die, positively die, if Papa didn't say yes on my behalf. I felt certain that this was exactly how a love story should go.

Two weeks later, Bernhard promoted Fritz to vice president of the textiles business, and Fritz came to see me. He wore a white evening jacket, and the familiar cinnamon scent of his skin was as welcome to me as air.

"I've had a good long time to think about you while you were away," Fritz said. He took me in his arms and said he loved me.

"Your home will be with me now," I whispered.

On our wedding night he took off my clothes one by one until I was naked under a blanket. He kissed my body slowly, beginning at the neck and going down to my toes. I was trembling with happiness. Any reluctance he'd shown seemed a thing of the past, and our life together started out like a happy fairy tale, just as I'd dreamt.

But with Nazi soldiers living in our newlywed apartment, and the two of us soon crowded into three narrow attic rooms, Fritz became silent and withdrawn. I began to remember the darker Grimm's stories: the ones where the children died.

ADELE

1899

I was a virgin on our wedding night, and when Ferdinand made love to me, I closed my eyes and struggled to breathe. His fat fingers were gentle, his fumbling sweet, and his caresses sincere. There was an instant of pain, the awkward weight of his body on mine, and then it was over. It wasn't so bad, I almost blurted aloud. At least it was quick.

We went to Paris as he'd promised, and stayed in a hotel that overlooked the Champs-Élysées. Toulouse-Lautrec's bright posters of dancing women in ruffled dresses hung in coffeehouses and kiosk windows, and there was heady flirting in the cafés where women and men mixed freely. In Vienna most women still kept their necks and arms covered, but in Paris the women wore low necklines, rouged their lips, and stared boldly from beneath bright hats.

It was after ten o'clock when Ferdinand slipped the maître d' a ten franc note and we were led to two narrow chairs at a long table close to the cabaret stage. The Moulin Rouge was smoky and smelled of cheap perfume. Ferdinand ordered absinthe, and I had claret. It was too dark to see his face, but I smiled at him and looked for the tilt of his mustache that would indicate he was smiling, too. The gaslights dimmed and blinked, and music whirled in a kaleidoscope of color and noise. Soon the curtains parted and a marching band rolled onto the stage. The musicians wore funny striped jackets and played a crazy, tilted rhythm. Ladies in short skirts and fishnet stockings pranced a cancan, kicking high above their heads as the music got louder.

The performers made bawdy jokes and double entendres in French that were beyond Ferdinand's comprehension—and I was thankful for that, because I knew he would be shocked. Certainly, *I* was shocked. But I was also riveted. There was pungent sweat, bulging décolletage, and miles of crazy laughter.

I finished my drink, and then I finished Ferdinand's.

"Isn't it exciting?" I asked when there was a short break in the show.

Before he could answer, a woman in a long red gown stepped onstage and began to sing in a smoky voice. Behind her, a line of women in short pink and black ruffled dresses swayed from side to side.

The singer slowly stripped off her long black gloves, peeling back the fabric an inch at a time. When her hands were bare, the band slowed its tempo. The gaslights went out one by one until there was a single smoky spotlight on the red dress and a rumble of low laughter coming from the line of dancers.

To the single beat of a deep drum, the woman slid her bare knee and then her thigh out between a long slit in her gown. I felt a jolt through my whole body.

Ferdinand put a hand on my shoulder, and I turned, my face flush.

"I'm sorry, Adele," he said in my ear. "This is beneath you."

I thought he was joking, and asked him to order me another glass of claret. Then he stood abruptly, taking me by the elbow. I followed helplessly as he pushed his way between the narrow tables, pulling me along until we'd reached the doorway. A line of women in Egyptian costume was making its way onto the stage when he gave the coat check girl our ticket and wrapped me in my sable coat.

"I wanted to stay!" I said when I could finally make myself heard out on the street. The red windmill was spinning against the starry sky, and wind from the river whipped around my ankles. Carriages were still arriving with gay Parisians in furs and top hats.

"It was scandalous," Ferdinand said. "I had no business taking you in there."

He set his jaw in a stubborn line. I could see he was angry, but I was angry, too.

"We went in there together," I said, standing up to him in a way I'd never dared speak to my father or even to my brothers. "I'm not a little girl—I can decide for myself what is proper."

Back at the hotel I went straight to my bedchamber and shut the door between our rooms. I fumbled in the dark before I found the lamp and turned on the key switch. I hung up my coat, and slipped off my shoes. I took down my hair and let it fall around my shoulders.

I could still hear the music in my head, and smell the sweet perfume and cigarette smoke on my clothes. I could see the woman in the red dress showing her bare leg to us, the slit in her dress going higher and higher.

It was late, but I wasn't ready to sleep.

I'd ordered a box of books delivered to the hotel, and they'd arrived that very afternoon. I ran my hand across the leather-bound volumes piled on a table near the window: Descartes, Schopenhauer, and Wagner. Two novels by Jane Austen. A fat anatomy book from London.

I rang the bell for a chambermaid, and asked her to bring up some tobacco and cigarette papers.

"Matches, also," I added at the last minute. "And coffee."

I'd watched Berta rolling her own cigarettes, and seen my brothers do it at home, as well. It was easy enough. And I was alone. I could do it. I needed no one's permission.

I heard Ferdinand making noises on the other side of the door, but I ignored him and soon enough he must have gone to sleep. I did not. I lined up the dark cigarette paper, laid out a line of fresh tobacco, and pressed it tightly into a long cylinder that I sealed by moistening the edges. I let it dry while I changed into one of my new white sleeping gowns. After midnight, coughing and dizzy, I smoked the first cigarette of my life. I drank coffee that burned a second night into my first one. And I read two books side by side: Austen's *Emma* on my left and *Gray's Anatomy* on my right.

I read deep into the night as the heroine of Austen's tidy novel made one romantic mistake after another. When I wanted to think over a line, or had trouble puzzling out the English because I was tired, I

paged through the brilliant anatomy book. I studied veins and ligaments, the system of bones and joints, and the red organs beneath a
white rib cage cut in half. I found a page with the four chambers of the
heart laid bare, and felt my own blood moving from one chamber to the
other, the thump of my heartbeat moving with the pace of a clock over
the mantel. I felt how easily life could slip from my body, as quickly
as the heart could stop beating.

The hotel went from peaceful to eerily quiet. The heat slunk from
the room, and the coffee failed me. So did my anger. I became homesick
for my brother, and for the simple years of my childhood. I didn't know
what I was doing so far away from home, with a man I didn't love and
didn't know if I could love. Karl had been right when he'd warned me
about the box—but he'd been wrong when he'd told me that beneath
the skin everything had already begun to heal.

I wept quietly at first.

"You were wrong," I said aloud, as if Karl could hear me. "You were
wrong, everything isn't healed beneath the skin."

I must have made more noise than I realized, because soon I heard
Ferdinand insisting that I open the door.

"It you don't let me in, I'll ring for the bellman and they'll use a key
to open the door from the hallway," he said. And so I let him in. I let
him find me weeping.

"What is it?" He took me by the shoulders. "Why are you crying?
Is it the cabaret? We can go back tomorrow if it means this much
to you."

I couldn't make it out. I couldn't begin to explain how the woman
singing in the cabaret had made me long for something I didn't understand, or how it had been hard for me to breathe when he'd lain on top
of me our wedding night. I must have choked on my tears, because
he gave me a drink of water, and when I couldn't swallow it down he
pressed my lips to the glass and tipped it toward my throat. Naturally
that only made me choke harder, and as I was still crying, I began to
gasp for air.

In a panic, Ferdinand rang down to the front desk. Soon the hotel doctor swept into the room with his black bag and monocle glass, and gave me a bitter dose of laudanum.

"Drink it slowly," he said in French. He was a soft-spoken man, older than Ferdinand, and nothing in my behavior or appearance seemed to shock or upset him. "It will calm you."

He took a seat beside the bed and inspected my books one by one. I felt the medicine course through me, soothing my nerves. Ferdinand faded to the doorway between our rooms, unsure of what to do.

"What are you reading here?" the doctor asked. "Schopenhauer is a madman, no one reads him unless they're fond of suffering."

Ferdinand's French was clumsy, but mine was fluid. I spoke quietly to the doctor about my brother's death, and about how I'd wanted to study at university. I told him I'd become frightened that I was to live a life I didn't want.

"I want to read and study," I told him. "I want to be an intellectual. Why shouldn't I study just because I'm a woman?"

The doctor adjusted his monocle. He seemed to give my words careful consideration.

"You're a young woman, and you have needs of the body as well as the mind," he said. He spoke as a father might, if I could have spoken that way to my father, and he had understood. "You must eat and sleep well, and take in the air. Go to our museums, and see our art. Walk the street, and enjoy your days. You're intelligent and you're beautiful. Don't rely on your face more than your mind, or on your mind more than your beauty. Your life will come to you. Don't be in a hurry."

But I was in a hurry. I was afraid if I didn't learn everything, and quickly, somehow life would pass me by as it had passed by Karl.

"She's spirited," I heard the doctor tell Ferdinand as he was leaving. "Be careful with her. You wouldn't want her to break on you."

I thought perhaps the doctor's German was lost in translation, or that I'd heard him wrong. I was going to ask him to explain, but the medicine pulled me into deep sleep. When I woke it was early afternoon, and Ferdinand was sitting in a chair by the window.

"Let's go see the museums," he said. "If you're up to it."

The crying jag had frightened me. I dressed in my warmest clothes and carried my cheerful white fox muff. I put on the hat that I knew made my eyes look more green than brown, and we set off.

By day, Ferdinand and I visited museums and braved the cold to stroll through the Luxembourg Gardens and the Tuileries. We went down crooked cobblestone streets and ducked into bright little galleries where we saw canvases filled with colorful fruit and flowers tipped at dizzying angles, yellow skies, and thick brushstrokes of blue and red. The names Van Gogh, Degas, Monet, and Cézanne were on every art dealer's lips, and Ferdinand liked their paintings.

"Beautiful and modern," he said. We were standing in front of a line of Monet's haystacks, each one fading into a changing sky of purple, yellow, pink, and blue. "I'd like to see more of this in Vienna. You've convinced me that this is what our city needs."

I saw the gallery owner making his way toward us.

"The Impressionists aren't of the moment anymore, Ferry." I took his arm and led him to the door. "They're not pushing the edges of what art can be."

In the winding streets, where the white peaks of the Sacré-Cœur rose above us like a goddess, galleries were exploding with paintings of naked pubescent girls cloaked in anxiety and mystery. Gauguin was showing a piece called *The Spirit of the Dead Watching* in a small space on Rue Laffitte: a brown-skinned girl staring out from the canvas, one eye blocked, the other shrouded in secrecy. Her naked bottom was round and firm, as ripe as a piece of fruit. Behind me was Paris and the smell of baking bread and fresh croissants, women in stylish hats, and singers whose jokes made me blush. In front of me was power and fantasy pulling me in, the way the sea tides will pull in anything that stands at the edges of the shore.

"Symbolism—that's what's new," I told Ferdinand. "I've been reading about it in a journal I bought yesterday on Saint-Honoré. The painters are trying to send us messages in symbols."

"Messages about what?" Ferry asked.

He was genuinely trying to understand, and I was touched. I struggled to put into words what I barely understood myself.

"About the meaning of life." I spoke with more confidence than I felt. "About everything that we can't see and don't know."

He encouraged me to go on—that is one of the things that I valued most about him right from the start. I told him our modern painters were looking beyond books and knowledge and peering into the unknown corners of the heart and the mind.

"And even beyond that," I added, "into the realm of spirits, death, and desire."

Ferdinand seemed satisfied with my answer, but I was not. I wanted to see it all for myself. I wanted to know and to understand, not to guess.

With a map in hand, and the sun as a halfhearted compass to guide us, I went in search of my first painting by Edvard Munch that same day. At the top of the funicular we turned away from the cemetery, going behind the church and round and round past dark little shops where women lounged in doorways and the air smelled of something sweet and thick. We stopped at a creperie and had a savory cheese crepe, followed by a sweet chocolate dessert. As I was wiping my mouth and preparing to begin searching again, I spied the place I'd been looking for almost directly across the street.

The gallery was small and cramped, and there were two cats sunning themselves in the window. The proprietor was a tall, elegant man with a salt-and-pepper mustache. Immediately he recognized that we were Viennese, and spoke to us in German. He went on about Munch's popularity in Berlin, and how we would be bringing the modern right to Vienna if we brought his works home with us. I didn't hear much more of what he said. I was as horrified as I was captivated by the two pieces on the wall. One was an anxious mermaid pulling herself from the sea, and the other was a naked girl sitting on a bed as if she were a butterfly pinned under glass.

"This symbolism seems dark." Ferdinand's voice was clear and sure.

He put a hand on my elbow, as if waiting for me to concur or object, but I was lost in the paintings: the mermaid caught between two worlds, and the naked girl staring out from the white sheets with her arms crossed between her legs as if she knew what was coming, and she was afraid.

"Certainly this is not what you mean we should be doing in Vienna?" Ferdinand asked.

"I think Klimt is already doing it," I finally said.

"Well then," Ferdinand said. Then he fell silent, too.

We spent a month in Paris. We did not return to the Moulin Rouge, and I did not pick up Schopenhauer again. By the time we returned home in February, I was nineteen years old, and a show was about to open at the new Secession gallery. I felt sufficiently prepared to join society as a woman of substance—and I was sure that Gustav Klimt and Berta Zuckerkandl were exactly the people I wanted to know.

*T*he white building on the Vienna River is finished. It stands directly over the Ottakring stream, where its foundations are eight meters deep and held in place with large concrete weights. Olbrich's exhibition pavilion cost a mere 120,000 crowns because all the artists worked without payment. The dome is a bower crowned by a gigantic laurel tree painted in gold leaf, with 3,000 leaves and 700 berries. It is an enchanting sight. Through the gaps in the dome branches one can see the sky above and the townscape below. Herman Bahr's words round the exhibition hall run thus: "Let the artist show his world, the beauty that was born with him, that never was before and never will be again."

A novelty is the interior walls, which can be shifted around at will. Even the great columns that separate the middle room from the back are removable. Thanks to this flexibility it will be possible for Klimt and the other artists to have a new ground plan each year over the next ten years. Even the lighting can be varied from overhead to side. Naturally, it will take time for public judgments to settle out feelings of confusion and perplexity, but as a whole the Secession gallery stands ready to host the young artist's first international exhibition of new works.

—LUDWIG HEVESI, FEUILLETONIST AND ART CRITIC, VIENNA 1900

ADELE

1900

After my bath, I settled on a sleeveless green and gold-trimmed cocktail dress. The evening was to be my debut as a married woman in Vienna, and I wanted to strike just the right balance: rarified, but also bright and modern.

I powdered myself carefully, surprised at how much effort it took to make my underarms smooth. My new dressing maid was even younger than I, and she was nervous, too. I tried not to rush or jangle at her as she slipped the dress over my head and lifted my hair so that nothing would catch in the necklace clasp.

The heavy gold choker by Koloman Moser was a wedding gift from Ferdinand, and I was glad for the chance to show it off.

"Radiant," Ferry said when we met in the foyer. "Just beautiful."

"Moser will be there tonight," I said. "I'm sure he'll be thrilled to see I'm wearing his piece."

"I meant you," Ferdinand said. "You are beautiful."

As we'd done that first day of our courtship, we took Ferdinand's carriage across the Ring to the gleaming new Secession gallery. We were early, which I preferred. There were two footmen at the doors, and Ferdinand and I climbed the red-carpeted steps slowly, passing beneath the motto above the doorway in gold letters that read, *To Every Age Its Art; To Art Its Freedom.*

The Zuckerkandls were waiting for us beside the reception table. Berta wore a loose turquoise dress and a colorful turban around her hair. I said I was certain no one would rival her daring costume, not even the Flöge sisters.

"And you look ravishing," Berta said. "The dress is perfect on you."

All the important artists would be there—Klimt, of course, and also Carl Moll, who acted as the painter's agent in all matters of commissions and sales, Josef Hoffmann, Olbrich, and maybe even the elusive Albin Lang. I was looking forward to meeting them, but I was also intimidated. I'd done my best to read up on the Secessionists, but while I knew the artists concerned themselves primarily with truth in art, I wasn't quite sure what that meant.

"Relax," Berta said, as if she could read my mind. "Everyone will love you."

Just then Koloman Moser hurried toward me and nearly bowed. I wanted to laugh, but it would have been unsuitable.

"Frau Bloch-Bauer, how happy I am to see you," he said. He was a handsome man, with a pencil-thin mustache.

"I'm thrilled to be wearing your exquisite necklace," I said, fingering the gold at my throat. "It's stunning craftsmanship, and so uniquely Viennese."

It was an expected formality, but also the truth.

"Your beauty does it great justice," he said.

Moser had also designed the stained glass window that dominated the gallery lobby. I asked him about the colors, and we enjoyed a lively conversation as the room filled. New people flooded in, and fashionable women were everywhere. I saw them turn to look at my dress, but it was Alma Schindler, holding forth about the libido and the death drive, who'd soon attracted a small circle around her.

"Eros and Thanatos," Alma said in a high, bright voice. "Dr. Freud understands what no one has dared to grasp before."

I leaned into Alma's circle and looked at the women gathered around her. Some appeared shocked; others looked frightened or confused. One, a widow, was smiling slyly. Dr. Freud's new ideas about sex and desire had brought people to blows, and I was both stunned and amazed by Alma's brazenness. It was hard to believe that only a few years ago I had been forbidden to study anatomy and now people—women!—

were talking openly and in public about sensual appetite. Ferdinand's fuss at the Moulin Rouge seemed pedestrian in the face of it.

"Here you are." Ferdinand tapped my shoulder. He handed me a catalog of the show, and I missed whatever it was that Alma said next.

Berta appeared behind me, and threaded her arm through mine.

"Let's go in," she said.

I took a deep breath and stepped into Vienna's avant-garde in my sleeveless green dress, with my heart thrumming.

"There are two hundred pieces here," Berta said, tugging me close. "Besides Klimt's mural—the centerpiece of the show, of course—he has some wonderful landscapes, and there are bold new pieces by the Belgian Symbolists, too."

The Secessionists wanted the exhibition to be an experience that pleased as many senses and sensibilities as possible—a complete art work of art, music, color, sculpture, and nature. A string quartet was playing Mozart in the center room, and the show had been divided into smaller areas that looked like intimate galleries or parlors. There was sleek, modern furniture designed by Josef Hoffmann, and electric light fixtures over tables arranged with flowers and sculptures.

"I'd like a garden mural painted on my dining room walls," I heard a woman with silver hair say. Her friend, who was staring at a pair of stiff white chairs, nodded. "And some of those Mackintosh chairs, too."

Beyond the small, stylized spaces there were four movable panels hung with large, colorful pieces. Berta and I stopped in front of a frightening painting of a bird-woman against a black sea background.

"Jan Toorop's *Medusa*." She tapped a pencil against a slip of paper where she was jotting some notes. "What do you think, Adele?"

I whispered that it seemed like two ideas mixed together into the grotesque. She liked that, and made a note.

"I prefer this one," I said, looking at a larger piece that showed three brides preparing for a procession. The women's faces were alternately European and Egyptian, regal and exotic.

"So do I," Berta agreed. "It's like Vienna right now, poised between the old and the new."

The dressmakers Emilie and Helene Flöge made a late entrance and caused a stir with dazzling new dresses that showed their ankles. Soon, Berta and I found ourselves in front of Klimt's landscapes. Right away I fell under their spell. With their turquoise water and crooked, lively rooftops I felt as if I'd stepped right into the countryside.

"And what's behind there?" I pointed toward an enormous blue curtain that hung floor to ceiling. Two of the emperor's soldiers were standing in front of it, on guard.

"The new mural," Berta said. "Klimt will open the curtain around nine o'clock, just when everyone is dying of curiosity. He has a flair for theatrics," she added with a smile. "But we can see it now, if you'd like."

My friend slid a brown ticket out of her purse and showed it to a guard. The press pass had the date—March 4, 1900—stamped in large black print, and was signed by Gustav Klimt in a flourished hand.

The guard studied the pass and gave us a nod.

"The mural is going to the Paris Exposition after this," Berta said as we slipped through an opening in the curtain. The blue fabric covered my face, and for a moment I was lost in a sea of velvet.

"Of course it is," I said, my voice strangely muffled. "Everything exciting is in Paris."

"That's not true." Berta put a warm hand on my bare arm, and spoke with a sense of urgency. "What the Secessionists are doing in Vienna is worlds ahead of anything that's happening in Paris. I can promise you that what's happening here will shape the art world for a very long time."

Berta didn't promise things lightly, and I felt a shiver of nervous excitement as she guided me into the center hall. There were two others in front of the mural: I recognized the critic Karl Kraus and the writer Peter Altenberg, but they were standing shoulder to shoulder and barely seemed to notice us.

Klimt's *Philosophy* was thick and dense—taller than four men and as wide as three. Red and blue figures seemed to swim across the canvas, and there were dark lava swirls and twisted naked bodies clutching their heads or crouching in fear. It was overpowering and terrifying, and I had to stare at it for a long time before I saw a ghostly face burning in the center of the canvas—a shimmering sylph looking coolly above the suffering without giving it thought.

"But it's ugly," I heard Kraus murmur.

Altenberg said nothing. Berta frowned.

There was more in the mural than I'd seen at first: a gaunt, naked man straining toward nothing with his arms above his head; a nude woman, bending toward the outer edge of the frame where she could find no escape; bare, spackled space filled with a red and golden haze like the fires of hell or the expanses of heaven and the whole world a roiling, uncontained place of misery and mystery.

It made *Adam and Eve* seem like a child's primer.

"Well?" Berta asked at last. The others had left, and we were alone. "Do *you* think it's ugly?"

"It's terrible and magnificent," I breathed. "It's astonishing."

When I was young, I'd searched the sky for God's face or closed my eyes and tried to pray him into my heart, but I'd always failed. When Karl got sick, God didn't answer my prayers—he'd let Karl die, and I'd decided right then that if God existed, he was a phantom in the sky looking past our suffering, never hearing our supplications. Since we didn't go to synagogue and we certainly didn't attend church, no one had contradicted my beliefs; no one had even asked.

Klimt's unblinking honesty in the face of human suffering was a truth I understood—and as I stared into his swirling eternity I saw the certainty of my life rise up to the glass ceiling, hover for a moment, and vanish. I felt the circle of time open into a possibility I had never dreamt of. In that moment, I saw exactly what Klimt meant by truth in art.

"It's everything I believe about God and suffering," I said.

"Is that a good thing, Frau Bloch-Bauer?" a man asked.

I turned to find Gustav Klimt standing right behind me. We'd never met, and I was very pleased that he knew who I was.

"Herr Klimt," I said. My throat filled, and no more words came.

Berta came to my rescue.

"I think your work has made her speechless," she said.

"No." I recovered myself, and cast about for phrases I'd read and heard. "It's like music, but it's also a meditation on . . . truth. Is that right?"

He smiled broadly, and I liked him right away. Quite a few men at the party, especially the painters, had a sickly look about them. Klimt was robust, with curly brown hair and wide shoulders. He was handsome, close to forty years old, with an elfin beard that came to a trim point. His fine three-piece suit was perfectly tailored, and his muscles were evident beneath the tweedy fabric. Although we'd not seen the sun in Vienna for most of February, his complexion was ruddy and healthy.

"I try not to make my work a meditation on anything," he said. "I like to think about color and balance."

He touched the gold necklace at my throat. I noticed bits of blue paint under his fingernails. Up close he smelled of the turquoise air in the countryside, blue water and snow, and the suggestion of animals waking from hibernation.

"I look for things that are in contradiction but are somehow in harmony," he said. I could feel the heat from his fingers, and did not let my eyes leave his. "Like this gold on your shoulders, and the glow against your dark hair."

Klimt's charisma was exceptional. I stammered out something about the woman's face staring out from the corner of the mural.

"She looks wise and fierce, to me," I said.

"If you've read Wagner's essay on Beethoven, I'm sure you'll know who she is," Berta chimed in. She was a dear: she knew I'd read the essay, and thought about it deeply.

"I have," I said to Klimt. "I've just come from my honeymoon in Paris, where I did read Wagner's essay."

I cast about for something more to say. I wanted to sound clever.

"We saw art there, too," I added. "Some of the images here tonight put me in mind of Munch, especially the mermaid."

"I haven't seen his mermaid, but I did see Munch's *Scream* in Berlin," Klimt said. "I think I know how that poor fellow feels."

He put his two thick hands alongside his mouth and pulled his face into a comical scream.

I laughed out loud.

In Vienna we took our ideas and ourselves very seriously. Klimt was brilliant, but he was also devilish and debonair.

"Honestly," he said, while we were still laughing. "What did you think of Munch's mermaid?"

"It was disturbing," I admitted. The laughter had made me relax. I felt my tongue loosen. "It was provocative. It made me think. Like your painting does. Only your piece is far more exciting."

"I hope the others will be as generous as you are," he said. He clapped his hands. "They'll be seeing it soon enough."

Someone popped a head through the blue curtain and called for the painter. He excused himself, but turned back for an instant and smiled.

"I hope you'll visit my studio, Frau Bloch-Bauer," he said. "I'd like to see you there."

I flushed from head to toe, and was very glad I wasn't wearing a long-sleeved dress.

"Well," I said to Berta, after he'd gone. "Is he always like that?"

"He does know how to coax a smile onto a pretty face," Berta said.

"And what about his fiancée?" I asked.

Berta laughed. "Emilie Flöge? Dear, they're like brother and sister. I thought everyone knew that."

"I didn't," I said.

Berta explained that Emilie's sister had been married to Klimt's brother, and that when Ernst died, Klimt had become close to all of the Flöge women. He and Emilie weren't engaged, she said, but people seemed to think they were, and they'd never done anything to discourage the rumors.

I was trying to piece it all together when Berta put her arm through mine again, and pulled me close.

"The truth is that Emilie prefers the company of women in the bedroom," she said. A strange expression came over her face. "Although of course that's scandalous to say, and nothing more than gossip."

"Of course," I said. "It's only hearsay." I felt a jolt go through me, just as it had in Paris. Sexual transgressions and secrets seemed to be everywhere, and my friend's face was very close, and very warm.

The next hour passed with wine, cigarettes, and hors d'oeuvres. Friends who'd been at our wedding in December wanted to talk about the ball season we'd missed, and to hear about our honeymoon in Paris.

"We saw everything," I told Alma. I ticked off a list of artists we'd seen on our honeymoon. "And the Moulin Rouge—Ferry took me to see the dancers."

Alma shook her hips and smiled knowingly.

"I've been there," she said. "It was thrilling."

No matter whom I was talking to, it seemed Klimt was always in my line of sight, and always surrounded by admirers. He grew more animated and enigmatic as the evening went on, as if he were flirting with men and women alike and holding the whole room enthralled. Once or twice I saw Emilie Flöge stand near him, but there was nothing that suggested anything intimate between them.

At nine o'clock Klimt called for everyone's attention, and the new minister of culture made a few remarks to the crowd.

"Emperor Franz Joseph is proud and pleased to support the efforts of true Austrian art such as we see in Gustav Klimt and the new Secessionist movement," the official said.

Klimt shook the minister's hand and thanked the crowd for coming. His voice was clear and strong. I thought he might make a few remarks, but he simply reached for the curtain and drew it open himself.

"I give you *Philosophy*," he said.

In the full gallery light, the mural was even more powerful than before. The figures were gaunt and tortured; the swirling atmosphere haunted. There was a hush in the room, and a few gasps. A cry rose from the professors who'd commissioned the mural for the university's Great Hall.

"I don't understand," I heard one of the professors say. "Where is Aristotle? Where is the Greek temple?"

"Is it an allegory?" another man asked. "I thought it would be an allegory to wisdom."

"Good God," someone cried. The minister of culture backed away from the painting, but he did it slowly, inch by inch, moving in such tiny increments that the change in his position was inconspicuous.

"They expected a party scene," Berta said in my ear. "The philosophers through the ages, eating grapes in a sunny Austrian garden. Now they're disappointed."

"It's ugly," I heard Kraus say again. A few men around him agreed, and loudly.

Emil Zuckerkandl, who was standing with the other academics, was one of the first to clap his hands together. Soon a few others began to applaud, too. Someone shouted *bravo!* And the applause grew.

I looked at Ferdinand, and he at me.

"I think it's brilliant," I said.

"Well then, I'm sure it is redeeming," my husband said. "Although I have to admit I don't quite see what's brilliant about it."

The last thing I saw that evening was Klimt, taking a long drink of wine and gazing up at the sylph in the center of his painting. It was as if he wanted an answer from her, and knew there would be only silence.

◎◯

I lived with Ferdinand on Schwindgasse in those early years of our marriage, in the very same apartments I'd visited with Mother during our courtship. Our home filled a good portion of a city block, with two parlors and a dining room suitable for grand parties, private rooms on the second floor, and Ferdinand's business offices on the third floor below the servants' quarters. From my bedroom windows I could look across the Ringstrasse and see the lights from the emperor's palace winking on at dusk. Sometimes I could hear the royal horses whinny as the guards made their rounds at first light.

My rooms were my own and my bed was grand, piled with pillows in all shades of blue and white arranged so that I could lie back and look up at the sky. The green velvet chaise from my childhood bedroom was in front of a cupola window. I watched the sunset from my bed on spring evenings, and on nights when I couldn't sleep I lay there rolling cigarettes and smoking until the sun came up.

The morning after the Secessionist party I woke easily, reached a toe out from under the blankets, and pushed aside the curtains. I was shrugging into my robe, deciding what to wear and whether or not I should send a calling card to make an appointment with Klimt, when Ferdinand knocked and came into my room. He was dressed in a brown jacket and tweed vest, and was carrying a pile of newspapers. I could tell by the way he held the newssheets against his chest that something bothered him.

"They've written another editorial about Sarajevo," he said. "They're advocating for suffrage throughout the empire."

"It's too early in the morning to worry about Bosnian radicals," I said.

I took the newssheets from him, and found Karl Kraus's culture journal.

"Here," I said. "Kraus has reviewed the Secessionists' show."

I scanned the page quickly, running a finger under the lines about Klimt.

"It's an attack—he says Klimt has no understanding of philosophy." I read the rest aloud—*In his ignorance, the painter has offended the intellectual and aesthetic principles of his sponsors at the university, and invited a new darkness to descend upon the Secessionist movement.*

"He didn't understand the painting or anything about it." I was surprised that my voice was shaking. "We need this kind of art, Ferry—we need a way of thinking about the things that we're afraid of or don't understand."

The emperor had supported the Secessionists, and Ferdinand supported the emperor.

"What kinds of things?" he asked.

"Sorrow," I said, thinking over the painting, and what I'd felt last night. "Death. Pain. A world without God that's still wise and beautiful."

He shook his head. He didn't believe in God, but he believed in the emperor and the order of our city and of our lives.

"I'm not sure this is a good thing for you to be worrying about," Ferdinand said. "Remember what happened in Paris."

"This isn't like that." I was prone to heady pronouncements, and I summoned one then. "This is the future of Vienna."

"I'm not sure I agree," he said again, but he did not insist on anything further.

After breakfast Ferry went up to his offices, and I told the maid that I would be out until after lunch. I bundled into my ermine cloak, kidskin gloves and warm boots, and set out on the Ring. The sun had broken through the clouds, and the city looked bright even though the trees were bare. Triton and Naiad Fountain in front of the Museum of Art History was dancing, and even the pigeons were clean and white. I took the path through the Volksgarten past the café where I knew Berta and some of the others would be meeting at eleven. I knew they'd be talking about Kraus's review, but I didn't stop.

Klimt's studio was far from the First District, in a neighborhood where workmen lived with their families. As I got closer, the sidewalks narrowed and there were fewer carriages on the road. I passed housewives and laborers in burlap coveralls, schoolchildren in gardens catching snowflakes on their tongues, and men shoveling coal from rumbling delivery carts.

A low, white fence surrounded Klimt's yard on Josefstädter Strasse. The gate was open, and I entered without shutting it. There was a brown flower garden that had not been turned or weeded, and a wreath of holly shrubs against the fat, yellow house.

I thought Klimt might be something of a madman to have created such a work of art. I wanted to see him alone in his studio; to see what was behind the face he presented to the world.

Beside the hedges I saw a wide window, and I stepped off the path to peer inside. Through the glass I saw a pretty young woman, about my age, sitting on a high chair. Klimt was standing in front of her, his long robe dragging on the floor, his eyes rapt on her face.

Without thinking, I hid behind a shrub.

Standing, I watched Klimt's mouth move. His voice carried through the cracks around the edges of the silvered glass—the words were muffled, and yet they seemed perfectly clear. I pressed further back into the shrubbery and ducked my head. In my green cape, I was camouflaged by a tangle of ivy and branches.

"Take off your dress," Klimt said.

A look crossed the woman's face—some expression I hadn't yet learned to read—and she crisscrossed her arms and drew the clean blue dress up over her head in a single motion.

Her brilliant red hair cascaded across full breasts, and her heart-shaped face tipped toward the painter. She looked eager. She wasn't wearing a corset, so there were no tight strings to loosen and no buttons to unhook. Her shoulders were pale and freckled, the folds of her belly soft and loose.

My whalebone corset had never felt so terrible against my waist as it did at that moment.

"Your garters and your stockings, too," Klimt said, followed by something I couldn't make out.

It was cold outside, but I flushed as I watched her fingers roll the fabric from her thighs. The soft flesh sprang to life, pink and ready. I'd never undressed fully in front of anyone, not even my husband.

"It's freezing," the woman moaned, but she didn't look cold. She wrapped a bright shawl around her shoulders and licked her lips. I could see the imprint of the brass snaps still on her skin; I could feel my own garters pinching the inside of my thighs. What had been invisible and imperceptible before that moment now seemed impossible to ignore—the heat between my legs, cool morning air reaching up through my own stockings and bloomers, the feel of garden ivy brushing against my shins.

"That's beautiful, the scarf is . . ." Klimt's voice trailed out of range as he reached for his sketch pad. "Now lay down, Mimi. Lie down and spread your legs."

She did it: she lay down and opened her thighs. I saw the bold streak of red hair and the dark hollow of her opening, and I went breathless as Klimt's pencil flew across the page.

"That's right," he said softly. I had to strain to make out his words. "Now touch yourself."

A shock rocked through me: I felt as if I were back in Paris, alone onstage with the woman in the red dress. When my schoolmates had whispered about lust and desire I'd listened with a detached coolness, never understanding what it was that excited them so. I'd studied my anatomy book with barely a thought about sexuality, and nothing in my time with Ferdinand had made me dizzy or breathless. But as the woman brought her fingers to her mouth and then back between her legs, my hips began to move. Heat spread from my thighs to my navel, making me light-headed. Klimt's pencil flew across the page and the woman's fingers moved slowly, then more quickly, between her legs.

I nearly pressed my nose to the glass as he drew furiously, pulling the sketches from the pad and dropping them to the floor one by one—snatches of thighs and hip bones falling at his feet. At last he spoke in a low growl.

"Come here."

"The boy will be awake soon," Mimi murmured—it seemed I could hear the tiniest whisper of her breath, the call of a winter bird in the distance, the soft drop of snowflakes that had begun to land on the bushes around me, and the sigh of Klimt's exhale as if in my own ear.

"We have plenty of time," he said. She moved toward him as a fish through water—writhing her body as if swimming in a river—and in a fluid motion climbed up his torso, hiked up his robes and wrapped her legs around his waist.

He grabbed her bottom and they closed their eyes. I stood as I was, watching his buttocks tighten and hips thrust as he growled her name and pressed her against the wall.

It was too late to turn away. I watched until Mimi threw back her head and moaned sharply, and then the two fell apart as quickly as they'd come together. I backed away—the spell broken—terrified that her eyes, flashing toward the window, had seen me with my mouth open, panting.

ADELE

1900

I turned from Klimt's window and hurried back out through the open gate.

I didn't want to go home, but I knew I couldn't stand there.

Time had to pass. My blood had to cool.

I walked furiously through unfamiliar streets, past men digging in a ditch and a stockyard full of sheep. The houses thinned. A few brick homes with thatched roofs lined the road and then gave way to open fields. I walked beside them without seeing anything. More than an hour passed—I heard the church bells chime twelve—before my body finally settled and I went back to the studio on Josefstädter Strasse, back through the white gate.

There was no knocker on the door. I rapped as loudly as I dared.

"Go away," Klimt called. "I'm working."

I kept knocking until he pulled open the door. What possessed me, I have no idea. Maybe it was desire. Maybe I wanted to feel the heat inside that room.

Klimt was wearing his strange brown robe. I saw none of the softness I'd seen in his face earlier, nor any of the amusement that I'd seen in his eyes the night before. I wished, then, that I'd gone straight home. But it was too late. He was close enough to touch. I couldn't go back.

"I've come," I said in a rush. "You asked me to come to your studio."

"Yes." He softened when he recognized me. Behind him, cats padded over sketches that had been carelessly dropped on the floor. I saw no sign of the redhead.

"I read Kraus's review," I said.

"Kraus is an ignorant mule," he said.

He looked tired—not at all like the man I'd watched through the window or the man I'd met last night.

"I wish you'd sent a card ahead, Frau Bloch-Bauer," he said gently. "Or made an appointment."

"But I'm here now," I said, more boldly than I felt. "And it's cold outside."

Slowly he opened the door and invited me in.

A cat mewled at my leg. I looked down, and found I was staring right at a pair of splayed legs, sketched with a hand between them at the crotch. I smelled the sex in the air, and dared to glance through a doorway at the back of the studio.

Mimi was still there, but she was dressed. She had a child on her lap, and she was breastfeeding him. The juxtaposition of mother and lover inhabiting a single body within the space of an hour was stunning to me.

"That's my model, Mimi," Klimt said without a hint of intimacy. "She'll be leaving soon."

I tried not to stare as Mimi gently separated the child's mouth from her nipple. She pulled her hair into a scarf and bundled the boy into a coat and hat. When she stopped to let Klimt give the child a pat on his head, I saw that her hands were rough, like a washerwoman's. But her skin was glowing, and her little boy had big, winsome brown eyes.

"Send for me when you need me," she said.

The boy raised his arms to Klimt.

"Hug Pa-pa," he squealed.

Papa?

Klimt put his arms around the boy, and nuzzled his pale neck with a tiny growl. The boy giggled. Then the two were gone.

In the quiet atelier, the memory of Klimt's bare bottom tied my tongue. I felt none of my heady giddiness as I twisted a cigarette into the holder and fumbled for my lighter.

"I didn't mean to scare away your model," I said at last. I decided to say nothing about the child. "I came because your painting says everything that I feel inside."

Klimt had a changeling's face, and I saw it then for the first time. He was an urchin one moment, a seductive lover the next. On that morning he looked decidedly untamed, as if the man wrapped in the tweed suit had broken out of his clothes and was free to run wild.

"Go on, please," he said. "You sound much more intelligent than Kraus."

"The whirl of terror and longing," I said. Sex and fear seemed closely linked to me that day, as they'd never been before. "The loss of control—all the things I've read about in my philosophy books."

"I'm not a scholar," he said. "I'm sorry if I gave you that idea last night." He found a piece of graphite and searched until he found the knife to sharpen it. "I make art, that's what I do."

"It's all there," I insisted. "I've been thinking about the face at the bottom of the mural. She's Wagner's *Wissen*, isn't she? She's Wisdom, but she stands outside the whirl of our emotions—she's there, but she's so small you can miss her."

"I'm a simple man," he said, almost wearily. "I work every day, from morning to night. I have no time to talk about philosophy when I should be working."

He was tired, there was no doubt about that. I felt foolish for even thinking he'd want to see me on that day, after such an eventful night.

"I'm sorry," I said. "I was impulsive. I can go, if you like."

He kept talking, as if he hadn't heard me.

"I spend every day in my studio." He gestured as if to say *look around, don't you see my work is everything?* "The university professors are already threatening to withhold payment for the mural. If they don't like *Philosophy*, I can only imagine what they're going to say about *Medicine* and *Jurisprudence*, which I've barely begun. So you see, I don't have time to sit and read—I don't even have time to worry. All I can do is paint."

When he finished his short monologue, I smiled. I don't know why. I can only think that it was flattering to hear him say so much, as if he were confiding in me.

"I'm sorry," I said. "I didn't mean to smile, I know you're a serious man."

His pencil was sharpened, and he reached for a sheath of paper.

"And you're a very serious young woman."

There again, I saw the changeling. I wondered if I, too, seemed different than I'd been the night before. I certainly felt different. I'd seen things in the past sixteen hours that I'd never even imagined.

"Yes, I do take myself seriously," I said. "Maybe too seriously."

"How does a serious young woman like you spend her time?"

His pencil was whispering across the paper. I wanted to keep his eyes on me.

"I read—I read all the time," I said. "I go to the opera, to the theater, to museums, to Berta Zuckerkandl's salons. I attend lectures, too."

"What kind of lectures?"

Neither of us stood still; we were moving in concentric circles then, getting closer to one another and then moving apart.

"I love British and French literature—I especially adore Jane Austen."

I thought of Emma, Austen's heroine, who made all kinds of mistakes when she involved herself in romantic affairs where she didn't belong. I mentioned Dickens's *David Copperfield.*

"He's the hero of his own life," I said. "That's an idea I like very much."

Klimt's gaze was intoxicating. I'm embarrassed to remember how little it took to keep me talking. I smoked one cigarette after another as he dropped his sketches onto the floor and table. I caught glimpses of my hair, my mouth, and my arms in motion as he worked.

By the time he put down his pencil, almost two hours had passed. He sorted through the sketches quickly, and thrust one toward me.

"This is how I'll paint you," he said.

I was shocked to see myself naked from the waist up, my face a blur but my breasts exactly as they were in my own mirror.

"Nude?" I cried. "I haven't asked you to paint me at all—and especially not nude."

"Isn't that why you're here?"

The time I'd spent in his studio had passed almost without passing at all—it was as if we'd stepped together into the endless circle of time, or some other timeless place.

"No," I managed to say. "I'm here because I read Kraus's review, and I want to answer it." I took a breath. "I'm thinking I might write a rebuttal and try to place it in the *Neue Freie Presse*."

There, I'd spit out the words. They didn't sound so crazy after all. I knew enough about philosophy and anatomy, which was also important to the painting. I wanted to be like Berta; now, perhaps, I could begin.

"There's no solution in words," Klimt said slowly. "The only answer is in art."

I tried not to feel discouraged or dismissed. I looked around his studio. There were women everywhere, in every state of dress and undress. Some were drawn hastily on paper, others were painted carefully on canvas. Turned away from the window was an almost-finished portrait of regal Rose von Rosthorn. Her body was sheathed in a glittering black gown, the jewels at her neck still wet with white paint glistening as a snowflake on a leaf.

"Others will write in my defense," he said. "Your friend Berta, for one. I still have a few friends at the university who will speak for me and my work. I've already heard this morning that a scholar wants to present a public response to the critics who are calling the mural ugly."

"Please understand, I want to support you however I can."

He gazed at me with what seemed to be electric attention, and in that moment I became something like spirit and gold. I felt completely and absolutely lifted out of the world in which we stood.

"You're a woman of substantive style, and more influence than you may know. You will come into your own very soon, I think. That can help me, Frau Bloch-Bauer. Your friendship can help me."

"Then we will be friends," I said, the words catching in my throat.

"And I'll make a painting for you."

What did he see in me that I didn't see in myself?

"I'm not a femme fatale," I said. "If I'm going to pose for you it will be for something new," I searched for a word. "Something powerful."

"Something powerful." Klimt nodded. He scratched at his pointy beard and drew a few more lines on another sheet of paper: a rough shield, a knife, a breastplate. "A heroine. Like Judith," he said.

"A Jewess?" It was one of the only times I used the word to describe myself. I'd endured the jest of girls who thought they were better than me because they were Catholic and I was not. I felt that same teary desire for denial as I'd felt then. "Why a Jewess?"

"Judith is a heroine." He stood straighter, and used his whole body to create a victorious pose. "And a seductress. She goes where she's not invited, and stirs passion in powerful men."

I'd seen Hebbel's play about Judith and Holofernes at the Burgtheater. I'd seen the actress taking off her layered scarves as she seduced the enemy general in his tent. Like everyone in the audience, I'd known the story of Judith slaying the general. I had been prepared for his decapitation—and still it had shocked me, the way sex and death met on the stage.

"My husband will never pay to have me painted as a bare-breasted Jewess, even if she is a heroine."

I remembered Alma, and the way she'd looked when she was talking about Dr. Freud.

"It won't be a commission." Klimt took the sketch from me. His hand brushed mine, and I felt a spark. I hoped I didn't gasp aloud, but I could not be sure. "The painting will be ours, it will belong to me," he said. "Your husband will have nothing to do with it."

For a rare moment I was speechless. I was also thrilled.

"And you'll be a heroine," he repeated. "Bold and beautiful."

So there it was. I was a heroine. I was bold and beautiful. I was a Jewess, and Klimt would paint me that way.

"Come back to me when you're ready to begin," Klimt said.

I wanted him to touch my neck again, right above the collarbone. But he didn't. He picked up his sketch pad, and disappeared into his work. It was as if he'd already dismissed me, and I was gone.

It didn't matter, though. I had not felt so perfectly alive and fully visible since Karl had taken my hand and traced it over his anatomy drawings many years before.

———

I had a secret, and it burned through me all afternoon. Like Judith preparing for Holofernes, I was aware of my face, my hair, the way my body moved through the streets and how I looked in the mirror. I thought I certainly must look different, but no one seemed to notice.

I dined with Ferdinand, Gustav, Thedy, and my parents at the Hotel Metropole that night. The evening was pleasantly predictable—the dining room was filled with flowers, my mother ordered her favorite cold vichyssoise soup for a first course, and we enjoyed an hour of conversational French over dessert.

Almost everyone we knew spoke French, and read Voltaire in the original, and my mother liked to practice with us as often as she could. Even Ferdinand did his best to keep up, mentioning Klimt's mural in passing, and the editorial about Sarajevo, which clearly troubled him.

"We all support the emperor," my father said, pacifying Ferdinand as he often did. "The Bosnians and Serbs are nothing to worry about."

"On the contrary," Ferdinand said. "They'll take every bit of power that they can."

"Thedy, did you enjoy the symphony last night?" Mother asked, changing the conversation from politics to music.

No one asked how I'd spent my day, and I mentioned nothing of my visit to Klimt's studio.

Alone in my room at the end of the night, I blew out the candles and slipped between my sheets without bothering with a nightgown. I pulled up the blankets and imagined I was Judith, parting the tent flaps to find Holofernes beside a fire in fur boots and a long robe.

I was a seductress, Klimt was Holofernes, and in my fantasy I dropped my scarves one by one until I was wearing only a thin white toga, I was opening his hungry lips and plying him with wine and sweets. My head filled with Klimt's lithe redhead and his fingers weaving through her long hair, her hands between her legs, the look of bold pleasure in her face as she stroked herself.

Sex with Ferdinand was uneventful, but I had another picture of desire as I slipped my hand between my legs and imagined being taken by the redhead and the painter at once, their limbs swimming through mine, their skin hot against me. I'd heard of such a thing happening to other women, this feeling of excitement at the moment of surrender, but I'd never felt anything like it with Ferdinand—never this surge, never this rocking, never this power as if I was climbing a mountain and ringing a bell, ringing and ringing as I rocked and shook with a crown of pleasure.

MARIA

1938

A Nazi flag was raised at the factory gatehouse, the whistle blew at eight, and our business reopened under German control in the third week of March. Fritz and I watched from our attic rooms as hundreds of workers streamed onto the grounds carrying lunch boxes and paper sacks. They laughed and called to one another in loud voices. Some were our old employees, but they walked by our windows without glancing up.

"It doesn't seem right," I said. I moved away from the window and pulled on a favorite blue sweater.

"It isn't right, but what can I do?"

"You can't do anything." I meant it to sound gentle, but Fritz jerked as if I'd slapped him.

"It's not like they gave me a choice, Maria."

I rushed to say, "That's not what I meant," but his face had already shut, and I hadn't the energy to say more.

All of us were losing our resilience. Friends and family were leaving the city without a word. Men were being flogged in the streets. My cousins Eva and Dora had disappeared in the night with their parents, and we had no way of knowing if they'd fled or been arrested. My parents and I told one another that Louise and her children were safe in Yugoslavia, and that Robert and his family would be fine in Grinzing. We told ourselves that Leopold had escaped, and that we would hear from him soon. But we couldn't be sure of anything, and the silence was terrifying.

Fritz waited that first morning until the workers had stamped their timecards and the machines in the shops were humming. Then he disappeared out the kitchen door without another word.

I knew where he was going, because every day he did the same thing: he stood on line at the post office, hoping for a letter from Uncle Ferdinand or Bernhard. He went to the bank, where the lines poured into the street and few reached the teller windows before they closed at noon or one o'clock. Then he joined a long line outside the police station, where everyone was trying to get an emigration visa.

"It's the same thing everywhere," Fritz said when he came home that afternoon. He slouched in a kitchen chair, and I knelt in front of him to take off his shoes. "It's like I'm invisible."

"Not to me," I said. I cradled first one brown wingtip in my hand, and then the other. His socks were damp at the heel. I inhaled the scent of leather and sweat. I put my head in his lap and waited for him to stroke my hair, but he didn't raise his hand.

That evening, as they'd done the prior nights, Felix Landau and his men knocked at the door after we'd eaten our supper. We answered because we had to. The Nazis smelled of beer, and we could hear music playing in our apartment downstairs.

"Where are the button and thread accounts?" Landau asked, pressing his way into our parlor.

"I don't know," Fritz said. In Landau's shadow, he looked small and frightened.

"What are you owed for the wool and satin exports? Where are the account books for the cashmeres?"

"I don't know." Fritz kept his face blank. He had to be polite. "Don't you think I would give them to you if I could?"

"No," Landau said. The scar on his jaw was pulsing. "I think you are lying to me, Herr Altmann."

But Fritz wasn't lying. He didn't have the account books because he had burned them to ash in the factory's boiler.

Fritz finally reached the bank window on a rainy afternoon the last week of March. The teller looked at his bankbook, and put it into the tally machine.

"Your accounts have been Aryanized," she said, dismissing him with a single sentence. She stamped the passbook and handed it back to him.

At home, Fritz fell into the kitchen chair and showed me the deposit book. *JUDE. JUDE. JUDE.* Three pages, one after the other, stamped in blood red ink: *JEW, JEW, JEW.*

"We have nothing left," he said.

But we didn't have nothing; not yet. We still had the rubies and emeralds my mother and I had sewn into the black gloves, and the tiny diamonds I'd hidden in my brassiere. We had silver candlesticks that we'd been given as a wedding gift, and a pewter clock my parents had given me to mark our engagement. We had time, ticking and ticking, marking our days and evenings. We had the gold watch from my gymnasium graduation, and the pearl earrings my mother pressed into my hand.

I sold them, one by one.

I tied a plain scarf around my head and crossed the river into Josefstadt, pressed my hands into my coat pockets and filed into a sour-smelling kitchen. I watched the woman weigh my silver and count the coins into my palms. I watched her lick a pencil and make a mark in her dirty notebook. I slipped the money into a hidden pocket, and kept a tissue in my sleeve. When I wept, I blotted my eyes so that no one would see my tears.

I was reaching for a small package of butter in the market one morning when a woman slipped a blue envelope into my market basket. The woman didn't look at me, and I barely saw her before she turned out of the aisle.

My first instinct was to hurry after her, and my next was to snap the purse shut and go directly home.

I did the latter.

At home, we saw the enveloped didn't have a stamp or postage mark;

it had come to us hand-after-hand, friend-to-friend, all the way from Paris. Fritz read it carefully.

"Bernhard says we're to contact a man at the bookbindery on Heu-mühlgasse," he said. "He'll help us get out."

Then he lit a match and burned the letter over the sink.

That same week, the phone trilled in the middle of the afternoon, and it was Uncle Ferdinand calling from Jungfer Brezan.

"Thank God—we've been worried sick," I said.

"I had to leave right after the chancellor's speech," my uncle said through the scratchy line. "I had a call from a friend—he said they were coming to arrest me, and I needed to go immediately."

I held the receiver away from my ear so Fritz could listen, too.

"The lines have been down or I would have called sooner," my uncle said.

"Is it safe in Czechoslovakia?" I asked.

"I'm safe here. I'm trying to get Fritz what he needs, but it's harder than I expected."

"We've had word from Bernhard," I said carefully. There could always been someone—a neighbor or a telephone operator—listening to our phone. "But we don't know what will happen with my parents."

"Do whatever you have to do," my uncle said. "And I'll keep trying on my end, too."

"And what about Leopold?" I asked.

"What about him?"

"We haven't seen him," I said.

"Nor have I."

"Then he's not with you?" I felt suddenly lost and afraid. "Leopold isn't with you?"

"I'm alone," my uncle said, his voice almost as hollow as I felt. "I've been alone for a long time."

Fritz paid a hefty sum at the bookbindery in exchange for lengthy information that involved roundabout meeting spots and path that would take us out of Vienna at night.

"At least now we can do something to help ourselves," I said when he spelled it all out for me. But it wasn't as if we'd been handed an immediate plan of action. We had to wait, and waiting was terrifying.

Every day someone we knew was betrayed or caught trying to escape. My parents came home from a walk in the park to find the Nazis had come and taken everything—even Papa's cello. A friend passed by Bernhard's *palais* on Franzensgasse and saw men loading my brother-in-law's art into a military truck. Someone told me there was a German flag hanging at 18 Elisabethstrasse, and a row of black cars lined outside along Schiller Park. There was no news of my brother, and nothing more from my uncle. But there was never silence, either.

One of our old foremen came to the kitchen door one morning and told Fritz that Mathilde had been taken into custody along with her husband. I'd never seen Fritz's old lover, but I'd heard she was a beautiful woman with a beautiful voice.

"What do you mean?" Fritz asked.

"I mean the Nazis have her and she's in trouble," the man said.

Fritz turned from the door as if he'd seen a ghost, and locked himself in the room where we'd stored our phonograph and records. I pressed my ear against the door and heard the furniture moving. I heard him scratching around like a mouse in a cupboard, and then I heard the whir of the record player. The needle dropped, a soprano wailed, and Fritz began to sob.

The woman sang her heart out, and Fritz wept for hours. He wept through lunch, and he wept through dinner. When he finally came out of the room, it was dark. I handed him a piece of toast with butter, and a warm cup of tomato soup. I loved him, and was sorry to see his sadness. What was happening in Vienna was happening to all of us, and I didn't see any reason to pretend otherwise.

"I'm sorry," I whispered.

"I'm sorry, too," he said.

"Tomorrow or the next day." Fritz looked tired in the dim kitchen light. "Keep everything close at hand. We have to be ready at a moment's notice."

He'd barely spoken those words when we heard steps in the hallway and then a sharp knock that made me jump. Instinctively I checked for the last diamonds hidden in my brassiere, as if feeling for my own hammering heartbeat. Fritz put a finger to his lips, a warning to reveal nothing. Then he opened the door.

Felix Landau stepped into our flat followed by two men in brown uniforms. The air in the room stood still, the light changed. I could not take a breath.

"We're taking you into custody," Landau said to Fritz. "We're done being patient."

Fritz went white, and I'm sure I cried out before Landau's hard glare silenced me.

"Under what charge?" Fritz asked.

"You're withholding assets and account books," Landau said. His men went to either side of Fritz. I felt as if I might vomit.

"My brother is in charge of the business," Fritz said in a weak voice. "I've had nothing to do with it for weeks, as you well know."

"I know that Bernhard is running everything out of Paris now," Landau said. "Those are German assets and German accounts—you are stealing from the Führer. Until it stops, Herr Altmann, you will be held accountable."

"I need my shoes," Fritz said quietly. He sat on a kitchen chair and slipped off his house slippers. His sock had a hole in the toe that I'd neglected to mend.

"Where will you take him?" I managed to ask.

"Rossauer Lände Prison," Landau said.

At least Rossauer was in Vienna. At least we'd heard that it was possible to survive there.

"Until when?" I whispered.

Fritz tied his wingtips slowly, as if in a trance.

"That's up to Bernhard," Landau said. "When we have all the assets and books, we'll let him go."

"Hurry up." One of the storm troopers pulled Fritz up by the sleeve. I jumped at the same time, as if he and I were two marionettes joined at the wrist.

"Let him take a coat," I said.

Fritz shook his head.

"It's warm out, Maria."

"It will be cold," I said. My hands began to shake, and I felt tears coming. I pushed his brown cashmere jacket into his arms. "It will be cold in the prison, there's no heat, Fritz, there's no hot water."

Fritz looked at Landau.

"Go ahead—kiss your wife."

Holding the coat crushed between us, Fritz pressed his lips on mine. Then he was gone.

*T*he painter slips off his brown robe and hangs it on a hook by the door. He stands naked in the studio, but he's not cold. Above his bowed legs, his belly is a furnace. He splashes water on his body and washes under his arms. On another hook he finds his white shirt, vest, and pants. He slips them on and snaps the suspenders into place. Tonight is his French lesson, but he doesn't want to go. French is troublesome, the verbs and conjugations always an impossible task. Emilie will mind, he thinks, but he writes her a postcard—I'm tired, and the French lessons are a dreadful bore—and begs off.

He drops the card in a box at the corner of Josefstädter Strasse. The mail is quick, the tubes are efficient. He knows the note will reach the Flöge dress shop in less than an hour.

He walks slowly home through the twilight, past the empty schoolhouse and the noisy beer hall. He thinks about Judith, the warrior Jewess, and about a golden shield. By the time he reaches his low brick house, the sky is dark. Through the door he can hear his sister Klara talking loudly about the price of sugar. He smells fried onions, and his stomach growls. The sky has darkened, and the moon rises.

Inside, he sits at the table, tucks his napkins into his collar, and eats his bread and lentil stew.

"I heard the university might reject your mural," his mother says. "Does that mean we'll have to give the money back?"

He shakes his head. "That won't happen. And if it does, then they can go to hell."

He sleeps deeply, until the cock crows.

ADELE

1900

Not long after my visit to Klimt's studio, the maid brought the morning post with a note from Berta.

Gustav Klimt asked me to invite you to our salon next Sunday evening, she wrote. *You must have made quite an impression on him.*

I arrived ten minutes before the appointed time to find Berta wearing a striped apron tied over her dress.

"I have a few things to finish in the kitchen," my friend said. "But Klimt is already here."

The Zuckerkandls' second-floor apartment wasn't as lavish as our home, but it was warm and inviting. Berta's parlor was a bright mix of old and new furnishings, colorful rugs, and floor-to-ceiling shelves overflowing with books. The windows overlooked the Town Hall Gardens, where carriage drivers waited while their charges visited the Hofburgtheater or Café Landtmann. Cigarette smoke and the sound of whinnying horses was part of the apartment's charm.

I found Klimt sitting in a big blue armchair by the fireplace, sipping a glass of wine. My heart jumped when I saw him. Preparing myself hadn't helped at all. Like a wild horse, or a hill that ran too fast and steep for the toboggan, I was as equally drawn to him as I was wary.

"I'm glad to see you," he said, rising.

He was dressed in a creamy suit and rumpled white shirt, and seemed a different man than I'd met before: quiet, even subdued. He kissed my cheeks—or at least, he brushed them with his beard—and asked after Ferdinand.

"The salon life isn't for him," I said. "Ferdinand likes to be up at dawn."

Klimt nodded.

"Early risers accomplish more," he said. He put his hands in his pockets and rocked on his feet when he spoke. "I'm up every morning at the cock's crow," he added.

"I imagined you would keep a more lively schedule."

"A dull life is good for an artist," he said, more sincerely than I expected. "I walk with Moll every morning at seven, and many nights I'm asleep before my sisters have cleared the supper table."

I thought I'd misunderstood him, and begged his pardon.

"I live with my mother and sisters in the house where I grew up," he said. I'd once heard a rumor to that effect, but hadn't believed it. "My father and brother are gone, and I take care of everyone now. We're not a rich family. We still have the bedrooms we had when we were children—to be honest, there's something comforting about it."

I told him that nothing had ever comforted me more than the nights when I'd stayed up reading, knowing that my brother Karl was studying in the next room.

"I still have my favorite childhood chair—it's in my sitting room now," I said. His expression warmed, encouraging me to go on. I told him that I used to sit in the chaise long past midnight when I was a girl, dreaming of myself as a woman of the world—a scholar, an arbiter of culture, someone important and intelligent.

"And here you are," he said, as if to say *voilà*.

"My brother studied anatomy with Emil," I said, almost without knowing what I was going to say next. "He showed me the veins beneath the skin, the world that's always moving inside of us. I don't know if I can explain it."

In another room, I could hear Berta's little boy saying good night to his mother, and the nursemaid leading him off to bed.

"But sometimes I feel no time has passed at all." I heard my own voice swimming in my ears. "It's as if part of me is still a girl, waiting for my life to begin."

The front bell rang, and Emil hurried to get the door.

"Does that make any sense to you?" I asked. I felt strangely un-chaperoned, and wondered if I had made a mistake by coming without Ferdinand.

"It makes perfect sense to me," Klimt said.

Something new had come over his face. I could tell he wanted to say more, but the others arrived, and the moment was gone. Carl Moll came directly over to us. If he noticed that Klimt seemed subdued, he gave no indication. He was hearty and loud.

"Are you still looking at your husband's sentimental Biedermeier landscapes?" Moll asked with something of a guffaw.

"I suppose we are." I glanced at Klimt. "Although I'd like to have a new landscape for my sitting room."

"Gustav has a number of them," Moll said. "You can see them at the Secession, and have your pick. I think *Beech Forest* is the best."

I said I remembered his beech trees, and thought they were cheerful and happy.

"That's because when I'm in the country, I'm cheerful and happy," Klimt said.

"As am I," I said.

It was an intimate salon that evening: we were joined by the art histo-rian Franz Wickhoff and his plump wife, Sadie; two professors from the university who supported Klimt; and Serena Lederer, who was married to a wealthy industrialist.

I'd never liked Serena much, mostly because she had a foolish gig-gle that grated on my nerves. She was a pretty woman, but her rouge was too red and her mouth too pouty. Klimt had recently painted her portrait in the style of Sargent; I hadn't seen it, but I'd heard she was wearing all white, and that the portrait was held in high regard.

"I'm so glad you enjoyed Paris," Serena said, giggling. She was drink-ing a tall flute of champagne with two strawberries floating at the top. "Alma told me you went to the Moulin Rouge."

"We saw the cabaret," I said. "But what I really enjoyed was the art."

"I like the dancing best." Serena began to sway as if to music. "I hear the whole city is exploding with primitive costumes and exotic dancing."

Behind her, Klimt smiled and nodded. Then he put the sides of his palms flat against his face, opened his mouth, and mimicked Munch's silent scream. It seemed we had our own private joke.

"Frau Bloch-Bauer enjoyed seeing the new Symbolists in Paris," he said with a devilish grin. "But I'm more envious that she went to Montmartre, where the crepes and chocolate are the best I've ever had."

At half past eight we took seats in the parlor, and Berta opened the salon.

"I'm very pleased to welcome Herr Professor Wickhoff," she said. Her elocution was perfect, and she held the room with an easy grace. "The professor recently defended Herr Klimt's new mural to the members of the Philosophical Society, and we're honored to have him share that talk with us tonight."

I saw Serena smile at Klimt. Berta gave the floor to Professor Wickhoff, and there was a round of polite applause.

"I'd like to address, in particular, the criticism of modern art as ugly," the professor began. He used note cards, as he might have used at a podium, and spoke for a long time—perhaps much longer than necessary—about primitive man's fear of all things ugly, which he said had led to idealized beauty in early art.

"Now that we're evolved far beyond Darwin's apes, we're able to see that truth in art is much more important than beauty," he said. "To use art to help us explore every poetic, spiritual, and physical aspect of life—both pleasant and unpleasant—is the greatest use of our knowledge and creativity. Modern—even ugly—art is worthy of Vienna's place in history, and we should embrace it."

"Bravo," Emil and his colleagues said when the professor was finished. "Bravo, simply brilliant. The connection between evolution and art is something I've never considered before. You've opened our eyes, Herr Professor."

The four scholars immediately fell into a deep conversation about the body and its relationship to art. I tried to follow along as well as I could, but I really wanted to hear what Klimt thought about the professor's ideas, and how he was feeling about all the criticism of his mural. I tried to catch his eye, but he seemed to sink further and further into the blue chair until he was almost entirely in shadow.

When the professors finally wore themselves out, I turned eagerly as Klimt cleared his throat.

"Thank you, Professors," he said. "Your words and thoughts are truly appreciated, and I can't thank you enough for defending me to the critics, and for supporting my work."

"Tell us about your other murals," Berta asked.

"I'm continuing with them," he said. "*Medicine* will be done by next year, and *Jurisprudence* after that."

"And will they be in the same style?" Emil asked.

"That's what I've planned."

"Then you'll ignore the critics?" I asked. "That's brave."

"I won't change my work for them," Klimt said.

We all waited for him to say more, but he sank back in his chair, obviously finished.

"I'm sorry you didn't speak in more depth about your work," I told him when we broke for refreshment. "I was hoping you'd respond to the professor's points."

We were standing at an elaborate buffet table carefully laid with sweets and savories on silver dishes and heavy pottery that Berta had brought home from her travels in Morocco and Algiers.

"The professor put me to sleep," Klimt said in a conspiratorial whisper. "I hope I wasn't snoring. That's happened to me before."

I barely stifled a laugh. It came up through my nose in a strangled chortle. He laughed, too, and pretended to rub the sleep from his eyes.

"I'm sorry I haven't seen you back at my studio," he said as he filled his plate with scallops, cheeses, and salted almonds. "I thought we'd reached an agreement."

I lit a cigarette, and took a glass of sherry. Almost all the nerves from our first meetings were gone. I felt that I could tell Klimt the truth.

"I'll be honest, Herr Klimt, I'm not sure what to think of your sketches or of your proposal," I said. I saw a flash of myself wrapped in scarves, taking them off one by one while Klimt watched.

"I think you'll understand, soon enough, why the time for the Judith is right now," he said. He ate a few of the scallops in quick succession, and washed them down with another glass of wine. Then he reached into his jacket and pulled out a folded journal. Fresh ink smeared on his fingertips as he thumbed the pages.

"A fellow I know at the printing presses got hold of an early copy of tomorrow's *Volksblatt*," he said.

The *Volksblatt* was a far-right newssheet that espoused the ugly politics of Mayor Karl Lueger.

"Here's what they're saying about *Philosophy* and Professor Wickhoff's defense of it," Klimt said.

He began to read quietly, but the others soon gathered around and we all listened in horror.

Klimt's art is Jewish art, and adulation of such immoral art is destroying the fiber of our city. It should be stopped, and the art should be burned.

The room erupted into shouting. We were all a bit loose from the wine by then, and the cries had a carnal sound. Klimt had to raise his voice to continue.

Klimt's supporters, especially the members of the Philosophical Society, are of the same indecent Semitic heredity, which we know as the greedy and perverse Jew. If only the Philosophical Society's membership cards were made of yellow cardboard triangles, and worn on the patrons' lapels, we would be satisfied. Then, at least, they would be wearing the patches by which, in happier times, Jews were distinguished from Christians. If this practice were to return, we would be able to know the Jews when they walked down the streets and into our public meetings, and we could recognize them before we let them pollute and ruin Vienna's beauty.

"There you have it," Klimt said. He looked around the room. "The mayor's party has spoken."

"You aren't even Jewish," Serena said faintly.

It wasn't that we'd never heard anti-Semitic screeds before, or that we didn't know there were men in Vienna who hated the Jews and envied our success. It was the suggestion that Klimt's art invited punishment, and that it should be destroyed, that outraged us.

"You have to offer a rebuttal," Wickhoff said.

"The *Volksblatt* doesn't deserve a response," Emil said. "Ignore it, the way we ignore all of their screeds. That's the only way to stay above it. But we have to address the critics at the university. We can't expect Klimt to stand up to their criticism alone."

"I'm going to respond to all of my critics," Klimt said, when the others let him be heard. "Actually, I'm going to make a number of responses. You're the first to know what I'm planning."

"Tell us, Gustav," Berta said. We were all leaning forward, waiting.

"My answer will be on canvas." His eyes got a faraway look, just as I'd seen in his studio. "I'm going to paint a beautiful, dangerous, Jewish seductress. And I'm going to paint a gorgeous redhead showing her naked derrière to the crowds."

Emil Zuckerkandl laughed. Serena let out a giggle. Wickhoff took off his glasses and wiped them studiously on his handkerchief. The others murmured their supporting assent. I flushed, but in the dimly lit room, where everyone was red-faced from excitement and outrage, no one noticed.

As we were leaving, Klimt stopped me in the foyer with a hand on my arm.

"You'll come now, won't you?" he asked quietly.

The maid was handing out the coats, and everyone was congratulating Berta on a successful evening.

"Why me?" I kept my voice low.

"Because you feel everything so deeply. And because you inspired it." His face was intent and close. "When I look at you I see something fierce awakening. You, right now, when you're discovering your power—that's what I want to capture."

"I need to think about it," I said. I wanted it very much. I wanted it more than I should, and for the wrong reasons—seduction, desire—as much as for the right ones about art, freedom, and my place in Vienna's society.

"When you come, bring the gold necklace you were wearing at the opening," Klimt said, as if it was already decided. "If my critics want to see a Jewess in yellow and gold, then I'll give them one."

"You said it wouldn't be a portrait," I reminded him.

We'd moved into the shadows, and the others were gone. We had only a few minutes before we'd have to pour out the door, where my coachman was waiting.

"There's the real world, and the world of art as representation," he said. "It will never be you, and it will always be you. Just like you'll always be the little girl sitting at the window, looking down into the streets where you're walking now—a beautiful woman."

There was no reason to protest. I knew I would go to him, and he knew it, too.

The following week I told the maid to put away my corset, and to help me into my new dress. When she realized the loose frock required neither buttonhooks nor a cinched belt, her face twisted like a question mark.

"You may as well get used to it," I laughed. "The new style will be everywhere soon enough."

She slipped the teal dress over my head, and I pulled it down over my chemise; then I piled my hair on top of my head and crowned it with a tiny ruby pin.

The dress hung to the floor in a single, easy layer. The sleeves were wide and loose, with a bell-shaped opening at the wrist. Ferdinand did a double take when I went into the breakfast room.

"What on earth are you wearing?" he asked.

"It's from Emilie Flöge's dress shop," I said. "Do you like it?"

I spun around slowly.

Ferdinand had been to my bedroom twice the week before. He always told me to expect him, and arrived fresh from the bath in a belted robe and house slippers. He was gentle and tender, kissing me on the mouth and whispering my name. He thanked me when he was finished, and said he hoped we would have a child soon. I always told him I hoped we would, too. It was truly what I wanted. But I also wanted more.

"Berta had one made just like it in another color," I said. Beneath the dress I could feel my legs, my waist, the breath moving in my lungs.

"You will be quite a pair walking along the Ring together," Ferdinand said, smiling as he spooned up the last of his soft-boiled eggs.

There was a pile of leather portfolios beside his morning newspapers, and luggage on the landing. Ferdinand had business at the sugar factories in Moravia, and the carriage was being prepared for the six-hour journey.

"Before you go, Ferry, I'd like to talk with you about something," I said lightly. "Do you remember Klimt's landscapes at the Secession show?"

I knew he'd hardly looked at them the night of the opening, but he nodded for me to go on.

"After Kraus's review and the other attacks against Klimt, we all think it's our duty to support the Secessionists. Especially Klimt. The university is threatening to reject the mural, and even to cancel the others. If he loses the support of the academic establishment, he'll need new patrons."

"Who is *we*?" he asked.

"The Zuckerkandls, the Lederers, and us. We talked about it at the salon—it's our responsibility. And we have the means," I added. It was all true. Everything I said was absolutely true.

"It sounds fine, Adele," he said. He put his napkin on the table and pushed back his chair. "We'll talk about the landscape when I get back. I'll be gone for four nights, maybe five if there are things to attend at the factory. I hope you'll find a way to amuse yourself while I'm away."

"Don't worry," I said. "I think I'll look at some of Klimt's paintings while you're gone."

I did, too. I went to the Burgtheater in the afternoon when rehearsals were under way, just so I could look at the mural Klimt had painted with his brother in the grand lobby. I went to the art history museum, where I spent a long time studying the Egyptian women they'd painted above the central staircase. When I finally went to the Secession and saw his *Pallas Athene*—a ferocious goddess behind a golden mask—I was certain Klimt was capable of painting a woman who was both beautiful and powerful. With the light streaming through the glass ceiling, I felt that I was becoming invincible. And I knew that I was ready for Klimt.

"Frau Bloch-Bauer," someone called to me as I was walking down the steps outside the gallery. The street was noisy, and at first I couldn't tell where the sound came from. The voice called again, and there was a giggle.

"Frau Lederer," I said. Serena was wearing a yellow hat that framed her face, and she was with her little girl and the nursemaid. To my surprise, she looked the perfect picture of motherhood and grace.

"Did you enjoy the Zuckerkandls' salon?" I asked. Her little girl stood right at her side, holding a parasol over her pretty head.

"The professor was erudite, but a bit dull," Serena said. "Even Herr Klimt was dull, and he's never dull."

There was something in the way she looked at me that made me want to squirm.

"I hope Gustl does answer the critics with a shock, don't you?" she asked, using the painter's familiar name. "We need as much excitement in our art and in our lives as we can manage in good taste." Then she giggled again.

I took the trolley and went to Klimt's studio that afternoon, as planned. It was late spring in Vienna: horses and carriages were everywhere, cutting across the tram tracks and racing in front of pedestrians who had to scurry to get out of the way. The Volksgarten was in bloom, the orchestra was practicing in the Opera House with the doors flung wide open, and university students were spilling out of coffeehouses shouting about the poetry of Rilke and Hofmannsthal.

Klimt was waiting, as we'd arranged by post, and he opened the door before I knocked. He was wearing his brown robe and thick sandals, and smelled of shaving cream and turpentine. When I saw his bare feet, I was surprised at how pale and vulnerable they looked.

"You're here," he said.

"And so are you," I said with a nervous laugh. He was as magnetic as he'd been the first night, as if he'd rested all week since I'd seen him last. His color was back, too. He took my coat and remarked on the new dress.

"Emilie Flöge made it for me," I said, watching to see if his face changed when I mentioned her name.

"No one else is making dresses like that," he said. If I knew how to judge a man's voice, I would say that he sounded proud of his friend. "I'm sure she'll have you to thank when all the fashionable women are rushing to her shop next month."

A quick glance around the studio told me that Klimt's redhead had been back. There was a series of sketches of Mimi—or at least I thought it was Mimi—curled on her side. Her back was to him, and her red hair was swimming across the page as if she were underwater. On a soft corkboard, he'd tacked up another series of a woman with her bare bottom filling a good portion of the paper. It was exactly as he'd described at the salon.

"My goodness," I said. "Your Mimi is bold."

Outside the large window, the shrubbery where I'd hidden in March had blossomed into thick rhododendrons hung with huge purple flowers. The courtyard garden was full of tall lupine and wild orange irises.

"Mimi's the one who brings me news from Lueger's church meetings, and the one who brought me the early copy of the *Volksblatt*."

"Then she's useful to you," I said. I'm not sure why I said it, or what I meant by it. Except that I felt somehow jealous of her, as if we were in a competition.

"Mimi is the mother of my son," he said. "And we understand one another."

I almost told him that Ferdinand wanted a son more than he wanted anything, but bit my tongue. I poured myself some water from a silver pitcher, and Klimt shuffled through a pile of drawings. There I was— my face drawn in four lines, a full mouth, large eyes.

"You know the story of Judith and Holofernes," Klimt said. It wasn't a question. Of course I knew. "So you know what the painting has to be, don't you?"

"Not really."

"There has to be triumph and power. And there has to be seduction."

I understood triumph and power. But seduction was something I'd never fully understood. With Ferdinand I had been the pursued, and had yielded as expected.

"Seduction and gold?" I asked.

I found the velvet pouch and slipped out the choker. Klimt opened his hand, and I poured the necklace into it. It was like heat moving between our palms, like a thousand gold coins.

His fingers were flecked with yellow, red, blue, and white. Something sparkled under his thumbnail.

"Put it on," he said. "Let me see it in the daylight."

I had to have help with the clasp. There was no way I could do it myself. I lifted the loose pieces of hair off of my neck, and turned my back to him. From where I stood, I had a perfect view of the sketches of the redhead, her naked spine curling in an S from head to bottom; her torso slinking across the page as if she were crawling toward us; a face that was only a smile and a tongue between her lips.

Klimt put a hand on my neck, and I shivered at his touch. The neckline of my dress was loose, and the tops of my shoulders were bare. The window that had been closed on that first cold day in March was open. I could smell hayfields in the distance, and the swollen lupine below the window.

"Here," he said, in a voice that had a gruff catch in it. "Lean your head forward."

I did as he said. I felt him very close behind me as he put the necklace around my neck. I suspected that he was wearing nothing underneath his robe. Without a corset, my garters and the tops of my stockings were the only thing that covered the skin beneath my dress and silk slip. If he moved forward or I moved back, we would be touching.

"Is that good?" he asked. His breath was right in my ear. My body spoke for me. A sigh escaped my lips, and I said, "Yes."

"My fingers are used to working with metals," he said.

His words whispered around my neck, they coiled with the gold. The necklace was close around my throat, he was closing the clasp; his hands were sure and warm. I felt the hook meet the latch and sink in. *Snap*. And then the next, *Snap*. And the one below that. All four, set in place. *Snap, snap*. My heart was pounding.

"There," he said. "Now let me see."

I turned. I was almost in his arms, and his lips were almost on my face. I could smell the fresh air on him, and cool, deep lake water. If a person could be a color, Klimt was deep turquoise.

"You're transformed," he said. He was very close to me, but he didn't speak softly. He spoke in a sure voice, only a decibel less than if we'd been seated across the table from one another.

I closed my eyes and tipped my face.

He licked my lips, light and tiny touches. His tongue was soft and warm, and it pushed into my mouth like a diver breaking the surface of a lake. He wrapped his hands around my shoulders, and took a step closer. His body was against mine and I could feel him beneath his robes.

"I can't," I said. My eyes flew open.

His eyebrows were crazy, the hairs went in all directions. His two front teeth were crooked, and one was chipped. He was as close as that, and yet I hadn't quite looked at him full on.

"That's all right," he said.

He let go of my shoulders.

I pulled back an inch.

"Can we do what I came here to do?" I was shaking, not with fear but with desire. I didn't know I could feel that in my body.

"Of course."

He reached for his pad, and I reached for the stool behind me. It was the same high stool that I'd seen Mimi sitting on that first day.

"Can you stand tall, please?" he asked. "Can you look at me, just as you are now, just as you feel right now?"

I blinked, and was blinded for an instant. Was it sunlight? Was it happiness? Was it longing? Was it the shivering between my legs, where I knew that if could only rub my thighs more tightly together beneath my dress I could have friction and then more, and more, and more again?

"You're so young, Adele," he said. It was the first thing he said when he stopped drawing. "I sometimes forget how young you are."

"I'm almost twenty," I said, but he seemed not to hear.

He shuffled through the sketches. I was hardly recognizable—my eyes were closed or half-closed, my mouth was a round O, my neck was arched back, there were fragments of arms, hands, and my dress falling in loose layers.

"This is enough to get me started." He gathered the sketches in a neat pile. If he'd been turquoise water an hour ago, now he was brown trees, distant and solid.

"I'm going to Paris next week," he said. "And then it will be summer. But we've started, and that's the most important thing."

He walked me out into the garden. An oppressive heat was coming. I felt it in a trickle of perspiration between my breasts, and a wet slide between my thighs. The cats were climbing in the bushes, swatting at yellow butterflies and bees. Somewhere up the street, a girl was singing a nursery rhyme about Magdeburg Bridge falling down. We listened together. Klimt knew the words, and when she came around to the refrain he sang along in a sweet, surprising voice, ". . . the goldsmith, the goldsmith, with his daughter."

I'm sure it was only my imagination, but he looked shy for a moment. He smiled as if he'd just realized something about me that he didn't know before.

"What?" I asked.

The girl was still singing.

"Nothing," he said. He leaned in, quickly, and kissed my cheek. "I'll need you to come again. You'll come, won't you?"

K limt's Philosophy *mural reaches the Paris Exposition in April 1900, where it thrills the judges with its graphic representation of human misery and ambiguous morality.*

In June the painting is awarded a coveted Gold Medal and Klimt travels to Paris to accept the prize. Scholars and the emperor's ministers have scorned him in Vienna, but in France he is well received. Parisians dance to African music at the reception party, and a pretty redhead watches him with bright eyes. She is wearing a boa hat with a silver feather, and he opens his arms and smiles as if he knows her.

By evening she's lying in his hotel bed and he is drawing the sharp line of her chin, the purplish blush under her eyes, her moist orange lips. She's a maid and a model—not nearly as complex or proud as Adele Bloch-Bauer—and for relief from that Viennese dance of wealth and desire, Klimt is very glad.

Adele offers him the trifecta of affection, protection, and inspiration. But the muse must be fed, and Klimt finds his sustenance in the redhead's arms.

MARIA
1938

The morning after Fritz's arrest I set out for the Hotel Metropole, where the Nazis had set up their police headquarters. The word *Gestapo* was new to me, but I'd seen it on the front page of the paper, and heard it whispered from friend to friend: *the Gestapo came for my husband, the Gestapo took our car, the Gestapo shot my brother when he tried to burn a stack of legal papers.*

"Do you know Hitler was born in Austria?" a familiar woman asked while I waited for the tram. I'd been at parties with her; I couldn't remember her name, but I knew she had two small children.

I pulled my kerchief tight under my chin.

"He grew up near Linz, and lived in Vienna was he was a young man." She kept her voice low. "This is where he learned to hate us."

I told her where I was going. I had Adele's letter opener at the bottom of my purse, and I was wearing my mother's black gloves with the diamond sewn into the seam.

"Don't do it," the woman said, her eyes darting from side to side. "I'm serious, no one in his right mind is going into Gestapo headquarters unless he's dragged there."

"I have to," I told her. "It's the only place to go if you want to get answers."

"Answers?" The tram screeched to a stop in front of us. "There are no answers, Maria."

———

105

Four huge Nazi banners hung from the Metropole rooftop, sweeping almost down to the sidewalks. A line of official black cars stood along the riverfront, and red swastika flags flapped in the wind. The streets were swarming with soldiers and men in black coats, and when I stopped to summon my courage, a black car screeched to a stop across the street. Two men in brown shirts pulled a cowering couple from the backseat. I gripped my handbag tightly, and pressed my lips together so I wouldn't scream.

The woman was crying and dragging her feet. The man had lost a shoe, and his pants had a dark stain at the back.

"You smell like shit," one of the Brownshirts shouted as he shoved them up the steps.

It seemed impossible that I'd celebrated my thirteenth birthday in that very building with my uncle Ferdinand only nine years ago. On that clear winter day the Metropole steps had been swept free of snow, my boots had been black patent leather, and my uncle's car had come to stop at the very curb where I now stood trembling.

Then, the hotel lobby had smelled of winter lilies and pine boughs. A parade of red and white canna lilies in tall urns had led to a dining room filled with glamorous ladies dressed in flapper finery. There was short hair, beaded dresses, and harp music floating in from another room. Snow was falling onto the glass dome above the dining room, and beside my chair my uncle had deposited a huge box wrapped in silver paper with live ferns tucked into purple ribbons.

The ferns seemed to shiver whenever a waiter rushed by, and I giggled each time it happened.

"I can't sing worth a darn," my uncle said when the waiter carried out the chocolate cake with thirteen candles. The candles danced in front of me as the entire waitstaff sang "Happy Birthday" in English. I closed my eyes, made a wish, and blew out the candles in one breath.

"Do you want to know what I wished for?" I asked.

"You can't tell me your wish," Uncle Ferdinand said with a smile. "Or else it will never come true."

I was quite sure that my wishes would come true whether I told them or not. Everything I'd ever wanted had come to me without asking. It was 1929, I was thirteen years old, and I thought everyone in the world was as rich and happy as I.

"I won't tell you my wish," I said, glancing at the pretty box, "but I bet you already know."

Inside, I'd found the navy blue bouclé coat with dark mink collar that I'd been admiring in Gerngross's department store window for a month. My uncle sent the rest of my cake up to the lobby for the hotel staff to share, and I'd walked out of the restaurant on his arm feeling like a lady for the first time.

Now the wind picked up, and the air outside the hotel snapped with energy. I took a breath and tried not to hang my head. I dashed across the street just as a woman—another Jew, alone like me—came out of the revolving door in a hurry. Her coat was hanging open and her face was streaked with tears. She stumbled and spilled her pocketbook, and I stepped around her just as a German shouted, "Clumsy fool!"

I used my whole body to push against the heavy door.

Inside, the old floors were polished to a high gloss, just as I remembered. The familiar reception desk was there. The lobby ceiling soared; all that was the same. But there was a strange smell in the air. A line of screaming schoolboys in knickers ran by me, followed by three snapping German shepherds on leashes. The men holding the dogs were laughing.

"*Heil Hitler*," the woman behind the desk said loudly. "Why are you here?"

I clutched my handbag and stammered out a reply.

"My husband was arrested. I've come to inquire about his release."

"Release?" she asked.

I blinked and nodded. The woman pointed me in the direction the boys and the dogs had gone, and I moved quickly toward the old dining room where I'd blown out my birthday candles.

Even before I reached the doorway, I could smell the foul stench. I stood at the top of the stairs for a moment and felt like I was about to fall into hell. There must have been more than three hundred people crushed inside the old restaurant. The carpets were gone, and the tables, too. Terrified, desperate men and women holding suitcases and briefcases were standing in tight lines, their faces pinched into bloodless silence, their necks straining as if watching for a train that would never come.

Someone directed me toward a table for the dispensation and surrender of Jewish assets, and I joined a long line. I looked neither right nor left. A man fell to his knees, and a soldier struck him in the face. I heard dogs barking in the distance, and doors slamming. There was shrieking, and pleading. No one dared look around to see where the sounds came from; no one in line spoke unless it was absolutely necessary.

It took two hours, and by the time I reached the clerk seated at a long table, I badly needed a restroom.

"My husband is in Rossauer Prison." I forced my tongue to move. "If I can send a cable to my brother-in-law in Paris, he'll give you everything you ask for."

The woman behind the desk barely looked at me.

"I was told to come here—" I said. I fingered the jewels in my glove, wondering if it was the right time to use them, and how I could show them to her quietly.

"Your papers," she said. I handed them over and she glanced at them for a second.

"Jews can't send cables without special documentation," she said.

"That's why I'm here," I whispered. "Bernhard Altmann will give you what you need. I just have to reach him."

She shrugged. "I can't help you."

"We don't have the ledgers," I said in a rush. "We don't have them—"

"Move along," the woman barked, calling for the person behind me. "You Jews need to learn some manners."

Gentle snow had been falling when my uncle and I left the Metropole on my thirteenth birthday. He'd told his driver we were going to walk, and guided me up the long block that sloped toward Rudolf Park.

Back then, Uncle Ferdinand rarely mentioned Aunt Adele's name without choking up. Sometimes when I visited 18 Elisabethstrasse, I'd found him gazing up at her portrait as if expecting the picture to speak. But his memories seemed happy that day, and he went on about the books my aunt had read and enjoyed, the philosophers, "dark," he said, "but worth a look at least," and the British and French novelists.

"I want to take you to your aunt's favorite bookshop," Uncle Ferry said. "Since you can read French now—" he began, and I laughed.

I couldn't read French at all, then.

"Don't laugh." Uncle Ferry smiled. "I thought we might get you a copy of Proust in the original. If your aunt were alive, that's what she'd want for you."

I beamed at him. He treated me very well, and I loved him very much.

"That sounds lovely," I said, taking his arm.

We walked quickly in the snow, chattering away. Before we reached the bookstore I thought I heard someone cry out in pain, but my uncle was talking and he didn't hear it. He kept going, and we turned onto Sterngasse. Right in front of us, not less than forty feet away, men in brown shirts were beating a small group of men in front of a storefront. One used a baseball bat to knock a man to his knees. Another kicked him in the face.

"Jewish swine!" someone shouted.

That stopped my uncle cold. His eyes narrowed, and he put an arm around my shoulder. In that moment I saw everything clearly: the front of Schuster & Sons Booksellers, the torn sign in the shop window that read *Young Socialists Meeting Today*. A chain swinging through the air and catching a man's cheek. Blood splattering.

"Brownshirts," my uncle said. He was already pulling me backward. "Let's go, Maria."

"Filthy Socialist pig," a man roared. He cracked a stick on a small man's head, and then my uncle and I were around the corner and we were running.

We went at least two blocks until we turned onto the main boulevard and my uncle bent over with his hands on his knees, trying to catch his breath. In the distance I could see the army barracks at the top of the hill, and I could hear a military band playing a familiar battle march. The men's shouts echoed in my ears. I heard the two-note cry of a police car, and hoped it was heading toward the bookstore.

"Who were those men in brown shirts?"

"National Socialists," he said, still struggling to breathe.

"Socialists?" I asked. I thought maybe he was confused. "Not the men who were being beaten. I mean the other ones."

My uncle wiped a hand across his face.

"The Brownshirts aren't Socialists, they're *National* Socialists—Nazis." He spat the word. "They follow Adolf Hitler and they hate Socialists."

I'd heard my parents speak of Adolf Hitler once or twice before, but his name had meant nothing to me until that moment—and even then, it didn't mean enough.

"They called those men filthy Jews," I said. "Are all Socialists Jewish?"

"Socialists are from all backgrounds," my uncle said. He'd begun to catch his breath, and he was straightening his coat. "But Jews are the ones being blamed."

"Blamed for what?" I asked.

"For whatever is wrong," he said. "Poverty, hunger, the state of the German economy."

"The state of the German economy." I repeated his words, barely understanding their meaning.

"The Nazis are trying to take control in Germany," my uncle said. He'd stood up fully by then, but his face was still very red. "They hate anyone that's not like them—especially Jews."

"Why are they here?" I asked. "Why doesn't the chancellor make the Nazis leave?"

"He's trying," he said. "A lot of us are trying to keep the Nazis out of Austria."

I thought my uncle could do anything, then. If he was working against the Nazis, I didn't think I had anything to fear.

My black gloves were still on my hands, the jewels still sewn into the lining, as I returned through the factory gates and hurried back to my empty apartment. The telephone line clicked and buzzed and rang across the miles to Czechoslovakia, and finally a voice answered. For a second, I felt as if I could reach back through time and bring everything back as it had once been. But of course I could not.

"Uncle Ferry?"

"Maria?" It was hard not to cry when he said my name. "I've been trying to reach you."

Quickly, before we lost the connection, I told my uncle that Fritz had been arrested, and asked if he could reach Bernhard in Paris.

"We need him to release the accounts," I said. "They want all of our assets."

"I'll do whatever I can," Uncle Ferdinand said. "I still have some friends in Vienna."

He sounded very sure of himself, and I believed he would help us. But when he called the next day, his voice was grave.

"I went to the bank in Prague yesterday," he said. "The Germans had everything transferred to the Austrian Länderbank. Even the Swiss accounts. The Nazis have everything now."

"Were you able to reach Bernhard?"

"Your brother-in-law has gone very quiet in Paris," my uncle said. "No one seems to have a telephone number for him."

I didn't say anything.

"There's more," my uncle said. "You'll have to prepare your parents."

My knees gave out, and I sank to the floor. Every last bit of my courage slid away.

"The Germans have Leopold," Uncle Ferdinand said. "He's being taken to Dachau."

"Leopold? My brother is in Dachau?"

"I was told that my accounts may help secure his release."

"Then what about Fritz?"

The line was silent. Somewhere, I could hear the buzz of another conversation, in another life. A woman's laughter came through the line, and the ghost voice of a child I would never meet.

"We won't give up," my uncle said. "I promise, I'll never give up."

"But Fritz isn't here." I felt very young and scared. "I'm alone."

"They allow packages to go in and out of Rossauer Prison," Uncle Ferdinand said gently. "You can bring Fritz clean laundry, and hide notes inside the shirts. At least that's what I've been told."

When I hung up the phone, I began to gather Fritz's shirts. I thought they would smell like his cinnamon aftershave. I thought they would smell like him, but they didn't. They smelled like fear. They smelled like the people in the Metropole. They smelled like all of us.

*T*he painter shuts his work trunk and stacks it on top of the brown leather suitcases. The cats are mewling against his legs, brushing their tails along the blank canvases he's tied together with a long rope. The canvases are four-feet squares, and he intends to paint a landscape on each one. That's his indulgence every summer—never portraits, only landscapes.

While he waits for his carriage, Mimi comes to the studio carrying the boy in her arms. They kiss hello and he hands her a fat envelope.

"It's more than enough for two months," he says. "If you need anything, you can see Moll. He'll get word to me."

The toddler is sucking on a candy, and looks up at his father through wide brown eyes.

"Papa will miss you," Klimt says. "I'll see you when I come back."

Mimi tucks the money inside her dress, and slowly walks away in the heat.

When the carriage comes, Klimt and the driver lift the heavy trunks into the back. The courtyard garden is hot and dusty, and he's happy to leave it behind. He closes his eyes, and imagines diving straight into the cold, blue Lake Attersee water.

ADELE

1900

Everyone escaped Vienna in July and August. Berta and Emil went to Salzburg, where they had a summer apartment close to the Mozarteum. Klimt took the Flöge sisters and his niece to Seewalchen on Lake Attersee. And we went to Bohemia with Thedy and her family.

At Jungfer Brezan we had picture windows that overlooked the valley. Church bells rang in town every morning at seven, and when I went down to the breakfast room, iced cinnamon pastries and dark coffee were always waiting. Crisp linens were hung out to dry in the sun. It was heaven.

My sister and I wore loose cotton shifts with only bloomers and a chemise underneath, and long swimming costumes that draped below our knees. We all wore hats, even in the shade, and everyone's skin smelled of sleep that was rinsed away as soon as we took that first dive off the dock into brisk water.

Thedy's little boy was almost a year old, and a red ball and colorful wooden blocks kept him busy for hours.

"When will you have a child?" my sister asked as we watched her little Karl toddling across the lawn in a white and blue sailor suit.

"I hope it will be soon," I told her, feeling a bit sad. "So does Ferdinand," I added. "He wants sons. He wants heirs."

Ferdinand seemed to pay little attention to Karl that summer, but maybe I wasn't being fair. He had a lot on his mind: the price of sugar had fallen, new catwalks had to be built between barrels and tanks, and one of his young workers had been burned with scalding water when a valve burst. Ferry often had to stay overnight in an apartment beside the factory offices, where he took his dinner in a country café or at a picnic table with the men. Whenever he came home from one of those trips, he was exhausted.

In the long evenings my brother-in-law practiced his cello while Thedy and I did cardboard jigsaw puzzles or played gin rummy, and on the weekends we all went into Prague for dinner and entertainment. The restaurant at the Cheval Noir had a wonderful menu, the Rudolfinum Hotel had a grand dance floor, and the national theater put on charming summer plays. I loved the astrological clock in the Old Square, where we sat for a cold ice cream and watched the mechanical figures mark the hour.

The countryside was tonic for everything. I didn't forget about Klimt, though. Something was awake in me—it was hungry, and I needed to feed it. Ferdinand and I were married six months by then, and I'd gotten used to having him in my bed. We had thick, wide mattresses stacked with goose down pillows at Jungfer Brezan, and when he came to my room in the dark, I closed my eyes and pretended he was Klimt.

Was it wrong? Certainly he never objected to any of it. I wrapped my legs around him and thrust up, moaning. I climbed on top and rubbed into him until that relief broke through me in waves. Then I threw back my head and laughed.

"What just happened?" Ferdinand asked, blinking into the dark. He seemed to genuinely not know.

"I think maybe we just conceived a child," I said. I didn't know how else to explain something to him that I barely had words for myself.

One night when I touched him in a way that made him shudder and writhe, my husband held my face in his hands and called me a vixen.

"You've bewitched me," Ferdinand said.

It was August, and almost my birthday. His face was close and red. I could see I'd made him very happy, and I was glad.

"I have a surprise for you," he said. "And I don't want to wait."

I pulled on my bathrobe, and he led me through the dark house to his library. The air smelled of tinder and ash, and my husband's particular scent of perspiration. We didn't have electric lights in the country, but the hurricane gaslight illuminated the far end of the room where a large, square painting tied up in brown paper was leaning against the wall.

Ferdinand tugged at the strings, happy as a schoolboy.

I was hoping it would be one of Klimt's village landscapes. Instead, it was one of the unfinished pieces I'd seen in his studio—a brilliant patch of blue water against a sliver of sky.

"I arranged it with Moll," Ferdinand said, beaming. "You'll have a say in how it's finished. It's unusual, but they agreed to it."

I tried to imagine what I would say if I were simply happy and excited about the painting, and not flooded with a rush of longing.

"It's already a masterpiece of color and new perspective," I managed.

I knelt close enough to see each of Klimt's individual brushstrokes. There was pink in the blue water, and green, white and yellow, too—the very colors I'd seen on his fingertips.

"I bought *Beech Forest II,* also. It will be delivered after it's finished," Ferdinand said. He was happy and proud. "You see, Adele, I didn't forget."

I hugged him. He was generous and thoughtful, and I was very grateful. I felt I owed him honesty, at the very least.

"I want to tell you something, Ferry."

I fished a cigarette from the pocket of my robe—by then I'd switched to a French cigarette that came in a box of ten—and slipped it into my cigarette holder.

"Go on." Ferdinand pushed an ashtray across the desk.

"Klimt asked me to model for one of his paintings," I said. I hesitated for a few seconds. "And I've agreed."

"I don't understand," Ferdinand said. "Moll didn't mention anything about it."

I lit the cigarette and took a long inhale. I could see he was going to put up a fuss, as I'd expected.

"Probably because Moll doesn't know." I blew a plume of smoke into the air. "It's not a portrait, Ferry, and it's not going to be a painting of me. I'm going to be Judith—the Jewish heroine who slayed Holofernes."

He frowned.

"It doesn't seem right," he said. "Doesn't he have models for that kind of thing?"

I had to think about exactly how to phrase my reply.

"His models aren't Jewish women," I said. "He needs someone who looks the part."

"But why didn't you ask me before you agreed?"

"Why would I need your permission?" I tried to keep my voice calm. "It's not a commission, it's my own time, and I'll learn a lot. You said I could have the avant-garde, and this is it, Ferry."

He glared at me as if I'd caught him in some kind of trick.

"I said you could have art, and I've bought it for you."

"You said I could have freedom," I said. "Remember the women walking alone in Paris? They ride bicycles in the summer there, too. They don't ask their husband's permission before they make a friend or choose a piece of art. Berta Zuckerkandl doesn't, either."

"Berta is an unusual woman. She and her husband are practically equals," he said.

I pulled myself up tall. I imagined Judith standing up to a man in her tribe—someone who might have challenged her even after she'd killed the general.

"Are we not equals?" I asked.

By the way he looked at me, I knew the answer.

"I'm going to do it," I said. "I've already agreed. It's what I want—it's what you promised me, Ferry."

"We'll see about that," he said.

Ferdinand left early the next morning, and stayed at the factory apartment for several nights. Thedy and Gustav didn't think anything of it, and I was glad. I saw how attentive my sister was to her husband, and how she deferred to him on so many things. I was sure that Ferdinand wished that I were more like her. But that wasn't what I wanted, and I could not pretend.

"I love the painting," I told Ferdinand when he came back.

"Then you should decide which you want," he said. "The landscapes, or the Judith."

He stayed away at the factory for three more nights the following week.

"What is the trouble?" Thedy asked one morning. Summer was drawing to an end, and it was clear that something wasn't right.

"He's angry because I've agreed to sit for a painting with Klimt," I said. "It's not a portrait, and it's not a public agreement. It's private, between us."

I told her all about the Zuckerkandls' salon and the *Volksblatt* reviewer who said Jews should wear yellow triangles. I explained that Klimt was painting a powerful woman—a Judith in gold—as a response to the anti-Semites.

"But why you?"

"Because I inspired it," I said. "That's what he told me."

Thedy pulled her son onto her lap, and sighed.

"I'd be very careful with a man like Klimt," she said. "I've heard stories about him, and if even half of them are true, he's dangerous for a woman of good standing."

"I know what I want," I said.

Dr. Freud said that every decision, every dream, and every creation were driven by unconscious impulses, but what did that mean, exactly—and what fed those impulses?

"You always have, Adele," Thedy said. "But even so, I worry about you."

I went back to Vienna with Thedy and her family the first week of September, but Ferdinand stayed behind. He said there were new centrifuges on order, and that he needed to be at the factory when the machinery arrived. I wasn't sure if I believed him, but I didn't put up a fuss.

"I'm sorry if you're disappointed in me," I said before we left. I had on my traveling clothes, and we were standing alone near the rear porch where no one could see us.

"I'm sending the Attersee back to Moll," he said. He was formal and distant, as if he hadn't called me a vixen only a few weeks ago. "I'll tell him you didn't care for it."

"But I like it very much," I said. "You can't say that—it isn't true and I won't say it is."

A flock of geese flew overhead, honking noisily.

"Then I'll return it without an explanation," he said.

"That will make you look like a man who doesn't know your own mind," I told him. He was stubborn, but so was I—and I could see by the way his face shuttered that I had hit a nerve.

"I know my own mind," he said.

"Of course you do. And you know excellent art, Ferry. It's as important to you as it is to me."

Back home, the theater and opera seasons were beginning. The flower gardens were in their last blossoms, and the leaves on the trees along the Ringstrasse were beginning to blush into the first shades of autumn. January ball committees were called, and invitations came in from across the city. Berta asked me to spend a day at the grape harvest festival in Grinzing, and I had a postcard from Klimt: *Will you come?*

My heart soared.

I studied the sepia drawing on the front of the card, and his blue scrawl across the back. There was nothing in it that seemed improper, but just to be certain, I tucked it inside one of my novels, and sent him a reply without signing my name.

I will come, I wrote, and set a day and hour.

All the wine gardens in Grinzing hung grape boughs and lanterns on the fence posts to welcome visitors, and garden gates were flung open on the day of the harvest fest. Polka music played in the squares, and the village roads were filled with men in lederhosen and women in smocked dresses. Berta wore a peasant-style skirt and hat, and my hair was coiled on top of my head in a twisting braid.

It was a brisk autumn day, and there were rich and poor families with picnic baskets and blankets. In a clearing at the edge of the vineyards, my friend and I made our way to a white tent decorated with vines and flowers, where long rows of wooden tables were set with red-and-white-checkered cloths. Little boys ran hoops through the streets on long sticks, and girls danced.

"It's good to be home," Berta said. She was in an affectionate mood, and slipped her arm around my waist. I'd missed her company, and was glad to have her to myself.

An accordion player with a dog tied to a rope sidled up to our table, and bowed. He showed us two black teeth when he smiled, cranked the bellows and ran his fingers along the white keys. I was about to shoo him away when Berta snapped open her purse and handed him half a week's worth of wages.

The man's eyes widened comically, but he made quick business of pocketing the coins and striking up a loud, new song.

"So much?" I asked under my breath.

"My great uncle was an accordion player in Galicia," Berta said with a shrug. She tapped her fingers to the music. "He was the kindest, saddest man I knew."

We ordered a carafe of new Grüner Veltliner and a plate of bread with chopped liver and pickled onions, and caught up on our summer months. I told Berta about the theater in Prague, and she told me about the Salzburg music festivals.

"We went to Attersee in August, and stayed in a little house across from the Villa Paulick," she said. She told me the Flöge sisters were making new blue dresses with Japanese designs, and that Klimt spent his afternoons swimming and rowing with his niece—"the little girl is in love with him," she said—or tromping through the woods in his long robe.

"The local people call him their Wood Sprite," she said, laughing. "Or maybe they call him their Wood Devil."

I told her about the Attersee painting—*there,* I thought, *now Ferdinand can't return it*—and asked after Emil and their son. She said her little boy was ready to start school, and was showing a keen interest in anatomy, like his father. I thought of my brother Karl, but blinked away the sadness.

We were finishing our food and wine, feeling merry and loose, when I heard a familiar giggle.

"Frau Zuckerkandl and Frau Bloch-Bauer," Serena Lederer exclaimed. She was dressed head to toe in a traditional peasant costume, with her little girl on one side of her and Alma Mahler on the other. Alma's hat was decorated with grape leaves, fresh flowers, and ferns.

"It's remarkable to see you here," Serena said after we'd exchanged the usual pleasantries. "When I just saw you two nights ago in Prague—really, what are the chances?"

"Are you speaking to me?" I asked. I couldn't imagine what she meant.

"You must be exhausted," she said, sliding her gaze just a bit too far to one side as she spoke. "The way you and Ferdinand were dancing at the Rudolfinum."

I bit my tongue, and tipped my head to one side. I saw that Alma was looking at me with bright eyes.

"I tried to catch you, but Ferdinand said you'd gone up to bed and that was that," Serena added. "Tell me, why would you stay at a hotel in Prague when you have Jungfer Brezan?"

An answer was required, that was clear. I felt all the women looking at me, and I smiled.

"It's Ferdinand," I said. "He likes to . . ."

"Dance," Berta said, as if she'd just woken up. "Yes, Ferdinand likes to dance."

Serena giggled again.

"That's funny," she said, staring at me. "It's hard to imagine that he can outpace you on the dance floor."

The accordion player with the black teeth came back, and I glared at him. The music was too loud, the wine too sweet, the air too warm.

"Yes, it is," I said. "It is hard to imagine."

When Serena and Alma left us to find their companions, I paid the bill and told Berta I had a headache.

"Don't let them bother you," my friend said. "It's all nonsense, you know."

It had never occurred to me that my husband could have a mistress. Now it seemed clear—the nights at the factory, the way he'd come home exhausted.

"It's nothing to make a fuss over," Berta said, putting her arm around my waist again. "I suggest that you leave it as it is."

"I feel so foolish," I said. I felt hurt and angry, too. "Why would you have me leave it as it is?"

Her face was bright under her hat, her cheeks flushed from the wine. She was close enough to kiss, if that's what I wanted.

"Ferdinand was a bachelor for a long time, Adele. And this is the way things are done."

"Even Ferdinand sees that you and Emil are equals," I said. "Does that mean that you're both free to take lovers?"

My friend demurred, but she didn't say no. And that gave me something else to think about: the possibility that I, too, could take a lover.

"Ferdinand has a mistress in Prague," I blurted out to Thedy. "I feel ridiculous that I didn't know."

We were walking through the Volksgarten, and Karl and the nursemaid had gone ahead. Thedy was wearing an old-fashioned pink dress, without the belt that went around the waist. I told her what had happened in Grinzing, and what Berta had said.

"I agree with Berta," she said. Thedy didn't seem the least bit surprised or shocked by my news. "If his mistress is in the country, it means she's probably clean and devoted."

"Devoted?"

"Yes." My sister looked at me as if I were still a child. "Faithful to him—so that she won't give him a disease that he'll bring home to you."

The last of the daylilies were losing their bloom, and the grass was browning at the edges of the lawn. My sister's face was lined and puffy.

"You say it so easily—as if it's already settled."

"You'll have children soon, and then you won't mind," she said. "You know, Adele, sometimes I wish . . ." Her voice faded. "I wish . . ."

We stopped next to a small fountain. Thedy put her hand to her chest, and startled me with a long, dry sob.

"What is it?" I asked. "Is something wrong between you and Gustav?"

"No." She buried her face against my shoulder, and I lead her to a garden bench beside a hedgerow. "There isn't anything wrong."

"Then what?"

She covered her face with her hands.

"I'm having another baby." Her words came out in a teary blur, but what I could make out sounded something like, "I'm tired . . . she'll do things you don't want to do . . . if he has a mistress, he'll leave you alone . . ."

I stroked her head, and tried to make sense of it all.

"Are you saying you want Gustav to take a mistress?" I asked.

Karl came toddling back in our direction, waving two pinecones in his plump fist. The nursemaid was right behind him.

"Maybe," my sister said quietly. "It would make things so much easier for me."

I'd married too young, it was clear. I'd married without knowing the world.

"Let Ferdinand keep her," she said. "Soon enough you'll have your children, and then everything will be as it should."

Karl put a fat pinecone on my sister's lap, and one on mine. I thought about the doctor in Paris, and the way my brother had said *don't let them put you in a box.*

"You can decide a thing without deciding, you know," Thedy added. "You can just keep it to yourself."

"I saw Serena Lederer in Grinzing on Saturday," I said after dessert was served.

Ferdinand lifted his eyes from his chocolate mousse. He'd been home for three days, and hadn't yet come to my bedroom.

"I always thought she was a silly woman," he said.

There was candlelight, and the sound of the cook in the kitchen.

"Did you go dancing in Prague?" I asked. I was surprised at how calm I felt.

He blinked and put down his spoon. That was all. He didn't even clear his throat.

"Yes," he nodded. "I did go dancing."

In the silence I felt as if we were deciding something together. Something modern, I suppose. Something like the dappled swirl in Klimt's painting, or the way the bare winter trees against a cobalt sky are as much about life as they are about death.

The butler came into the room and refilled Ferdinand's teacup. The clock struck seven. We had tickets for the opera, and the butler said the coach was ready and that Thedy and Gustav were waiting downstairs.

"Please don't return the painting, Ferry," I said in a rush. "Please let me have my life, too."

His face turned red. It was only for an instant, but I saw his expression crack, and I saw how much he cared for me.

"Everyone in this city watches what you do," he said.

"But I will have the art, Ferry." I forced myself to say it bravely. "You promised me that. You know you did."

He wiped his mouth, and pushed away from the table.

Downstairs, Thedy was already in the carriage, wrapped under a blanket. I sat beside her, and watched our husbands talk easily about the evening's performance.

"Tonight it's *Tristan and Isolde*," Gustav said. "What a treat."

We got out of the carriage on Operaring and joined the throng. I watched the way Thedy held Gustav's arm, and the way he leaned toward her. He was protective of her, and she relied on him.

Ferdinand put a hand on the small of my back, but I held the banister and stepped up to our box without my husband's help. As far as I was concerned, whatever he thought was settled, and whatever I thought was settled had been left largely unspoken. I thought this was to become the way we lived our lives. But when the curtain came up, Ferdinand put his hand on my knee. As the violinists lifted their instruments, and Mahler raised his baton, my husband put his lips against my ear.

"I expect fidelity from you," he whispered.

MARIA

1938

My father and mother were getting old and fading quickly, and there was nothing I could do to stop it. We had relied on Uncle Ferdinand all of our lives—Papa most of all—and it was impossible to imagine what we would do if Uncle Ferry couldn't help us anymore.

So when the Nazis released Leopold at the end of June—just as my uncle had said they would—a tiny bit of our faith and hope was restored.

Leopold had lost a lot of weight, and there were deep, dark rings around his eyes. But he said he hadn't been hurt, and that he'd never been to Dachau.

"I was in a room on the third floor of the Hotel Metropole the whole time," Leopold said. We were in my father's study, talking by the light of a single lamp. My brother was smoking a cigar, and drinking the last of my father's brandy.

"There was a banner hanging over the window, and all the light in the room looked red," he said. He was folded into his chair, almost bent in two. "I was alone all the time, but I think that was better than anything else."

"I went to the Metropole," I whispered. "It was unspeakable."

Leopold glanced at our parents, and shook his head.

"It was bearable," he said, but I knew he wasn't telling the truth. I'd heard the screaming. I knew why he looked as if he hadn't slept in weeks. It seemed a miracle that he'd not been beaten and broken, but it gave me hope for Fritz.

"Thank God Uncle Ferry gave them what they wanted," he said.

Leopold told us he was going to Canada. There was no way to soften the news. He didn't even try.

"I was able to get papers for Robert and his family, too," he said, reaching for my mother's hand. "I'm sorry, Mama, that's all they would give me."

"Don't worry about us," my mother said. She'd wept so many tears, I think her ducts were dry. "We're all waiting for Fritz. We can't leave without Maria and Fritz."

"I'm not leaving," my father said from the deep recesses of his armchair. "I'm not strong enough to go anywhere."

Leopold had nothing to take but the clothes on his back. My mother gave him a scarf and an extra pair of socks, but he couldn't carry anything more. When he'd buttoned up his coat, and wrapped Papa's scarf around his neck, my brother pulled me into a hard, long hug.

"Take care of them, and don't give up on Fritz," he said in a low voice. "Most of all, Maria, take care of yourself."

"Don't say that," I said, hugging him harder. "I'm not giving up on anyone, do you hear me? No one."

Every week I brought clean clothes to Rossauer Prison and took away Fritz's laundry to be washed. We exchanged trinkets in the bundles. Fritz drew funny little doodles for me, like a comical mouse eating a piece of cheese. I slipped a fresh biscuit into his basket, and a note that I sprayed with my perfume.

I waited in line against the dirty prison walls with hundreds of wives, daughters, and mothers all holding packages. Everything was orderly and civilized, and no one asked why the others were there. We knew that asking questions only caused trouble. Our talk came in snatches of shared conversation, some of it hopeful but most of it terrible.

"Bettina Flux and her brothers killed themselves last week—all four dead in their beds."

"They seized the Rothschilds' palace and arrested the father and son. The richest banker in Europe and there was nothing he could do to save his family."

"They're starving Jewish prisoners in Germany—giving them bread made of sawdust and mud."

Soldiers patrolled the laundry line, sometimes stopping to flirt with a pretty woman. A hard-faced officer with very large hands singled me out one afternoon.

"Fräulein," he called me, and I didn't correct him. "Fräulein, who are you washing clothes for and waiting on line to please?"

"Fritz Altmann," I said.

"Your brother, yes? Or your father?"

I wasn't wearing my wedding ring. Everything had been hidden or sold.

"My husband." I meant to hold his gaze, but I dropped my eyes and I whispered, "Fritz, my husband."

"The Jews have such good wives," he said. "To wait all these hours only to bring clean clothes and take away the filth."

One morning the line at Rossauer was shorter than usual, and I quickly found myself at the front window.

"Package for Friedrich Altmann. Prisoner 61875," I said by rote.

The officer riffled through a stack of papers.

"There is no Altmann here."

The morning coffee burned in my stomach. In an instant, I was wide awake.

"He was here last week," I said. I could feel the blood behind my eyes. My mouth tasted of metal. "Maybe there's a mistake."

The officer frowned. I tried to smile and look pretty.

"Wait here." He disappeared into a back room and emerged a moment later.

"He's been moved to Landesgericht Prison. No packages. One letter a week, that's all."

"Why was he moved?" I asked in a voice I hardly recognized. "I don't understand why he was moved."

"Landesgericht is in the Eighth District," the clerk said. He was already looking behind me. "There are no visitors. No laundry. One letter a week."

For the next two days I braved the Landesgericht Courthouse, praying for a sympathetic officer who would tell me something or agree to pass my note to Fritz.

"*Verboten,*" I was told again and again. Forbidden.

On the third morning I found a letter in our mailbox with Fritz's familiar handwriting. I tore it open and found his words slashed with black *x*'s by the censors.

> *Beloved Maria*
>
> *I'm at XXXXX and am still all right. Stay strong for both of us and I'll return to you soon. Please, Maria, I beg you not to come here. My cellmate's wife was arrested last night at the prison door XXXXXXXXXXXX must XXXXX my brother to release everything. It's the only way. Your Fritz*

On a bright June day, I found my father in bed in the middle of the afternoon. His dark room stank of black cough and something I couldn't recognize.

"I'm scared," my mother said.

Jewish doctors had been stripped of their right to practice and non-Jewish doctors could not enter a Jewish home, but there was still a black market and help was still possible with the right offer of jewels and gold.

Just before sundown on Friday, Dr. Schoenbart showed up at the kitchen door dressed as a handyman. He carried his medical tools in a workman's satchel, and washed his hands in our kitchen sink. He was incognito: a doctor disguised as a plumber.

My father didn't make a sound as his blood was drawn.

"He doesn't have to eat," the doctor said as he capped the small vial and slipped it into his bag along with two of my mother's ruby earrings. "But make sure he's is drinking some broth and weak juices."

We did what he suggested, but it did no good. A week later, Dr. Schoenbart returned to tell us my father had stomach cancer.

"What is the treatment?" Mama asked.

"If he can pass as a Christian, maybe you can have him admitted to the central hospital. Otherwise . . ." The doctor's voice trailed off.

I saw Felix Landau in the factory grounds the next day, and told him my father was sick.

"I wouldn't mention it if it wasn't very serious," I said.

"Your father is old," Landau said, drawing his back up very straight. I'd gotten used to the scar on his face, but I noticed it on that day because it was pulsing. "If your brother-in-law doesn't see reason, your husband will be sent to a German prison—that's what you should worry about," Landau said. "Write to Bernhard and tell him to return what belongs to us—then I'll try to get your husband released for you. I can't do anything if you won't cooperate."

"I don't have an address," I said. "How can I write to Bernhard?"

"I know where he is," Landau said. "Give the letter to me."

When I delivered my letter to Landau the following morning, he let his hand brush against mine.

"You're a smart woman, Maria." He smiled at me. "Pretty and smart, a very good combination—especially in a Jewess."

"You know," I said slowly, "we're barely Jews."

He turned so that he was facing me squarely.

"Tell me what you mean."

"My parents didn't practice Judaism, and neither do I."

Landau leaned closer, and drew in a breath. I'd heard the Nazis used strange, cruel methods to determine who had Jewish blood. They said we smelled like pigs and that our big noses and heavy lips gave us away.

"You smell like roses," Landau said. I pulled away as if I'd been slapped. "Very pretty roses. I'm glad you told me that, Maria. I will bear that in mind."

There was something in his eyes that I didn't want to see: pity, maybe, or affection. I didn't let myself look at it for even one second more.

By the end of June anyone who'd been able to get an exit visa was gone. The sun came up each morning but the green parks, crowded squares and voices of happy children in the streets were a mockery to me. Every routine comfort faded and I waited only for word of Fritz. His letters came in ripped envelopes with half the sentences blacked out by censors, but at least I knew he was alive and thinking of me. He closed every letter with the same words: *Until we're together again I am, as ever, Your Darling Fritz.*

Then the letters stopped. After a night with no sleep, I went down to my newlywed apartment and knocked until Landau answered. It was barely dawn. Landau was wearing white long johns. I wanted to rip the smirk off his face. Instead, I begged.

"Please tell me if he's alive?"

"He's alive for now. But prison does strange things to men."

"Strange things? What strange things?"

He gave me an indifferent shrug.

"What can I do? Please tell me —" I put a hand on his shoulder and he looked at the place where I was touching him.

"Tell your brother-in-law to give us what we want," Landau said.

"I did that already," I said. "What else can I do?"

I didn't think I wasn't offering him anything, because I didn't think I had anything to offer. But I did touch him. I admit that I touched him. And Landau stepped back, leaving my hand hanging in the air.

"It's late—or rather, it's early. Nothing can be done now."

I walked all the way to the Metropole. It was a hot day and you could tell who the Jews were because they hugged the sides of the buildings as if hoping to disappear between bricks and mortar.

The Metropole was even worse than before. There was horror in the hard faces of men in uniform, and terror in the children who were led behind closed doors while their mothers were sent in another direction pleading and crying.

"Find a line," a Nazi barked, and I got on the closest one without looking up.

When I reached the front, I spelled Fritz's name and waited, looking neither right nor left. A woman beside me fainted, and a man slipped his hands under her arms to keep her from hitting the ground.

"Friedrich Altmann has left the city," the clerk said.

"To where?"

Telephones were ringing. I smelled my own perspiration over the lavender handkerchief I'd tucked into my shirt.

The woman looked me up and down, tapping an index card against the large metal box. I saw Fritz's name and a number neatly typed across the white card.

"You must know," I said. It was hard to breathe. I thought I might faint.

"Dachau," the clerk said, filing the card away. "Friedrich Altmann is in Dachau."

I moved away from the clerk without knowing I moved, and left without knowing how I left. On the hotel steps I slid past the other ghosts weeping or moaning or begging for their lives. The red banners flapping in the wind roared like wild animals. Black cars swept through the street like hawks, the Germans' hard vowels shot through the air like spears. I rushed across the street without looking. A car swept around the corner, and as I hurried out of its way, my foot caught on the curb and I fell, hard, on my knees.

"Fräulein!"

A black glove, shiny boots, crisp green pants. He reached down for me. My knees were screaming.

"Get up," the man said. I tried to push myself up. Pebbles cut into my knees, my hands could hardly lift me.

His glove wrapped around my arm, and he pulled me to my feet.

"Are you all right?"

"I'm sorry," I whispered. His hand was large and black. I forced myself to stand on my own feet. I didn't look at his face. "Thank you, I'm fine, thank you."

"You're bleeding," he said. He must have thought I was a Gentile. I wanted to get away as fast as I could.

"I'm fine," I said. "I'll be fine."

He let go of my arm and I rushed away without looking back. It wasn't until I got home that I saw my stockings were torn, my knees were cut, my shins and shoes crusted with blood.

By day my mind traced over escape routes, friends I could contact, favors I might be able to call upon. At night I dreamt that Fritz and I had sprouted wings, sailing above giant crows with slick black feathers. But it was all in my mind, a manic casting about for hope that faded until Felix Landau showed up at my door one night in his black jacket. The scar on his face a painful red under the bare hallway bulb.

"I've come with a message," he said.

I tugged my dressing gown around me. He took an official-looking document out of his coat pocket.

"Lieutenant Hans Erlichmann of the Central Agency for Jewish Emigration requests your help in securing the transfer of all Altmann Textiles records to the Reich. In exchange, Fritz Altmann will be released from prison." Landau's diction was crisp and formal. "You may do a service to the Führer and also help your family."

The name Erlichmann was not familiar to me, but I knew it wasn't good to have a Nazi officer take any special notice of my family's affairs. Landau saw the panic on my face.

"Lieutenant Erlichmann wants to help you," he said without even a hint of irony. "Let me explain."

He said the orders were simple: I was to accompany him to Berlin, where Bernhard would come with all the account books and sign over everything to the Germans.

"Haven't you already taken everything?" I asked. "The factory and all the money that goes in and out of here are yours."

Landau eyed me coolly.

"Not mine—the Reich's," he said. "And I'm not a fool. We know there's an entire subsidiary of Altmann Textiles being run out of Paris. That subsidiary also belongs to the Reich. It's my responsibility to ensure that every single asset is relinquished in full cooperation of the law."

I didn't know if I had a choice, or if I was about to be arrested and taken to Berlin.

"But why Berlin?" I dared to press him. "And why do you need me to go with you?"

"Because your brother-in-law isn't very keen on coming back to Vienna," he said. "That's why. And because we think your presence will be particularly persuasive."

"Then I will be a ransom," I said. I didn't ask, because it seemed apparent to me.

Landau heaved a loud guffaw.

"I can have you arrested now, tonight, tomorrow—anytime—for failing to cooperate with the mandatory Aryanization of every Altmann family asset." He spoke as if he were struggling for patience. "Instead, the Reich is inviting you to Berlin. We feel quite sure that your presence at the table will entice your brother-in-law to cooperate to the fullest and sign all the proper documents."

"You don't need his signature," I said. "Just take it, the way you've taken everything else."

A strange, cunning look came over his face.

"The Reich doesn't seize property," he said. "As you know, everything is done by the letter of the law."

It made no sense, and yet it made perfect sense: the Nazis' brilliance, the thing that kept everyone doing what we were told, was the way they made everything—even a coercive trip to Germany—sound extremely logical and lawful. This was their first great cruelty: strict adherence to laws that served only themselves.

"And if I go, Fritz will be released?"

"When Bernhard signs the papers, Fritz will be released."

I packed as if for a funeral, with somber dresses and a dark hat. Just before dawn I locked the apartment door, although of course I knew anyone could enter if they wanted to. Landau met me beneath a lamppost by the gate, and put my overnight bag in a taxi. I sat between Landau and a man in uniform who didn't say a word to me. Close to the train station, we passed a barroom that was still open. Women of the night were hanging on to officers who were stumbling out of the brightly lit storefront. The prostitutes' lipstick looked orange in the strange dawn.

At half past eight, the three of us boarded a Berlin-bound train. There were Nazis everywhere in brown coats and black uniforms, traveling with women wearing dark lipstick, long raincoats, and manly hats. Red lights flashed and bells rang as we pulled out of the station. I closed my eyes and recalled the song Fritz had been singing the day I met him.

You are peace, the gentle peace, you are longing and what stills it.
I consecrate to you, with all my joy and pain, a home in my eyes
    and my heart.

When we crossed into Germany, Landau insisted I eat with him in the dining car. I choked down a few bites and watched the wet countryside turn into flat houses, small villages, then rows of Nazi flags as we approached Berlin.

Rain was falling steadily as I followed Landau through the German streets into a hotel, where a porter showed me to my room. I locked the door, and tossed through the night. In the morning, nauseated and frightened, I trudged behind him up a flight of stone steps and down a hall into an airless room where Bernhard sat stiffly, his mouth in a grim line.

Outside, it began to thunder.

"Be brave, Maria," Bernhard said.

I gave him a nod but couldn't manage a smile.

A man in a business suit handed a dossier to Landau.

"Your brother-in-law is a stubborn man," Landau said to me. "We want him to understand the consequences if he tries to hold back anything this time."

Bernhard understood. He signed and dated the documents. It took less than five minutes. Then I was led out with Landau.

"Can't I speak to my brother-in-law?" I asked.

"No," Landau said. He put his hand on the small of my back—a protective gesture, one a man might do with his wife. "Now we go back to our hotel."

We walked together under one umbrella, through crowded streets and past perfumed women and handsome men who barely glanced our way. The smell of grilling meats belched from sidewalk cafés.

"Will we go home tonight?" I asked. "Will that be to your liking?"

"My liking has nothing to do with it, Maria." He smiled, and I saw his crooked teeth. "Our train doesn't run back to Vienna tonight."

At our hotel he closed the umbrella before ushering me through the revolving door. Inside, the lobby was bright and strangely empty.

"You're a smart Jewess, you should understand that the Altmann property legally belongs to the Reich now," Landau said, as if explaining a lesson to a schoolchild. "We could have seized it, but we showed your brother-in-law the courtesy of a formal exchange so he's no longer a criminal in our eyes."

We were in the lift by then, a tiny space that was wet with rainwater and sweat. The elevator walls were mirrored with a dark, smoky glass. Landau spoke to my reflection.

"Now Bernhard will be free to go about his Jew business elsewhere," he said.

The lift stopped at the third floor, and he put a hand on my waist.

"Maybe you'd like to freshen yourself now." He walked me to my room and waited for me to open the door. "A bubble bath, or some lipstick? I ordered you a bottle of Chanel No. 5. It's a lovely scent. So womanly."

Landau followed me into my room and shut the door behind him. On the gleaming settee there were a dozen pink roses in a cut crystal vase. Beside it, on a silver tray, was a pitcher of red juice and two glasses.

"Roses for you," he said. He reached for my coat. "Because you always smell like roses."

I knew it was going to happen then.

"You don't have to be scared," he said, reaching for me. "We have perfume, roses. Lipstick for your beautiful mouth. Would you like to take a bath?"

I shook my head.

"That's fine. You can take a bath later."

He poured a cup of juice, and held it out to me.

"Pomegranate juice is an aphrodisiac," he said. "Come, Maria. Drink."

He held the cup to my mouth until I took a sip. Then he put a hand on my shoulder and turned me toward the bed. When I tried to resist, he put a hand on my chin. He smelled of onions. He made me look at his face, and my skin burned.

"I'm not going to hurt you," he said.

The bed was a four-poster canopy princess bed, like the one I'd had when I was a little girl. I stood against it, and he let go of my hand.

"Now take off your dress."

I shook my head.

He reached for the top button of his shirt, and opened it. He unbuckled his belt, and then the buttons on his trousers. I could see that he was aroused.

"Please," I said. I meant to shout, but it came out as a whisper. "Don't."

In the small room he was a large, dangerous animal, a tiger at the zoo. When he stepped out of his pants and kicked them behind him, I heard my aunt telling me to be fierce.

"I'm glad you came to Berlin," he said. "We have an understanding, don't we? Don't pretend you didn't know."

"No," I said, shaking my head. "I'm afraid I'm a fool."

"A pretty fool," he said, grabbing my wrist. "A very pretty little fool."

Then he pushed me onto the bed, and forced himself between my legs.

By the time Landau returned me to Vienna I'd been gone almost three days. The rain had stopped and late afternoon sunlight was cascading over the city. I couldn't wait to bathe in scalding water and burn the clothes I'd been wearing. But I didn't have time to clean Landau off my skin—because at home I found a note from my mother slipped under the door.

She asked me to come directly to Stubenbastei, and when I saw the blackened windows, I knew right away what had happened.

"There are no rabbis, no *minyan*." Mama was stoic as she wiped away my tears. "We have to say the Kaddish ourselves."

Poor Papa was small and yellow-skinned in his coffin, the dark evening jacket swimming on his wasted body. The coffin itself was a luxury, and my mother was proud to have found one.

Despite what I'd told Landau about not being Jews, in ordinary times we would have called on a rabbi from the synagogue where I'd been married, and he would have organized ten men to pray over my father's body. We knew no one would come to sit shiva or to pray the Kaddish now. Instead, Mama found a heavy black prayer book in my father's study. She turned the pages backward, then forward. The Hebrew letters were like hieroglyphics to me, scribbles and symbols that I couldn't decipher.

"Leopold should be here," Mama said quietly. "Leopold and your uncle Ferdinand are the ones who should lead the prayer. Do you know the Kaddish?" she asked. "Do you know the prayer for the dead?"

I shook my head, and did the only thing I could think of: I held her and sang the one song I knew that gave me comfort.

"You are peace, the gentle peace, you are longing and what stills it. I consecrate to you, with all my joy and pain, a home in my eyes and my heart."

I couldn't bear to tell her what happened in Berlin. I felt the shame as if it had been branded onto my body, and swore I would never speak of it.

*I*n her dream] she puts a candle into a candlestick; but the candle is broken, so that it does not stand up. The girls at school say she is clumsy; but she replies that it is not her fault. . . . An obvious symbolism has here been employed. The candle is an object which excites the female genitals; its being broken, so that it does not stand upright, signifies impotence on the man's part (it is not her fault). . . . But does this young woman, carefully brought up, and a stranger to all obscenity, know of such an application of the candle?

—*SIGMUND FREUD,* THE INTERPRETATION OF DREAMS, *1900*

ADELE
1900

Outside, it was a brilliant October morning. Inside the studio, Klimt stoked the fire and it roared. The curtains were drawn and the small back room was dim and close, like a tent at night. The floor was covered in animal skins, and the walls were hung with dark canvas. Candles flickered. The light was amber and gold, the flames buzzed and snapped, candle wax popped and melted.

"Close your eyes," Klimt said.

I closed my eyes and opened my lips. Alone in my bedroom I'd held the mirror to my face and watched how I looked at the moment of climax. I was brave, but I wanted to be braver. I raised a fist, imagining Judith's knife slicing through the air.

"Frau Bloch-Bauer." Klimt said my name gently, and circled my wrist with his thumb and forefinger. I could smell the turquoise air that was always around him. "You need to be softer."

There was a catch in my throat. For weeks I'd been waiting for him to kiss me again. Ferdinand might expect fidelity of me, but with a mistress of his own in the countryside, his demand didn't seem fair. And I was capable of keeping secrets. I'd always been capable of that.

"Judith is a warrior," I said.

My mangled hand was folded in my lap beneath the end of a scarf. Klimt felt for it among the fabric, and I let him take it. He ran his finger along the edge of the purple scar and the ladder of dark stitches. He traced the blue lines beneath the skin, just as Karl had once done.

"She shows him that she's vulnerable," he said. "That's how she seduces him."

He ran his fingers along my palm, and then threaded them each between mine. He moved closer, and his bare foot touched my naked heel. My toes curled, deliciously.

I knew he had lovers. I knew he wouldn't belong to me and that I would never belong to him. But he was so heady and so near. He was more alive than anyone I knew.

I murmured something about being fierce.

"You have to be soft," he said.

My heart was racing. I could feel it beneath my dress. One last blue scarf slipped to the ground.

"Show me," I said.

When his mouth came it was warm and hot, one tongue, two lips. He touched my clavicle and ran his hand beneath the necklace. He put his finger on the pulse at my neck, and the line between my heart and groin tightened like one long muscle.

"You smell good," he said. I had to strain to hear him. His words were so faint they were almost my words; his voice was almost my voice. His hand was moving my hand and sliding up my thigh, pushing aside the folds of my dress.

His tongue slid down to my breast.

I pushed the dress off my shoulders and it fell to the floor. I was naked and he was pressing against me, he was licking my stomach and his tongue was between my legs and then he was rolling a sheepskin condom onto himself like a cap and lifting me off the chair.

He was strong.

There were animal skins for the setting. There was dense shearling rubbing against my naked buttocks, a soft, bushy friction that I'd imagined a hundred times. He kissed my shoulders, parted my thighs, and pressed into me slowly until I cried out—it was pleasure, but it came in a full, deep cry—and then he turned me over and took me from behind, just as I'd dreamt, and I was split wide open. I was screaming and he was bellowing and then I was laughing and crying because I'd taken him and I'd surrendered, and nothing would be the same for me, ever again.

"You have a lovely figure," Klimt said. I was stretched out on the animal skins in front of the fire, a blanket pulled over me.

On the table in the front room I'd seen the usual cluster of new sketches: bare limbs, splayed legs, shock of red hair.

"I'm sure you see a lot of lovely figures." I meant it to be a joke but it fell short, and my words faltered.

He put his hand under my chin.

"Let's understand one another," Klimt said. His expression was serious. His mouth was pulpy and wet. I wanted to toss my head and say something clever, but words refused to come.

"All right," I said. Was this how lovers spoke? "Let's."

"You're brilliant and beautiful, and I adore you. But we can't be possessive of one another. I'm not like that. I can't be."

It hurt, a little, but I also understood that I didn't have to promise him anything, either.

"There's also the small matter of my husband," I said, finding my voice and hoping it sounded light.

"Who has an astonishing and charming wife," Klimt said. "And excellent taste in landscape paintings."

I laughed.

"And who expects fidelity from me," I added. "As well as a child of his own."

He kissed both of my palms, flat in the middle where the skin tingled.

"The sheepskins won't fail you," Klimt said. "And you can keep careful track of your menses, it's just as reliable."

Then he pulled on his robe and seemed ready to work again. It shocked me for an instant, but I saw it made perfect sense.

"Here are my plans for the Judith," he said. We looked together at a long row of sketches laid out along his worktable. The measurements and colors were indicated in penciled notes and fat dots of paint—there was to be a wide golden frame, my jeweled necklace, a halo of dark brown hair. My eyes rolling up into my head. One naked breast. My mouth in two red pencil strokes.

"And here," he waved a hand toward a corner of one page. "You'll have Holofernes's head in your hand. You'll be holding him by the hair."

I held a sketch to the candlelight.

"Ferdinand won't like it if I'm shirtless."

I was surprised that I felt protective of my husband. Even then and there, with the fire roaring and my screams still in my throat, I felt quite keenly that I did not want Ferdinand to be shamed by anything I did. I had what I wanted, and I would have much more if I did not make him angry.

"I'm serious, Gustl." I used his nickname, just as I'd once heard Serena speak it to him. "You can't make it look exactly like me."

Klimt traced his finger along my hand, and across the scar.

"It's you, Adele, but it's not you," he said. "You're the model, but it's not a portrait. It's just as I said that night at Berta's."

"I understand," I said. "But I want Ferdinand to be able to understand, too."

Even before I was dressed he was at his canvas, whistling and laying out the measurements for the painting. I didn't mind. I kissed him good-bye, laced up my boots, and walked home with a new joy in my stride.

I went back again the following week and lay down on the animal furs in my chemise. I told myself to remember every flicker of his tongue, every charged and swollen desire, because how long could it last? How long would I dare?

"You could become like opium to me," Klimt said. "An irresistible drug."

We were dressed, and I was looking through the sketches he'd made that morning. I hardly recognized my own face.

"But I won't be."

I'd brought us two cinnamon buns from breakfast, and we were sharing them with a cup of tea he'd warmed by the fire.

"Why not?" he asked.

As he spoke there was a knock at his door, and then a woman's voice.

"We're here," she called in a Czech accent. I saw her peeking through the window where I'd stood hidden less than a year ago. Her hat was jaunty, her eyes a bright, narrow green.

Klimt opened the door and two models danced in wearing white dresses and smelling of the bakeries or the pastry shops where they worked.

"That's why," I called over their heads, but Klimt was already taking a white sheet off a canvas, revealing a rough painting of two women curled together in long, flowing robes.

"Next week," he said, locking eyes with me as I let myself out. "I need you, Frau Bloch-Bauer."

I went to his studio every week that autumn. I was giddy with our secret, and consumed by all that was new in my life. With unbound energy I scoured the Graben for art books and devoured everything I could find about the Symbolists, new architecture, and art history. I learned about Michelangelo's tormented brilliance, da Vinci's *Vitruvian Man,* Brunelleschi's miraculous dome, and Botticelli's evolution of idealized female beauty.

"The Italians were great patrons of the arts," I said to Ferdinand one evening as I studied a daguerreotype of Michelangelo's *David.*

I'd asked nothing of my husband since the summer. I'd done nothing to indicate that I'd taken a lover of my own, and he'd asked nothing about the progress of Klimt's painting. But our intimacy had cooled, and I felt it was time for our standoff to end. I felt that he was ready, too.

When I asked if we could visit Florence—"To study Renaissance art," I said, "they had their golden age, and now we will have ours in Vienna"—Ferdinand quickly made the arrangements and ordered me a new fur coat in preparation for our excursion.

We traveled in a luxurious sleeper cabin through the Alps, and arrived at the Grand Hotel in the middle of a snowstorm. Roast pheasant and cheese ravioli filled our bellies the first evening in Florence, and we slept in four-post canopy beds piled high with goose down pillows.

The next morning our carriage slogged through the wet streets and deposited us at the Uffizi the moment it opened. In my excitement, I barley glanced at any of the antiquities but went directly upstairs to the Botticelli room.

It was just as I'd expected, but even more powerful than I could have hoped. Looking from Venus to *Primavera*—each as naked as Eve in the garden, each full of life and seduction—I felt a kinship with Botticelli's women that made me blush from neck to knees.

Our footsteps echoed along the Uffizi's long hallways, and the Italian's cheerful chatter was contagious. After Botticelli we found a small crowd was already gathered around Titian's *Venus of Urbino*. Venus's skin was supple and lush, and the white dog at her feet was almost quivering with life. Even hundreds of years hence, I could imagine how she must have felt as she stared at the painter, staring back at her— consuming and consumed, frozen in place like Munch's girl on the bed but also cunning, also wise: unashamed and in full possession of her own erotic allure. I imagined the young model looking boldly at the painter as he placed her hand between her thighs. I saw it all—the scene in the studio, the life in the drawing, the wet paint, and the full orb of light that illuminated the canvas.

"In Paris we saw the new art," I whispered to Ferdinand, struggling to keep my voice calm. "But this is where it all started."

"I love visiting museums with you," he said. He looked at me with so much tenderness, I almost felt sorry for what I had done with Klimt.

After our Italian sojourn I had new art supplies delivered to the house, and sent a note to Franz Cizek to ask for a private drawing lesson. Herr Cizek was teaching Austrian children to see motion and energy in all things, and in two short lessons he showed me how to draw a candle, a chair, and my own shoe so that each object seemed alive on the paper.

I wasn't very good, but the simple act of drawing excited me.

I stayed up all night smoking and sketching as the city prepared for the Christmas holiday. Klimt's redheads, the Italians with their goddesses, the French and Dutch Symbolists, the Norwegian with his virgin pinned to the bed—they were all dancing in front of me, their faces mixing with scenes that I'd dreamt, things I'd done, and moments I'd only imagined.

When Ferdinand pushed open my bedroom door just after dawn, he turned pale at the sight of me.

"Have you been up all night?" he asked. He grabbed my hand—it was covered in red pastel. "Are you bleeding?"

I threw back my head and laughed.

"I'm not hurt," I said. I felt a bit manic when I saw that I'd been sketching the same red flower over and again: a red flower, bursting out of the place where my hand had been torn open. "I'm drawing my dreams."

We'd all begun to speak of our dreams by then. Dr. Freud's lectures were still quiet affairs on Saturday evenings at the university, but his book had cracked open our imaginations—our *unconscious*—the way Klimt had opened my body. Everywhere we went, people were talking about the meaning of their dreams: *Water is sensual. Fire is desire. Blackness is death. A waterwheel is sexual consummation, and dreaming of milk is the longing to be a child again.*

I wrote it all down, I drew my hand again and again, I visited Klimt in his studio and tracked my dreams in a little diary that I kept hidden in my room.

I tracked my menses there, too.

I'd barely pushed my leather diary beneath my pillow one December night when Ferdinand came into my bedroom carrying a blue velvet box tied with a white ribbon.

"Tomorrow is our anniversary," he said, as if I'd forgotten.

He sat on the edge of my bed. His robe, and the scent of his pomade, told me he was there for romance.

I pulled open the ribbon and found fat gold earrings to match my choker necklace. I put them on and looked at my reflection in the mirror.

"You should have seen how thrilled Moser was when I told him what I wanted," Ferdinand said. He touched the nape of my neck. His hair was turning gray, and his face was strained as he fumbled with my dressing gown. I put my arms around him, and murmured his name. He closed his eyes, opened his robe, and climbed on top of me.

When I woke in the morning, he was still in my bed.

"Go on," I said, pushing at him playfully. "Go get dressed."

"You come, too," he said. I could see he wanted to say something more, but he changed his mind and put on his slippers with his usual precision.

At breakfast, I found him frowning over the newspaper.

"What is it?" I asked.

It was a bright day. The sky was blue, and there were clouds fluffing merrily outside our window. The servants were decorating the Christmas tree in our front parlor. I'd ordered dozens of gold and silver baubles for the tree, and red ribbons for the banisters. Our staircase was decorated with nutcrackers and fat red devils dancing on top of sugarplum boxes wrapped in bright foil.

"There's a mutiny at the university," Ferdinand said. "It looks like Gustav Klimt is in trouble."

He showed me the declaration against Klimt, and the long list of academics who had denounced and rejected his university murals.

"He'll have to give the money back." I felt sick. "And I doubt he can afford that."

Ferdinand studied my face, and I studied his.

"I've given it a lot of thought," he said. "If you admire Klimt this much, we should commission a piece from him when you're ready."

I more than admired Klimt, and I remembered each afternoon as if it had happened in slow motion. But I'd trusted my fate to Ferdinand. I was his wife and he was my husband, and I owed him at least a fair warning.

"You know he hasn't finished the Judith yet," I said carefully.

He busied himself stirring sugar into his coffee. My sister had told me that I would grow to love him, and at that moment I did. My tenderness surprised me.

"There are some things you should know about the painting," I said.

Ferdinand narrowed his eyes.

"Go on," he said.

"It's my hair and features in the picture. But he also imagined things that he hasn't seen."

A deception seemed not only prudent but necessary.

"Go on."

"It's me, and it's not me."

He put down his spoon, and folded his hands together.

"Please say what you mean to say, Adele."

"It's a seduction scene, and so the painting is seductive."

"Is it indecent?"

"I've only seen the sketches," I said. "There's a bare breast. But that's all I know."

By then my husband had half a dozen expressions that I could easily recognize—pride, anger, impatience, desire, happiness, shrewd understanding. But the expression that crossed his face at that moment was a mix of confusion and sadness that I had never seen before.

"I told you that the whole city watches what you do," he said.

"I know, Ferry." I put my hand on his—I chose the mangled hand, although I knew he wouldn't notice. "And because we've befriended Klimt, it puts both of us at the center of Vienna's new art world. Just like the Medici in Florence."

"Don't use my generosity against me," he said.

"If everyone is watching me, it's only because of you," I said, knowing how true it was. "You can build a legacy for both of us if you'll support the best artists and help them grow."

It was easy to see Ferdinand remembering how the Medici had built their fortunes with one hand and their legacies with the other.

"With your resources and power you can influence art more than any other man in Vienna," I went on. "I hope you will do that, for both of our sakes. And for our children when we have them, too."

As a girl I'd been denied the education I'd wanted, and my choices had been keenly limited. That morning I felt those limitations beginning to splinter. If I could strike the right balance between courage and surrender, I might have all that I'd ever desired in the way of books, knowledge, art, freedom, family—and a lover, too.

MARIA

1938

A sharp pain woke me in the dark. The bedroom felt small and close, and the air smelled like rust. Rain was tapping at the window with long, hard fingers and there was thunder in the distance. I'd been dreaming of Landau and Fritz, the two of them singing a terrible, screeching opera. My head was pounding, and my heart was beating too fast.

I dragged myself out of bed and into the bathroom. I was dizzy. The tiles felt cool and sticky on my feet, and I started to cry because I was sick and alone. I'd had tomato soup for dinner, and it came up into the sink. The overhead light was blinding: I snapped it on, and quickly off again. In the flash, I saw a dark smear on the floor. My nightgown was wet, and when I put my hand down to feel what it was, my fingers came back covered in thick, clotted menses.

I sank to the floor and wept in long, gulping sobs: my bleeding was a week late, but it had come.

When the birds began to sing outside, I crammed my soiled bedsheets and nightgown into the bathtub and watched the water turn pink.

It rained all day, and all day I bled as if I was turning inside out. But I knew I would survive. Of course I would. Nature was doing what had to be done, ridding my body of every last shred of Landau.

In the lonely days that followed, I did everything for myself. I did my laundry in a yellow basin in the bathtub. I baked potatoes for breakfast and boiled the peels with an onion for my evening meal. I sold my silver pieces one at a time, and checked in on my mother. I trained myself not to cry about what happened in Berlin, and if I dreamt about it, I washed until my skin was raw. Whenever I saw Landau, I held my chin high and asked him about Fritz.

He always told me the same thing. "Trust me, Frau Altmann. I am a man of my word."

"I hope that's true," I always said.

Fritz had been gone almost a month when I heard a scratching at the apartment door—a cat or a maybe a rodent, I thought. Rats were suddenly plentiful in Vienna, and I kicked my foot against the door and hissed. The scratching turned to a knock and a voice said, "Open."

When I did, Fritz tumbled in.

His eyes were hollow and his clothes threadbare. A strange sound came from my throat, like an animal that can finally make a noise after being breathless for a long time.

I bolted the door and fell beside him on the floor.

"They said it was thanks to you," Fritz said in a whisper. "How did you do it? Tell me the truth—"

The shame was almost more than I could stand. The air whistled down my throat, a sound of sadness and relief.

"The truth is that I didn't think I could live another day without you," I said, rocking him in my arms.

"Tell me what happened." His breath was rank. There were sores around his mouth and all over his scalp. "I stayed alive for you and I'll go mad if you don't tell me."

"They made me go to Berlin," I said. "Bernhard was there. He signed everything away—"

Fritz whimpered.

"—and he was glad to do it," I said, taking his chin in my hands. "He did it for you. And thank God they kept their word and sent you home."

I helped Fritz into the bathroom, and pulled off his shoes and pants. There were lice in his pubic hair—I'd never seen lice except on the public health flyers, but the scuttling bugs and red welt bites were unmistakable.

I used a scissor and then a razor. I shaved off what was left of the hair between his legs, and dabbed the skin with kerosene to kill the bugs.

I ran my hands across the bristle of his shaved head and the patchy stubble of his beard. I soothed him. I filled the bathtub with steaming water and he slipped into it, soaking until the tub was gray.

"They burn the dead," Fritz whispered when I'd gotten him into bed. The window was open, and there was the smell of summer in the evening air. He made me pull the shade and darken the room. His body was stark and narrow against the clean white sheets, like a Schiele painting I had seen a long time ago.

"I was with the workers," he said in a strangled voice. "On the other side of the camp was a hospital. I heard screaming all night long."

Of course there was no lovemaking. He was too weak, and so was I. It seemed a lifetime ago that we'd been in Turnergasse Synagogue signing the ketubah and exchanging our vows. We'd promised to love and protect one another in sickness and in health, but I had never expected so much sorrow and pain. I lay beside him in the dark and tried to imagine how I would forget what I'd done with Landau.

From the moment of Fritz's return we were under house arrest. A guard was stationed at our door day and night, and I had to ask permission each time I needed something from the market.

With Nazis everywhere, the streets were dangerous and unpredictable. Jews were pulled out of their homes, dragged into the streets, and beaten. Friends were dying and children were starving.

We opened the newspaper one morning to a full-page photograph of the Nazi Hermann Goering and his wife Emmy at a gala in Vienna.

"Look at her," I said. Fritz leaned over me. His eyes had been weakened in prison, and he used a fat magnifying glass.

"The necklace is familiar." Fritz leaned closer to the table. "I've seen it before."

Adele's golden choker was one of kind. It was unmistakable. My uncle had given it to her on their wedding day, and he'd given it to me when I married Fritz.

"A keepsake from your aunt," my uncle had said so tenderly.

The Koloman Moser necklace had been mine until Landau took it. Now it belonged to a Nazi's wife.

I looked through the magnifier.

"The earrings, too," I said. They glittered on Frau Goering's ears like cruel stars, one more thing that Landau had taken from me and destroyed.

All I had left from 18 Elisabethstrasse was my aunt's silver letter opener. Sometimes when I was alone, I held it up to the light and imagined it was a weapon. I imagined walking downstairs and putting it through Landau's heart.

I was boiling the last of our eggs for lunch when a man in a uniform came up the rear fire escape and knocked on our kitchen door. My instinct was to hide, but I'd been seen through the window, and had no choice but to go to the door.

"It's me, Frau Altmann." I recognized our old factory guard, Otto, beneath his black cap. "I'm here as a friend," he whispered. "I don't have much time."

He waved a sealed envelope at the window, and my hand shook at the lock.

"Bernhard sent this from Paris," he said. He was gone before I could thank him.

Bernhard's letter contained careful instructions for our escape. The plan called for us to go through Germany and Holland, to follow secret messengers like breadcrumbs through a dark forest and tiny villages, to wait in farms and barns for a man he called Cousin Paul, who would guide us to safety by moonlight.

I thought it sounded far too dangerous, but Fritz was buoyed. It was the first spark of life I'd seen since his release.

"We don't have any other options," he said.

"What about Mama?"

Fritz took my hand.

"You can bring her if you want to. But it's going to be dangerous and we don't know what we'll find in Germany. If there are only two of us, we'll have a much better chance of making it."

He was right. I knew he was right. The journey would be hard, and we'd have to move quickly.

"We'll send for her as soon as we can," he said. "I love your mother, Maria. I won't leave her behind, I promise you that."

We memorized the instructions. That week, when Landau stopped me on the stairs with a hand on my arm, I forced myself to stop.

"Maria." He dared to speak my intimate name. "Maria, you don't look well. Are you ill?"

"It's Fritz," I said. "He's been weak since he came home, and now he's up half the night moaning with a toothache. You know how much that can hurt."

"Then it's nothing," Landau said, turning away with a sniff. "It's nothing for me to worry about."

"But he'll have to see a dentist, Herr Landau," I called after him. "Can you do that small thing for me?"

❧

On a cool September morning I went to my mother's house with two apple cakes that I'd baked with the last of our butter and sugar.

"I want you to leave, like we planned from the beginning," Mama said. "It's the only way. Fritz is right—you go together and then send for me. If your uncle sends for me first, I'll go to Czechoslovakia. If it's Bernhard, I'll come to you," she said.

She was firm and strong, and I was strong for her. It was only after I'd hugged her good-bye and walked that I broke into a trembling sweat that lasted all afternoon.

The next morning I screwed up my courage and knocked on the door of our old apartment. A fat Gestapo officer answered.

"My husband needs a dentist now," I said. "It's an emergency."

The man belched. I pushed back my shoulders, and tried to speak firmly.

"I'm sure Herr Landau told you about it. There's a Jewish dentist in the Bristol Hotel, we need to see him as soon as possible."

His gaze fell from my face to the neckline of my dress.

"May I take him, please?" I asked.

I felt sick. Since I'd been to Berlin with Landau I'd heard countless stories of women wrested in doorways, women bent over desks, broken garters and torn stockings and lean young legs wrapped around the enemy's thick thighs. It may be hard to believe, but it was cold comfort to me, by which I mean it was a comfort, if not a balm.

"We need to get Landau's approval," the officer said.

"There's a telephone," I said. "Perhaps you can make the call, please?"

The man grinned and relented. An hour later, Fritz and I were walking on the Kärtner Ring, chaperoned by that same officer in his wrinkled black shirt. Fritz was wearing a long coat and a hat, his jaw clenched above his collar. He hadn't been on the streets very much since his return, but he did his best to hide his nerves.

Just outside the hotel, Fritz paused in front of a colossal portrait of Hitler. The Führer's face was everywhere, watching everything we did. Fritz looked dazed; I took his elbow and guided his hand to the revolving door, pushing hard.

In the lobby the carpets were the color of blood.

"Make it quick," our escort said, but his eyes were already watching a pretty girl walking across the red rug.

"Dr. Holstein is on the second floor," I told him. "We'll be down as soon as we can. You can always come up," I said, taking another chance. Fritz squeezed my hand, but said nothing.

The Nazi smirked as another girl, this one wearing a severe suit and black-seamed stockings, slipped past. Landau had given me a pair of stockings exactly like them, but I'd shredded them into rags and braided them into a rope, and then I'd hidden that rope in a bottom dresser drawer along with the letter opener. They were dagger and noose to me: weapons I might need one day. The rope was back in the apartment, but the letter opener was at the bottom of my purse, reminding me to be fierce.

"I'll wait here," our guard said.

We moved toward the elevators. Fritz pressed the button and we watched the dial spin backward from the ninth floor, eighth floor, seventh floor. Our guard was out of sight. Fritz tugged my arm and we stepped into the restaurant behind the elevator bank.

It was almost lunchtime, and the mirrored room was set with flowers, pressed linens, and silver. There was a table full of Nazis in a corner, speaking softly.

"Don't look their way," Fritz murmured, pressing his lips to my ear. "Just keep going, nice and slow."

I'd never been in the Bristol Hotel, but Fritz knew it well. He guided me through a rear door and out onto Mahlerstrasse, where the sun fell on the sidewalk in broken patches. The bellhop blew his whistle and a taxi slid to a stop.

"To the airport, please," Fritz spoke smoothly.

The driver glanced at us in the rearview mirror.

"No luggage?"

My heart skipped. I imagined Landau walking up the narrow staircase, knocking on the apartment door, calling my name.

"We're in a bit of a hurry," Fritz said, waving a fat stack of bills. "Our bags are there already."

We were going to Germany, the most dangerous place I could imagine. We had no idea what to expect, and yet we had to act as if everything was calm and easy. Under the bright airport lights, we forced ourselves to link arms and pretend to laugh like new lovers. Our reservations for Cologne were retrieved at the ticket desk, and we were given our passage under assumed names.

"Thank you, Mr. Burgess," the pretty girl at the desk said as she handed Fritz the tickets. She smiled at him, and I saw something of his old sparkle come back.

The airplane was cramped and small, and every seat was filled with Germans. We sat back as the engine began to roar. A little girl behind me started to cry, and I shut my eyes.

"Frau Burgess, let me help you."

My eyes bolted open. A flight steward was kneeling beside my seat, collecting items that had spilled from my purse.

"Please don't trouble yourself," I said. I snatched up my false documents, the wallet with my true identification, the letter opener carved with initials that were not my own.

I kept my eyes open for the rest of the flight, watching clouds pass before the window, watching the pretty stewards in their trim blue skirts and jackets offering snacks and drinks and, to the little girl behind me, a bag for her vomit. Soon my own stomach was heaving.

"Steady now," Fritz said as we stepped off the steep black steps onto German soil. "Remember, you're Frau Burgess and we're meeting our cousin in the square. We're having dinner at Aunt Hilda's tonight."

"Yes, I remember," I said, pressing a kerchief to my forehead. "I remember, don't worry."

From the airport we took a taxi to the Cologne Cathedral. The square was filled with soldiers, swastikas, and Nazi banners. When a man Landau's weight and height walked by in a black jacket, I felt sure it was him, and that he'd come to arrest me.

"You'll feel better if you eat something," Fritz said. He bought two salty pretzels from a street vendor, and we sat on a bench to wait.

"Cousin Paul," Fritz said, using the quiet singsong voice we'd used when we'd rehearsed our plans.

"Cousin Paul and Aunt Hilda," I said, reciting the names we'd memorized.

"Aunt Hilda, who lives in Aachen," he said. "Where we'll sleep tonight."

The pretzels were finished, and my throat was dry.

Cousin Paul was thirty minutes late.

"Is there anything else we can do?" I asked.

He shook his head, no.

An hour later, Cousin Paul still had not shown.

"Stop checking your watch," I said softly.

Evening was falling, businessmen were leaving for home, and the square was filling with shopgirls and officers calling to one another and hurrying off in every direction. Fritz stood abruptly and pulled me to my feet. I followed blindly, moving deeper into Germany with every step.

ADELE

1901

D r. Frank was a small man with clean white hands and impeccable round spectacles that reflected my face in his. He put a stethoscope to my abdomen, and asked the stiff-faced nurse to hold a clean white towel across my waist. I couldn't see him insert the cold instrument between my legs, but I felt it—and it hurt.

"This will only take a few minutes," he said. I gritted my teeth, and when he was finished, he told me what I already knew.

"You're expecting a child." He wiped his hands on the white towel. "You'll need to be very quiet for the next month, just to be sure everything goes well."

The nurse showed me how to put a pillow under my knees and an extra one at the small of my back when I sat up in bed.

"She's anemic," the doctor said to Ferdinand before he left. "She needs creamed spinach and rest."

"And something for my migraine," I called after him.

"Not in your condition," the doctor said.

"My head feels like it's splitting open."

"Turn off the lights and close your eyes."

After he'd gone, Ferdinand kissed my cheeks. He was positively radiant.

"A son," he said fiercely and then, more gently. "A son."

He was forty years old, and wanted an heir.

"Or a daughter," I said. "Girl or boy, Ferdinand, I want our child to have every advantage, and to study everything there is to learn."

Then I sent him out of the bedroom and had the lights turned out.

I sent two notes to Klimt—*I'm sorry I can't come today . . .* and then . . . *I'm sorry, I'm still under the weather,* but to reveal more seemed indecent, especially through the post.

My head pounded, and morning sickness stretched from dawn until after teatime. I was too exhausted to do more than read a book or sit by the window while Thedy tried to teach me how to needlepoint a bib for the baby. The threads were tiny strings of color, the needles pricked my fingers, and the hoop to hold the cloth kept pinching my palms.

"Try to be patient," Thedy said, her head bent over the pillowcase she was working on. Her stitches were a neat row of abstract flowers and a blue waterfall in the Japanese style, and I could see how much pleasure it gave her. But for me, needlepoint was misery.

One afternoon, after Thedy had gone, the maid handed me a postcard of the Prater gardens. There was a single sentence scrawled across the back: *Judith is almost finished and will be on her way to Munich soon.*

"Help me get dressed," I said. I threw off the blankets and swung my feet to the ground.

"Madame," the poor maid cried. "My job is to keep you resting."

"Do as I say," I insisted.

She looked wildly about for someone to call, but Ferdinand was out and I was already stripping off my white housedress. Fresh undergarments went on, and then a loose blue dress. I pinned up my hair and washed my face, put on my winter boots and started down the stairs.

"I'm going out," I said. "Have the carriage ready."

I got as far as the front step when I was overcome with nausea and dizziness and had to be helped back to my bed.

"I don't feel very strong," I told Dr. Frank. "And there was blood this morning."

He produced the despicable instrument, and I didn't accept the discomfort gracefully. I demanded a cigarette as soon he'd stepped away from the bed.

"The foundation is weak," the doctor said. He busied himself in his black bag.

"I'm not a house or a museum," I said. I was feeling cross and frightened. I took a long drag on my cigarette. "Please say what you mean."

"I mean that you're miscarrying."

His coldness took away my breath. I tried to formulate a question, but within seconds he'd covered my mouth and nose with a chloroformed rag.

"Easier this way . . ." I heard him say. "Breathe normally, don't struggle against it."

He kept the cloth pressed against my face, and I watched his features disappear into a set of spinning red lights.

When I woke, Ferdinand was sitting in the dark, holding my hand.

"I love you, Adele," he said. A tear slid down my cheek and into my mouth, and then Thedy was whispering, "I'm so glad that whatever came between you and Ferry has passed." I didn't know if she'd been there the whole time, or if Ferdinand had come and gone. I didn't know if an hour had passed, or a day.

"I don't know, Thedy," I said. "I don't know anything."

They gave me Bayer's Heroin for the pain, and I floated in a jumbled twilight for days. I dreamt of red sugar beet juice and clean white shelves, sloe-eyed Egyptian women sliding across my bedroom walls, a genie stretching her hands toward something she couldn't reach, and a choir of women with golden haloes standing at the window, singing. I heard poetry set to music, and sopranos hitting high notes in clear, bright voices.

It was like sleeping inside one of Klimt's murals. By comparison, the real world that awaited me was temperate and barren, but it was filled with dark coffee and the allure of bathing, dressing, and slipping into warm cotton stockings and a loose velvet dress.

"I'd like to get back to the land of the living," I said after the doctor finished an early-morning examination. I lit my first cigarette.

"Then you should go about your daily routine." Dr. Frank waved away my plume of smoke. "You are healed."

Pale February sun shone through the clouds like a light in a smoky theater. Boiled eggs, toast and apricot jam, liver on bread, fruit and cheese were all put in front of me. I poured steamed milk into my coffee and liberally stirred in the sugar. The newspapers were folded on the table, unread.

"I'm happy to see you up and dressed," Ferry said, rather formally. His face was blank, as if he'd intentionally wiped it clean for me. "You look beautiful. I'm so sorry for what you've been through."

He fumbled in his jacket pocket and pushed a small box across the table. Inside was a gold ring with two pearls and a ruby.

"Dr. Frank said we can try again," he said. Something must have flashed across my face, because he added, "In time, of course."

"I want a doctor who speaks kindly to me," I told him.

"Choose who you want," he said. "As long as he's an excellent doctor."

"I've heard there are young physicians at the university who are filled with new ideas."

"You'll have whatever you want." He slipped the ring onto my finger.

I thanked him, but I knew the antidote to my sadness wasn't in jewels or a new doctor. The antidote was across the city, in the sunny studio on Josefstädter Strasse.

After breakfast I wrote a quick note—*I am better and will be there shortly*—and asked the maid to drop it into the box on the corner. By the time Ferdinand had gone to his offices, I was dressed and the carriage was waiting.

I smelled their perfume as soon as Klimt opened the door. There was a dark-haired beauty, a redheaded sylph, and a very tall blonde. They were dressed in diaphanous pastel sheaths—something I couldn't imagine finding in Vienna—with daisies and feathers in their hair.

"This is Martha—she's Madness," Klimt said. The girl's long, messy braid fell past her shoulders. She looked pleasant until Klimt said the word *madness,* and then she contorted her face in a way that made me laugh but also cringe.

"Now Gerda," he called to the redhead. Her waist and neck were long, her bust full under the thin fabric of her dress. "Gerda is Lust."

She looked like a woman who could carry and birth many beautiful children, and I had to turn away.

"And you?" I asked the last one.

"I'm Debauchery, madame," the blonde said, so seriously that I burst out laughing. There were merry squeals from everyone, and soon Klimt was telling the girls to be dressed and on their way, "until I send for you again, my lovelies," he said.

Only after he'd closed the door behind them did I see how strained and tired he was. His face was thin, and his beard was untrimmed. There were dark circles under his eyes.

"I'm sorry—maybe you know what kept me away," I said. I spoke in a nervous rush, as I'd done that first morning on his doorstep.

"You don't need to explain," he said. "I don't expect you to."

"I would have come if I could," I said.

"I told you, you don't owe me anything."

He motioned me to sit, and I did. I felt a bit woozy.

The studio was as I'd expected to find it, littered with sketches and cats, a landscape filled with white birch trees and another of a garden path filled with chickens. There was a new formal portrait on an easel, and I recognized Gertrud Loew's pale, pretty face.

"Why didn't you wait before you finished our Judith?" I asked.

"I'm sorry, Adele." I could see that he was truly sorry. "Moll practically took it off the easel while it was still wet—I didn't have a choice. With all the trouble over the murals, I have to keep producing."

I looked to the back room where we'd spent our time in afternoon candlelight. The animal furs were gone, replaced by twisted branches from the garden and two tall vases stuffed with fresh holly.

"You know the Academy turned me down?" he asked.

I knew he'd applied for a teaching position and been rejected.

"That was a mistake," I said.

"When you don't keep the ministers happy, they do whatever they want."

"Now what?" I asked.

He gave a sort of shrug, and I was shocked at how drained I felt. Fatigue set in like a stone in my pocket, and I sank deeper into the chair. On the table, there was a book of poetry facedown, split open. I picked it up.

"Are you reading Schiller?" It was foolish, but I felt a stab of jealousy. I had a ludicrous image of the redhead nursing her child and reading aloud from the book. "Or does it belong to someone else?"

Klimt groaned.

"It's for the *Beethoven Frieze*." He finally came toward me, and I could smell unwashed nights under his robe. "I've got to have the mural designs and materials ready by April."

I'd read about the Secessionists' plans for a Gesamtkunstwerk—a complete artwork—with music, painting, sculpture, and poetry.

"That's why the girls were here," he added. "I have to fill three walls and I'm stuck on the last image. Everything I'm picturing seems too much or too little."

He showed me the poem he'd marked—it was "Ode to Joy"—and I read it slowly.

"What about the kiss?" I asked. I turned the book to him—"You circled it, right here—*be embraced, millions—this kiss for the entire world.*"

"Right," he said. "I've read those lines over and over, but I can't make the crescendo feel real."

I remembered lying in his arms after our passion had been spent.

"What about an embrace instead of a kiss?" I asked slowly. "What about what holds lovers together after the passion is slaked?"

"Keep talking," he said.

I felt unsure, but the look on his face encouraged me.

"I don't have a picture in my mind," I said. "But doesn't everyone want to be held just the right way, and for just long enough? If we don't have it, we're sad, but if we're held too tightly, then we feel bound."

He drew slowly at first, then more intently. He drew a man's broad naked back, and his arms wrapped around a woman. He used red chalk and blue, and soon he'd filled a long sheet of paper that stretched the length of his workshop.

When he stepped away, his eyes were shining. On the page were the same flying genies and naked women I'd seen in my heroin-laced dreams.

"A kiss for the whole world. A kiss to *save* the world," he said. "For you, Adele."

It was as I'd suspected all along—my mind, more than my body, was what would keep me alive and away from the edges of sadness.

"It's going to be magnificent," I said.

I was wrapping my scarf around my shoulders, preparing to go, when I said quietly, "I was pregnant. That's why I didn't come."

He looked up from his work.

"But I'm not anymore."

"I'm sorry, Adele. I know it's what you want."

"Yes, it's what I want," I said. "I want everything. I want this, and I want that, too. I'm greedy, Gustav."

"I'm greedy, too," he said. "We're all greedy for something—only you and I, we're willing to admit it."

MARIA

1938

We were in Germany without traveling papers or proper identification, and afternoon was sliding away quickly. Fritz put his hand on my waist, and guided me in front of a festive-looking restaurant with a small poster that said *Hitler is good for Germany!*

Soldiers and women with black stockings and netted hats walked by, laughing merrily. I was wearing my best blue hat, and I was glad for it.

"What if Paul was caught?" I asked quietly. "If he was caught, then we should stop right now."

"And do what?" Fritz asked. "We have no choice, we have to keep going."

A man in a black fedora narrowed his eyes when he heard Fritz's voice, and circled back around us. What could I do? If I spoke, he would hear my Austrian accent. If I didn't speak, surely Fritz would say something more.

I squeezed my husband's arm and pulled him into a candy shop. I felt myself growing faint. The man in the fedora stared at me through the window. I pointed at a box of chocolates and fumbled for my wallet. I turned away from the window and murmured quietly, "I think we're being followed."

I knew Fritz heard me, but he didn't even blink.

"A black fedora, at the shop window," I said softly. "He heard you speaking."

I paid for the candy, and waited while the shopgirl wrapped it in silver foil and put it in a bag.

Outside on the street, the man in the black hat had moved to the end of the block. Fritz hailed a taxi, and we got in.

"We're going to Kohlscheid," he said in his best, guttural German. I didn't dare look out the window as the taxi pulled away from the curb.

Thirty minutes later we were following the cobblestone paths outside of Kohlscheid. My shoes were cutting into my heels and my head was aching, but we had to act calm, as if we were on a little outing together.

We arrived at a farmhouse just after dark.

"Are we sure it's right?" I asked.

Fritz recited the instructions we'd memorized: *Follow the lane past two boulders, take the road that splits to the right and look for the house with the red barn and the crooked weathervane.* He pointed to the weathervane: it was bent nearly in half, and looked like a swastika. The farmhouse door was blue, with peeling paint. Fritz tapped timidly. When the door swung open, my knees buckled. If Fritz hadn't caught me, I would have fallen onto the hardwood floors.

"You're safe here," the farmer said, once we were inside. He was younger than I'd expected, and there was a carved wooden cross on the wall behind him. "You'll eat and sleep. Then it will be time to go."

He gave us buttered rolls and ham, and we ate alone in his kitchen. I heard children somewhere in the house, and a mother hushing them. Simply by having us in her home, she'd put her family in danger. I felt deeply grateful as I curled into a root cellar with Fritz and slept until a hand on my arm woke me in the dark.

"It's a moonless night," the farmer whispered. "You're lucky."

As I smoothed down my dress and gathered my coat and purse, I remembered the chocolate. I left it on the folded blankets for the woman and her children.

Silently we followed the man into the dark fields. We walked in single file, with me behind the farmer and Fritz in the rear. I tried not to think about anything but one foot in front of the other as we moved through the cool night. A low wire fence marked the border between Germany and Holland. It was as far as the farmer would take us.

"Go about ten meters," he said. "My nephew will meet you there before morning."

He faded into the darkness before I could thank him.

Fritz stepped across the wire fence, then turned and held it down for me. I heard a loud, sudden noise—like the ricochet of a gunshot. My stocking caught on a snag of wire, and I fell to my knees. Fritz shut off the flashlight, and dropped down beside me.

"I heard it, too," he said in the faintest whisper.

Small animals scurried in the nearby shrubs as we lay on the ground. My ankle throbbed, and I was trembling. My hands were cold, the field was damp. There was something alive in the night, and something dying, too.

The night grew still, and the sounds of small insects filled my ears. The stars overhead twinkled like bullets, and I remembered the first time Fritz kissed me, when I'd tasted cinnamon stars.

An hour passed before Fritz spoke again.

"We should go further," he said. "The sun will be up soon."

We rose to a crouch and ran toward a cluster of farm buildings.

A truck roared to life, and a dog started barking.

As a faint light broke on the horizon we washed in a stream and inspected one another quickly. My hem was streaked with mud and my stockings were ripped, but I'd managed to keep my coat out of the mud and it was passably clean. So was Fritz's.

"You're beautiful," Fritz said.

"I love you," I told him.

We walked into a small Dutch village just as it was beginning to wake. The smell of fresh bread came through an open bakery window, and we heard someone whistling.

We stopped and the whistling stopped. That was our sign.

"Fritz?" the young man said in a hush. "Maria? It's all right—Cousin Paul sent me."

Fritz asked him a question—something about our passage that only someone who knew our plan could have answered.

The young man seemed confused. He gave a stammered reply.

"You're Fritz and Maria, aren't you?"

"We're looking for the train," Fritz said.

"I have an aunt in Aachen," the young man said, brightening. "Do you know my aunt Hilda?"

"Yes," Fritz said, visibly relieved. "Aunt Hilda, who lives in Aachen."

"You can take the train to Aachen from here," the young man said. "It will be coming shortly."

I washed my face and rinsed out my stockings in a basin behind the bakery. The Dutchman gave us fresh bread and a lunch pack, and we made our way to the small station. With its rustic wooden doors and colorful shutters, it looked more like a fairy-tale cottage than a country railway station.

Our guide leaned in as if we were old friends.

"May God be with you," he said, and then he melted away just as the farmer had done.

When we heard the low whistle of the train, Fritz turned to me with a terrified expression.

"We forgot to change our money," he said. "All we have are reichsmarks."

The train hissed to a stop, and we climbed aboard. I was thankful that it was empty as we slid into a red seat. The conductor, stout and elderly, arrived a few minutes later.

"Our apologies," I spoke as steadily as I could. "I'm afraid we only have reichsmarks. My aunt Adele in Amsterdam is very ill, and we barely had time to throw some things together before we left."

The conductor looked from me to Fritz and back again. I saw him look at my feet, and I followed his eyes. My shoes were caked with mud. It was clear that I was lying.

"I hope your aunt feels better soon," he said, taking the German currency and handing me two second-class tickets.

"Thank you," I said, nearly in tears.

"Aunt Adele?" Fritz asked with a weak smile, after the conductor was gone.

"It just slipped out," I said.

I flushed to imagine what I looked like—a far cry from the strong and proper woman my uncle spoke about so longingly. But I'd been courageous and fierce, as she'd always urged me to be, and I believed she would have been proud.

We forced ourselves to stay seated and look calmly out the window as the patchwork of colorful trees and fields slid by. Fritz even closed his eyes for a time, although he surely didn't sleep.

Four hours later, when we reached Amsterdam, I scanned the tracks. Neither of us said a thing as a German couple pushed in front of us to step off the train. As my foot touched the platform, a strong hand took hold of my arm.

"Thank God," Bernhard said. The three of us hugged quickly. "We have the plane waiting."

A taxi took us to a small new airport, where we climbed into a tiny silver airplane.

"Nettie and the children are already in Liverpool," my brother-in-law said. "She's found you a flat. You'll be safe there."

As air and clouds bled together and we rose over the earth, I saw a white moon rising in the blue sky to the north. Somewhere under that same sky my mother was preparing her afternoon dinner. She was looking out her window, she was getting smaller and smaller as the ground slipped away and our airplane flew like a lone bird across the North Sea.

ADELE

1902

"What comes after Hope?" Berta whispered in my ear as the crowd pressed around us at the Secession gallery.

"I think that's Ambition," I said. I recognized a young beauty I'd seen at Klimt's studio, and pointed to her face high above us on the stucco wall. "The other one is Compassion."

People crushed around us with their necks craning, fingers pointing. Overhead, Klimt's magnificent *Beethoven Frieze* filled three walls with seductive and frightening figures rendered in black, white, and gold. There was a beastly ape with snakelike arms reaching toward Sickness, a skeletal Death personified, ghostly women floating as if in a dream, and a heroic knight in shining armor fighting his way toward Lasciviousness, Wantonness, and fat, bloated Intemperance.

Behind me, Ferdinand was reading aloud from the program that explained the 14th Secession exhibition.

"'Executed in plaster, paint, graphite and gold leaf at a height of seven feet and a width of 112 feet,'" he said. "'The frieze commemorates Beethoven's tribute to Friedrich Schiller's poem, 'Ode to Joy.'"

From the reception room came the sound of flutes being tested and violinists warming their bows, and then the small orchestra began playing Beethoven's Ninth Symphony.

"It's a thousand times better than his University of Vienna murals," I heard someone remark.

"An act of self-preservation, I'd say," was the tart reply.

By then, Berta and I were standing below Klimt's naked man and woman embraced in a kiss to save the whole world. The man's back was muscular and powerful, his buttocks clenched, his head bowed. The woman was pale and dark-haired, her face hidden. Curled at the top of the man's broad shoulders I saw what seemed—to me, at least—the clearest thing in the room: the woman's bent and scarred thumb at the nape of the man's neck.

"Do you think that's a self-portrait?" Berta eyed the powerful lover. "A flattering one, if it is."

My friend looked at me for a second longer than necessary, and the room grew hot and close. I didn't think Berta could have noticed the thumb; certainly Ferdinand did not.

"That's for certain." She laughed. "Klimt may be strong, but that man looks like a Greek god."

Sometime later I found myself pressed against a white wall, staring out at a blur of plumed hats and men in dark suits. I spoke to Elena Luksch-Makowsky, whose startling piece on death and time dominated the third gallery, and was kissed by a sweaty Gustav Mahler. Alma Mahler's heavy perfume overwhelmed me, Thedy and Gustav appeared briefly, Berta disappeared, and Ferdinand was lost in the crowd.

When Klimt finally found me alone, it was nearly nightfall.

"What do you think of the embrace?" he asked.

I kissed my scarred thumb. He smiled and winked.

That was all we had time for, but it was enough.

Following behind Berta Zuckerkandl, Auguste Rodin runs supple fingers through his long white beard and slips into a garden chair at the Prater Café. It is a warm June day. Hummingbirds hover at the honeysuckle planted in pots around the fountain, and a small string quartet adds to the soundscape of summer gaiety.

Beside the aging sculptor, Gustav Klimt looks like a young man in his white linen suit and straw hat. The two artists could be brothers, or even father and son: they have the same broad foreheads, their bodies are both thick and strong, and their eyes blaze with the same intensity.

"Coffee with cream," Berta tells the waiter. "Cheese and fruit, and apple strudel."

"Champagne," Klimt adds. "On ice."

It is their first meeting, and the men are in good cheer.

Klimt's lithe models slide into empty chairs beside Rodin. Martha and Gerda's dresses are light and fluid, and their hair is decorated with flowers. Zuckerkandl opens her notebook to record the scene. The sculptor closes his eyes and seems to breathe in the bakery scent of the young women, the honeysuckle that perfumes the air.

"I've never experienced such an atmosphere—your tragic and magnificent Beethoven frieze, your unforgettable, temple-like exhibition," Rodin says to Klimt. "And now this garden, these women, this music. What is the reason for it all?'

Klimt understands Rodin's delight. He smiles, and answers only one word.

"Austria."

ADELE

1902

Ferdinand and I summered at a lakeside villa in the Salzkammergut region the year of the *Beethoven Frieze*. We adored our estate at Jungfer Brezan, but the change was good. The hilly landscape was verdant and soothing, and I felt something fresh and peaceful arise with me each dawn.

We rowed in a silver boat on Lake Nussensee in the mornings, took afternoon naps in the hottest part of the day, and began trying for a child again. Invitations came, but while Ferdinand worked at his desk I preferred to spend my time reading, walking through the hills, and swimming in the warm baths at Bad Ischl.

In July we took a carriage through the foothills of the Alps to visit Salzburg for the music festivals. We stayed in a small apartment near the Imperial Palace, where Berta and Emil delighted in introducing us to their friends as "the Bloch-Bauers, who are important art patrons in Vienna."

I could see that pleased Ferdinand very much.

My days in Klimt's studio seemed far away, and I thought perhaps my husband's mistress was a thing of the past, too. We hosted a large party for Ferdinand's business associates in Vienna that autumn, enjoyed a grand Christmas, and celebrated the last night of the year with Thedy, Gustav, and their two little boys. The whole city extinguished its lights at the stroke of midnight, revealing a sea of silver and velvet gold stars against the velvet sky.

"A shooting star," Little Karl cried. As the red tail dropped into the heavens I wished for a child—a little girl, then a little boy.

Klimt's *Judith* was sent back from Munich after the New Year. I knew, because Ferdinand received an announcement in the morning mail, along with an invitation from Klimt to see the new exhibit at the Secession before it opened to the public.

Herr Bloch-Bauer, the pleasure of your company is requested at a private showing for our esteemed and valued patrons.

"Is Klimt mocking me? Does he know you modeled for him against my wishes?"

I leaned over Ferdinand's shoulder and read my friend's familiar scrawl.

"We own two of his landscapes now, and everyone knows you just bought a Rodin," I said. "You're a patron of the arts, and you are esteemed. I'm sure his invitation is sincere."

Berta and Emil were invited to the private showing, too, and we four went together. I wore a high-neck dress and a new hat with a wide brim. Berta wore a turquoise shawl, and a new necklace that Moser had designed. When I admired the long pendant, she said, "You know how I adore the gold choker Moser made for you."

That was when I became nervous. Somehow, I had forgotten that everyone knew the fabulous necklace Ferdinand had bought for me. The same one Klimt had clasped around my neck that very first day I sat for him—the one in the painting.

"Remember, no one but you knows that I was the model for *Judith*," I whispered to Ferdinand as we entered the gallery.

He said nothing. His face was tight, his fat mustache stiff as a horse-hair brush. The gallery was dimly lit, but there was a bright light on my *Judith,* and even from afar I could see that she was everything Klimt had promised: fierce and seductive; sheathed in gold; her face—*my* face—ecstatic in victory. It was true that it was not a portrait of me, but my gold choker was plain as day around her neck.

The four of us stared at the painting until Berta finally put a hand on Ferdinand's arm and broke the silence.

"You must have him paint your wife's portrait," she said. "If he can do something this spectacular with an allegory, imagine what he'll do with our Adele."

I held my breath. There were a few other people in the gallery and they were coming toward us.

"Really, Ferdinand, you can afford the grandest portrait of all," Berta said. She was gay but emphatic, and once again I was very, very glad she was my friend and ally.

"We'll see," Ferdinand said gruffly.

He did not wait for me to get out of the carriage that evening, but left me with the footman and disappeared inside the house.

I was at breakfast alone two days later when I picked up the newspaper Ferdinand had left folded beside his half-eaten plate of eggs, and found Felix Salten's review of the exhibit.

One sees our Judith *dressed in a sequined robe in a studio on Vienna's Ringstrasse,* Salten wrote. *She's the kind of beautiful hostess one meets everywhere, whom men's eyes follow at every premiere as she rustles by in her silk petticoats. A slim, supple woman with fire in her dark glances, a cruel mouth; mysterious forces seem to be slumbering in this enticing female, energies and ferocities that would be unquenchable if what is stifled by bourgeois life were ever to burst into flame.*

I was horrified; it was as if Salten had seen right through me—as if he knew what was in my heart. I canceled my appointments, stayed at home all day, refused my callers and waited for Ferdinand to return.

When he arrived long after the supper hour, I checked my face in the mirror, and met him in the hallway between our bedrooms. He stopped, and pinned me with his eyes. It was unnerving, but I held his gaze.

"I want a proper portrait of you," Ferdinand said. "Not a half-dressed seductress, Adele."

He came very close. I smelled whiskey on his breath, and cigars and cinders on his clothing. I thought there was a smudge of unfamiliar glitter on his jacket lapel.

"A real portrait, like the one Klimt painted of Rose von Rosthorn with her pearl necklace and diamond ring," he said.

"I don't want a portrait like hers." I summoned my composure. "I want something entirely new and dazzling. Something that will make a name for us."

"You have already made a name for us," Ferdinand said.

"It's not me," I said. "It's an allegory. I explained it to you before."

I turned back into my room. I thought he would go to his own room, but he followed me inside and closed the door behind him.

He took me by the shoulders, and ran his hands down my dressing gown. I was astonished at his ease with the buttons.

"It looks like you," he said. "Only I've never seen that look on your face."

In a rough motion, he threw off his evening coat. He kissed me hard, and slid the gown off my shoulders.

"Lie on the bed, Adele."

I did as he said. He turned out the light, and made an animal noise as he lowered himself on top of me.

"You will have what you want," I said. Then I threw back my head and pretended that Wantonness and Greed were looking down at me from Klimt's frieze, taking heated measure of me as my husband growled my name.

MARIA
1938

I survived. That's not all. I was glad to be alive and away from Vienna. I tried to pretend that a man named Landau had never existed. I made him dead in my mind: I lay in bed at night and watched him burn, watched him choke, watched him drown, watched him die. And every morning, I was alive.

Bernhard had a new fabric-import business up and running in Britain, and he put Fritz to work as soon we arrived. Even in autumn the Liverpool streets were gray and overcast, and there were none of the cheery red double-decker buses that I'd expected. The buildings were squat, the people kept their heads down and their hats pulled low over their eyes, and their English was unfamiliar gibberish to my ears. Still, I was glad to be there. Whenever I felt homesick, I thought of church bells ringing for Hitler and the red Nazi flags hanging from every building along the Ring.

It wasn't our Vienna anymore. It was theirs.

We settled in. Fritz went to the office or called on Bernhard's cashmere accounts every morning, and I found a market and a butcher that I liked. The butcher was named Rudy, his wife was from Leopoldstadt in Vienna, and the women who shopped there cooked sauerbraten the way our cook used to make it at home. I bought a heavy stockpot and a potato peeler, took down recipes from Rudy, and learned to be a wife in our new world.

I used day-old bread for breadcrumbs and made something close to veal schnitzel with creamed potatoes and fried onions for Fritz. When he cut into the fried meat and took a bite, he closed his eyes and sighed.

"Do you like it?" I asked. I was wearing a new blouse with magenta ruffles I'd stitched on by hand. My hair was newly done, and I'd dabbed eau de toilette on my wrists and behind my neck.

"It's like my mama's," Fritz said. There was a bit of cream on his mustache, and I wiped it with my napkin.

Very quickly I met other ladies in Liverpool who'd fled the Nazis. Soon enough we were going from the butcher to the corner bakery together, making jokes about the weak coffee and worrying over our families back home. Everyone had a sister, brother, mother or child who'd stayed behind or slipped out from under the Nazis and disappeared. We were brokenhearted, but we weren't broken. We told stories of our escapes, and we felt stronger.

Our apartment was in a three-story brick walk-up in a neat row of buildings on a modest street. It was an unremarkable place, and that was fine. There was an extra room for my mother, and I wanted to bring her to live with us. Mama was willing. Her letters were rare, but when they arrived, she wrote of stores closing and bread shortages.

"Every day life is harder for the Jews left behind," my sister-in-law said. We were in her kitchen, and she was using a heavy metal masher to make potatoes. Like me, Nettie had been raised with servants, and like me, she was learning to fend for herself. "If they don't go out of the houses, they'll starve. And when they do go out, they risk their lives."

"We have to get my mother to Liverpool," I said. I looked to Bernhard for help, and he made it clear it wouldn't be easy. Britain, the United States, even Luxembourg—the final hope for so many—had issued their last visas.

"What about your uncle?" Bernhard asked. "What have you heard from Ferdinand?"

"Nothing," I said.

I had not spoken to my uncle in months. I wasn't even sure if he knew we were in England.

Waiting is an anxious thing, but that's what we had to do. We walked along the river Mersey and watched the leaves turning in the park on the corner. We read the small pages in the weekly papers that listed the names of new immigrant arrivals, and studied the ship dockets that were published every Monday. Oskar Kokoschka, the crazy painter who my aunt had loved, arrived in London with his wife. Dr. Sigmund Freud came with his wife and family. There was talk of children arriving without their parents, but I didn't believe it would come to that. I still expected someone to stop the Nazis.

At night while Fritz was sleeping, I peered up at the ceiling and remembered how long I'd waited for him. *Good things come to those who wait*, I told myself. I'd read those words in a ladies' magazine, and liked the way the English sounded on my tongue. I believed it. I whispered it to myself until I fell asleep.

"I wish my husband would come," my new friend said to me one morning. We were in the bakery, eating pastries and pretending the coffee was tolerable. My friend was a large woman who wore sturdy black shoes and covered her head with a flat blue hat. Her husband was a rabbi in Amsterdam, and he'd sent her ahead to Liverpool with the children and his parents. I'd never have befriended her back home, but the world was changing, and I liked her very much.

"Good things come to those who wait," I told her.

She was the first person I'd ever met who could translate from English to Hebrew and German or Dutch. She rolled her eyes toward the bakery window, and said something in Hebrew.

"I don't speak Hebrew," I reminded her. So she said it in German, and then in English.

" 'The Lord is good to those who wait for him, to the soul who seeks him,' " she said. "Lamentations 3:25."

I had no use for God. I looked at her blankly, and she laughed.

"You know there's a new synagogue on Greenbank Drive," she said.

"There are so many refugees, they say there's already an instant congregation. I'm going there tomorrow, you can come with me."

"Maybe Fritz will want to go," I said, pressing a few dots of powdered sugar into my finger. "If it pleases him, then we'll go."

But I didn't tell Fritz about the synagogue, and he didn't find it on his own. My husband and I each had our secrets. I just didn't know it yet.

ADELE
1903

If he was nervous about being invited to our home, Klimt showed none of it when he arrived for dinner that evening in May. He was spry in a pale linen suit, and Emilie Flöge wore a turquoise dress that spiraled around her ankles like a mermaid's tail.

"I want a dress just like yours," I said.

She'd just been to London, and was eager to talk about the new women's sporting costumes she'd seen.

"It's going to be white frocks with blue ribbons for Wimbledon," Emilie said. "It's all about freedom. You need movement in your clothing if you're going to do anything physical."

She made us laugh by demonstrating a terrible tennis swing, and tripping on her dress.

"You see, this is a perfect example of the wrong kind of costume," she said, and then fell into an overstuffed chair.

We had hors d'oeuvres and champagne in the parlor, and Ferdinand showed off his porcelain collection. I'd once watched my husband caress a delicate teapot as if it were a fragile child. That evening he grabbed the largest gold-and-ivory platter in the collection, and put it in the center of the table like a trophy.

"Maybe I can use that gold pattern in your wife's portrait," Klimt said.

"That's an excellent idea," Ferdinand said.

We lit the candles, opened the red wine, and served warm foie gras. I was relieved to see that Emilie put Ferdinand at ease. She was attractive and charming, and seemed a perfect companion for Klimt.

"I've always wanted to make a portrait in gold and silver," Klimt said as he tucked his napkin into his lap. "But the cost is prohibitive."

He was a man of many faces, and on that night, he was the perfect supplicant to Ferdinand.

"Spare no expense for us," Ferdinand said. He covered his own glass, but motioned for the butler to pour another cup of wine for Klimt. "Use gold and silver, too. As much as you need."

Emilie began to tell me about the divided skirt that was debuting in Paris that year, but I was listening to my husband, who'd leaned forward and was speaking to Klimt in a quiet voice.

". . . make it proper," he said, sounding almost stern. "Within all bounds of decency. Make it like the *Mona Lisa,* but make her . . ."

"Queenly," Klimt said.

"Yes, precisely. Make my wife a queen."

"Queen of Vienna," Klimt said with a raised glass. "We'll start after the summer—will that suit your schedule, Frau Bloch-Bauer?"

"Of course," I said. Autumn seemed very far away. I hoped my disappointment didn't show on my face. "Whatever you and Ferdinand have agreed."

॰◌

The city was crowded and busy on the first cool day of autumn. Everyone had packed the summer months away into cedar-lined chests and taken their cloth coats out of storage. There were new black automobiles belching smoke as they chugged along the Ring, and chattering young women in bright, loose dresses. The Triton and Naiad Fountain in Maria-Theresien-Platz was making a million tinny drumbeats as the water splashed and sprayed at our feet.

"Vienna means everything to me," I said, slipping my arm through Klimt's. "But I don't want to be her queen."

"Maybe not," Klimt said. "But it's what Ferdinand wants, and so I will give it to him."

I'd come to believe with all my heart that Vienna was the most important city the world had ever known—greater than Rome, which had been ruled by conquerors; even greater than Paris, which had so much to offer. When the emperor had demolished the old city wall and built the Ringstrasse atop its footprint, Jews from across the empire had come to Vienna seeking freedom and opportunity. The city had made our very lives—*my* very life—possible.

"I mean it," I said. "The city is a symphony, and I'm only one small musician in a grand orchestra."

"Modesty doesn't suit you," Klimt said cheerfully.

He stopped in front of the fountain and tipped my chin to him.

"You love the city and the city loves you." His eyes were shining; his hand was warm on my shoulder. I felt as if we were in a tableau, moving through a script that I had imagined and wished for when I was a girl. "Why can't I make you a queen, if only on canvas?"

I looked into the fountain, and the sun blinded me for a moment.

"It has to be done in the finest taste," I said. "It cannot be gauche or loud. It cannot be anything but exquisite."

Inside the museum, Klimt guided me to the coat check window. The girl took my cloak and handed me a wooden disc printed with the number 22: my age, exactly. I took it as a lucky sign, and slipped the disk into my purse before we climbed the staircase.

At the top, we stopped along the balustrade to look at the frescoes Klimt had painted with his brother. My hand held the same banister I'd held a hundred times, my eyes rose to the same Egyptian women with their smudged eyes and stiff hair I'd seen when I was a girl.

I knew how much Ernst had meant to Klimt, and he knew how much Karl had meant to me. For a moment we stood together in our shared sorrow.

"It seems a lifetime ago," Klimt said, as if reading my thoughts.

"But that's in the past, of course."

"And we go on," he said, brushing a finger along my cheek.

Soon enough he was talking about the symbols he'd used in his early work and the hieroglyphics he'd put in the frieze. At an Egyptian tomb engraved with a goddess holding a circle overhead, Klimt fished a pad and pencil out of his pocket and copied the carved figures while he explained their meaning. "A circle, a glyph, the moon—it's all about fertility," he said.

He was beautiful to watch when he worked. I was still trying to conceive a child, but it didn't change the way I felt about Klimt. I didn't think anything ever would.

"Can we agree on an Egyptian motif?" he asked. "A modern mosaic, with ancient symbols?"

"Gold and silver, and spare no expense," I said. "Isn't that what Ferdinand told you?"

"My job is to make both of you happy," he said.

"I'm happy now," I told him.

I felt the longing for him in my breastbone; I felt that happiness quivering in my arms and legs. As we said our good-byes in the court-yard, I put my arms around him and lingered ever so lightly as I kissed the edges of his lips.

"I'm so glad to have you back," he breathed into my ermine collar.

My head was spinning as we parted. My boots crunched along the gravel, and I passed the fountain and the imperial gates. Perspiration trickled between my breasts as I walked through the Volksgarten, past elegant sculptures and the glass walls of the royal greenhouses.

I turned at the cathedral and went into the Döbling District, where I soon found myself at Währing Cemetery. My breath felt hot in the cool air, and I kept going until I was on an unfamiliar street that was cluttered with horrid-smelling food stalls.

Only then did I realize I was lost.

I made my way toward a newsstand where a ragged man was blow-ing into his hands to keep them warm. I was about to ask for directions to the Graben, when a fat headline stopped me cold.

GREEDY JEWS GROW RICHER AT VIENNA'S EXPENSE.

Beneath the ugly letters was a drawing of two hook-nosed men pull-ing a frightened child by his hair.

"This one?" the seller asked.

It took me a moment to react. I struggled for words.

"Who would want such trash?" I finally shouted, and spun away.

"The anti-Semites are everywhere," I said to the friends who'd crowded into Berta's parlor.

Automobiles were idling along with the carriage horses below the Zuckerkandls' window, and I could smell the driver's cigar smoke rising from the streets. Musicians were warming up in the Burgtheater—the string instruments sounded like preening women, the trumpets and horns like bellowing men.

The subject for the evening was the assimilated Jew in Austria, and it had drawn an eager crowd. Instead of a dozen people, Berta's apartment was crowded with nearly twice that number. Women were pressed together on the sofas, and men sat on stiff-backed chairs crammed in front of the sofas and bookshelves. We were drinking iced Pernod, and I'd already begun to feel its effects when I stood and shakily recounted what I'd seen in the Döbling District.

"The cartoons are getting uglier," I said. "I believe we must fight back."

Then I put a copy of Theodor Herzl's Zionist pamphlet on the coffee table.

"We can't talk about Herzl's ideas here," Berta said quietly. "Emil forbids it."

"I'm not saying I support a Jewish State," I said. "But I think Herzl's pamphlet is at least worth discussing."

"No," Emil said, catching sight of the book. "Herzl's ideas aren't welcome here."

Ferdinand also opposed a Jewish State, but for practical rather than political reasons.

"It's hot in the Sinai Peninsula," he said that night, clearly hoping to defuse Emil's anger with humor. "It's a desert, Adele—you'd hate it there."

"That's fine," I said. "We don't have to talk about Zionism"—I was the first in my circle to say the word aloud, and I saw a few of our friends flinch—"but let's talk about Mayor Lueger's torchlight rallies and what he's telling the workers about us."

Only the week before, Mayor Lueger—Handsome Karl, they called him—had rallied his supporters to burn an effigy of Albert von Rothschild with a sign around his neck that said FILTHY JEWISH MONEY.

"Lueger is a very shrewd politician," Emil said. "He doesn't believe what he's saying, he's just using rhetoric to keep the workers in line."

"Do you know what I heard from my bookseller?" I asked.

There were two hired servants in and out of the room. It was likely that they went to church on Sundays wearing the red carnation of Lueger's Christian Socialist party pinned to their jackets. It was likely they believed everything Lueger said about the Jews: that we were greedy, that our good fortune was their misfortune, and that we were taking over the city and leading it to ruin.

The thought of it made me lose my taste for the Pernod and the salty nuts I'd been nibbling.

"Edwin Schuster told me that Lueger and his friends show up at the Grand Hotel carrying walking sticks carved with Jewish faces—big noses, ugly ears, some even have devil horns," I said.

"For God's sake," Emil said. "We're not Jews, we're capitalists. We're society's engines, and Lueger knows it."

A woman who rarely said anything without checking first with her husband put a hand on my arm and said, "Frau Bloch-Bauer, you don't need to be worried, haven't you already declared yourself without faith?"

I turned to reply when one of the other men spoke up at last.

"You may not think of yourself as a Jew, Emil," Georg Bergman said. "And I know the rabbis in the city hardly think those of us in this room are worthy of the name." A few of the men laughed at that. "But we are Jews to Lueger, and if he's burning an effigy of von Rothschild, he has a certain class of Jew in mind."

So there was all of that to worry about. And then there was Klimt.

I didn't waver very hard or long. As soon as we were alone in his studio, I went right into his arms. It was easier than ever, as if two weeks had passed instead of more than a year. It was also more dangerous, as we were both aware. I felt Ferdinand's watchfulness in the mornings, and when I arrived at the studio Carl Moll was often there with his smudged eyeglasses and his coat pockets weighted with things that clanked when he moved. Once I saw him pull out a small measuring tape in a silver case, and another time he fished around until he found a pocketknife that he used to scrape paint off his fingernails.

I couldn't help but wonder if Ferdinand had asked Moll to keep track of me and of the progress of the portrait. I suggested as much to Klimt.

"He's watching me, there's no doubt," Klimt said. "I have four commissions to finish, and he wants me to be working on all of them at once. He says I don't have time for any indulgences."

Klimt knew what he wanted to see in my face, and he coaxed it from me. He told me to cross my legs and smile and then he sketched furiously. He told me to worry about the state of the empire, and his pencil raced across the page. He told me to think of something I wanted more than anything, and then he drew.

"Think of something that you want, and that you know you can have," he said, and I imagined myself as the leader of my own salon, with dozens of friends asking me what to read and talk about.

"That's good. Now think of something you're afraid you'll never have," he said, and I thought of my child, still to come.

"Now think of something you know that you can never have," he said, and I thought of him in my bed every night.

I wore a golden dress, and walked through his studio pretending I was a queen.

"A smiling queen," he said. "Now a bold one. Now a great patroness of the arts. Now Ferdinand's wife. Now my lover."

He drew the way I twisted my hands. He drew me draping a scarf around my neck; he drew me unpinning my hair and letting it fall across my shoulders.

Sometimes he didn't touch me. On other days, when he knew Moll was occupied elsewhere, he made love to me and I felt I had been bathed in gold and fire.

ADELE

1903

I t was a quiet afternoon in Cafe Central, and the coffee was hot and strong. I had spent three long days posing for Klimt, and was eager to sink into my new journal. I smoothed the paper wrapping from the September issue of *Deutsche Arbeit* and admired the modern typeface.

"Have you read Rilke's new poem?" asked a gentleman in a black suit as he hung his coat on a hook.

"Not yet." I smiled.

Straightaway I scanned the table of contents, and turned to Rainer Maria Rilke's poem. There I found three devastating stanzas, each one taking me farther backward to my youth, to my brother's bedside, to the sadness I had felt after he was gone.

I reread one line in particular—*and behind the bars, no world*—until tears ran down my cheeks.

"You have so much passion," Berta said when I showed up at her home, eager to talk about the poem. "You should start your own salon."

It had been my dream—the thing I had wished for when Klimt had prompted me to imagine what I desired. But Rilke had caught me by surprise; my vision was blurry from tears, and I felt uncertain.

"Who will come?" I asked.

"I will come, of course," she said. "And so will all the others."

I made a list of topics that could not fail to entice: Rilke's poetry of objects; Klimt's university murals; Oscar Wilde's arrest and homosexuality. I invited theater people, musicians, and writers. Berta brought me journalists, and the Mahlers brought me Stefan Zweig, whose brilliant little stories about unhappy suicides were wildly popular.

How I loved to see Zweig in my home. He was a funny, compact man who had been discovered by Herzl at the *Neue Freie Presse* and was building a great body of work.

"If you will indulge me," Zweig always began, before astonishing us with his newest story.

Many years and political differences had separated Zweig and Herzl, but he was devastated when Herzl died in the summer of 1904, and he wept openly at the funeral. While bouquets of dead flowers were still piled on Herzl's grave, my dear Zweig agreed to lead a discussion of the Jewish State at my home that autumn.

This was turning point for me: what had been denied in Berta's salon was welcome in my own.

The evening began with Zweig reading the opening page of Herzl's pamphlet and was followed by raucous and deeply divided debate. Everyone agreed that the Dreyfus Affair that had spawned Herzl's idea for the Jewish State was a travesty, but almost no one thought that it was practical or desirable for modern Jews to make a homeland in Israel—or anywhere. I was relieved that no one came to blows that evening, and equally thrilled when my suggestion for the following month—Nietzsche's Eternal Return—was accepted without a single objection.

At my childhood dinner table, I had been forbidden to speak of philosophy, but in my home on Schwindgasse that November, we lingered together for hours on the passage that had lingered for years in my mind: "*The ring in which you are but a grain of sand will glitter afresh forever. And in every one of these cycles of human life there will be one hour where, for the first time one man, and then many, will perceive the mighty thought of the eternal recurrence of all things—and for mankind this is always the hour of Noon.*"

I was fortunate—so fortunate to have found this moment, this hour of noon, when I was master and mistress of my own days and nights, of my heart and of my mind as well.

One afternoon after he and I had shared lunch in his studio, Klimt showed me a thick stack of burnished gold and silver leaf. Each sheet was separated by brown paper, the whole stack no more than twelve inches thick.

He separated a single gold sheet and held it out for me. It quivered as if it were alive.

"For the portrait?" I asked.

"I'm practicing on something first. I'd like you to see it."

He took me into the room where we'd had our first trysts, and pulled a sheet from a large canvas to reveal a kneeling man and a woman, their bodies diaphanous and ethereal, floating in a blank canvas. The man was kissing the woman's face. Their features were missing, but the shape of their embrace mirrored the shape of the kiss in the *Beethoven Frieze*.

"I've managed to keep this a secret—even from Moll," he said.

There was a large sketch beside the canvas, where he'd drawn elongated black columns on the man's robe and round purple and red flowers on the woman's.

"Dr. Freud will appreciate your choice of symbols," I said with a smile.

"No one will see it if I don't get it right," he said.

"Then get it right, Gustl."

He worked slowly, with a Bunsen burner and a pot of glue. First he painted the glue onto a small patch of the canvas, then he melted gold over the flame. When it was just the right liquidity, he applied the gold paint with a flat brush. The man's body and the woman's became bound together in a single golden sheath: there was not even a line between them, only the melding symbols and robes floating together into one.

"You once asked me how I want Vienna to see me," I said. "This is what I want—this grandeur and richness. This kind of complexity: an endless merging of myself and the city."

"This is exactly what I'm going to give you," he said.

What we had between us was nothing as simple as longing or sexual desire. It was a hunger for beauty and meaning, and a willingness to search in the world and in ourselves to find it. We had a sense of permanence and the fear of oblivion. We knew, of course, that everything was transient and nothing could last—and yet it didn't stop us from wishing for something eternally beautiful.

Winter rages outside the studio as he fills a fat sketchbook with hiero-glyphs, symbols, and letters. He designs a ring of gold and white tri-angles for the neckline of her dress, and draws elongated eyes of Horus until he finds just the right shape and size. He studies his notes on the mosaic at Ravenna, and puts Adele on a gold throne that echoes Empress Theodora's.

He paints the jeweled necklace severing her head from her shoulders to show that she's separate from her fortune and yet bound by it. He paints a diaphanous curtain of an unknown universe floating around her. He paints yearning, intelligence, and beauty. Weeks pass in a chilling sleet and Klimt works in the hazy glow of yellow-gold and dappled metals. He forgets to eat lunch, and goes home at the end of the day cold, hungry, and exhausted. He uses all of his gold and silver leaf, and sends for more.

He brushes loose pieces of gold from the canvas, collects the fallen flakes, and melts them again. Nothing can be lost. Everything must be used and reclaimed, again and again.

ADELE
1906

Vienna's newspapers ran cruel cartoons of hook-nosed Jews squeezing the life out of German babies. Anti-Semitic churches flooded with men, women, and children who eagerly believed the angry screeds that rained down from the pulpits. As I hurried past one of those churches on a cool spring afternoon, a slim redhead carrying a large canvas bag came out a side door, followed by a boy in a patched coat. The boy held a flag in one hand and reached into the doorway for a little girl in a red coat and black shoes. It had been years since I'd seen her, but I recognized Mimi's hair beneath a blue hat, and her lithe body under her dress and cloak. I watched her call to the little girl and smile as the child toddled toward her across the cobblestones.

I'd had another miscarriage the year prior, and Mimi and her children reminded me of all that I'd lost. They made me tremble with envy. I turned my face from them, and hurried past.

"I saw Mimi and the boy," I told Klimt.

"The boy?"

I was sitting on a stiff chair with my elbows propped on a table. He was drawing my hands, the left twisted around the right, the good protecting the injured, and I had to keep them perfectly still.

"Your son," I said. "It looks like he has a sister, too. Is she yours?"

For a moment it looked as if he was going to shrug. In that instant I hated him a little bit.

"They were coming out of a church in the Third District," I said. "Your son was waving a little German flag, and he was chanting."

Klimt was hardly listening.

"Don't move your hands, Adele. Just hold still a little longer," he said.

"Does Mimi know your patrons are mostly Jews?"

"Why would you ask that?"

"Because your son was mimicking Lueger's speeches, that's why. He was saying, 'Jews, everywhere you go—Jews, Jew, Jews.'"

"He's a little boy." Klimt touched the stack of gold bracelets on my wrist, and turned one so it caught the light. "I don't think of my friends that way. And I know Mimi doesn't, either."

"Mimi thinks of us?" I snapped.

"That's enough for today," Klimt said, as if he could sense how far my mind had wandered.

"I think you should tell her your patrons are of the Jewish lineage," I said as stood to leave. "I think you should let her know that you don't feel that way about us. Do you?"

"Adele, Mimi doesn't hate anyone," he said. "But if it will make you happy, I'll talk to her and the boy."

"Yes," I said. "That would be a very good idea."

He pulled me to him before I left.

"Don't leave angry," he said.

"I'm not angry," I said, although of course I was. "It's just that everything is taking a very long time."

With Klimt I'd used sheepskin condoms and rinsed with a vinegar douche at night. With Ferdinand, I kept trying to conceive. The doctors told me that pregnancy was best achieved with a woman's legs in the air after sex, and that coupling should be done two weeks after the menstrual cycle was complete. And so I was diligent with Ferdinand, bringing him to my bedroom every month and putting my legs in the air as soon as he was finished.

"Hand me a cigarette," I'd say with my legs resting against the wall. Soon he began to take one out of the case even before I asked, striking the match and bringing me an ashtray as well.

After those nights, he was always most attentive.

"Klimt said you can see the work," I told Ferdinand at breakfast one morning after he'd shared my bed.

"Is it finished?" Ferdinand asked.

"Almost," I said. "When he gets close to the end, he doesn't want anyone to see it."

"Then you won't have to go there anymore," Ferdinand said, looking up from the stock market pages. "You'll be free to go about your days as before."

I tried not to look at him too closely; I tried not to reveal any sense of sorrow. Ferdinand had been elevated to president of the empire's unified sugar industry, and there was talk of regulating the prices so that there would be no market collapse as there had been twenty years earlier. I knew he was busy with negotiations in Budapest and also in Moravia.

"Maybe I'll stop by the studio," he said. "I'd like to see how the portrait is coming along."

Besides Moll and myself, Ferdinand would be the first to see the portrait—at least that's what Klimt had told me—and I was eager to share it with him. But in the end Ferdinand was called away on business, as was so often the case, and I went alone.

Even unfinished, my face was far lovelier on the canvas than it was in life—my eyes wider, my lips fuller. I looked regal and intelligent. I looked proud.

"You're making me too pretty," I said. The words felt strange on my tongue.

"This is how I see you," Klimt said. "This is who you are to me."

Did he know how I wished to be seen? Or was it that under his gaze I became what I wished to be?

"And what will go here?" I waved across an empty expanse of beige gouache and yellow paint.

"Silence," he said. "And the things we've spoken of that have no name."

He showed me stacks of gold and silver leaf, and told me there would be letters and symbols, and the eyes of Horus that I'd asked for.

"When you start the gold, I'll have no reason to see you again," I told him. "No excuses to come here."

He touched my cheek.

"You don't need an excuse, Adele. You're always welcome here—I hope you will come when it's done."

I left knowing that I would not return for some time. My bleeding had stopped; my breasts were swollen and tender.

I arranged to see a new doctor. Dr. Julius Tandler was a well-known Socialist at the forefront of medicine and social reforms. He was known to speak to women with kindly intelligence. I knew that he would tell me that I was pregnant, and he did.

"After two miscarriages, you have to be very careful," Dr. Tandler said. "You have to stay in bed. I know it's hard, but you must."

I stayed in bed with my legs propped up on pillows, and watched the winter rage outside my window. Ferdinand doted on me: he had fresh juice sent up to my room every evening, and bought me violet-scented soaps and creams imported from London.

"We'll have a son," he said. I smiled and let him hope for a boy.

I'd read books on childbirth, which sounded painful and horrifying; and on childcare, which seemed as if it would be exhausting without the help of round-the-clock nannies.

As the weeks stretched on, I wrote an advertisement for the perfect nanny, and put it in my bed-stand drawer where I kept my bookplates, letter opener, and stationery. I reread all of Jane Austen's novels, and decided if I had a girl, I would name her Emma. I imagined her walking proudly beside me through museums and galleries as she grew. I pictured her at the gymnasium, then the Lyceum, and finally at university. I knew I would give her every opportunity and encouragement that I had never been offered.

I sent for a sketch pad and colored pencils, and tried my hand at images of bounty: harvest wheat, golden apples, juicy pomegranates, and ripe figs. Everything was alive, exactly as Franz Cizek had taught me to see even the most inanimate objects. Soon I was drawing prams, pregnant bellies, and colored blankets. I pored over advertisements for baby furniture and made a scrapbook of the things I liked most. The German buggies were the best, and I had Ferdinand order one to be delivered in early spring.

I waited for the baby to kick and when she finally did, Dr. Tandler let me get up.

Early hyacinths were poking through the hard ground when I showed up at Klimt's studio in the late morning. My pregnant body was well concealed beneath my loose dress. I knocked, called Klimt's name and then went inside.

"I'd like to see it now," I called.

In many ways I had changed, yet in others I had not. I still wasn't patient, and when I wanted something, I would not be deterred.

"Adele? I wasn't expecting you," he said. It was good to see his familiar brown robe and thick feet in leather sandals and socks. But he looked as if he'd been up through the night, and the studio smelled of an acrid burning.

"Did you send a note?" he asked, rubbing a hand over his bald spot. It seemed he'd lost more hair since I'd last seen him. "Do we have an appointment?"

"No," I said. "But I'm here now. The show is only a few months away—I'm sure you're almost finished."

I saw the portrait behind him on a low easel, turned away from the door.

"It's not finished," Klimt said, putting himself squarely in front of me. "It needs one final breath of life."

"You have to let me see it today." I put a hand on his neck, surprised to feel a small lump there. I didn't ask about the boil. I didn't want to know.

"Why this urgency?" he asked. "I said you were welcome, and you stayed away for months."

"Show me—then I'll tell you."

Klimt waved a weary hand—*no*—across his face.

"Really, don't make me beg," I said. "Please. We've already given each other so much."

"All right," he relented. "But will you close your eyes for me, please?"

How many times had he asked me just that when we were naked? *Open your eyes, close your eyes, open your mouth, open your legs.*

I closed my eyes and he guided me across the room with a hand at the small of my back.

"Now," he said. "You can look."

The painting was astonishing. Shocking. The gold and silver glowed. My face was luminous, floating like the moon over a glittering night-scape. My eyes were brimming with raw desire and need, and yet I seemed to be a goddess lording over a brilliant universe decorated with stars and lights.

"It's beautiful," I breathed. "I love it."

He beamed.

"I came to tell you something, Gustl," I said. His eyes went to my draped midsection, as if he already knew what I was going to say. "I'm having a child. I'm five and a half months along."

"Five months?" I saw him calculating the cycles of the moon. "You haven't been here since Decemb—"

"Of course it's not yours," I said quickly. "We've always used the sheepskins. The child is Ferdinand's."

He put a hand to my cheek.

"I know this is what you've wanted. Are you happy?"

"I'm frightened," I whispered. "I've lost two pregnancies already, and I want this child so badly."

"Then you'll have a child," he said. "I'm sure this will be your time."

I'd always known that he understood my vulnerability. He'd seen it from the start—that first day, when I'd seen his mural.

"Do you remember what you said about the Sistine Chapel and the moment of creation? You said Michelangelo painted God handing life to Adam—not a breath, but a touch." I spoke in a rush, not waiting for answers. "That's what you said, I remember and I believed you. And that's what I need from you now."

His eyes lingered on me. I knew enough to be quiet, and I knew how to be still. It was something every woman in my world had learned to do: sit quietly, and wait.

He rummaged through a clutter of pigments and mixed his colors. He used a slide rule to carefully measure out and paint first one, then two deep red squares level with my face. He stepped back and studied the effect, twisting the ruler one way and another, tipping the right angle first up, then down, and then toward my face. He added three more squares.

"The *ka* is a symbol for the soul," he said as he painted one final three-sided square. "Egyptians believed there was a piece of a living soul in every work of art—something eternal that animates the inanimate. I've turned the opening toward your face, here"—he touched my cheek, and then dipped a single drop of red onto the same place on the canvas—"and here."

I listened and I watched, waiting to see the moment when the life sprung from his hands into the work. I'd spent hours with him in silence as he seized on something invisible and intangible and rendered it as color and form in his work. But even as I watched and waited, it seemed to happen in a mysterious way that I could not see. I blinked, and it was there. It appeared in silence, without movement or sound.

That silence is in my portrait; that waiting is in my expression; that mystery is in the eyes of Horus and the *ka* and all the symbols in silver and gold that he carved into my dress.

"I see it now," I said.

"Now it's finished," Klimt said.

He kissed me tenderly. It was good-bye, and we both knew it.

After that day I felt a powerful inner awareness that came slowly, as a plant grows imperceptibly to the human eye.

Within a month, I knew I was carrying a boy.

When my birth pains began, I knew he would not survive.

❧

Unlike the miscarriages, which had been private affairs, everyone knew I was expecting a child, and everyone knew when the baby was stillborn that spring. And unlike the moment of creation, when rich silence is everywhere, my sorrow felt like a howl and a scream that went on and on into the dark void at the center of myself.

Ferdinand was crushed, and my mother came at once offering comfort, but the doctors were unflinching. Even Dr. Tandler. He was kind, but held my hand and told me with no uncertainty that another pregnancy would kill me. I could not try again.

"What will I do?" I asked in a hollow voice.

Dr. Tandler put me in mind of the wise, old doctor who'd come to my room in Paris. He took a seat beside my bed, and ran a hand along the books on my shelf. He looked at the art on my walls.

"You have a good mind and a good heart," Tandler said. I felt almost that we were friends, or that we would be, after this. "There are so many places and people in Vienna who need someone like you."

I was devastated and exhausted.

"When you're ready, you can start your salons again. And we can talk about ways to help the city that are meaningful to you."

"I want you to call the maid in to wash your hair and help you get dressed," Thedy said. "Or I'll do it myself."

I had not looked out the window for more than a month. I hadn't even opened the blue curtains.

"You can't help me, not five months pregnant," I told her. "And there's nothing I want to do and no place I want to go."

"You have your art," Thedy said. "I know how much the portrait and your friendship with Klimt means to you."

My sister already had three children. She'd carried each one easily, and we had no doubt that in a few months she would have another child in the nursery and another nanny in the servants' quarters.

"Not enough," I whispered.

She glanced at the newspapers fanned on my coffee table.

"Everyone is talking about the *Kunstschau*," she said, picking up the *Neue Freie Presse*. "Your portrait is going to be star of the show, Adele."

The *1908 Kunstschau* would mark the sixtieth anniversary of Emperor Franz Joseph's rule, and Klimt was the spirit and master of the show. As my sister read the description of the grand white buildings that were being built in an empty field in the center of Vienna, I closed my eyes and imagined the crowds standing before my portrait, imagining they knew me, then turning away and calling me—what? Beautiful. I felt sure they would call me beautiful.

"They say Klimt is showing two large golden paintings," Thedy said. "Did he paint you twice, Adele?"

"No. The other work isn't a portrait. It's called *The Kiss*."

She looked at me strangely, as if she were going to ask a question and then thought better of it.

"I haven't seen it finished," I added.

"But you will see it soon," Thedy said. "We'll go to the *Kunstschau* together, it will be gay and lovely."

My sister cared little for modern art. She said it for me, and I loved her for that.

*P*eering into a communal mirror in the damp rooming house, a hungry seventeen-year-old carefully trims his toothbrush mustache, draws an old razor across his face, and slicks back his hair.

As church bells chime eight o'clock, he arrives at Vienna's Academy of Fine Arts and follows the guard into the building. In the admissions office, he gives his information to a seated clerk.

"Hitler, Adolf," he says. "Application date May 10."

The clerk pokes his glasses onto the bridge of his nose, and finds a card on top of a thick pile.

"Application unsatisfactory," he says. He riffles through a bin, and hands the young man a folder.

Adolf's face burns. He makes his way past green fields where the white Kunstschau buildings glimmer in the distance, sits alone under a tree, and opens his folder. It is his second rejection from the Academy, and he's sure there has to be some mistake. Some kind of conspiracy. It's the only thing that makes sense.

MARIA

1938

The first thing I did every morning was put on the kettle and run down to fetch the newspaper. While the tea steeped and Fritz got dressed, I snapped on the radio and practiced my English. There was no decent coffee to be had in the Liverpool markets, but I added chicory to the tea and waited until it turned black, then poured out a can of condensed milk and pretended it tasted like home.

Every day after Fritz left for work, I tried to do at least one thing to make our little home welcoming and inviting. I labored over the newspaper advertisements, carefully converting the prices from pounds to reichsmarks and keeping my budget in a black and white notebook. I whipped cream with powdered sugar and baked apple strudel. I found a sausage shop where they stuffed every bit of the cow and pig into lamb casings, and a market that sold spiced kraut and red potatoes. I bought a piece of red-and-white-checkered cloth and used my mother's needle and thread to sew a cheerful curtain for our kitchen.

But something was still missing in our evenings together. Fritz didn't say he was sad or homesick, but I could see that he was unhappy, and sometimes he turned away from me in bed and pulled the blankets over his head, saying he needed to sleep.

"When I sleep, I forget," he whispered.

Wandering through the market district on a cold autumn morning, I spotted a windup phonograph in the window of a secondhand shop. A bell rang when I pushed open the door, and a man with a big, round belly came out of a back room wiping his hands on a greasy rag.

"How much?" I asked, hoping that my English wouldn't fail me. He stared just above my face, and seemed to consider my question for a moment.

"Five pounds," he said.

I had two pounds, three shillings in my purse.

"No," I said, disappointed. "I'm sorry."

"Too much?" he asked. "What can you offer?

"I have two pounds," I said, taking care to string the sentence together properly.

"Two pounds, and the hat you're wearing."

I was wearing the fashionable fedora I'd worn when I left Vienna. It was blue felt, with a jaunty black brim and a net tucked inside that I could pull down to dress it up in the evening. I'd bought the hat for my honeymoon trousseau, and paid six crowns—a very dear price. The lining was black satin, and the Gerngross label, stamped in gold, was still fresh.

"I'll give you the hat, and one pound."

He considered my proposition. There was a green light filtering through the shop window, and rows of old cigarette cases and silver sets lined up on neat, clear shelves.

"That will do just fine," he said, finally.

I sorted through a collection of records until I found what I was looking for, and breathed a relieved sigh when he let me take two records and the phonograph for the remainder of my coins. He even had a boy help me carry everything home.

When I heard Fritz's footsteps on the stairs that night, I cranked up the phonograph and dropped the needle. The sound of an Italian tenor singing Puccini met Fritz when he opened the door.

"How did you do it?" He smiled at me with happy amazement. "You're the greatest, Duck. I always knew you'd be the best wife a girl could be."

We spent the night listening to music by candlelight, and when he woke up in the morning, Fritz was still humming happily.

———

On the last day of September the British and the French signed an agreement that gave Hitler the Sudetenland in Czechoslovakia. In exchange, Hitler vowed never to invade England or France.

"Hitler will never keep his word," Bernhard said that night. "The Sudetenland won't satisfy him."

We were playing cards at Bernhard and Nettie's kitchen table. The radiator was piping comforting steam heat, and the kitchen smelled of chicken soup. Bernhard had been right about Hitler all along, and I didn't doubt him this time. My uncle was in Jungfer Brezan, deep in the heart of Bavaria, and I hoped that he would have the good sense to leave before Hitler's armies crossed the borders.

"Ferdinand will have to get out of Czechoslovakia quickly," Bernhard said.

"I'm frightened," I said.

Sometimes when my brother-in-law looked at me, I thought I saw a questioning pity in his eyes. I saw it that night while Nettie was putting the children to bed and Fritz was in the washroom.

"Maria," Bernhard said quietly. "You said you're frightened, but you're the bravest woman I know. Coming to Berlin—"

"That's not true," I said. "Everyone is brave now. We're all brave."

"My brother is very lucky to have you."

I looked at him with an expression that was as naked as I'd ever shown anyone, and whispered, "Please, that's enough, Bernhard."

Soon after that, when I tried to call my uncle in Jungfer Brezan, the line was disconnected, and there was no way of knowing where my uncle was, or if he was safe. Like almost everyone else from home, he was lost in the Nazi's shadows.

We'd been in Liverpool for a little more than two months when I woke one morning to find Fritz's side of the bed empty. I rolled over in the dark, pulled on my bathrobe, put on the kettle, and went to retrieve the paper from our landing.

It was November eleventh, and the frosty air rose up to greet me even before I opened the door. On the stoop, a woman who lived on the second floor was standing with the newssheet open in her hands.

"Look, Maria."

The headline screamed up at me: *NAZI ATTACK ON JEWS: Orgy of Hitler Youth—Synagogues Burnt, Destruction and Plunder.*

"What does it mean?" the neighbor asked. Her two young children had been secreted out of Germany into Amsterdam, and she was still waiting for them to reach Liverpool. "What can it mean for my children?"

I read: *In Vienna the synagogues were blown up with bombs—thousands of Jews were arrested.*

She ran a shaking finger along the news story.

"What does it mean, Maria?"

I looked up and saw Fritz hurrying up the street unshaved, a cigarette dangling from his lips. I ran to him.

"Did you hear?" I asked. "Did you hear what happened at home?"

When he held me close, I smelled Chanel No. 5 on his jacket—I could never mistake it. All the blood rushed to my head.

"Where were you?" I asked, pulling away. "Why do you smell like perfume?"

He hung his head and mumbled something. The streets were beginning to come alive with the news. People were on their doorsteps, and there was a siren in the distance.

"Fritz, please tell me where you were," I said.

"I went to the pub for a drink."

"No you didn't," I said. "The pubs aren't open now—"

He tried to pull me into his arms, but it was too late. I turned away, dizzy and angry, my vision slipping away as if someone had put a black cloth over my eyes.

They called it *Kristallnacht*: the Night of Broken Glass. I did not forget the empty side of our bed, or the smell of Chanel No. 5, but I pushed it from my mind.

In Liverpool we gathered in the markets and the bakeries and could speak of nothing else. People broke down in tears in the middle of the squares, and gathered before sunset to wait for the evening newspapers to reach the corner stands.

News from Vienna slowed to a trickle, and it was impossible to reach my mother. Bernhard had been working through friends to get her an immigration visa, but after that he exhausted every legal way of bringing her to safety.

"We don't even know if she's alive," I said.

"She's alive," Bernhard said. "I know that much. And as long as it's humanly possible, I will get her out."

Of course he said that. He knew that I would accept no other answer. But what was possible and what was impossible was all a matter of luck. And I knew far too much about secrets and lies to trust in luck.

ADELE

1908

The day of the *Kunstschau* dawned clear and inviting. I chose low-heeled shoes, and had scones and fruit sent on a tray to my room with my morning coffee. At ten o'clock, Ferdinand and I climbed into our carriage with Thedy and Gustav and joined the emperor's procession of gold carriages and noisy new automobiles decorated with red and gold imperial buntings. Ferdinand wore the royal commendation sash he'd received from Emperor Franz Joseph, and I wore a lavender crepe dress with yellow trim.

My brother-in-law hummed under his breath while his fingers played an imaginary cello, and for a brief moment a flock of starlings trailed behind our carriage, piping out a song to accompany him. The fruit trees along the Ringstrasse were in brilliant pink blossom, and the flower gardens that rimmed the Hofburg Palace were a rainbow of color alive with hummingbirds and butterflies.

Thedy wore a lovely hat decorated with two fresh white chrysanthemums; she was six months pregnant, and radiant.

"Tell us what you think of Adele's portrait," my sister said to Ferdinand. He had attended a private preview of the show the night before, and come home bursting with enthusiasm.

"I'm very pleased," he said. "The emperor told me personally that he finds it remarkable. The word he used was 'brilliant.'"

"That's wonderful," Thedy clapped. "Isn't it wonderful, Adele?"

"It's wonderful," I agreed.

I saw Thedy and Ferdinand exchange worried glances. They were eager for me to recover my happiness, and I was grateful to them. But I was still in mourning for my unborn child, and unprepared for festivities. The time Klimt and I had spent on the portrait had belonged to us alone; now the painting would belong to the public, where anyone could pass judgment on us. With the weight of loss upon me, I felt sad and nervous. As much as I wanted to enjoy the day, what I wanted most was to go back home and crawl under my soft blankets.

The others chattered about the new artists who'd come to Vienna for the show, but I kept my eyes trained on the flat green horizon, where the new white exhibition buildings rose in the distance like a sprawling fairground.

"Adele knows who they are." Ferdinand put a hand lightly on my knee. "She'll be our guide if she feels up to it."

I blinked at him, at a loss. In the distance I heard a marching band.

"The other artists," Thedy said. "Klimt's protégés—what's the name of that young, wild one?"

"Kokoschka," I answered. "Oskar Kokoschka."

"I caught a glimpse of his work last night," Ferdinand said. "I suppose I should trust Klimt's judgment, but orange faces and blue hens seem like the product of a crazy man."

"People are saying that," I said. "But they called Klimt far worse, and we know they were wrong."

There was a long line of open-topped cars and carriages full of women in new hats as large as beehives; mothers and nannies pushing prams with new babies and fathers holding their sons by the hands. I had to blink away sadness as best I could as our driver stopped at the welcoming stand and two footmen helped us onto a red-and-white carpet that stretched across the grass.

Inside the gates, refined Viennese were walking side by side with foreigners from every edge of the empire: Magyar silk importers and their wives wrapped in colorful scarves, Bosnians in dark brocade, Slavs with sharp cheekbones and deep blue eyes. There were Nords, Ukrainians, Germans, Parisians, and even a few Italians speaking in loud voices and waving their hands. On everyone's lips, in a chorus of tongues, I heard Klimt's name.

When we reached the inner courtyard, my friend was about to deliver his opening speech. After so much rejection and disappointment, this was a great day for Klimt, and I was glad. He was well turned out in a fine three-piece linen suit, and was carrying on a lively conversation with two officials from the culture ministries. Emilie Flöge had her arm wrapped through his, and Moll was behind them with his hands in his pockets.

I hugged Ferdinand's arm more tightly, and took a seat at the end of an aisle. It was hard not to think back to the first night I'd met Klimt, when I was a newlywed and everything had still been in front of me. Now I was afraid everything was behind me.

"I can't wait to see the portrait." Thedy put a hand on my arm. "I'm sure it's splendid—I'm sure it will mark the beginning of a wonderful new phase of your life, Adele."

Thedy knew what I needed to hear, as always.

Klimt welcomed everyone to the show and thanked the ministries for their support. Every piece of art in the show was for sale, he announced—eliciting a burst of laughter from the crowd. He thanked the emperor and the two hundred artists who'd come from far and wide to display their creations, and the city itself, "for making a home for visionary art and artists, who've been able to explore the edges of creativity thanks to the support and enthusiasm of Vienna's generous patrons and ministers."

When he was finished, Ferdinand and I inched slowly through the crowd behind dozens of well-wishers, until Klimt saw us and pulled Ferdinand into an embrace.

"The reception is spectacular," he said. "Come, we'll go to the gallery together."

My husband wasn't used to taking directions from anyone, but Klimt's excitement was contagious. We followed him into the central gallery, where five new paintings hung beneath modern spotlights. In a magnificent gold frame, my portrait looked like something from a different universe, and I like an exotic woman from a mysterious dreamland. I had seen it in the studio, but in public it was a shock: my mouth was luscious and red, my eyes limpid with an expression of longing and desire that even I could not decipher.

A crowd was staring up the painting, and waiters were circulating with trays of champagne. When I was handed a glass of champagne, I drank it in three quick gulps.

"Easy, Adele," Ferdinand said. "That will go right to your head."

I *wanted* it to go right to my head. When he turned his back, I took another glass, and tossed it down quickly. As I handed the empty glass to a passing waiter, I saw Emilie Flöge smiling at me.

"It's disorienting to see your face up there, isn't it?" She slid close to me. Klimt had once painted her dressed in a blue gown with her hand on her waist, and her hair a reddish halo around her pale face. "I don't think anyone is ever prepared for what it's like to see it in public."

I nodded, but no words came.

"Just remember that's not really you on the canvas," she said in my ear. "That was the hardest thing for me—that people kept insisting it was me, when it wasn't me at all."

"Who was it, then?" I asked.

"It was Klimt, of course," she said with a funny laugh. "It's what Klimt saw when he was looking at me, looking at him."

"But isn't it more than that?"

The same stillness I'd seen on Klimt washed over her, and she closed her eyes. She seemed to travel somewhere inside of herself, and then to come back when she had her answer.

"He works and works until something alights on the canvas that's much more than either one of you," she said, opening her eyes. "That's his genius."

Just then there was a loud cheer, and Klimt's voice rose above the crowd.

"I've done your wife's beauty great justice Herr Bloch-Bauer," he called out. "I hope we can agree on that."

"Indeed, we do agree on that," my husband said.

"He has done you justice," Emilie murmured. "And now, thanks to him, you'll look that way forever."

Ferdinand put a protective arm around my shoulder, and Emilie faded away just as Thedy put out a hand to steady me.

"The painting is a masterpiece," my sister said, fanning herself with a printed program. "You look positively regal, and your eyes are burning . . ."

The end of her sentence was drowned out by laughter and a new surge of the crowd, and in another breath, Berta was beside me in a bright red shawl.

"It's indescribably gorgeous," Berta pronounced. "Your face is floating over the city—he's made you the queen of Vienna, Adele."

I looked from Berta's smile to the faces that filled the gallery—from Klimt's new portrait of Fritza Riedler to his naked *Danaë* with her bare bottom. Directly opposite my portrait was the golden *Kiss*; it was as spectacular as it had promised to be.

"Of course your portrait is better than all of the others," Thedy whispered. "And Ferdinand loves it. That's really what matters, isn't it?"

Behind Thedy I spotted Fritza Riedler in the flesh, smiling at Klimt from the edge of a small group of admirers. I saw Serena Lederer, Rose von Rosthorn, and even Hermine Gallia, who'd come from Prague for the show. Like me, they had flooded into the galleries with their husbands by their sides, little dogs in their arms, children tugging at a hem. Like me, they were Klimt's admirers and patrons. The possibility that they'd all been his lovers was so obvious that I should have seen it clearly all along—and yet it felt like a startling revelation as the women's voices rose around me like a swarm of sirens.

Klimt wiped his forehead with a handkerchief and mopped at a boil on his neck that I hoped no one else noticed.

While everyone gathered around my portrait—and I *did* love it—I forced myself to study Klimt's *Three Ages of Women* more closely. It was a beautiful painting, in some ways superior to my portrait. He'd considered the entire life cycle and painted a child, a mother, and a crone with limbs entwined as if they were three faces of the same woman, or three phases of the same moon.

What Klimt depicted there was true—a woman leaves her childhood behind when she becomes a mother, and ages as her children and grandchildren grow. But my life would not be that way. I would never be a mother, and I could not go from child to crone—I was too young for that; I was too smart, and too curious about the world.

In a room crowded with friends and family, I felt suddenly bereft. I was lost in my thoughts when a man's voice broke right in my ear.

"Why is this art so ugly?" he demanded.

I turned to see a burly German staring up at Fritza Riedler's portrait.

"I beg your pardon?" I asked.

"They say this art is about truth," his friend said, ignoring me. "But I don't see what's true about painting an ugly woman."

A third man glared up at my portrait and said something about the Jew's gold. He had a thick Bavarian accent.

"You have no taste—no refinement whatsoever." I glared at him.

The man who'd spoken first glanced at me.

"They worship the Jews and their gold," he said in a stage whisper.

"If you don't like the art, perhaps you should leave the show," I said, but my words were lost among other voices, speaking in other tongues—not only German but also Czech, Polish, Romani, the hum of the Hungarian's Magyar, and a choir of strange sounds from the edges of the empire.

The room was filled with women in fine clothing and glittering jewels, satisfied businessmen and pompous dignitaries, artists and patrons congratulating themselves on a display of magnificent new art. But there was something else in the room, too. That sense that I could perceive what the naked eye could not returned, and I scanned the gallery until I saw two bedraggled young men standing away from the others. They were staring up at my portrait with a look of hatred and horror on their faces. The taller one wore a cap and gloves; the smaller of the two had a stiff toothbrush mustache and cold blue eyes. His face was a mask of barely controlled fury.

"Where's Berta," I asked. I reached for my sister's arm. "Can you find Berta?"

I felt sure that if I could tell my friend what I'd heard, she would help me understand it.

"You look overheated," Thedy said. "There's a garden café with shade trees and a fountain, let's go sit there."

"I want to tell you something," I said. "You and Berta and Ferdinand."

Berta came to my side, and Ferdinand to the other. All they heard was "I want."

"You can have anything you want," Thedy whispered.

"What do you want? I'll get it for you," Ferdinand said.

I wanted to know what I'd just witnessed, and what it meant. I wanted to know what I would make of my life now. But these things seemed impossible to articulate, and when I tried to explain, it sounded like gibberish.

"We'll go home," Ferdinand said. "You need to rest, this has been enough exertion for one day."

"Should we send for Dr. Tandler?" Thedy asked.

"I don't want to leave," I said. I'd seen something changing in Vienna and something had changed in me. "I'll be fine. Art always makes me feel better," I added, and I willed it to be so.

MARIA

1938

I didn't ask again where Fritz had been the morning of *Kristallnacht*, and he did not bring it up. I didn't forget, but I was too sick with worry about my mother and Uncle Ferdinand to face any other sadness.

My husband seemed to know that I couldn't bear to wake up or go to sleep without him. He made me tea and toast in the mornings before work, and at night he held me close. On Christmas Eve he gave me two jazz record albums wrapped in newspaper and tied with a piece of string, and I gave him a tuxedo I'd found at a second-hand store. We dressed up and danced to the new records, and in the morning we went back to making phone calls and writing letters, trying to reach anyone who could help get Mama out of Austria.

"I found someone to forge her papers," Bernhard finally said on a snowy Sunday afternoon. "If your mother is willing to take the chance, now is the time."

My mother had to make the decision and the arrangements on her own. All we could do was wait and hope.

"Once she leaves Vienna, we'll have no way of knowing where she is until she reaches Paris," Bernhard added.

I spent ten long, cold afternoons on Nettie's couch mending socks, listening to the radio, and trying not to cry. I bit my nails to the quick, and couldn't bring myself to cook supper unless Fritz was with me and there was music playing. I could not sleep at night without imagining my mother sleeping safely, too.

In February Mama arrived in Liverpool by train along with thousands of others, dragging a single suitcase along the ground and wearing the long mink coat she'd had for as long as I could remember. The coat seemed to weigh her down, as if she'd shrunk since I'd seen her last. She was thin, her eyes haunted, her steps hesitant.

My brother-in-law grabbed her suitcase, and Fritz put an arm under hers.

At home I folded her into slippers and a warm robe and put out cakes and pastries I'd made from our rations. She wanted only to drink a cup of warm tea, and to talk about home. She knit her hands together like gloves, and ran through their names: Louise still had not been heard from; Dora and Eva had not reappeared.

"I don't understand how our own people could do this to us," she said.

"They're not our people," I said.

The one bright spot of news was from my brothers Leopold and Robert, who'd finally reached Canada with their wives and children. Robert's wife was expecting another baby, and he'd sent a postcard from Vancouver that showed mountains as high as the Alps.

He wanted us to come live with him, but Fritz and I wanted to go to America, where some of our friends had already found work in California.

"If you go to America, your children will be American," Mama said one afternoon while we were folding laundry.

"I suppose," I said, although I had not thought of it that way.

"Will you teach them German?" she asked without looking up. "When you have children, will they speak our language?"

I looked at the bent crown of her gray head and realized how hard it was for her to imagine her children and grandchildren making a life away from Vienna, speaking a language she barely understood.

"Fritz and I speak German, so of course they will."

"Yes, of course." She put down the last towel, and gazed out the window. The sky was gray. Night was falling. "And will they be Jewish?"

Fritz and I had married in Turnergasse Synagogue for the sake of tradition, not for God. Now that synagogue had been destroyed by the Nazis. I could not fathom an answer for her. There was too much uncertainty, and more questions than answers.

"Do you feel Jewish?" I asked.

"I didn't used to be a Jew," Mama said. "I used to be Viennese."

"Are you a Jew now?" I asked. I felt angry, but whether I was angry at my mother or at something much bigger, I couldn't have said.

My mother looked at me a long time.

"You remind me of my sister Adele," she said, finally.

I remembered my aunt smoking her cigarettes and urging everyone to speak their mind without fear. I did not think I was like her at all.

"She was passionate," my mother said. "She was a fighter."

"I'm not that way," I said.

"Of course you are! You're tenacious," my mother said. "You wanted Fritz, and you got him. When you make up your mind, Maria, you get what you want."

I looked around at the flat where I'd made do. There was peeling yellow wallpaper and silver pipes that banged when the heat came up. There was a tiny closet for Fritz's suits, and an even smaller space for my few dresses. Everything I'd ever expected to have was somewhere else, in someone else's life.

"Well, what I want is to . . ."

"Yes?" My mother was waiting.

"What I want is . . ."

I thought of the perfume on Fritz's collar and how sick and alone I felt when he worked long nights in London. I suppose when a man has come close to death, he does what he needs to do to feel alive—but still, I wanted him to be faithful. I wanted to forget what Landau had done to me. I wanted my own home. I wanted children and a family. I wanted what I'd expected—what I'd been promised.

"I want to know if you think Aunt Adele had a lover," I said. I'd heard rumors about my aunt and Gustav Klimt, and yet my uncle had never stopped loving her. He'd never once seemed anything but proud. "Do you think she had an affair with the painter?"

My mother blinked.

"What kind of question is that?" she asked.

"You're asking me all kinds of questions," I said. " 'Will I have children? Will they speak German, will they be Jews?' Now I'm asking you a question. I'm asking if she was faithful to Uncle Ferdinand. And if you think that he was faithful to her."

My parents had been devoted to one another. I'd rarely seen my father stay away from home overnight without my mother. But I knew that men of their generation kept mistresses, and that their wives almost always looked the other way. I didn't think it was possible, but even my uncle might have looked the other way.

Was I supposed to look the other way? That's what I really wanted to ask.

"My sister wanted to have children," Mama said. "Instead, she had paintings. That's all I know. I don't even know if her husband is still alive."

I thought I was going to cry, but I didn't. Instead, I put on the kettle and made us some tea.

*T*he door pops open at 18 Elisabethstrasse, and eight men in dark suits step into the silent palais. *The rooms are cold and dusty. Spiders run from the center of thick webs and hide in shadows. Mice scamper into dark corners in the pantry. A young clerk in a long green coat marks the date in a ledger: January 28, 1939.*

Hitler's men fan through the dark rooms, each with a task: count the porcelain, inventory the Wiener Werkstätte silver, collect the fur coats and crystal glasses, the table linens and the leather-bound books. Tag each item, and cross-check it on the inventory list. Prepare the best works for the Führer's art museum in Linz.

In Adele's old parlor, two men from the Reich's Central Monuments Office pull open the blue silk curtains. Sunlight cuts through unsettled dust, and illuminates the golden portrait.

"Maybe the Führer will want this for his museum."

"I don't think so," says the first. "Maybe he'll melt it down for the gold."

"It's here, on the list. Adele Bloch-Bauer I *1907. Signed, lower right.* Gustav Klimt.*"*

ADELE

1909

My portrait traveled across the empire to Budapest and beyond, and it was celebrated everywhere. There were critics of course: a reviewer said I looked like something sprung from the dreams of a hashish addict. Another said the painting had "more brass than Bloch," as if the silver and gold were gaudy and overpowering rather than magnificent. But people of good taste and education called it a masterpiece. Some even called me the queen of Vienna.

"They love you as much as they loved Empress Sisi," Ferdinand bragged one rainy morning as thunder and lightning raged outside our windows.

"That's impossible." I smiled with embarrassment, but I was also delighted.

Imagine your face sent as an envoy to cities you'll never visit, your portrait gazing across stately museums you'll never see. Friends and strangers began sending notes and postcards to ask what I was reading and which lectures I was attending. They stopped me on the Ring and asked when I would start hosting my salons again. Everyone knew I'd lost the child, and I thought they were pitying me. Thedy said it wasn't time, but it was Alma Mahler who convinced me.

"Your parlor one of the few places in Vienna where a woman's ideas are taken seriously," Alma said when I saw her on the steps of the opera house.

Other women might have felt differently, but to me the recognition was a welcome balm to what I'd most feared: obscurity, purposeless-ness and the prison of an idle bourgeois life—especially one without children.

With my husband's encouragement, I sent handwritten invitations and welcomed two dozen more friends to my salon that year. Dr. Julius Tandler brought along three professors who lectured on political theory and economics, and Ferdinand invited two of his fellow industrialists to attend with their wives. The businessmen and professors eyed one an-other skeptically, but we served cheese and duck confit with fresh bread, and poured the wine liberally. Once people were sated and relaxed, I said I wanted my salon to go beyond art, literature, and music, and asked what subjects would be of interest in the months ahead.

"What is modern man?" Alice Saltzer proposed.

Her husband was a banker who'd invested heavily in my father's railroads, and I'd always enjoyed her view of the world.

"What is modern woman?" her sister counter-proposed, which de-lighted me even more.

Berta suggested we discuss women's suffrage, but when the business-men bristled, I quickly marshaled a consensus around the intersection of business, politics, and modernity.

I had not forgotten what I'd seen and heard at the *Kunstschau*. The city's economy was in a slump. Emperor Franz Joseph was growing old and had lost much of his vigor. Karl Lueger's Christian Social Party had gotten bolder, meaner, and more popular. We all felt Vienna's anxiety; we all wanted to understand why so many women were collapsing from nervous hysteria and why men were committing suicide in broad daylight.

"It seems we are in an age of great anxiety," I said.

"It's the specter of war in the Balkans," Professor Rosen said.

"It's the German economy that's threatening to bring down the empire's," one of Ferdinand's colleagues replied, and so our lively year began.

I could not entice Klimt to my new salon. He insisted that art and pol-itics were of two different worlds, and required different kinds of men.

"To be honest," he wrote to me, "I am painfully bored by politics."

This was the first time I saw Klimt as a man limited in his vision. His mastery of imagination and imagery had not dimmed, but to separate art from politics—and the political man of reason from the artistic man of passions—seemed wrong. Klimt and the other modernists had taken us from decorative art to true art; it felt essential that we do the same with our politics, and that those of us who were deep thinkers lead the way. But there was no changing his mind, and that was very disappointing to me.

I had purpose, though.

I went with Dr. Tandler to a series of lectures on Socialism, and read the pamphlets he put in my hands. Once my eyes had been opened, I saw the poor everywhere. I saw them coming from church, carrying day-old bread, and gathering at anti-Semitic rallies wearing the red flowers of Lueger's party.

When Mayor Lueger shouted, "You're hungry because of the Jews," and the crowds of laborers cheered, I knew we had to find a way to keep impoverished Austrians from hating us.

"Lueger won't live forever. Things will change after he's gone," Ferdinand said. "Then it will be the industrialists' time to rise."

Lueger died in 1910, and it did seem that a new age was indeed upon us. Ferdinand traded our carriages and horses for two sleek black automobiles, and had a telephone installed in my sitting room. We put electric lights in every room, and hired a driver for our cars. We doubled our art collection, adding another Klimt landscape, two Kokoschkas, and two beautiful white Minne sculptures.

When Ferdinand said he wanted a second portrait of me, I phoned Klimt to ask if he could make the sketches at home, in my own parlor.

"If that's what you want," he said, and I assured him it was.

What had happened in his studio had happened in another lifetime. I didn't want to have it all opened up again, when I knew that I was not the same woman I had been.

Klimt arrived early on a spring day with his son Chicky carrying a sketch pad and box of tools and supplies. The boy was twelve years old, with a head of curly dark hair and a jacket that was too small. He took furtive looks around my parlor, his eyes lingering on the silver tableware, the white and gold porcelain, the elaborate clock Ferdinand had commissioned from Josef Hoffmann. He stared, with his mouth open, at my portrait over the fireplace, until his father noticed and told him to get busy setting up the easel.

"You look tired," I said to Klimt when he came close.

"I'm having some treatments," he said. His eyes were rheumy, and he had a scarf around his neck: sure signs of an unchecked illness.

"Do you need money for a sanitarium?" I asked quietly. I saw the boy shifting from one leg to another, pushing back his bushy black hair. "Or maybe for the baths at Bad Ischl?"

Klimt lifted my hand, and pressed his lips against my scar.

"You've already given me so much," he said. I was surprised to see tears in his eyes. "You made my best work possible."

"Don't." I pulled my hand free. "You'll make me cry, and I've had my makeup done for the portrait."

"You're so bossy," he said with a teary laugh. "As always."

"As always," I said. "Now let's get started."

He asked for a pencil and pad, and had me stand away from the window.

"What colors do you want for the dress?" he asked as he made his first, long pencil stroke.

"Whatever you want," I said. "I trust you."

"You're just saying that because I called you bossy."

"Yes," I said, smiling. "That's true."

◌◌

Because another pregnancy could kill me, Ferdinand had stopped coming to my room at night. It was a relief, at first, to never have him in my bed, but after a while I found that I missed him.

"Sleep with me, Ferdinand?" I asked one evening, and there was so much tenderness in his face, I was sorry I hadn't asked sooner. I held and touched him as I used to, and when he was there when I woke, I was glad.

When he asked what I would like for my thirtieth birthday, I told him I wanted to build a public art collection. I knew art could speak to people in ways words often failed to do. I also knew that if there were ever to be art for the people, and a bridge between the bourgeois and the masses, it would have to happen through a decided effort of Austria's most enthusiastic patrons.

"It's something we can do for the city," I said. "And it will mean a lot to me."

Ferdinand's wealth and good standing with the emperor made it possible for him to ask for almost anything and have it. Within the year, he was a founding member of the Austrian State Galleries, and by 1913, when the first radio waves were crossing Germany and the Russians were secretly arming agitators in Sarajevo and Croatia, I was spending a good deal of my time considering all that did and did not belong in a national collection celebrating modern art.

Our curator championed some of the more daring Expressionists, but I jettisoned them for safer, more fundamentally appealing works by Van Gogh and Rodin. These were men whose work the average person could appreciate.

"Adele, you were once so bold," Klimt said when we met at the opening night of the opera. Flöge was beside him, looking like a strange peacock in a bright purple dress. "Why would you keep Schiele out of the Belvedere?"

"I didn't keep him out," I said. The strains of the flutists warming up somewhere behind the velvet curtain floated through the air. "I simply made sure there was enough room for your best work. Ferdinand is trying to buy *Medicine* for the museum. You don't object to that, do you?"

He leaned toward me, his familiar scent mixed with something sleepy and unclean.

"Touché," he whispered. "You haven't lost one bit of your fire."

My portrait finally returned from the international exhibition in Venice, and I had it installed in my second-floor parlor room. When the salon gathered in the evenings, my figure seemed to be seated just above us, my own eyes burning across the room the way the ghostly face in Klimt's *Philosophy* still burned in my memory.

I saw art, music, and science in the portrait; astronomy, anxiety, and desire. The passion that had been part of its creation became something that seemed to breathe in the house even when everyone was asleep. But I knew this: if I were the queen of Vienna, then my portrait must belong to my beloved city after I was gone.

"Ferdinand and I will give the portrait to the museum someday," I told Berta.

"And what about the second portrait?" she asked.

The second portrait had been a disappointment to me, as Berta well knew. In stark contrast to the first, I looked old and haggard in the second; instead of the queen of Vienna, I looked like her nursemaid mother wrapped in a pink and green robe.

The painting hung in Ferdinand's private rooms, between two Kokoschkas that he'd bought almost as a joke, but had come to love.

"That's Ferdinand's to choose," I said. "Although I suppose I would like them all together."

I remembered what my husband had said long ago, about his porcelain collection, and added, "Together, like a family."

MARIA

1939

In Liverpool my mother helped me sew beads and lace onto my clothes, and taught me how to use egg whites to make my skin bright. I scrimped and saved so that I could treat myself to a weekly trip to the hairdresser, and rinsed my undergarments with rose-scented water. I wanted to be beautiful for Fritz. I wanted to keep him home with me every night.

I was sitting under an electric dryer in a beauty parlor near Greenbank Drive one morning when I heard someone say the name Felix Salten.

"My sister just came from Paris," a woman said to her companion. "She saw Salten and some other Viennese—Zuckerkandl and the Kleins, and that wealthy sugar baron whose wife died young."

"Ferdinand Bloch-Bauer?" I was so excited I jumped up and sent my hair curlers flying. "Is that who you mean?"

It was. The blonde remembered the name of the hotel, and after a few hours of trying, I was able to place a call and reach my uncle in Paris that very afternoon.

"Maria? Is it really you?" he asked when he heard my voice.

"We're in Liverpool," I said. "Please come—we're all here, even Mama."

"Not yet," he said. He sounded tired, but there was still a fight in him. "The inventories are under way in Vienna, and I want to see if I can have your aunt's portrait secured and sent here to me."

"The most important thing is that you're safe, Uncle Ferry."

"Jungfer Brezan's gone now," my uncle said. "All the art your aunt loved, everything that made our lives so beautiful—they've taken it all."

"We'll get your things back, Uncle Ferry, I'm sure of it," I said. I desperately wanted to keep his hope alive. Too many people were dying or killing themselves. "I know you have it in you."

"I'm doing my damnedest," he said. "But they're ruthless bastards, Maria. Ruthless and cruel."

In the spring, my mother took a steamer ship to Canada to live with my brothers and their wives. Robert had started a new business there, and had a house with extra room. There were three grandchildren in Vancouver and my mother wanted to be near them.

"You come, too," she said, but Bernhard's business was growing, and Fritz wasn't ready to go.

After my mother left, my life fell into a lonely routine. Fritz stayed overnight when he called on his London customers, and the evenings I spent with Nettie and the children made me long for a child of my own.

Weekends were better. On Saturdays we all took English lessons in an elementary school, and when warm weather arrived Fritz and I began to spend Sundays strolling through Edinburgh Park.

One afternoon, two nannies in starched whites sat on a bench nearby.

"War's inevitable now," one said. "Churchill says so. It's just a matter of time."

Fritz and I locked eyes.

"That's a load of nonsense," the other nanny said. "Hitler's not given us any more trouble since the peace treaty, and I'll not send my son to die for a bunch of Krauts and Jews."

Six months later the Nazis stormed Poland, and within weeks it felt as if there had never been a time when England wasn't at war.

Liverpool officials began evacuating children just as the school year was about to begin, and every morning I saw parades of boys and girls carrying sad little suitcases toward the boat docks. By October there were no nannies or prams in the streets, no children playing hopscotch or football. Luxuries disappeared from the shelves. Sugar and milk were impossible to find, and coffee was just a memory.

On an overcast morning I stepped onto the crowded tram and asked the driver, in my best English, "Pardon me, sir, but will you be making stops along Boundary Street?"

The driver narrowed his eyes, and I repeated my question, thinking he must not have understood me.

I saw two older women put their heads together and whisper, looking in my direction. With my thick Austrian accent, the people on the tram saw me as the cause of their troubles, the reason their cupboards were empty and their children far away.

Fritz must have sensed my unhappiness, because he took me to London for the holidays that year. I was charmed by the city with its old-fashioned street posts wrapped in tinsel, and store windows packed with puppets and dolls. Big Ben was majestic, Westminster Abbey was decorated with red ribbons, and the famous double-decker buses were packed. Still, the war was never far away, and posters everywhere reminded us of it.

On Saturday evening we met a group of Fritz's colleagues for dinner at the Criterion. I tried not to show my surprise when the group included women—pretty ones, at that. When one of the pixie brunettes pulled out a cigarette, Fritz offered a light and she blew the smoke out in one long plume.

"Tell me, Maria, what do you think of London?" she asked, as if she were genuinely interested in me. I told her how much we'd been enjoying ourselves in the city, and she asked if Fritz had taken me to "that clever little pub over in Covington Gardens."

"No," I said. "He hasn't even mentioned it." When I looked at Fritz, he gave me a funny smile that I didn't like one bit.

At the end of the night I found myself standing next to the brunette, and as she wrapped her scarf around her neck, a shock of shame and nausea rocked through me. Chanel No. 5. Could it be so? I knew what I knew. I had known it, in a way, for months.

By the time Fritz and I got back to the hotel I had a migraine that kept me in bed for the entire next day. I kept seeing the woman's face and Landau's face; London and Berlin. Our return to Liverpool couldn't come soon enough for me. As we rode the train through the snowy countryside, I thought again and again of the pretty women in the Criterion. We were almost home when the lights in the train blinkered off, and plunged us into darkness.

I touched Fritz's arm.

"Fritz," I whispered. "I think my aunt Adele took a lover when she was a young woman."

I don't know what I hoped to accomplish by that. I only knew that something had to be said, and that was all I could manage.

"How do you know?" he asked. Light slashed across his face, illuminating his features for an instant. "Did someone tell you that?"

"I heard the rumors when I was young," I said. I remembered the party at Mada Primavesi's home, the whispers and raised eyebrows I'd pretended not to hear or see. "It was only a rumor, but now I think it must have been true."

I tried to think of what I really wanted to say to Fritz, and how to say it. Could I say I'd smelled perfume on his clothes again? Could I tell him that I thought he would live a long and good life, that he no longer had to fear for his own death?

"I don't want you to go to London anymore," I said. He took my hand and kissed my knuckles.

"I love you, Maria," he said. "You mean everything to me. I hope you know that."

"Then be faithful to me, Fritz," I whispered, without looking at him. "That's what I'm asking. Be faithful to me. No one will ever love you the way I love you."

Even in the dark, I could see that he was ashamed and angry. I bit my lip and waited for him to say something in return, but then the lights sparked back on, the conductors came down the aisles and opened the compartment doors, and we'd arrived in Liverpool. I followed Fritz's footsteps in the snow, knowing I had to find a way to reach him.

———

When I brought home a leaflet from the Red Keys Pub in Liverpool, Fritz read the advertisement twice through, and put on his best clothes that very afternoon.

"I miss singing," he said. "You know me so well, Maria."

There were cheerful white lights strung around the front door of the Red Keys, and a sleek baby grand piano waiting inside.

Fritz slicked a hand over his hair and asked to see the manager.

"I don't speak too good," Fritz said in broken English. "But I sing it perfect."

To prove it, he snapped his fingers and sang the first two verses of a holiday tune I'd heard on the radio dozens of times.

"I'm dreaming of a white Christmas," he sang with hardly a trace of an accent. "With every Christmas card I write."

By the time we left, he'd been hired to sing at the pub every Friday and Sunday evening.

I wore my prettiest blouses on the nights he performed, and sat on a stool close to the piano so that I could be the audience that I knew my husband craved.

Soon there was a crowd of regulars: men and women like us, who needed something to relieve the tedium and strain of their days. People danced cheek to cheek, their shoes making funny sucking noises on the sticky pub floor. In the dim white lights, with the music playing and Fritz's warm voice washing over me, I was able to put some of what had happened out of my mind. I was his girl again, and when we went home on those evenings, we dropped our clothes at the foot the bed and spent the rest of the night in one another's arms.

On a Friday night in early spring, Bernhard showed up at the Red Keys just as Fritz was starting his second set. It was a cold, wet night but there were plenty of people standing around the piano with their cocktails, and it felt happy and cozy.

"The Brits have declared me an Enemy Alien," Bernhard said, shaking a cigarette out of his packet. "I'm leaving right now—I'm going tonight."

His hair was sticking straight up and his jacket was rumpled. Even in the din of the piano bar, he was loud.

"They're arresting people and sending them to prison," he said. Fritz ran his hands over the piano keys, but it was clear to everyone that something bad was happening. Bernhard leaned in to say something in Fritz's ear, and my husband went white.

We'd read about the Enemy Alien act in the newspapers—it said that Germans and Italians were being sent to a detention camp on the Isle of Man, where no one could contact them.

"But we're not German," I said. "We're Austrian."

"To the Brits we're all the same," Bernhard said, crushing his cigarette out in the ashtray.

"But we're Jews!" I said, surprising myself. "We're refugees."

"They're shutting my factory," he said. "I'm going to America, and Nettie and the boys will be right behind me. I'll send for you when I'm settled."

Bernhard stuffed a wad of money into my hand and watched me push it to the bottom of my pocket book. He was out the door before I'd even finished my glass of soda water. Fritz played until the end of his set, counted up the bills in the tip jar, slumped over the bar and ordered a whiskey.

"We have to be ready to leave, too," Fritz said. He downed his drink in two quick gulps. "I'm not going to prison again. And it's better for you to travel now than to wait."

There was no arguing with what Fritz said. I was a Jew who didn't practice Judaism, a Viennese banished from Austria, and an enemy alien in Britain. I was frightened, and I was three months pregnant.

In Vienna the doctors used to come to the house when we were sick, but in England I took the bus to West Derby Road, where I saw a doctor in the Liverpool Clinic for Ladies Medicine.

Dr. Edwards was the first man to examine me with my legs in stirrups, and any idea I had to ask about damages or diseases from what Landau had done were quickly forgotten when he shone the light between my legs. I just wanted it to be over, and quickly. The doctor took a long tape measure and spanned the height of my belly. He placed a cold stethoscope against my skin and told me he could hear a faint heartbeat.

"The baby is fine," he told me after I'd dressed and was seated in his office. "Your skin suggests slight anemia, but it's nothing cod liver oil and a regular plate of roasted beef won't cure."

He handed me a booklet of special ration tickets for milk, meat, and vitamin A and D tablets. I tucked the tickets safely into my purse and took a long breath. His office was filled with posters of smiling, expectant women.

"I want to go to America," I said. Bernhard had already sent a cable saying there was work for Fritz, and a good, clean hospital where I could give birth.

"You should wait until the child is born," the doctor said somberly. Everyone was somber when they talked about the child, but I wanted him to be as fat and happy as the babies in the posters. "You're almost four months along now. An ocean liner is no place for a woman in your condition."

Liverpool, where there was noise and smog all hours of the day, seemed no place for a woman in my condition, either, I said. And every ocean liner had a medical doctor on board.

"A doctor, yes—but not an obstetrician who would know what to do in the event of complications."

"If I wait, I'll be traveling with an infant. Won't that be even more dangerous?"

"Traveling with a newborn is difficult," the doctor admitted. "But at least you'd have your strength if you wait."

"I have my strength now," I said.

When he saw I was determined, he unlocked his cabinet and handed me an amber bottle that fit into my palm.

"You'll need this when the seas are rough," he said.

ADELE

1914

I was having dinner at Hardtmann's with Ferdinand, in June of my thirty-third year, when the restaurant door burst open and a young man rushed inside.

"Archduke Ferdinand's been assassinated in Sarajevo," he shouted. "The archduke and duchess are dead!"

The whole room stopped. A woman dropped a dinner roll onto the floor, and there was the clatter of tableware followed by a loud eruption of voices.

"They've killed the heir to the throne," a woman cried in a shrill voice.

"We should have put down the Bosnians a long time ago," said a man wearing a pince-nez.

"The emperor will snuff out the rebellion," Ferdinand said loudly. He covered my hand with his own. "He'll stop them fast and hard."

Some of the diners glared at my husband, but no one spoke against him.

"There will be a war," I said quietly. I knew it, just as I'd known my child would be stillborn. For an instant, I saw a flash of my husband bent and alone while war raged around him. Then the image vanished.

"It won't come to that." Ferdinand said. He downed his whiskey. "The emperor will stand up to the Bosnians and the Russians. He'll restore order."

———

Nietzsche said that the will to power brings incarnate forces into collision with one another, just like Zeus and Poseidon throwing thunderbolts and brewing earthquakes. And so it was in Europe.

In the last week of July, the empire declared war on Serbia. The German Kaiser quickly took our side and rallied his forces, while France, Belgium, and soon Great Britain took sides with the Russians against us.

"The old order is falling away," I said when we learned they were drafting men far too old and sick to go into battle. "It's what Dr. Tandler and the other professors said would happen."

"The emperor will prevail," Ferdinand insisted. "We'll win the war."

Ferdinand believed in victory, but when battles began to spill into French villages, and cafés in Vienna began to close, he insisted we go to the country.

"We'll stay at Jungfer Brezan through the spring," he said. "Have the servants pack a summer wardrobe in case things drag on."

I must admit that I was relieved.

Richard Ernst, who'd written a monograph about our porcelain collection, was a curator at the Belvedere and a good friend. With his help, I had all of my Klimt paintings sent to the museum for safekeeping.

It was November and I was sorry to say good-bye to my friends and see the house shuttered, but I did my best not to complain. The drive northeast took us through farmlands and country villages that had been emptied by the war. When we stopped for lunch not far from the Czech town where Ferdinand had been born, the village was deathly quiet. The cobbled streets hadn't been swept in a long time. Pails of garbage had been tipped over, and black crows pecked at the trash.

Our nephews had been spared the draft, but in the countryside the poor boys were all gone.

"Look around, Ferry," I whispered as a thin waitress showed us to our seats in a small café. "There are no young men in the village—no men at all."

The war went well for the empire in the beginning, and the news that reached us in the comfort and safety of Jungfer Brezan was always of victory. We weren't ignorant, but we were in good cheer as the snow piled up and our thick walls kept out wind and cold.

Ferdinand brought food to his factory workers, and continued production until the last beets had been processed and run through the machines. When the war began to turn and profits tumbled, he refused to fire any of the men. He paid them at a loss from his own accounts, knowing that their sons would be called to the battlefields and soon even the old men would be ordered to fight for the empire.

My niece Maria Viktoria was born in 1916, in the depths of the war. Thedy was past forty, and too old for another child, yet she delivered a beautiful, healthy girl—a gift in the midst of darkness. I knew Maria was surely the last child, just as I had been the youngest in my own raucous household. I couldn't help but feel Thedy and the new infant would need me, and that I could be of use to them.

"Come to Jungfer Brezan," I said when I was finally able to reach my sister on the telephone. I knew she was tired; she'd been tired ten years ago. I was younger, and had no caretaking responsibilities of my own.

"I wish I could come," Thedy said. "I wish you were here, Adele."

I would have gone to Vienna if it were possible, but snow blocked the roads, petrol was in short supply, and it was unreasonable to travel unnecessarily. I had to be satisfied with the post.

I hungered after news of the child, and when it came, it cheered me a great deal. I visited my bookseller in Prague, and began a library for my niece. Picture books and a crisp new copy of Hans Christian Andersen's folktales made me feel hopeful even when the Battle of Verdun was raging in France and the world was on the brink of destruction.

Three years into the war, when the butler brought a telegram to our afternoon dinner table, I was terrified that something had happened to baby Maria. Ferdinand read silently, while I chewed on my fingernail.

"Klimt had a stroke," he said, putting the cable down on the table. "I'm sorry, Adele. He's in Loew Sanatorium. They don't expect a recovery."

"It's Klimt," I said. "Not Maria."

I was almost relieved. Then I burst into tears.

By then we all knew the disease that turned men inside out with pustules and tumors, taking their vision, their sanity, and their ability to speak or move. I didn't want to see my dear Klimt in the agony of advanced syphilis; I was shamefully thankful that the snow-covered roads kept me from going home to Vienna.

In January Berta telephoned at dawn.

"Our friend is gone," she said. She was weeping, but for me the grief had the opposite effect: my throat dried and closed up, my hands went numb, and I could barely say a word. All the days and hours we'd spent together had seemed far in the past, but when he died they all came rushing back—his hand on my face, his tongue on my belly, the paint on his fingertips and the fresh blue air that had once seemed to follow him everywhere.

Everything was different after that. Klimt had belonged to life before the war, and after he died, the world was uglier and sadder. I'd taken to sleeping long and hard in the country under the dark sky, and under that same dark sky I mourned. I filled half a dozen journals with things I'd never dared to write before—all the things Klimt and I had done and said together. It was my way of grieving.

By the time I'd finished, Klimt had been gone for almost ten months, and the war was almost over.

When the emperor surrendered in disgrace, the Treaty of Versailles dissolved the thousand-year empire with a single stroke of the pen, giving birth to the fragile new nations of Austria, Czechoslovakia, Yugoslavia, Poland, Romania, and Hungary.

I burned the journals in the fire, poking at the pages until they'd all turned to ash.

ॐ

In Vienna, the Ringstrasse was littered with sad veterans who limped along with missing limbs or tapped at the sidewalk with blind men's canes. Amputees and the wounded filled every street corner, shaking their cups at me. Once I would have passed them without hesitating, but I found myself opening my change purse and dropping silver coins into their upturned palms.

A few months after the end of the war, we moved into our new home at 18 Elisabethstrasse, and I had our Klimt collection returned from the museum. It was like a gathering of old friends, as if Klimt had left the best part of himself for me, alone.

I hung *Beech Forest II, Apple Tree,* and the *Schloss Kammer* with my portrait in my private rooms, ordered new green velvet chairs from the Wiener Werkstätte, and had Koloman Moser design new decorative paper for my walls. I framed Klimt's photograph and put it on a table beside my stained glass lamp.

When it came time to declare our new nationalities, Thedy and I chose Austrian—as did our mother—while Ferdinand and his brother chose Czech. We all agreed that having passports for both new nations ensured our options for the future.

"If there's ever a question of bloodlines, our children can claim whatever is safer and more prosperous," Thedy said. She was holding little Maria on her lap. The girl was dressed in pink frills, her hair in a big ribbon. We toasted the future, and I vowed to begin Maria's education that very day. Her brothers were boisterous; her beautiful sister was already distracted by the trivialities of ornament and society. I did not want Maria's future left to fate or chance.

"Let's hope the peace lasts," I said.

"Don't be a pessimist," Thedy said. "There's no reason to think anything but the best is ahead for us."

Thedy was wrong.

I'd barely finished putting the final touches on my new library when the Spanish influenza swept through Austria and across the globe. Young and old died, rich and poor. At night I lay alone in bed and heard the collective weeping, coughing, and wheezing of Vienna, the wail of ambulances going slowly through the evening and the death rattle of the trucks gathering bodies for the morgue.

I developed a troubling cough that winter that wouldn't settle, and rang for Dr. Tandler, who came before dawn on a white-cold January morning.

"This is the only time I could make for you," he said. "I barely have time to sleep."

He'd lost weight during the war, and his hair had gone completely gray. He gave me camphor for my chest and an expectorant for the cough, and told me to stay inside.

"There's sickness and desperation everywhere," he said as he closed up his black bag. He refused to give me a bill for his services. "Donate money to the poor instead, Adele. There are thousands of young mothers who've lost their husbands and have no money for food or heat."

With half of Austria sick or dying, businesses and restaurants closed their doors again. Thedy refused to leave the house with her children, and I didn't blame her one bit. Caution was her rule. When my cough was gone I promised to go directly from my bath to her home, and to wear a face mask in the streets, and my sister agreed to let me visit.

I went for Maria. I believe Thedy knew that it was the little girl who enchanted me and troubled me; the little girl of whom I dreamt at night. My sister could teach her daughter how to run a perfect household and perform brilliantly as wife, mother, and hostess. But it was I who could teach Maria about literature, books, and a life of the mind. It was I who could tell her about truth, beauty, and tragedy, and how one depended upon another just as night depended on day.

I'd paid little attention to Maria's older sister when Louise was young, but it was not too late for Maria. I would be her Karl, and I would be alert to the older children drowning out her voice at the dinner table, as my brothers' had nearly drowned out mine.

On Maria's fourth birthday I wrapped a new wooden chess set, a harmonica, and a fat picture book in brown paper, and tied them with colored ribbons. It was a Sunday afternoon, and the streets were swirling with snow.

"Look, Thedy, I wore the face mask," I said, yanking off the ridiculous thing as we stomped the snow off our boots. "Ferdinand did, too."

As soon as the maid took our coats, my sister began updating us on the gossip about friends and family.

"The Aschers' son was accepted at Zurich medical school," she rattled on. She was wearing her hair clasped in a broach, as I'd seen in the fashionable stores along the Graben. "And I'm sure you've heard what Arnold Schoenberg is doing at the music society."

I didn't care about any of that just then, I told her. I put the gifts on the coffee table, and hugged the little girl. Maria's hair was shining, and her shoes were clean and white. Gustav fetched his cello from the study, and my sister gave instructions for the luncheon to be served. My nephews and Louise came in and kissed me one by one.

"We'll have music this afternoon," Thedy said. "It will do us good."

Before the music began, I asked Maria to sit with me on the davenport. She unwrapped the illustrated book of Greek myths, and I turned to the story of Demeter and Persephone.

"Here's the daughter," I said, pointing to Demeter. "And here's her mother."

The drawing was reminiscent of a Klimt painting. The girl's swirling yellow hair was sprinkled with flowers and ribbons; her mother was serene and queenly in a white toga and leafy crown.

Maria spotted Hades poking his head up from the underworld, and stabbed at the page.

"He looks mean," she said. She pointed to Hades's three-headed dog. "And scary."

She pulled the book close to her face, and studied Persephone's terrified expression as Hades carried her below the earth. It struck me that the picture said the same thing about life that I'd seen in Klimt's mural on that first night in the Secession building: beauty and horror, side by side.

I turned the page. Persephone was standing in the Hall of Hades. Demeter was distraught. There was something important in the story that I wanted my niece to understand—not just about a young woman's vulnerability, but about the will to survive and endure.

Maria and I counted the six pomegranate seeds, and talked about the dark empty winter fields. We cheered when Persephone finally was freed. At the end, I put an arm around her, and whispered in her ear.

"You're a girl, but you can do anything," I said quietly. I wanted Maria to know there could exist in her a ferocious courage. I wanted her to know that inner strength might save her one day, just as it had saved me. "You can learn anything, you can become anything."

She looked up at me, and just as I thought I'd reached her, she burst into tears.

"What just happened?" Thedy took the child right off my lap.

"I have no idea," I said, but I did know, and I resolved to be even more attentive to Maria after that. I did not wish to frighten her, but she had to understand what was within her reach.

MARIA
1940

Fritz and I left our Liverpool home at daybreak, each carrying a single suitcase. I shut the door behind me without looking back, and whispered a little prayer for safe passage and happiness in America. The only thing I would miss about our flat was the phonograph and records that had filled our evenings.

"We'll get a brand-new phonograph when we get there," Fritz said, tucking a hand under my chin.

I wore a brown cloth coat, and a plain brown hat. At the docks, there were smartly dressed women who looked as though they'd never suffered during the war, and a marching band playing as we climbed up the long gangplank.

Just before I stepped onto the S.S. *Britannic*, it felt as if I were letting go of the land beneath my feet. My vision clouded, and I stumbled.

"Are you all right?" Fritz caught my arm. The next thing I knew, I was sitting in a wheelchair and being rolled up to the ocean liner.

At the top of the gangplank, two men in white helped me to my feet. I gently unwound my arms from theirs, determined to stand on my own. I thought of all the stories that had given me strength as a girl, and set my feet one in front of the other as Fritz wrapped his arm around my waist and guided me.

"You're strong, Maria," he said, and, "That's my Duckling, you're so brave," until we reached our cabin and I collapsed on the bed.

From that first moment on the ship I was in a new world. Many of our fellow passengers were Americans returning home. We drank Coca-Cola for the first time, and ate baked macaroni and cheese with sliced bread and butter. Some of the people on board were on holiday, so they dressed in gowns for dinner and danced into the evening.

The ship's crew did its best to keep things merry on board, but one didn't need to walk into too many corners to hear talk of the war and its horrors: the thousands who couldn't get travel visas, the dogs the Germans used to sniff out Jews, the trains that went east and came back empty. Women in black hats and red lipstick appeared at dinner with cruel-looking men, and I was reminded of the German women I'd seen tromping through Berlin with hard determination.

"Where do those women come from?" I asked Fritz. "Where did they learn to dress that way, and look so cold?"

"At the cabarets and on the streets," he said. "Those aren't women with families, darling. Those are women who've attached themselves to bad men to escape something worse."

Something worse? Something worse than Landau? I watched them parade through the ship with their dark mouths and sharp eyes and when I passed them on deck, I shielded my belly with both hands.

At the end of our first week at sea a storm came, and the roiling ocean pounded above and below us. The doctor's medicine worked for the first half hour, but after that there was no respite. Fritz called the ship doctor, who said I had to keep down whatever fluids I could manage.

"I'm sorry," the doctor said. "There's nothing I can do."

I fell into a dark tunnel then, aching for my father as if he'd just died, wailing some long-forgotten prayers that I didn't recall ever learning. The storm was unforgiving, and as it pounded against the portals I saw Landau reaching for me. I smelled Chanel No. 5 and imagined I was one of the dead.

When Fritz came at dawn with lipstick smudged on his collar, I put a finger to it and fought back tears.

"An old Polish lady insisted on dancing with me, Duck," he said. "She was from Warsaw, with a big saggy bust and too much lipstick. I didn't have the heart to turn her down."

The lipstick was dark red, from a hard mouth.

"I've been sick all night," I choked out. "How could you?"

"It's hard for me, too, Maria," he said, looking away.

"You have to stop this, Fritz," I said. I was tempted to tell him what had happened. I was tempted to tell him what I'd done for him. I tried to drag myself from the edge of the violent sea, but there was nothing to resist it. The world was at war, and everything was black.

*F*orty-three-year-old Gustav Ucicky leads the deliverymen into his cherrywood-lined parlor overlooking Vienna's Volksgarten. His swastika pin shines on his lapel, and his new, young wife is waiting for him in the bedroom in her pink peignoir.

"Be careful with that one," Ucicky says to the men.

They unwrap the painting and wait while Ucicky inspects the frame, the golden castle, and the blue waters of Lake Attersee. When he's satisfied that the painting is authentic and undamaged, he signs the delivery papers and tips the men.

Feeling ebullient, he telephones the Nazi attorney who made the deal for him.

"I knew you would be resourceful," Ucicky says.

"I traded Klimt's Lady in Gold for your painting," Ferdinand Bloch-Bauer's lawyer says. "You can see it now in the Belvedere."

"I don't have to go to a museum to see my father's art anymore," Ucicky says. "I have five of his best pieces right here in my home."

ADELE

1921

The porch at Jungfer Brezan was cool and shady in the July afternoon, and I pushed the glider back and forth in the breeze. Maria was snuggled against me with an alphabet primer, and we were reading a new word for every letter. The little girl's toes were bare, and she smelled of the bath. When she got to the letter *Z*, she jumped up and started to buzz around the room like a little bug, flapping her hands for wings and running in a circle that made me dizzy.

Thedy came in from the garden wearing a summer dress and an old straw hat, and put out a hand as if to catch her little bumblebee in a net.

"There's a groundskeeper for that," I said when I saw the dirt smeared on my sister's apron.

"But I love the flower garden," she said, grinning. "I enjoy digging in the dirt."

"Only because you don't have to," I said.

She was holding a big bunch of purple hydrangea that matched her little girl's dress. Outside, I could hear the older boys calling to one another as they got ready to drive to a beer garden in Prague. Louise was away at a conservatory, studying dance and the flute.

"I want to go with the boys," Maria said, popping out her bottom lip.

"No you don't," Thedy said. "You want to stay here with Mama and Aunt Adele."

"Maybe she wants to go swimming," I said. "Do you want to go swimming, Maria?"

"She wants to go wherever the boys go," Thedy said. "Just like you always did."

Maria ran to the doorway and peered out into the bright day. I saw my young self in the way she held herself up as straight as she could, on her tiptoes.

"I want to be big," Maria said.

"I'll take her down to the lake." I pushed myself out of the swing, and felt a pain shoot through my hips. I was almost forty years old, and sometimes felt as stiff as an old woman. "I'll go with the nursemaid if you don't want to go."

Thedy put the flowers down on the wooden table, and called for Maria's nurse.

"In this heat, she still needs an afternoon nap," Thedy said. "But as soon as she's older, you can take her on all the outings that you like."

♒

Two years later, Maria and I stepped out of the car at the foot of the Belvedere gardens on a spring morning. My niece was wearing a red-and-white dress, and her long braid was tied with a polka dot ribbon. The formal gardens stretched behind us and pebbles crunched underfoot. I couldn't decide if I was impressed by the way Maria carried herself so carefully in her new brown shoes, or if I wished that she had the spunk and energy of the boys who were kicking fat new footballs ahead of exasperated nannies.

"Will there be pictures of ladies in beautiful dresses?" Maria asked, tipping her face to me. She was missing two front teeth, and her tongue caught and lisped on all those sibilant sounds. "I love to draw ladies in pretty dresses."

"There will be many women in beautiful dresses," I said as we stepped up into the castle galleries. "But art doesn't have to be about ladies in pretty dresses, you know."

I saw her puzzle over this.

"I know," she said, her face brightening. "There are pretty paintings of trees and gardens, too. Like the trees you have in your parlor," she said. "But you know I like your portrait best, don't you, Aunt Adele?"

"Art doesn't need to be pretty," I said. "Sometimes art can be about things that are scary or even—"

She tugged on my hand.

"Can we get ice cream and go to the zoo later?" she asked.

"That might be enjoyable," I said. "But first we're going to the museum. Don't you want to learn about art? It means everything to me," I added. "Art is a tonic for even the saddest days."

"Are you sad?" Maria asked, cocking her head.

"No," I said. "But everyone is sad sometimes, and art is one of the best remedies for a bout of melancholy. Art speaks to you, and you don't have to say anything in reply."

Inside the Belvedere we went right upstairs to Van Gogh's *Plain Near Auvers,* where I was sure the bright colors would appeal to her: green grass waving in the wind, clouds running across a deep blue sky, and a bright orange patch of wheat in the distance.

"What do you think of this one?" I asked.

"I like the green grass," Maria said carefully, looking to me for approval. "But why are the clouds green, too?"

Her question was simple, and I wanted my answer to be just as clear.

"Because that's what the artist saw when he looked across the fields," I said. "Have you ever looked at lake water and seen the trees and all the clouds reflected there?"

She nodded, and her face brightened at a memory. "I remember once it looked like our rowboat was floating in the sky," she said.

"That's exactly right." I took her hand. "You know there's no rowboat in the sky and no clouds in the lake, but that's what you remember when you saw it, and so that might be what you would paint if you were an artist."

"When the painter made your portrait, he saw you in a dress made of gold?" she asked.

"Maybe," I said. "Maybe that's what he saw."

She looked at me as if she'd never quite seen me before.

"I think he loved you, and that's why he made you look like a queen," she said.

"No, sweetie," I said, startled at the ache in my throat. "He made me look like a queen because that's what Uncle Ferry told him to do."

After we'd looked at a few more paintings I buttoned up her coat, climbed back into the car, and took her to the Schönbrunn Zoo. We found the ice cream stand, and had two big scoops of vanilla piled onto a sugar cone.

It was late afternoon. Across the graveled courtyard, the zookeeper was throwing raw meat into the lions' cage while the tigers and panthers paced and roared for their food. I couldn't help but think of Rilke's panther, who'd seen no world beyond his iron bars.

I pointed to a lone tigress clawing at the bottom of her cage. The beautiful, trapped animal made me sick with regret.

"She wants her freedom," I said.

"Like Rapunzel," Maria said. "And the girl in the story, who eats the seeds."

"Yes," I said, pleased that she remembered. "Like Persephone."

"Her mother saves her," Maria said. She looked up at me with wide eyes. "Do you think someone will save the tiger, too?"

"No," I said. I didn't believe in lying to children. "No one is going to set this animal free."

"Maybe we can," she said. "You and Uncle Ferdinand know all the important people. Can you set her free?"

Maria was holding her melting ice cream cone and peering at the tiger with an entirely different look on her face than she'd had before. I thought perhaps I'd been too frank with her, and cursed myself silently.

"I would, if I could," I said. I took her sticky hand in mine, and pulled her gently away from the cage. "You have to be fierce, Maria," I said, leaning down and looking into her bright face. "Don't let anyone put you in a cage, Maria. Not ever. Because once you're in a cage, it's very, very hard to get out."

A few days later, I thought of Maria's sunny, determined face as my driver pulled up to the address Julius Tandler had given me. We were in the Meidling District, where the buildings were stark and close together and the sidewalks were cracked and uneven. When I opened the car door, I could smell rotting garbage in the alleyways.

Inside the Hospital for Unwed Mothers, the hallways were dark and there was a strong smell of antiseptic. I was relieved when Tandler met me near the front desk.

"I'm so glad you've come," he said, taking my hands in his. The hospital was new, and he was struggling to raise funding. The walls were bare, but the floors were scrubbed and there was a hushed air about the place. We walked through a narrow corridor without windows, and my eyes slowly adjusted to the dark.

"Right now we've got sixteen women in residence," he said. "In the morning, the girls take classes on childcare and we make sure they get plenty of exercise and good food. We have nurses on staff, but we always need volunteers to help with the infants."

"Not I," I said, forcing a laugh.

"Of course not," Tandler said. "You're important because you have people's attention. They respect you. You can tell them about the work we're doing, and help us raise money."

"Really, Julius," I said. "That's almost too direct."

"Look around," he said. "We need bedding and medicine. Last week we lost two newborns. I don't have time to be politic, I'll leave that to you."

A pretty redhead with a heavy belly smiled meekly at the doctor as we passed. The slope of her shoulders and her smooth skin reminded me of the girls I'd seen in Klimt's studio a long time ago.

"Imagine what it would mean to these girls to have a real library," Tandler said. We'd reached the end of the hallway and came to a bright room full of windows. There was a simple wooden table and chairs, and a shelf full of dog-eared books. "Not just books on health but literature, poetry—things that can open their minds. You'd be giving them such a gift."

We were close to the nursery; I could hear children mewling and crying, and mothers trying to soothe them. I thought about all the models I'd seen at Klimt's studios, and the fact that I had never once worried over their fates.

"We can raise money for medicine and also for books," I said. "I think that's a wonderful idea."

⁓᷍

I lit the candles in my parlor moments before the guests were due to arrive. It was the beginning of the salon season, and I'd spent the day preparing an introduction and champagne toast for Karl Renner, who would be my guest of honor.

"Champagne for Karl?" Ferdinand asked when he came into the parlor.

"Socialists are happy to drink champagne with the rest of Vienna," I said, knowing he was only teasing. "And I'm sure you'll be very hospitable to my friend when he gets here."

"I will be," Ferdinand said. "But only because it will please you."

"That's good enough reason for me," I said.

I'd asked Berta to come early, and after she'd been poured a glass of wine, I practiced my introduction for her.

"I'm proud to welcome a modern leader whose wisdom has brought our country into a kinder and more prosperous era." I tried to speak spontaneously rather than to read from my notes. "We once led the world in modern art, and now we will lead Europe in social and political causes as well."

"It's perfect," Berta said. "You know your material inside out."

Just then the bell rang, and the butler showed in Renner, Tandler, and the Schwartzenbergs—who were already tipsy and gay enough to turn the whole evening into a party rather than the serious event I'd imagined.

Two dozen friends followed, including the Lederers and the Pulitzers, the Saltzer sisters, and a few of Ferdinand's banking friends' wives. The wealthy bourgeois women expected another spirited evening of conversation, but by the time Tandler finished describing the terrible conditions in Vienna's orphanages, they'd agreed to donate more money than Serena and I combined.

When Renner put on his top hat and set out for home at the end of the evening, we had secured nearly forty thousand crowns for a new X-ray machine, a library for Tandler's hospital, and funding to help the poor.

"They gave more than I hoped," I said after the door had closed for the last time. "Enough to keep the hospital for unwed mothers in operation for some time."

I fell into a divan by the fireplace. Ferdinand sat beside me, and took my feet into his lap. He was almost sixty years old, but he was still robust, and at the peak of his financial powers.

"The rest can go for other social programs—for a children's health clinic that we're building—Ferry, you don't object to these things, do you?"

He kneaded the arches of my feet.

"I don't object, of course I don't," he said. "You have your causes and I have mine."

"Will you promise to keep my commitments, even if something happens to me?" I asked.

"You'll outlive me by ten years or more," he said as he pressed my feet together and squeezed the toes gently. "But if you're worried about it, you can write your own will, and I promise you I'll honor it."

MARIA
1942

I traded everything for a safe home in the California sun. I did it
because I had no choice. I learned to cook bacon, eggs, and sliced
white bread toast for breakfast. I counted out trolley fare and got
on and off the tall black steps, tugging my baby stroller with one hand
and holding on to my toddler with the other.

At least in California there were plenty of others like me, and when
I spoke with my Viennese accent, the Americans knew why I was there.

"Refugee?" they asked when I signed my little ones up for a free
milk program.

"I'm an Austrian Jew," I said, straightening proudly. "And I'm very
grateful to be in America."

Bernhard and his family lived north of Los Angeles, and we moved
into a bungalow ranch in Cheviot Hills. I hung red-and-white-checkered
curtains in my kitchen windows, and cooked apricot tortes and apple
strudels that made the house smell like my childhood home. Fritz found
a good-paying job selling airplane machinery for Lockheed, and for a
very long time he came home every night. We had our two little boys
one after the other, and as soon as they could walk they rushed out to
meet their father when his car pulled into the smooth new driveway.

"Papa, play baseball with us," they called, and Fritz learned to throw
a baseball so that he could teach our sons.

But the war wasn't over, and not everyone was sympathetic or
friendly. More than once I saw people mouth the word "Jews," when I

walked the children to the park, and there was a regular Sunday radio hour about Jews, "the Jesus-killers." Still, I felt safe in my little white house surrounded by refugees from home. Arnold Schoenberg—the composer who'd been a friend of my parents'—lived nearby with his second wife and family. Alma Mahler and her third husband made a stir when they came to Los Angeles and bought a house like ours, and then Eric Zeisl, who wrote music for Hollywood movies, moved just three blocks away from us with his wife, Trudy.

Trudy became one of my closest friends, and when she rang me on the telephone, it always cheered me.

"Let's go to the park," she'd say on bright days, and, "let's take the children to the cinema," she'd say on rainy days.

When the phone rang one fine spring morning after a week of rain, I was preparing a picnic lunch for our outing to the park.

"Good morning, darling, I'm making the chicken salad," I said when I answered.

"A collect call for Maria Altmann," the operator said in Swiss-German. "From Ferdinand Bloch-Bauer."

"Uncle Ferdinand?" I whispered. It was seven in the morning. My little boys were just waking. I tried to do the calculations in my head: Was it yesterday in Switzerland? Was it tomorrow?

"Maria, they've taken my Adele," my uncle said. The line went scratchy. There was the sound of an airplane overhead and I heard my uncle's breath growing raspy. "The lawyer lied . . . only thing he sent is my Kokoschka."

"Who?" I asked. "Who's taken the portrait?"

"The Nazis," he said. "Of course, the Nazis."

I wanted to help my uncle. It seemed something that my aunt would have done if she were alive. But I'd been caught in a cage with no way out but America. And I'd run without looking back.

"I want my Adele," Uncle Ferdinand said. It sounded like he was weeping.

Fritz appeared beside me in his blue pajamas, and I held out the receiver so that he could hear my uncle, too.

"Uncle Ferdinand, you should come to California," Fritz said loudly.

"I'm sick," my uncle said. "I'm losing my vision. You're young and strong. I need you to help me, Maria."

I knew that I should care very much about my aunt's painting, but it was my uncle's heartbreak that hurt me more. It was Uncle Ferdinand, once so brave and strong, who haunted me long after we'd disconnected the line.

*O*n opening night of the 1943 Gustav Klimt retrospective exhibition, scores of proud Nazi officials crowd under Koloman Moser's stained glass roundel in the lobby of the newly christened Friedrichstrasse Exhibition Hall and raise full glasses toward the portrait of Adele.

"To Gustav Klimt," Vienna's new governor says. "One of our greatest painters."

"To Klimt," the crowd says in unison. The men's silver and gold medals shine under the lights, the women's jewels glitter. "Heil Hitler."

A string quartet plays Beethoven, waiters circulate with caviar on water crackers, bottles of French Taittinger are popped open, and pungent cigar and cigarette smoke clouds the air. Women blot bright red lips on linen cocktail napkins. The men who emptied 18 Elisabethstrasse gather around the city's leaders.

"I remember when the Secession gallery was new and bold," a woman says to her husband, but he hushes her with a warning, saying, "This is the Friedrichstrasse Hall now."

Golden Adele, bare-breasted Judith, smiling Fritza Riedler, and Margaret Wittgenstein draped in angelic white, like sisters at a ball, waiting to dance.

The label beneath Adele's portrait says only "Lady in Gold—Gustav Klimt." No one knows anything about the Bloch-Bauers or the lady in gold; no one asks her name.

ADELE

1923

By law, everything I had belonged to Ferdinand. But he encouraged me to write a will, and so I did.

I was only forty-two years old, and did not make a fuss of it by involving our attorney and so on. I sat at my desk, picked a smooth sheet of linen paper, dipped my quill in the ink, and began. I asked for my jewels to be divided among the nieces and nephews, a portion of my estate to be donated to the children's hospital, and the remaining assets to be dispensed to Ferdinand.

My two portraits and four landscapes by Gustav Klimt, I kindly request my husband bequeath to the Belvedere National Gallery after his death, I wrote. Because I could not rightfully and legally bequeath what I did not own, I considered those words carefully and made my wishes as clear as possible. I wanted what I was creating with my own courage and vision to be remembered and honored.

When I finished the will, I signed, dated, and sealed it, sent a copy to our attorney on Schwindgasse, and did not think of it again. I was busier than ever with the business of social reform, reading about the Palestinian territory, and shaping the expansion of the Belvedere's modern collection. Every Saturday, Julius Tandler, Karl Renner, Berta, Alma, and the others came to Elisabethstrasse to discuss social issues. We talked about Jerusalem, the importance of bringing books and art to everyone (even the poor, especially the poor), and the vast public health program that Renner and Tandler were advancing through the city's health council.

So I was surprised and disappointed when my friend Tandler, who had asked for my support in building the library for unwed mothers, objected to some of the books I sent to fill the shelves.

"They're working women—the city's poorest prostitutes and rag-pickers," Julius said when I mentioned a crate of philosophy books. "They do not need Goethe."

"But they do—"

"No. We need the shtetl Jews and poor barmaids to avoid child-bearing."

He was angry, but so was I. He'd begun using the health system to sterilize the city's poorest women, and while I might once have encouraged a program that prevented the lowest people from breeding, I could not condone anything that would deny a woman the joys of mother-hood, or make her suffer as I had. I had truly begun to understand what my brother had told me: that beneath the skin, we are all the same.

"You showed me how to be humane in regard to all women, and now you want me to endorse something with which I cannot agree," I said.

We argued, and I accused him of elitism.

"And *you* are a member of the elite," he said, eyes blazing. "Re-forming a society requires resources—and it requires that we not waste them on women and children who cannot carry the best aspects of the Viennese spirit forward."

It was Renner and Alma who stopped our battle.

"Let them read whatever they want, Julius," said Karl. "We have far more pressing political concerns."

It was true. I went myself to be sure the books were shelved in the li-brary we had built, and then turned my attention to the Russian exper-iment and the Palestinian territory. There was talk of a Jewish national home in Palestine, just as dear Theodore Herzl had once proposed, and we were all excited when Alma and her new husband announced plans to travel to Jerusalem.

The money my friends and I raised went to Renner's Red Vienna programs, and a good portion of my time that year was spent helping the new Belvedere director bring hundreds of modern Austrian paintings and sculptures to the collection.

Little Maria went to school, and proved that she was very bright. Even if she was a bit of a coquette she was also robust, and liked the outdoors. I had missed out on hearty excursions as a child because of Mother and Father's ideas about female decorum, and so I encouraged it as much as possible as Maria grew. I did not want her to grow weak and plagued with headaches, as I was.

"You remember how I longed to play like our brothers did," I said to Thedy. "I couldn't do it then, but your daughter has every opportunity."

◎◎

Ferdinand and I were set to take Maria ice-skating at Stadtpark on a cold morning in January 1925 when I woke with a blinding headache. The clouds were low, and the sky was promising snow.

"Please bring me calcium lactate and sodium bicarbonate," I asked the maid. "And pull the curtains shut."

I'd had matching fur muffs made for Maria and myself, and ordered her a new pair of white leather skates from Wurzl's. They were decorated with red pompoms and wrapped in a white box with a bow. The gifts were waiting on my mantel, above the roaring fire.

"You give them to her, please," I said to Ferdinand when he came up. "If I feel better, I'll meet you later."

After he'd gone, I drank a sleeping tonic, wrapped a cloth over my eyes, and burrowed under the blankets as the snow began to fall.

When Alma and her husband came to collect some of my books about Palestine and Jerusalem, I let Alma pick them off my shelves, and then burrowed back to sleep.

Many hours later, I heard the door pop open downstairs as Ferdinand and Maria came in from the cold. I felt feverish: my hands clammy, my chest damp and tight.

At first I was frightened, but then fear seemed to float beneath me like a sea of grass, as if my body was in the clouds but my mind was rising higher still; as if I were rising up out of the bed and looking down over my blue curtains and the place where I was resting.

I saw my portrait on the wall, the gold-rimmed porcelain tea set beside the chair where I'd sat up late the night before, the open book of Baudelaire poems and my new pack of Gauloises tossed beside the heavy ashtray.

It was strange, I thought, that I could see everything as if in a dream when I was wide awake and looking across my tangle of sheets and the splayed pillows and my loose hair spreading across them like a dark stain.

Then I saw Ferdinand in his office turning the pages of an enormous accounting book, I saw Schiller Park bathed in early-morning light and then I was becoming the light, I was in the courtyard outside the art history museum, I was looking down on St. Stephen's Square and the Danube River, and out of the corner of my eye were the thick woods that marked the edge of my beloved Jungfer Brezan, and far, far below was the cemetery where my name was being chiseled into a tombstone and Ferdinand—my Ferdinand—was crying as he ran his fingers over the letters in cold marble, ADELE BLOCH-BAUER 1881–1925, and a tiny piece of my soul—the soul I'd never believed in, the *ka* Klimt had painted—was looking out from the portrait and through the window of 18 Elisabethstrasse, where I could see the circle of time unfolding and folding upon itself, winding my story through Maria's until it stopped— it went black—and I could see no more.

MARIA
1945

The white airmail envelope was postmarked two days before my
uncle's death.

    I recognized the shaky handwriting, the Hotel du Lac statio-
nery, and the Swiss stamp. The war was over and Uncle Ferdinand was
gone, but as I read his words I could almost feel him in the room with
me, squeezing my hand.

> *My Dear Maria, I have little time left so I will be brief.*
> *Your aunt expected more of herself than of anyone else.*
> *For this I believe I owe her one last bequest.*
> *Save the portrait. Fight for her dignity. It will be up to*
> *you and to your brothers after I am gone.*

    I held the letter to my face and tried to inhale the familiar scent of
cigars and aftershave, but all I could smell was the dark distance of the
grave.

The ghosts were always with me after that. They were beseeching, they
were proud, they were whispering, they were angry. Sometimes I forgot
about them, but they didn't forget me.

    They were watching when Fritz and I became American citizens and
hung our red, white, and blue flag on our front lawn.

They were there when my brother called to tell me that we would never be able to bring Adele's portrait to America.

"Our lawyer in Vienna tells us the Austrians have a copy of Aunt Adele's will," Robert said. "He says that she left the portrait to the Belvedere."

Robert put my mother on the phone.

"Is it true, Mama?" I asked.

"I think it is true." Her voice was frail. "I remember my sister saying that she wanted her portrait to hang with the others at the Belvedere. She wanted the paintings to be shared with the Viennese."

I was thirty years old: younger than my aunt had been when I was born. I could remember her pinning up her hair and sitting in her parlor, talking about books.

"To be Viennese is the most important thing in the world," she'd said. I had not asked her what she'd meant then, and I could not ask her now.

All I knew was what my brothers told me: the Austrians were offering our family a few of my uncle's old sentimental landscapes and a dozen pieces of his porcelain. In exchange, we had to sign an agreement that acknowledged we had no claim to the Klimts.

"Uncle Ferdinand wanted something different," I said again to my brother. I could not bear to take the letter from the drawer and reread it, but I knew very well what he'd asked of me. "He told me to fight for Aunt Adele's dignity."

"No one is winning these cases in Austria now," Robert said. "If we don't sign, we'll never have another chance to get even these lesser paintings back for our family."

"The watercolors meant nothing to Uncle Ferdinand," I said.

"We can sell them," Robert said. "Every one of us can use that money now."

I fretted over this all night, pacing in our bedroom.

"My uncle wanted me to bring Aunt Adele's portrait to America," I said. There was a night-light in our hallway, and it cast my long shadow across the bed where Fritz lay.

"But your aunt wanted it in the museum in Vienna." Fritz sat up and reached for me. "And your brothers are clever negotiators."

Of course my brothers should have asked the Austrians send us each a copy of Aunt Adele's will. But they didn't. I took their word, and they took the word of our enemy.

My brothers sold the watercolor paintings and porcelain the Austrians sent, and we divided the proceeds among us. I bought a new sewing machine and signed up for a sewing class at the local citizens' center. Fritz bought a used violin, and began to play on Sunday mornings just as my father had once done. We used the largest sum to buy my mother a ticket from Vancouver to Los Angeles.

It had been nine years since I'd seen her, and I was stunned by how thin and slow she looked as the stewardess helped her down the airplane steps. She had aged, but when I ran to her on the tarmac, I was relieved to find her still graceful and elegant in her mink-trimmed coat.

"You look beautiful, Maria," she said, putting a hand on my face.

She touched me with her black glove and I remembered another glove, packed with colored jewels.

"You are beautiful," I replied.

I'd almost forgotten how good she made me feel.

"You once told me that you would teach the children German," Mama said.

She was wrapped in a blanket, and my little girl was resting against her shoulder. My boys were too full of wild energy for Mama, but my three-year-old daughter was entranced.

"Yes, I remember that day." I glanced at my little one. Her thumb was in her mouth and her eyes were closing. The boys were off in their rooms, and Fritz was in the back den, playing his violin and singing in German.

"They understand a little," I said. "They just don't speak it."

Mama nodded, and I could not wait any longer.

"Uncle Ferdinand wanted me to fight for the painting, you know," I said. "He loved Aunt Adele so much."

I saw my mother's eyes cloud, and remembered the rumors about the painter and my aunt.

"Mama?" I checked to be sure my little girl was sleeping. "What did Aunt Adele die of?"

I couldn't bring myself to say the word *syphilis,* but I knew that many people had succumbed to it, and there had been rumors about Gustav Klimt.

"Meningitis," my mother said without missing a beat. "She went to bed with a migraine and no one thought anything of it—she suffered terrible headaches all of her life."

"And?"

"And the next morning, she didn't wake." My mother teared up. "She was supposed to take you ice-skating."

I remembered that day; my uncle had given me a pair of new white ice skates with red pom-poms, and we'd flown together across the ice.

"They're all gone, now," my mother said. "I never imagined outliving them all."

I put my hand on hers. She wore a single gold wedding band. Her hands were wrinkled, but still nimble and strong.

"Please tell me honestly—do you think they were lovers?" I asked, half wanting her to tell the truth, and half wanting her to stay silent. "Aunt Adele and Klimt?"

My mother looked away.

"I'm grown up now, Mama. You can say it."

She nodded. She gathered the blanket around her more tightly, and talked about a long-ago spring day, grand white buildings in a green field, and Aunt Adele's golden portrait in a crowded room.

"I saw the way she and Klimt looked at one another that morning," she said. "I'd never seen her look at anyone that way."

"But Uncle Ferdinand loved her," I whispered. "He loved her so much, she was his dying wish."

My mother looked surprised.

"Ferdinand loved her, and she loved him," my mother said. "But every marriage has its secrets, Maria."

"Do you think Uncle Ferdinand knew?"

"I don't know," my mother said. "Adele was headstrong, but she was fragile. He held her the way he would have held a wild bird. And marriages were different then. Men had mistresses. I'm sure your uncle had more than one."

"And Papa?

My mother wiped an invisible spot off my little girl's chin. *I've only been with one man,* I wanted to say. But of course, that would have been a lie.

"Women are much stronger than men," she said quietly. "It may not always look like we're the strong ones, because our men would never let it seem that way. But every woman I know is stronger than her husband. Adele was. I certainly was. And so are you."

My mother was the one who'd put the needle and thread in my hands and shown me how to hide jewels and coins inside my gloves and brassiere. My mother was the one who'd told me to get out of Austria as soon as I could. My father had died, and she had gone on living.

"I'm not strong," I said. I was shocked to find a tear slipping down my cheek. "I didn't do what Uncle Ferdinand asked."

"You are very strong, Maria," my mother said. She wrapped her old hand around mine. Her grip was surprisingly firm. "Look how brave you've been—you're the bravest woman I know."

I wanted whatever it was that my mother saw in me to be alive and awake in my spirit. But when she died five years later, I still felt weak inside—haunted by the ghosts whispering to me, calling to me, asking me for something that I didn't know how to summon.

I made them be quiet, so that I could live my life.

MARIA
1965

I didn't see them at first.

Fritz and I stepped out of the yellow taxicab in front of the Guggenheim Museum, and joined a long line of people who'd come to see the first Klimt show in America. Bright banners fluttered from the lampposts, and everyone was dressed in colorful clothing.

"I've heard there are nudes in a back room," someone said.

"He was quite the ladies' man," said another.

Everything moved quickly, and soon Fritz and I were in a crowded elevator going up to the fifth floor. I'd bought the tickets, I'd made the arrangements with our travel agent, and I thought I'd prepared for the show.

But when the elevator doors opened, and I was looking directly into the face of a girl I'd known in Vienna, my feet stopped moving. The ghosts were there.

"What is it?" Fritz asked.

Mada Primavesi was wearing a white dress with flowers and ruffles, exactly as I remembered it. Her eyes were brown and steady, and the blue bow in her hair looked as fresh as it had been almost fifty years ago.

"My parents and her parents were friends," I whispered to Fritz. "I remember that painting hanging in their parlor."

The New York crowd moved around me, but instead of their voices, I heard music playing at brunch. Instead of their faces, I saw my mother and aunt moving gracefully in long loose dresses. I heard my aunt telling me that art wasn't always pretty. I saw my white shoes, a green sky, tigers at the Schönbrunn Zoo.

"Let's keep moving," Fritz said, putting a hand on my waist.

Klimt's apple and birch tree paintings were so real I could almost smell the fields in Grinzing right before the harvest. The patch of blue water in Lake Attersee was as cold as the day I'd swum there with my mother, and the colorful Unterach rooftops were the same ones I'd seen from Villa Paulick with my brothers.

I remembered things from home I had not seen or thought of since the war: white dishes and silver tableware; mink coats and the smell of pine trees at Jungfer Brezan; Uncle Ferry and my father laughing together; the church bells ringing when Hitler came; taxi horns blaring the day that we left. Even though I didn't want to, I remembered the way Landau's fingers had brushed my collarbone. I remembered how he'd hurt me.

"Have you seen what's in that room?" someone asked.

I came back to myself. I took Fritz's arm and went into a side gallery where nine pencil sketches were pinned onto a dark wall, each with a spotlight above it. They were nudes. A woman with her legs spread. A woman bent over the bed. A woman wrapped in tangled sheets.

"He had a lot of illegitimate children," a woman said in German. "I've heard ten or even thirteen."

"Klimt's son became a Nazi filmmaker," someone else said. "His name is Gustav Ucicky, I read about him during the war."

I thought I was going to faint.

"Let's go," Fritz said. He pulled me from the room, and led me to the elevator. As we made our way toward the exit, I was stunned to find a full-size reproduction of Adele's golden portrait in the gift shop.

"Buy it for me, please," I asked Fritz. "And a book of Klimt's paintings, too."

I carried that poster home and hung it over my sofa, where I studied my aunt's face as if for the first time. There were symbols in her dress, the letters of her name raised in gold. Her eyes seemed to look out at me from the picture, and her lips seemed ready to say something that she desperately wanted me to hear.

"Do you see it?" I asked Fritz. I was kneeling on our red sofa, studying the expression in her eyes.

He put a hand on my shoulder and leaned over me.

"See what?"

"She wants something from me."

"Maybe she does," he said. "But you'll never know what it is."

"I know what it is," I said. "I know what she wants from me."

That night I opened the book of Klimt's paintings, and turned the colorful pages one by one.

The women were beautiful and elegant, with flowers in their hair, and long white dresses. They were gazing out at me, each one calling across the years.

I read what critics had said about Adele's portrait when it was new. I read how it had traveled across the empire and become synonymous with fin de siècle Vienna and intellectual power. I read all night, and by the time dawn had broken, I could hear my aunt's voice telling me to be fierce and my mother's saying I was strong.

I turned one more page, and then another. I was tired, but the paintings were a tapestry of faces and places from the past, so brilliant and fresh they could have been made yesterday.

There was a tree of life made of gold and silver, pretty girls and bent old ladies, men holding women as if they could protect them from everything with love. There was a stranger in a purple hat, Serena Lederer's portrait, and there—I blinked; how could it be so?—there was my aunt's face looking back at me again above the caption, *Judith I*.

I knew the story of Judith: a Jewish widow, a general's tent. Seduction and murder.

"The original femme fatale," the book called Judith. "A true heroine."

Klimt's Judith—my aunt Adele—was surrounded by gold. She was holding Holofernes's decapitated head, and her face was full of pleasure and power. The book made no mention of a connection between Judith and the golden portrait, but it was clear to me that they were one and the same face. I was sure of it.

I was sure of the general's hand reaching for Judith.

I was sure of the painter's hands reaching for Adele.

I was sure of Landau's hand brushing my breasts in the dark.

"*Zieh dich aus,* Maria," Landau had said. "Strip for me."

And I'd done it. I'd done what he'd asked.

My memory was a castle of light and darkness, but that hotel room in Berlin was a locked cell. It was a room of unforgivable surrender where I could not remain for one more second.

But that night, I saw a way out. I saw that Judith had done the same thing I had done, and that she was a heroine.

"Good morning," Fritz said. Fresh from the shower, he was handsome in the crisp white shirt I had laundered and starched for him. "Did you have trouble sleeping?"

"I want to tell you something, Fritz," I said.

I'd spread the books around myself like guardians. There was the book from the Belvedere; there was a book by Nietzsche that my aunt had loved (although I can't imagine why). There was a book I'd found in our library about Judith and Holofernes, and there was the picture that had run in the magazine that had shamed me so long ago: French women with their shaved heads because they'd consorted with the Germans.

"Please sit down," I said.

"I've got a meeting up in Ventura this morning," he said, glancing at his watch. "I can't stay long."

"That's fine." I poured him some coffee, and took out the milk. "It won't take long."

He took a sip of his coffee, and I stood at the counter with my back to the sink.

"What are you so serious about this morning, Maria?"

"A long time ago, a man took something from me," I said. "Now I want it back."

"You mean the painting," he said.

"No, Fritz. I don't mean the painting."

I think he knew, even before I told him. Maybe it was the look on my face, or maybe part of him had always known.

Fritz was good in his soul, as I'd always known he was. And he loved me.

"I'm sorry," he said. He reached for my hand and pulled me to him, and then pressed his face against my belly. "I'm sorry he did that to you, Maria. I'm sorry you did that for me."

"I did it for us, and I'm not sorry, Fritz." I stroked the back of his head. "We have a good life together. But now I want something in return."

"What do you want?"

I waited until he looked up into my face.

"I want to be proud instead of ashamed. I want to feel brave instead of dirty. And Fritz, I want you to be faithful to me."

Ten months later I opened my dress shop in Brentwood, and in the many decades that followed I never saw another lipstick smudge on Fritz's collar or found a card from a stranger in his pockets.

Finally, I'd put what had happened in Austria and in Germany behind me.

MARIA

1998

If you're lucky, life teaches you to survive. The California sky is blue, you wake up, you make coffee, you fry eggs, and you don't look back. You don't think about the freckled maid who served smoked meats and pickled asparagus when you were a girl. You don't think about yesterday or what's been lost. Even when you hear the dead whispering, you go on.

I had my nice little dress shop in Brentwood for twenty years. The ladies who came were often immigrants, like me. We spoke in German or English and we ate miniature Linzer tortes, drank dark coffee, and thumbed through crisp new magazines. We talked about fashions and children, hairstyles, and the movie business.

Hemlines went up and I raised them. They went down and I lengthened them. I volunteered at the art museum, went to synagogue on high holy days, and wore lace to my children's weddings.

When the actor from California was still in the White House, my Fritz cried out for me in the middle of the night.

I sat up in bed, and saw his face was ghostly white.

He groped for my hand and said, "Thank you, Maria." Then he started to moan.

By the time we reached the hospital, his heart had stopped.

It had been a good heart, and we'd had many happy years together. I mourned and missed him, but I was lucky, too. Because I'd already learned to be strong on my own.

———

A Mahler symphony was playing on my kitchen radio when the phone call came from Austria. I was eighty-two years old by then—far too old for surprises.

"Maria? It's your cousin Eva."

"Is something wrong?" I asked. My cousin was frugal, and her phone calls were limited to news of sickness and death.

"Nothing's wrong. I'm reading the newspaper and there's a story about your uncle's painting—the portrait of your aunt," she said, pausing. "You know the one I mean?"

I had not gone one week of my life without thinking about that painting.

"This reporter says the portrait rightfully belongs to you," Eva said slowly.

"Of course it belongs to me," I said. "But we tried, and they refused to give it back."

"It looks like you can try again," Eva said.

"I'm old now," I said. My sister and brothers were gone, too. "And I'm alone."

"I don't think you're alone, Maria," my cousin said. "I think you have a righteous history on your side now."

When we hung up, I slid open a desk drawer in a corner of my TV room and found the yellowed envelope from the end of the Second World War. I took the letter into my kitchen, and put it on a clean place mat.

I opened the old envelope carefully. The glue had long given up its hold, and the Swiss stamp was beginning to crumble away. The Hotel du Lac stationery had gone from creamy to beige, and the black ink was fading. But the date was legible, and my uncle's words were still clear. *Save the portrait. Fight for her dignity.*

I turned my coffee cup round and round, replaying my cousin's words and writing the reporter's name, *Hubertus Czernin*, over and over until it looked like nothing but squiggled lines on the page.

"*Slowly one grasps the extent of the Nazi art thievery,*" Hubertus Czernin *writes in 1998. "Sixty years after the Anschluss, Austrian officials are slowly and tentatively beginning to open the book to this chapter in the nation's history. Stating a desire to correct 'immoral decisions' made after World War II, Minister of Education and Art Elisabeth Gehrer has formed a commission to shed light on Nazi art robbery."*

When Czernin's story runs in ArtNews *magazine, four Gustav Klimt paintings still hanging in the Belvedere Gallery are listed as gifts from Gustav Uicky, "in honor of his father."* The Adele Bloch-Bauer I, *also in the Belvedere, is listed as a "Gift from Ferdinand and Adele Bloch-Bauer," and is noted as entering the collection in 1936.*

These attributions and dates are false, of course. The painting was stolen from Ferdinand Bloch-Bauer, and his heirs are the rightful owners of Adele's golden portrait.

MARIA

1998

I t took me just a few hours to think of my dear friend Trudy's grandson. Randy Schoenberg was almost family—I'd watched him grow up, I'd been at his bar mitzvah and at his wedding, too. His paternal grandfather had been the composer Arnold Schoenberg, a friend of mine and of my parents'. When he was a teenager, Randy had gone with Trudy to Austria, and seen my aunt's portrait in person. He'd stood in my living room and looked at the poster with tears in his eyes, but he hadn't said a word. He'd seemed to understand that it was something I couldn't talk about.

Trudy, Eric, and Arnold were all gone, too. But I had Randy's telephone number, and I called him that afternoon.

"The portrait of Adele Bloch-Bauer," he said. "Of course I know the one you mean."

Randy came right from work that same evening. He was a passionate young attorney, not long out of law school. He had a freckled face, a thinning hairline, a pretty new wife, and two small children. I could see that he carried his grandparents' history heavily on his own shoulders, but the ghosts didn't seem to cow him; they seemed to cheer him on.

"My grandparents had to start over, like you," he said. He was sitting on my red couch, wolfing down a piece of pie with cream. "It would be an honor to help you get your uncle's painting back."

Austria's new law allowed for the heirs of dispossessed Jewish families to file new claims on their stolen property, Randy told me. There was better access to old files and hidden records, and it was clear that Austria would have to let some of the paintings go.

"Do you think I have a chance?" I asked.

"Yes, I do. And you're not going to be alone," he said. "Hitler stole hundreds of thousands of paintings and sculptures. All those families are going to be fighting for what's theirs, too."

I told him about the lawyer my brothers had hired after the war, and how little good it had done us.

"And we signed an agreement saying that we'd never make any more claims against Austria," I said.

"Those agreements are being challenged." Randy said. "That's what the new law is all about. Hundreds of people are filing claims in Austria right now."

Randy stood to stretch. It was almost nine thirty, and I knew he wanted to get home to his wife.

"Your aunt's portrait is the acknowledged masterpiece of her time," he said. "I'll file our first claims right away, this week. We'll let the Austrians know that you're coming to fight for what's yours."

MARIA

1999

I didn't want to go back and wake the sleeping ghosts. I didn't want to see the streets I'd fled, or the city that had betrayed us.

But Randy urged me to go to Vienna for the symposium on stolen art.

"It will be a very good thing, Maria, to show your face in Austria now," he said. And so, I did.

I scanned the faces at the airport and when someone called my name—"Maria, here!"—I spotted Eva's face right away, and hugged her so tightly that I frightened myself.

"Look at you," we said to each other, again and again. "Just look at you, alive and standing here in front of me."

A camera flashed, and someone called my name.

"Frau Altmann, please look here." I squinted in the flash, and another followed.

"Who are these people?" I asked Eva.

"You're famous," my cousin said. "Everyone knows you've come back to fight for the portrait. You're famous here, thanks to Hubertus."

A tall, thin man with round glasses and wild, wispy hair put a hand out to greet me and spoke in the courtly, formal German of my childhood.

"Welcome to Austria, Frau Altmann," Hubertus Czernin said. His glasses nearly eclipsed his huge brown eyes. His hands were warm. "I'll be covering your visit for the *Standard*. I hope we'll get to know one another very well."

He gave me directions to the Museum of Art History as if I'd never lived in Vienna, and handed me a folder with information about the program.

"This is my first return to Austria after more than sixty years," I told him.

"And how do you feel?" he asked.

I took a deep breath, as I'd learned to do in my yoga classes.

"After so many years of being helpless in the face of what was done to my family, I feel hopeful," I said.

The ghosts were awake that night. They whispered in my dreams; they were there in the morning; they rode with Eva and me in the taxicab to the museum; they sat on my shoulders as we turned onto the Ringstrasse and a maze of trolley cars crisscrossed the tracks.

On that beautiful spring day, Vienna was full of people on bicycles, people on foot, and tourists in groups following guides. The fountain in front of the Museum of Art History was dancing. I was relieved when there were no journalists waiting at the museum door; only Hubertus Czernin, stubbing out a cigarette and folding his narrow notebook open.

"Are you ready?" he asked

"As ready as I can be."

I was given a plastic name tag and ushered into a room with a small table and three rows of folding chairs in the museum basement. There was a coffee urn and pastries, and without thinking, I gobbled down two cream tortes.

Eva introduced me to the women who'd organized the symposium, and two ladies from the Austrian cultural ministry, who were courteous and welcoming. There were only about three dozen people in all; most of them Jews like Eva, who'd hidden in Austria during the occupation.

Before we began, Hubertus showed me a fat binder that he'd filled with an extensive index of items and provenance histories.

"This is everything that was in 18 Elisabethstrasse when the estate was seized," he said, turning the pages slowly. "The Nazis kept careful records. That's lucky for us."

Studying the thumbnail photographs, I recognized some of the things that had been in my uncle's home: the framed photograph of Klimt holding a cat, my uncle's cigar box, the porcelain pieces he'd treasured, the locked desk I'd tried to open the day the Nazis came.

"A lot of people are angry about the symposium," Czernin said quietly. "I don't want you to be surprised at that."

"Who is angry?" I asked, looking around. Everyone I saw seemed mild-mannered, even happy.

"Museums, art collectors, curators," he said. "The symposium was organized to help Holocaust survivors and their heirs successfully petition for the restitution of stolen property. No one wants to give up what they have in Austria."

"I'm not the kind of woman to make waves or put up a fuss," I said. I meant that genuinely. "I have letters from my uncle, begging for the portrait to be returned, and I have a copy of his final will from 1945. I think it's very clear that the portrait belongs to my family."

"You might find that people are angry, and that they'll make you angry, too," he insisted.

"I've always found that it's better to go after things with charm than with venom. But I am prepared," I said.

I was able to keep a low profile while legal experts spoke about the changing restitution laws and the paper maze that survivors and families had to navigate. People asked smart questions, and I soon realized that many of the others had never been wealthy. They'd been children during the war, and did not know how glorious Vienna had been, or the life that they had lost before they could even see it clearly. They'd inherited promises and lies instead of a *palais,* or old photographs instead of summers at their family's country estate. I was one of the oldest in the room, and my Bloch-Bauer name truly meant something to them. By the time it was my turn to speak, I knew that I had a special responsibility to speak for my uncle and my aunt, and to give everyone hope for what was ahead.

"We tried to be satisfied with the few things we were allowed to have after the war," I said. "But now I know that it all rightfully belongs to us. I will not give up until my aunt's portrait is returned to me."

I looked out at their faces and told them there were good people in Austria who wanted our paintings returned to us, and that recovering them was the best way to honor our parents and lost families.

"Adele Bloch-Bauer's name and face are famous here in Vienna," I said at the close of my remarks. "And I'm going to use her name to fight for justice for every one of us."

When I stepped down, people came to their feet and clapped. If I'd said those things just to please myself, I could not have felt proud. But I'd done it for all of them. I'd been fierce, just as my aunt had urged me to be. I couldn't wait to see her portrait at the Belvedere, knowing that I was worthy of her at last.

Walter Frodl, the director of the Belvedere museum, introduced himself to me at the reception following the symposium. He was a short, middle-aged man with a soft handshake and an Austrian flag pin on his lapel.

"That was a very emotional presentation you made," Frodl said. I thought his tone sounded a bit spiteful. "Well done."

I thanked him, and we exchanged a few pleasantries about the mild autumn weather and the new repairs to the Triton and Naiad Fountain. I could have gone on forever asking about the buildings in the Museum Quarter and the new visitors' trolley that made its way around the central Ring. But after a while, he cleared his throat and got down to business.

"Now that we know each other better, Frau Altmann, I propose we talk about our Adele," he said.

I glanced around for Eva or Hubertus, but they were both engaged in other conversations.

"I think we'd be more comfortable in the café upstairs," Frodl said. "Have you been up in the museum yet today?" The man's manner was formal and gracious, as if he'd stepped right out of my childhood.

"There's a beautiful view from the café. And we'll we pass right beneath one of Klimt's first murals on the way up."

We took the elevator from the basement to the second floor, and paused at the balustrade to look up at Klimt's frescos. From where we stood, we could barely make out the images above the staircase. But I'd studied Klimt's early paintings in books at home, and knew this one well.

"It's wonderful to know that Klimt took the Egyptian motif for Aunt Adele's portrait from some of his earliest work," I said.

"I see you're a fan of Klimt's oeuvre," Frodl said.

"Not a fan, Herr Frodl, an admirer. Like my aunt, I've made it my business to study Klimt's work and understand his ideas."

Frodl found us a window-side table in the café, and held a chair for me. Outside, the Ringstrasse buildings were dazzling against the blue sky. The fountain was sparkling and splashing in the sun, and just before I sat I had the strange sensation that I was about to fall into a moment from the past, as if I could be in two places at once, hearing voices that had spoken a hundred years ago running just above the hum of voices in the café.

"Now that we're alone, let's say what's in our hearts," Frodl said after we'd settled and ordered cups of tea. He leaned forward as if we were old friends. "I heard your speech downstairs. I recognize your attachment to the painting. But the portrait of Adele is a national treasure, and it's beloved here in Vienna. It belongs here."

"Is that what's truly in your heart, Herr Frodl?" I asked.

He nodded and smiled.

"Well, what's in my heart, Herr Frodl, is the hope that Austria will do the right thing and return my aunt's portrait to her rightful heirs."

"Sometimes people are confused about what is the right thing," he said, still smiling.

"I'm not confused," I said. I smiled, too.

"My dear Frau Altmann." Frodl put a hand on the table, very close to mine. "I will be frank with you. At the Belvedere, we have plenty of Klimt landscapes. We can spare a few of those. But Adele is special to us here in Vienna. I think on reflection you'll realize that the portrait belongs here in her rightful home."

"Her rightful home is with her heirs."

"I'm telling you as a friend, Frau Altmann, the portrait of Adele Bloch-Bauer is part of Austria's legacy, and it belongs here with us."

"Adele belongs to me, and I'll make sure the whole world knows it if I must," I said. I stood, more suddenly than I'd intended.

Frodl's face changed. It got hard and ugly. He stood, too. I could see then that he was a horrible little man.

"If you try to take our Adele out of Austria," he said, "we will stop you, and you will fail."

I marched into the Belvedere that very afternoon, across pebbled walkways I'd once tripped along with Aunt Adele, across a ballroom dance floor, and into the gallery where her portrait hung. Hubertus and Eva were with me, and a photographer trailed behind them.

It had been fifty years since I'd seen her, and as I crossed the gleaming floor she seemed to welcome me with every bit of her yearning. The sun was coming through the windows that overlooked the Belvedere gardens, lighting up her face and her golden dress.

"I'd like your photographer to take a picture of me with my aunt," I told Hubertus.

He spoke to the photographer and I smiled for the camera, but before it flashed, a museum guard rushed over.

"*Nein, verboten,*" he said. "Photographs are forbidden."

I straightened my spine.

"This painting belongs to my family," I said in German. A few visitors turned and glanced from my face to my aunt's. "This is a portrait of my aunt, my very flesh and blood. She's a Bloch-Bauer, and so am I."

Everything in the room stopped. The camera flashed. Someone even clapped.

The first step for my claim was to file a formal request for restitution with the Austrian Art Council. To do that, Randy had to untangle years of lost records and history and prove, as best we could, that the portrait had belonged to my uncle and that it had been taken from him wrongfully.

"The agreement you signed in 1948 isn't binding," Randy explained. "Attorneys for the Rothschilds and other Jewish families are all filing motions with the Austrian council, asking for those agreements and sales made under duress to be recanted."

Randy spent a long time accumulating everything from provenance records to legal findings. His office, hung with fancy diplomas from Princeton and the University of Southern California, filled with unruly piles of books and papers. His wife told me that some nights he worked until dawn and only went home to shower and put on a fresh suit.

After half a year, all we were waiting for was a copy of my aunt's will.

It was Randy's opinion that a copy of Adele's will should have been in the museum's archives, and the fact that it was missing suggested that perhaps the exact wording would work in our favor.

"Our friend Czernin seems to have friends in all kinds of shadowy places," Randy said. "He'll manage to get his hands on that will for us."

"There's only one problem," I said timidly. "Adele *did* want her portrait to go to the Belvedere. I'm sorry, but that's something she put in her will. Even my mother said it was true."

Randy's face went from flushed to bright red. The pile of papers on his desk threatened to topple over.

"Did she want her portrait to go to the Nazis?" he asked. "Was the Austria your aunt loved the same country that stole the work from your uncle's palace? I don't think so, Maria—I think that if Adele had survived, she would have been with your uncle in Switzerland and she would have wanted to get her portrait back."

Of course he was right. I'd agonized over my aunt's and uncle's seemingly divergent wishes, but the truth was crystal clear. Randy had to put it in a way that made perfect sense.

"You've never seen the will, have you?" he pressed.

"No."

"It's a simple matter of right and wrong. If I can prove the paintings were stolen from your uncle, then I can prove that keeping the portrait in Austria is wrong because it legally belongs to you. They built a wall of lies, and we're going to knock it down one brick at a time."

On the day of the Anschluss, my aunt's face in the portrait had seemed cold and silent. But that night in California, when I sat on the sofa with a cup of tea, I saw fear; I saw someone who seemed to know what was going to happen when Hitler came to Vienna.

"What did you know?" I asked her. "What did you know, and how?"

Of course she was silent. But her eyes were screaming. Someplace, in another world, I could hear her calling to me. Long after I turned out the lights and closed my eyes, her face hung in my mind like a head without a body, or a woman without a home.

*T*he archive room in the Belvedere basement is small and stuffy, but Hubertus Czernin is experienced at riffling through dusty old files for weeks on end. As a cub reporter, he proved that Austria's president Kurt Waldheim had been a Nazi. He's determined to right this Nazi wrong, too.

Pushing up his round glasses, Czernin leans on the counter and chats easily with the archive librarian.

"I hear you've done an incredible job organizing years of old files," he says. "It must have been a mess back there."

The librarian knows Czernin. She describes sifting through thousands of documents that hadn't been handled since the war, cataloging what she could and cross-referencing every document by year.

"The Bloch-Bauer files are kept in Frodl's office," the librarian says. "I can't access them. No one can."

Czernin lazily drums his long fingers on the tabletop.

"Do you really have boxes back there filled with miscellany from the war years?" he asks.

Soon Czernin is in a rear repository, sorting through boxes dated 1936–1945. After eight days, he finds what he needs.

At the Standard Press offices, Czernin hands his editor a fresh copy of an old letter with the Third Reich seal. The letter is brief and obsequious. The type is fading. The date on the letter is 30 September 1941. And it is signed by Erich Führer.

"Führer was Ferdinand Bloch-Bauer's Nazi-assigned lawyer," Czernin says. "He traded the Adele Bloch-Bauer I to the Belvedere in exchange for a landscape called Schloss Kammer on Attersee."

Czernin cross-checks his notes before going on.

"By 1943 that landscape belonged to Gustav Ucicky—Klimt's illegitimate son. Erich Führer must have sold it to him."

The newspaper editor reads the letter carefully.

"So this proves that Ferdinand Bloch-Bauer never gifted the portrait to the museum?" he asks. "It proves the painting was taken from him against his wishes, am I right?"

Czernin nods.

"And look here—that bastard signed the letter Heil Hitler," he says.

MARIA

1999

"Czernin got a copy of Adele's will, the real thing, from 1923," Randy said in a rush as he hurried through my front door. "Let me read you what it says here."

I took the paper from him, and read aloud.

"*My two portraits and four landscapes by Gustav Klimt, I kindly request my husband bequeath to the Belvedere National Gallery after his death.*"

I looked at Randy over the top of my reading glasses.

"My God," I said. "She never bequeathed the painting to the museum. It's right here—she requests my uncle—*ich bitte*—to bequeath it for her. And we know he never wanted the Austrians to have it after the war."

"Exactly," Randy said. "And that's not all—in 1923 Austria, a married woman didn't own anything. The law clearly stated that everything legally belonged to the husband then. Even if Adele had specifically given her portrait to the museum, it was never her right to do that. The bequest was always at Ferdinand's discretion. And we know what your uncle wanted."

We put a copy of my uncle's will and his last letter from Zurich into a fat legal binder with dozens of other documents, and prepared to send it off to Austria. It was amazing how excited I felt when I signed the letter that went along with my petition.

"So that's everything?" I asked.

"That's it," Randy said.

When a fax from Hubertus Czernin arrived at the last possible moment, we thought we had everything we needed to win our case.

" '*Heil Hitler,*' " Randy said as he put the final, damning letter signed by Erich Führer into the file. "I think that says it all."

MARIA

2000

The law was on my side, and the facts were lined up. But still, the art council denied my claim with a brief, impersonal statement: "*The* Adele Bloch-Bauer I *remains integral to Austria's cultural heritage and will remain in Austria. If you disagree with the decision of the Austrian Art Council, you are free to contest the decision in Austrian court.*"

Randy was so disappointed, I wanted to cry.

"If we want to go further, we're going to have to sue them in Austrian court," he said.

"Then we'll sue," I said. But suing in Austria required the plaintiff—me—to put in escrow a good portion of the money we expected to win.

"It doesn't make sense," Randy said. "But it's a fact. They want more than a million dollars up front, even before we make the claim."

"And if we lose?"

"Then we could lose the money, too."

It was an impossible situation, and I was angry.

"I'm afraid I have more bad news," Randy said. "My law firm said they've reached the end of the road on this case."

"What does that mean?"

"It means if we want to keep going, I'm going to have to quit my job."

I couldn't let Randy ruin his life. I couldn't let the Austrians break his heart and leave his family broke, the way they'd left mine.

"No," I said. "You can't do that. I'm not going to let you do that, Randy."

Randy slammed his hand on the table, and I jumped.

"Those goddamn Nazi bastards," he said.

"I'm angry, too," I said. "Do you have any idea what we had to do to survive?"

I saw Landau's face, Fritz's face, Frodl's face, my uncle when he'd waved good-bye to me across the crowded dance floor for the last time.

"They've turned my aunt and uncle's legacy into a collection of cheap souvenirs," I said. "They've made a lie out of my aunt's life, and I haven't stopped them."

I grabbed up the plates and cups with my aunt's face on them, and dropped them on the table. As I did, a coffee mug slipped out of my hands and shattered on the floor. I couldn't decide whether to pick up the broken pieces or smash all the others on the floor, too.

"Maria, you have just given me an idea," Randy said. I was surprised to see he was grinning.

When Randy told me we were going to sue the Austrian government in the United States Supreme Court, I thought it was a joke.

"We can't afford to sue in Austria," Randy said. "But I don't think the American courts are going to believe the pack of lies the Austrians are telling."

He dug into a fat canvas bag and pulled out some tacky souvenir plates and coffee mugs. Next to them he stacked a pair of ceramic candlesticks, a night-light, necktie, baby bib, and a gold scarf. Everything was decorated with Adele's face.

"Where in the world did you find all this?" I asked.

"Everywhere! I bought some on the Internet, and I asked Hubertus to send me a few from the Belvedere's gift shop."

Cheap souvenirs and expensive reproductions of Adele's portrait were being sold all over Austria, he told me. Each item reaped a profit. And that profit, it seemed, should have been ours.

"Austria isn't allowed to profit off images or properties that rightfully belong to an American citizen," Randy said. "The Austrian minister of culture might not think that we made a strong argument for the return of your painting, but I think the U.S. government will think otherwise."

He handed me a typed page that explained the American Foreign Sovereign Immunities Act.

"This law shields foreign governments from most lawsuits in the U.S.," he said. "But there's an exception to the law—it's called the *expropriation exception*. It was practically written for us—for a case like this one, when a foreign government is profiting off something stolen from an American citizen."

He rummaged around the bottom of the bag, and added a packet of coasters and some pens to the pile on the table.

"We can't go directly to the Supreme Court," Randy explained. "We start with a local court, and work our way there. We'll file a claim against Austria right here in California."

"It sounds like a long shot," I said.

"David killed Goliath," Randy said.

Judith killed Holofernes, too, I thought. I felt a strange and distant revulsion. Whatever it took, I would fight to have our dignity restored and the painting returned.

*I*n the shadow of the Hofburg Palace, where Lipizzan horses still dance
for tourists, tens of thousands of visitors troop through the royal gardens
and up the grand staircase in the Belvedere galleries to see the new show.

Klimt's Women *opens one month after Maria Altmann files her claim
against the Republic of Austria in a California courthouse. The faces
of long-gone women look out from the sumptuous canvases stolen from
haunted palaces and broken lives: Adele Bloch-Bauer, Amalie Zuckerkandl,
Mada Primavesi, Friederike Maria Beer, and more than fifty others.*

*"The Belvedere curators and the Austrian National Gallery are no better
than a gangster's moll, parading around after a bloody robbery, with jewelry
that she insists the victims gave her as a present," writes a British culture
critic.*

*"If they mean to shame us into surrendering the fight, they are wrong,"
Hubertus Czernin writes. "This has only shown us the cruel beauty of their
injustice. Art may belong to the ages, but it does not belong to its thieves."*

MARIA

2004

R andy staked everything on me. He quit his job, rallied a group of wealthy Americans to support my case, and put us both on television for interviews. Month after month, year after year, Austria sent their lawyers to face off against us in American courts.

"You say you're American one day, and the next day you say you're Austrian," one of their lawyers said to me on the steps of the Santa Monica courthouse. "I think you should make up your mind."

"I've made up my mind," I told him. "I will have my aunt's portrait returned to me."

"You embarrass yourself, Mrs. Altmann. You're an embarrassment to the people of Austria. We no longer recognize you as a citizen."

"I have heard worse," I told him. "I have survived far worse than your scorn."

When the time came, I watched Randy carry two enormous briefcases up to the United States Supreme Court building in Washington, D.C. He was carrying my ghosts and my spirits. They were calling to him, too, now, urging him on.

"You've brought us this far, and I know you won't fail," I said to him.

I watched from the courthouse gallery as Randy argued our case. I thought of my cousin Eva crouched in a dark potato cellar when Nazi soldiers came to the farm where she'd hidden during the war; of my uncle Ferdinand, who'd died alone in Zurich; of my aunt Adele, who'd once been the queen of Vienna.

I remembered falling across the barbed wire with Fritz, and the way the farmer had vanished into the night.

We were always alone unless we stood up for one another.

"Now we wait," Randy said when it was over. He was drenched in sweat, as if he'd run a marathon. The Supreme Court steps were behind him, like the rings of heaven or hell. "There's nothing left to do. You go home, I'll go home. And we'll wait."

I knew how to wait, I told him. I had waited a long time for Fritz.

Walter Frodl, director of the Belvedere National Gallery, calls a meeting in his conference room on a wintry morning.

"Maria Altmann has won the right to sue the government for our Adele," he tells his gathered staff.

The room buzzes; the curators' faces are a mix of horror and confusion. The day is a whirl of news reporters, cameramen, and bright lights. Austrians who've never given the portrait a second thought flood the Belvedere, some still carrying the news story in their hands.

As closing time nears and dusk is falling, Hubertus Czernin slowly makes his way out of the museum elevator with his wife and daughters. He is out of breath when he lowers himself onto a bench in front of the portrait of Adele.

"You won, Daddy?" his youngest girl asks. "Is that why we're here, because you won?"

Hubertus touches his daughter's soft, blond hair. The doctor's reports have been grave, and he knows he cannot fight his illness much longer.

"We've almost won, my darling. We're very close. When we win, the painting will leave Austria for good."

The little girl puzzles over his words.

"But how will we win, if the painting leaves home?"

Hubertus sighs. His wife kneels in front of the child.

"The pretty lady in that painting lived in Vienna a long time ago," she says. "But her family doesn't live here anymore. And they want the painting to go where they are. They want to have her with them in their new home, where she belongs."

MARIA

2004

We won. There was champagne and cake, and a small party in our honor, but it wasn't over yet. The portrait was still in Vienna, and the final battle with Austria was still to come.

With my sons and daughter beside me, and the last plastic cups full of champagne still scattered around my living room, I listened to Randy explain what he wanted to do next. It seemed I had been sitting there on my red sofa more than half my life, waiting for my aunt's face to give me an answer or a sign.

"We won the right to sue in the Supreme Court," Randy said. "But we have the option of putting the decision in the hands of three Austrian legal experts. We choose one member of the trio, and Austria chooses the second. The two, together, choose the third," he explained. "Everyone agrees that the decision is final and binding."

"What if they rule against us?" I asked. "Will there be any recourse?"

Randy shook his head.

"But I have a feeling that we can trust them to do the right thing this time," he said.

"Trust the Austrians?"

"If we don't do it this way, they're going to tie the lawsuit up in the courts for a very long time," Randy said. "That's what I would do, if I were them. I think this is our best shot."

I was eighty-seven. My health was failing. My friend Czernin was dying. I looked at my three children, and each one nodded yes. I looked at my aunt's face, and she urged me on.

"Yes," I said. "Let's trust the Austrians to do what is right."

And they did. They did what was right, and ruled in my favor.

MARIA
2006

When you're an old woman, memories and days stand up beside one another like rows of lights along the Santa Monica Freeway. They come while you sleep in your La-Z-Boy chair, and appear as clear as the carrot cake muffins lined on the baking rack in the kitchen.

They rain like notes from a piano, and fall among the pine trees in the yard. Bidden or unbidden, welcome or unwelcome, they come.

When Randy and I stepped off the airplane in Austria, I knew right away that the city had become my Vienna once more. It was spring. The lost days of my childhood, when Vienna had been most enchanting, seemed to be just above the treetops and in the scent of flowers blooming in the Volksgarten.

My cousin Eva was waiting just as she'd been before, and my friends from the symposium met us at the Belvedere with flowers and applause. When they parted, I saw Hubertus Czernin had come in his wheelchair. He smiled when I touched his hand, but he was too weak to speak.

"This is all thanks to you," I told him. "If you hadn't written that first story and Eva hadn't read it, none of this would have happened."

I was prepared to say more. *My dear Hubertus,* I wanted to tell him, *if you hadn't been such a brave and talented man, I would have died without saving the painting. My aunt would have been a face on teacups and kitchen towels, and my uncle would have been forever calling to me from another life.*

But before I could say any of that, Walter Frodl, who'd once told me he'd never let Adele leave his museum, stepped between us and cleared his throat.

"We have limited time for our meeting this afternoon, Frau Altmann. I'm sure you can understand," Frodl said. "The museum's counsel, Fräulein Mueller, will help you with the transfer."

Fräulein Mueller was a very pretty young woman. She was wearing a yellow blouse that matched my aunt's portrait.

"It's an honor and a pleasure to meet you." She shook my hand and then Randy's. "My name is Brigitte Mueller, and I think I have something that belongs to you, Frau Altmann."

She motioned for one of the guards, who stepped forward with a gold and white porcelain platter.

"I believe this was in your uncle's house," the young woman said. "Where my grandmother Brigitte was a cook."

I was overcome with the memory of that morning in Vienna, when I'd gone for my uncle and found he was gone. The cook's face had been as blank as a dinner roll.

"I remember your grandmother." I nodded slowly.

"I don't think you understand. The platter belongs to you," the young woman said. "My grandmother must have taken it from the house. I'd like to return it to you."

"I understand." I took a small step back. "But I want you to keep the platter, Fräulein Mueller. I'm giving it to you, rightfully. As a gift. Please accept my deepest gratitude."

Vienna of my youth had been a shining, vital city of marble archways and inviting streets. Everywhere I'd turned, there'd been music and people who loved me—my mother with her arms open wide, my father with his cello beneath his chin, my uncle Ferdinand saying, "Maria Viktoria, the little girl who makes my heart sing."

When I ran from Vienna, it was a city hung with swastikas and streaked with blood. The lions that stood at the entrance to the great museums had been mute and impotent, and in the end they'd roared like the bloody jaws of my enemy. There was still anger in Austria, and I knew that. But for one young woman to do the right thing meant there was goodness in Austria, too, as I'd always hoped there was, and always believed in my heart I would find.

Accompanied by two guards and three men from the freight company, Randy and I followed Brigitte Mueller along a gleaming hallway, through a sliding panel in a rear gallery, and up a long staircase to a gallery with no windows, where Adele was waiting.

In the small room, she glowed. Her jewelry seemed priceless, her face was beautiful. The necklace that Landau had stolen from me was around her neck. It was so true to life, I could remember its weight on my wedding night.

I hadn't wept when they'd taken Fritz, I hadn't wept in Berlin, I hadn't wept when I fled home or when I left Liverpool, or when they called me names in the Austrian press. But I wept then.

Randy nodded to the men from the American freight company, and they wrapped the portrait. They began with white linen, then shrouded her in black, then slid her into a wooden crate and onto a dolly. Then Randy, Adele, and I left the museum together.

Outside, the city was filled with posters printed *Ciao, Adele. Ciao* means good-bye, but it also means hello. Hello, Adele.

"What will you do with the painting?" a reporter asked as we left the museum. He had round glasses and kind eyes. He reminded me of Hubertus.

My aunt had been a great patron of the arts. She'd believed that art is one of the greatest things that a culture can build and create. In her final wishes, she'd said very specifically that she wanted her portrait to be in a museum.

"She'll be in an American museum, where everyone can know the truth about her life and the things that were important to her," I said.

"Then you will sell her?" he asked.

I was grateful for the truth when it came to me so clearly. I saw my aunt standing beside me in front of the tiger's cage, and knew exactly what she'd wanted of me, then and now.

"Yes, I will sell the painting," I said. "Because I never wanted to possess Adele. I wanted to set her free."

I was almost to the car when Fräulein Mueller caught up with me, breathless from running.

"Please take this, Frau Altmann," she said. "I almost forgot about it. This book belonged to your aunt, too."

She handed me an old book with a brown leather cover that felt smooth and cool in my hands. I tucked it into my tote bag almost without thinking.

"Come on, Maria, or we'll miss our plane," Randy said.

I got into the taxi, and we pulled away from the Belvedere. The pretty young curator faded from sight, and the journalists disappeared, too. Randy was quiet, the windows were rolled up, the excitement was over. Our task was done. The ghosts that had called and whispered when I'd arrived were quiet as if they, too, were stunned.

Somewhere farther along the road, I looked down into my lap. The book was *Emma*, by Jane Austen. I ran my hands across the cover, and opened to the first page. My aunt's bookplate was engraved there, the black ink fading, the letters the same style as the *ABB* on the letter opener that I'd kept with me for more than sixty years.

I flipped the pages, and the smell of the old ink and paper brought back the long, quiet afternoons we'd spent in the countryside reading on the porch and drinking lemonade. I remembered running barefoot across the lawn at Jungfer Brezan, jumping into my uncle's arms, dancing while my father played a polka on his cello, and being fitted for my first silk dress with my mother by my side.

I remembered kissing Fritz, and tasting cinnamon stars.

I could almost feel them in the car with me, as if everything that was going to happen had already happened and my aunt was urging me to be sure that none of it, and none of them, would ever be forgotten.

I was lost in that world when a sepia postcard fell from the book and landed in my lap.

On the front was a brown photograph of an old café beside a fountain, men in white suits and women in long, corseted dresses. On the back, in a strong bold hand, was a scrawled message—

Will you come?
—GK

*T*he auction hammer comes down with three resounding thuds, and Adele Bloch-Bauer I *is sold for $135 million to American collector Ronald Lauder.*

In 2006, the portrait is installed at the top of a sweeping white staircase on the second floor in the Neue Galerie in New York City. It hangs in a sun-filled room along with Kokoschka's cluttered landscapes and Schiele's gaunt self-portraits, surrounded by silver tea sets and carved furniture that once decorated Vienna's finest homes.

George Minne's graceful white statues stand beside Adele's portrait, just as they did at 18 Elisabethstrasse. A brass clock styled with two hearts at the ends of the sweeping arms mark the hour, and downstairs in the Café Sabarsky there is dark coffee, strudel, and sacher torte with cream. Little girls lunch with their grandparents, and lovers slide into velvet seats. Old women watch young waiters in white shirts and black ties, and remember dancing in ballrooms on the arms of their husbands and sons.

Gustav Klimt's spirit enlivens every room, and Adele's eyes seem to follow each of her visitors. When the lights are out and the moon shines through the windows, the golden symbols and red squares on her portrait dance with life, and the voices of yesterday seem to whisper about the world that they made modern, and the world that was almost lost.

Vienna was ours, they say, and we loved it almost as fiercely as we loved one another. We found truth in art there, and we bequeath it to you. Do not waste it. Remember.

AUTHOR'S NOTE

A modest oil portrait of my Hungarian-born great-grandmother hung for years over the couch in her old house in Seaford, Long Island. In it she was fair-haired and blue-eyed, a beautiful young woman in a corseted dark blue jacket.

I was ten years old when I learned that she had been raised Jewish and not Roman Catholic as my sisters and I, and our parents and grandparents, had been raised. Regina Solitar followed her brothers from Budapest to America in the late nineteenth century, and fell in love with an Italian barber. When she married him in secret, her family disowned her. Her Judaism, along with the rest of her past, was expunged and replaced by a life of raising Italian-American children, making a living as a seamstress, and, finally, quilting for her family.

When my great-grandmother passed away, the house was sold and her portrait vanished. But I held on to a secret ambition to write a story that would honor her heritage and independent spirit. Adele Bloch-Bauer and Maria Altmann gave me the opportunity to write about two strong-willed women united by art and family who, like my great-grandmother, lived separated from their faith and yet bound to it in ways both beautiful and terrifying.

To write a novel about real people is no small challenge. Maria's and Adele's lives and spirits proved worthy of the burden my fictional scrutiny put upon them. Many books, court records, news accounts, and films informed the story as I reconstructed real events and created internal lives for my characters. This includes an interview with E. Randolph

Schoenberg and extensive records that he made available online for a time, as well as *Portrait of Adele Bloch-Bauer* by Sophie Lillie and Georg Gaugusch, *The Lady in Gold* by Anne-Marie O'Connor, *Fin-de-Siècle Vienna* by Carl E. Schorske, *The World of Yesterday* by Stefan Zweig, and *A Nervous Splendor* by Frederic Morton. I also highly recommend the documentary films *The Rape of Europa* and *Maria's Story.*

The novel is fiction based on fact, with conversations imagined but dates, movements, allegiances, and betrayals all sourced in truth. Two liberties I feel obligated to report concern Maria. While she did tell the journalist Anne-Marie O'Connor that her sister was sexually intimate with a Nazi in order to save her family, there is no stated record of Maria having relations with a Nazi officer. Second, while there are many allusions to Fritz Altmann's wandering eye, details of infidelities are imagined.

Through the efforts of scholars, advocates, provenance researchers, and organizations—from Ronald Lauder, Sophie Lillie, and Hubertus Czernin, to the Commission for Art Recovery, the World Jewish Restitution Organization, the Institute for Art Research, and others too numerous to mention—thousands of stolen pieces of art have been restituted to their rightful owners. However, many thousands of works stolen by the Nazis remain lost or unclaimed. This fact compelled me to write this story through some of the dark and long days of its creation. Mostly it was a joy to discover and construct this novel, but the enormity of what was done to the Jews in the days immediately following the Anschluss in Vienna in 1938 cannot be overstated. My great-grandmother's portrait is but a tiny start in a galaxy of lost art, and this story is one victory in a universe of torches still waiting to be claimed and passed on.

ACKNOWLEDGMENTS

I'm so lucky to have a friend, researcher, and colleague as smart, talented, and industrious as Dr. Laura Morowitz. An expert on early twentieth-century European art, she introduced me to Gustav Klimt's work, and her scholarship and insights were indispensable to the foundation of this book. Laura and I traveled together three times to Vienna, where we studied Klimt's art up close, traced the footsteps of Adele and Maria's lives, and had a fabulous time in Café Central imagining spirited conversations between Adele, Berta, and their friends. Laura's shared knowledge about the aesthetics and politics of fin de siècle Vienna and the Nazis' rise can be found throughout the novel. I'm thrilled that her book in progress, on art exhibits in Nazi Vienna in relation to collective memory, grew out of our time together. I'm very proud that this woman is my intellectual partner and fierce friend.

I am grateful to my aunt, Rosemary Diaz, and to my father, Larry Lico, for telling me what they could about my great-grandmother and her life before and after she came to America. I miss my mother, and thank her for encouraging my writing from a very young age. For every family member who cheered me on during the writing of this novel, thank you. You all know I've always felt partly Jewish in my heart and this is why; this is how. That includes Rosanne and Jimmy Joos and Linda and Donna Lico, as well as my mother-in-law, Rosemarie (Roro) Helm, who is my role model in life, my dear sisters-in-laws Anna Albanese, Paula Brotman, Andrea Little, and Mary Albanese, as well as my brothers-in-law and extended Lico, Albanese, Lawrence, and Rovito peeps—you know who you are. Love to you all.

Heather Schroder, agent extraordinaire, thank you for recognizing what this could be and for making it happen. Sarah Cantin, editor of my dreams, you made the book golden in all ways. Leslie Wells, you helped bring Adele to life with invaluable and deft insight. Laura Morowitz, your friendship and scholarship mean the world to me, and to this book. Albert Tang and Donna Cheng, bravo, bravo for this brilliant cover. To Judith Curr, Peter Borland, and Suzanne Donahue; Ariele Fredman in publicity; Hillary Tisman in marketing; the awesome sales team including Wendy Sheanin, Michael Selleck, Janice Fryer, and Paula Amendolara; Kyoko Watanabe for a great interior design; Kimberly Goldstein and Mark LaFlaur for keeping the train running on time; and Haley Weaver for endless good cheer—thank you to the whole fabulous Atria team.

The novelist Pamela Redmond Satran and journalist Toni Martin went above and beyond to help me imagine this novel. E. R. Frank (aka Emily Rosenblum), Judith Lindbergh, and Dr. Ariella Budick read early drafts and shared keen insights. Christina Baker Kline, talented and generous, came through when I needed her most. Lisa Amoroso, gifted art director and lifelong friend—thanks for all of it, and for everything. Thanks to Dan Salzstein at the *New York Times* for running my travel pieces about Austria, and to the charming Erika Messner, owner of the Villa Paulick, for sitting with me on her veranda overlooking Lake Attersee and recalling days of yesteryear. Thanks to Adam Goss for the excellent Heuriger vineyard tours in the Wachau Valley. Klaus Pokorny and Dr. Robert Holzbauer at the Leopold in Vienna gave me their time and more than they know. Thanks to Sandra Tretter, curator at the Gustav Klimt Center, and to my guide Katrin Mekiska in Seewalchen. Marina Budhos, I'm sorry I never met your mother-in-law but am grateful for our shared affinity for the Viennese avant-garde. To my library writing partners Benilde Little and Anastasia Rubis, I love you and I love our Tower—I can't wait for your books to come out. Ditto journalists Leslie Brody and MaryJo Moran: our group is the best. Richard Satran, David Goldstein, and Peter Vigeland were helpful in very important ways, as were Martha Kolko and Nanci Naegeli—hugs and kisses, and thanks for the walks and talks. Jack Albanese and the other young people who tore through Vienna with us in June 2012, I'll never forget those days and nights.

Randy Schoenberg generously shared his recollections and thoughts on the case of Maria Altmann vs. the Austrian government. Charles Steinberg, a medical student at the University of Vienna when Hitler marched into Austria, shared the story of his escape during the Anschluss.

Many talented writers and teachers at Stonecoast in Maine, where I earned my MFA during the revision of this novel, contributed in myriad ways. My outstanding mentor Susan Conley is gifted, talented, kind and generous as a teacher and a writer. Aaron Hamburger put Collette in my hands and helped me find Adele's voice. Jaed Coffin said, roughly, "why write that, when you can write this?" and clarified so much for me. Robin Talbot, Matthew Jones, Justin Tussing, Suzanne Strempek Shea, Debra Marquart, Elizabeth Searle, David Anthony Durham, Ted and Annie Deppe on the faculty, and my friends Julia Munemo, Vicki Hamlin, Sally Donaldson, Shannon Ratliff, Clif Travers, Anya Mali, Ellie O'Leary, Maggie Almdale, Bill Stauffer, Lauren Liebowitz and the rest of the Howth gang, thank you for encouragement, camaraderie, and lots of bourbon, whiskey, and Guinness. My dear Montclair Writers Group friends Maureen Connelly, Alice Elliot Dark, Lisa Gornick, Nancy Star, Jill Smolow, Jill Hamberg Coplan, Kelley Holland, Laura Schenone, Peg Rosen, Diane Harris, Pat Berry, Dale Russakoff, Pam Kruger, Anne Burt, Cindy Handler, and Candy Cooper—thanks to every one of you. Friends, students, and fellow teachers at The Writers Circle, especially Michelle Cameron, I learn so much from all of you. Georgia Clark and the Brooklyn Writers Salon, there can never be too much of a good thing.

A research grant from the Hadassah Brandeis Institute provided financial assistance for the novel. A sabbatical from Wagner College in the fall of 2011 supported Dr. Laura Morowitz's research on this project. On her behalf, I thank her wonderful husband, Eric, and three incredible daughters for their love and support, and her beloved late aunt, Frances Morowitz Schwide, who inspired love of words, art, and Eastern European history.

Finally, forever, there is my beloved husband, Frank, daughter, Melissa, and son, John. Our home and your love are at the center of my life and everything I do. I am so proud of you, and so grateful for all the hours and years we've spent at the table talking about books, history, and ideas.

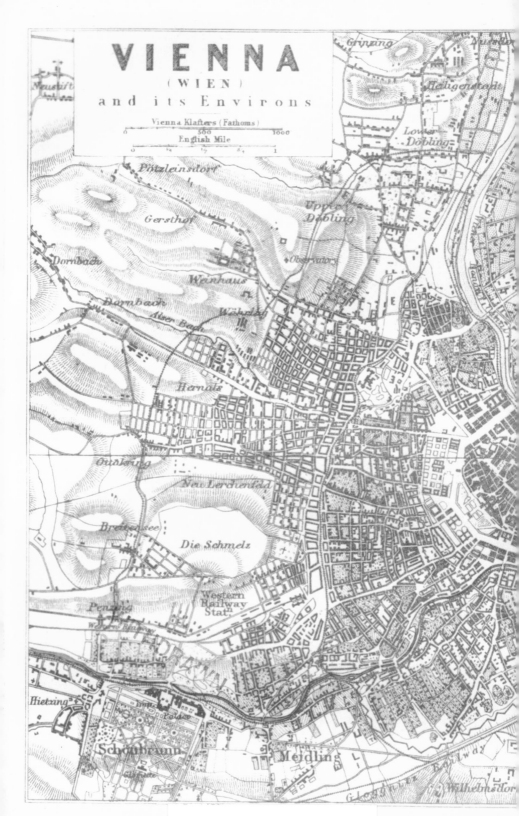